Max and the Gatekeeper

Book IV

The Dark Society

James Todd Cochrane

Special thanks to all my family and friends for their help and support. Thanks to all my fans who motivated me to keep writing.

Cover by Kalen O'Donnell
Sketches by Beth Peluso

www.darkmoonpublishing.com

Library of Congress Control Number: 2014919991
ISBN 978-0-9882110-5-6

CONTENTS

1

The Secret is Loose

Sam and Linda huddled close together under an old green tarp as the pouring rain seeped through several areas of torn fabric, penetrated their clothing, and chilled them to the bone. The rain and the steam from their breath obscured their view of the old motel across the street from the park, where they waited in a thicket of trees.

Sam—a thin, medium-height, freckled-faced male in his mid-twenties with straight brown hair had been on the run with Linda—a short, pleasant-faced black woman in her early thirties. For almost three months now, their existence had been a miserable one of eking by on barely enough food. Their tattered clothes matched their worn-out appearance.

"Are you sure they're coming?" Linda's voice chattered with the cold and she pressed closer to Sam's back for warmth.

"Yes," Sam responded, his eyes locked on the motel.

"How long can we keep this up?"

"As long as we want to stay alive." Sam cupped his hands and blew into them to revive them from their frozen state.

"Is Tanner with them?" Linda's voice cracked with fear.

"Most definitely," Sam spat as memories of his former coworkers flashed through his mind. They didn't know his full name, only that he went by Tanner and he had been their handler. He never let them out of his sight or his thugs' sight for almost two years. They didn't realize how ruthless he was until the day they and the others decided to run. Now they were the last two left. He had destroyed all the others. They knew if he caught them they would be tortured for information—and then eliminated.

"We're going to have to kill him," Sam stated, his sharp blue eyes stared straight ahead, "If we ever want to be free."

"I know," Linda acknowledged as she rubbed her eyes. "I'm not sure that he's even human."

"Me either. You set everything up?" Sam asked for what seemed at least the fourteenth time.

"Yes, the back window is open. The map indicates we are heading west." Linda yawned, fighting her exhaustion.

The steady rain turned into a downpour as lightning zipped across the sky, shaking Linda's nerves. The rain dampened her mood even more as they continued to wait for their tireless pursuers.

"Do you wonder if there are others out there? I mean people who have our talents or tricks or whatever?" Linda asked.

"Yes, I'm sure of it. That information had to come from somewhere. Where did they get it?" Sam answered. "As a whole, it has to be a lot more powerful than the individual pieces we worked on. Who would have thought it could fool an entire nation."

"Yeah, great change you can believe in. When it really meant misery and destruction. I think they would be ticked to learn they are giving up their freedoms for Lies of Comfort."

"Yes." Sam squinted to keep the rain out of his eyes. "Although their lies and deception run very deep now, and if we don't find a way to expose them they will maintain their control of the White House. The election is close. We don't have much time. Freedom and prosperity are at their greatest risk ever."

"It will be difficult to expose them. They control the media and the schools. They don't teach true American history in the schools anymore. If the youth really understood our past, they wouldn't buy these lies of social justice and redistribution of wealth," Linda added.

"They are converting people by the millions from productive self-sustaining individuals with a sense of unity and freedom to lazy entitled sheep, full of hate for anyone not like them," Sam snarled.

"Listen, I was thinking…" Linda inhaled a deep breath. "We should share our talents with each other."

"Didn't we agree that was a bad idea? If we know each other's tricks we don't need each other anymore. I think we have a better chance of survival if we stick together."

"Then we will have to make an agreement that we remain together no matter what, but I feel the more we know—the better chance we have of staying alive! I mean, look, we are both exhausted. It would be easier if we shared our responsibilities."

"I can't argue with you there. Okay, next time we get a break, we'll teach each other what we know," Sam agreed. "Okay, get ready. Here they come!"

Several dark figures converged on the motel from multiple directions. They wore black clothing and kept in the semi-darkness of the stormy day. A few of the figures held guns at the ready as they made their way towards a door in the center of the building.

"They have men watching the street in both directions," Sam stated, prompting Linda to look both ways down the street. Two dark SUVs waited on opposite ends of the street.

Linda's heartbeat kicked into overdrive and pounded in her ears. She would have to use her special ability soon. It was a skill she learned while translating sections of photographed papers. She didn't know where the paper came from, but it was written in an unknown language, and it appeared to be very old. The work she did had given a secret society the power to gain the White House and steal people's freedom.

She had received her Ph.D. from Columbia in linguistics and had received honors for her translations of ancient scrolls when a small unknown firm approached her with a lot of cash. The offer was too good to be true in a field where one had to constantly apply for grants and donations to stay employed. It was almost two years ago when she joined the team of ten other translators, working on different sections of what she had been told was from an extremely old book.

Their contracts forbade them from sharing what they worked on with the others, so none of them had the entire picture. They sent their interpretations on to a main supervisor who always had an armed escort. "It's a matter of national security," the supervisor said.

No one seemed worried after the first worker's mysterious death a few days before he was to leave for a new job. The company replaced him with a woman from Germany, and work continued as usual. Then Steve, an older gentleman from Texas, grew paranoid about the company watching him after he discovered several hidden cameras in his apartment and work area. He started passing notes to the others, asking them if they had found any such devices or anything else out of the ordinary. After his accidental death a few weeks later, and several secretive communications with the others, they all came to the terrifying conclusion they had signed on to their last job.

"I don't think this is about national security," said Lou, a grad student from Berkley. "I just finished a new translation. I think this whole thing is a grasp for power—through magic!"

The word "magic" surprised everyone, but somehow they all knew he was right. It just took someone vocalizing the word for it to sink in. Several translators demonstrated skills they thought no real human possessed. They had been playing with the things they discovered. A few days later the company rounded them up and sent them on a little bus ride into the forest. The revolt happened before they reached their destination, as the translators used their newly acquired talents to crash the bus and make their escape.

They agreed to travel in different directions in groups of two. Without knowing a destination, they became easy targets for Tanner and his hit squad. Sam and Linda didn't know if it was carelessness or the fact that Tanner wanted the others to know he was coming for them, because the victims had horrible deaths that always made the national news. They read about two in the newspaper, while seeing the other six on the national news. They all met with a grisly fate. Sam figured they were tortured first for information.

It wasn't until Sam and Linda had time to really chat that they realized the plans of the organization they had worked for. Their goals included the takeover of the United States from within. The secrets unlocked in the translations gave them power over the weak minded. The organization lulled people into believing they didn't want freedom and they couldn't take care of themselves. Slowly, through lies and deceit, they convinced the American people to give up their freedoms. The promise of free things without having to work for them and the turning of Americans against each other through race and social status seemed to be working to perfection.

These people were powerful and dangerous before, but with the assistance of what had been discovered they were entrenched, and it would take a miracle to root them out. The fact they spent so much time and effort in tracking down and eliminating everyone who had worked on the project proved their resolve.

"Get ready." Sam inhaled a deep breath as if steadying his nerves.

Linda glanced at her trembling hands as if somehow she could make them stop. Fear her magic might let them down and lead to their deaths

constantly flooded her mind; she had been taught all her life that there
was no such thing as magic.

"The minute they go in, you'll need to keep us hidden." Sam stated
the obvious. He stretched out his hand and Linda took hold of it. He
gave her a quick smile and squeezed her hand.

The dark figures arrived at the hotel. They hustled along in silence
until they reached a certain room. After exchanging several hand sig-
nals, one drew his gun and took up a position in front of the door.

"You can't hide from me," a cold voice from behind Sam and Linda
caused them to whirl around just as the man in front of the door kicked it
in.

A few feet away stood Tanner, the man who had been hunting them
since their escape. He stood well over six feet four inches tall. A dark
felt hat covered his features in shadow. He waited with his hands deep in
the pockets of his rain drenched trench coat. "Did you really think you
could beat me?"

Sam took a quick look at their surroundings and he stepped to the
side, pulling Linda with him.

"I wouldn't!" Tanner spat, and in a flash he had drawn a gun from
his pocket and leveled it at the two of them. "The game is over. You're
coming with me!"

"*Wind*," Sam muttered under his breath, and a blast of air slammed
into Tanner. The impact of rain and air current turned his head as the
gust threw his hat in the air.

"*Invisible*." Linda cast her spell and then pulled Sam down into a
crouch. Her heart raced as Tanner whipped around and his eyes floated
over them but didn't lock on.

"*@#$@*," Tanner swore under his breath. His head rotated in all
directions as he moved towards his hat, keeping his eyes in their general
area.

"We need to move." Linda chanced a whisper, feeling the downpour
would cover her voice.

"*Wind*," Sam said again, sending Tanner's hat flying farther away
from him.

Tanner rose to his feet, his hair already soaked and plastered to his
head. "I know you haven't moved!" Tanner stated as he rose to his feet.
He extracted a silencer out of his coat and twisted it on to the end of his
gun. "What do you say I fire my gun several times in your general area
to test my theory?"

"Drop it!" a police officer called off to their left, his gun drawn and pointed at Tanner.

"I have a permit," Tanner spat as he lowered it to the ground and set his gun on the grass. As he rose up he drew another gun from his other pocket and fired several shots into the unsuspecting officer.

Sam and Linda didn't hesitate and bolted from the trees. Bullets trailed their splashing feet, barely missing them.

Tanner whistled to the men coming out of the hotel and signaled them his way. "They're heading for the street," he yelled as he retrieved his other gun and his hat. "They're invisible. Watch for splashing water."

"Where should we go?" Linda asked in a hushed voice as they raced onto the sidewalk. "I won't be able to hide us much longer."

"The hotel! We stick to the plan," Sam said as he pulled her across the street. The search party had spread out along the street, leaving the hotel room door wide open.

"DON'T LET THEM ESCAPE!" Tanner shouted angrily.

Linda and Sam rushed through the open doorway as Linda's spell failed. They quickly dove out of the open doorway and crawled along the floor to hide behind the bed.

"What are we going to do?" Linda asked, her voice full of panic.

"I have an idea." Sam reached up and pulled the phone off the nightstand. He punched out 911.

"911," the operator on the other end answered.

"I want to report a shooting of a police officer in the park across from Motel 6," Sam spoke into the receiver. Sam relayed the address, a description of Tanner, and some details about the shooting. A few minutes after the call police sirens wailed above the storm, heading in their direction.

"We need to get out of here before the police arrive," Sam whispered. "I'm sure someone in this hotel heard the door being kicked in and they probably traced the 911 call to this room."

"You don't think we would be safe with the police?"

"No. This Tanner is too well connected and has too much power. If we are captured by the police it would be a death sentence. Are you strong enough to make us invisible?"

"I'm not sure." Linda trembled from head to toe. They had been running for several months, but this was their first real encounter with Tanner. The sense they were losing ground grew in her mind, weakening her resolve.

"Out the back window. Follow me." Sam crawled towards a window at the back of the room, with Linda right behind him. "Keep an eye on the door," Sam ordered, as he poked his head up high enough to peek out the back window.

"Do you see anything?"

"No. I think it's safe. There's quite a drop off in the back below the window. I'll go first and then help you down. I'm just going to take a better look first." Sam rose to his feet and leaned out the window.

"We need to hurry," Linda warned as the police sirens filled the air, their flashing lights bounced around the room.

Sam crawled out the window and jumped. He landed with a thud. "Linda, come on."

Linda stuck her head out the window to see what she had to do.

"YOU! FREEZE," a police officer said as he rushed towards Sam, his hand resting on his holstered pistol. "You in the hotel room, stay where you are," he ordered as his eyes made contact with Linda's. He pressed the radio button fastened to his shoulder to relay what he had found.

"Linda, hide!" Sam ordered out of the side of his mouth as he raised his hands above his head.

"*Invisible*," Linda muttered just as two officers stormed into the room. She quietly crawled into the open closet and sat on the floor with her knees pulled up to her chest. Inhaling a calming breath, she forced herself to relax and conserve her energy so she could hold on to the magic.

The officers checked the room for occupants. When one passed in front of the window a voice called from outside, "Did you get her?"

The cop in the room poked his head out the opening. "Get who? The room is empty."

"There was a girl. Did you check the room thoroughly? She was just there."

"Yes, there's no one here and we didn't see anyone exit the room either."

"Set up a perimeter, she can't have gone far. We are looking for a black girl. I'm guessing in her late 20's early 30's," the voice from outside ordered.

Linda breathed a sigh of relief as the policeman exited the room. "Sam," she muttered to herself as her mind locked on the fact the police had captured Sam. She forced herself to leave her hiding place and crawled to the window. While still under the power of her spell, she cautiously looked out the window. The officer had Sam standing with his legs spread and both hands touching the hood of the car.

"I'm the one who called in the shooting," Sam stated. "Check with the hotel. I'm the one who rented the room for the night. I was heading back to my room when I saw what happened."

"We have reports of several strange men in the area. And why did they kick in your door?" the officer asked as he frisked Sam, checking for weapons.

"I don't know," Sam answered.

"Somehow I think you do," the officer pulled Sam's hands behind his back, slapped handcuffs on him, and spun him around. "That was my friend who was shot, so I want answers," he barked, his nose an inch from Sam's.

"I don't know anything."

"Well, I believe you do. So you're coming down to the station. If you're lying to me, I'll personally make your life a living hell." The officer yanked Sam away from the car and escorted him into the back seat.

With the cop's attention on Sam, Linda lowered herself out the window and slipped behind some cars in a parking lot on the street opposite of the hotel. The rain continued to pound the area, and without the tarp for protection the water soaked into her clothing. She found a spot between two trucks and made herself visible again, wanting to remain fresh. An uneasy feeling spread through her like poison, turning her spirits dark, stealing her will. *What should I do?*

She hoped the officer would leave his car so she could attempt a rescue. She didn't want to have to spring Sam from jail. Now would be her best chance, if only the police would leave her an opening. Her mind spun as she hunted for ideas. *You could knock out the cop. You could sneak a ride. You could...*

Suddenly another police car arrived, stopping next to the one that held Sam. Linda could feel her options fluttering away with the arrival of the second car. She listened to the officers discuss the situation.

"Dan's alive but it's serious," the second said. "Do you think the prisoner is the shooter?"

"No, I don't, but I think he knows who the shooter is. He's not talking at the moment. What about the girl?"

"So far there's no sign of her. We also have a report of four men who forced their way into the hotel and a fifth seen running from the park."

Suddenly a distorted voice rang from the officers' radios.

"Come again," the first officer spoke into the radio on his shoulder.

"The area is clear. The suspects are gone. We've put out an APB for the men and four black SUVs."

"Roger that, I'm bringing in a possible suspect for questioning."

Do something! Linda's brain screamed inside her head. *Why didn't we share our tricks sooner? I could use some of your talents right now, Sam.*

"Where're you heading?" the first officer asked the other.

"I'm going to swing by the hospital, check on Dan," the second said as he opened the door to his car.

"Let me know the minute you have any information," the first said as he got into his car.

"*Invisible*," Linda muttered as she rushed forward. She wasn't exactly sure what she was going to do. Hang onto the top of a police car?

The second police car started to pull away. The instant the first officer closed his door a dark SUV flew down the street at a high rate of speed and slammed into the driver's side of the first car. The squealing of tires joined the sound of crunching metal and breaking glass as a second and third SUV blocked the path of the second squad car.

Linda lost control of her spell at the shock of the sudden violence and retreated back to her hiding spot. Fear that she'd been spotted gripped her and increased her heart's pounding as six men dressed in long black trench coats leapt out of the vehicles, armed with machine guns. They riddled the second police car with bullets, destroying the vehicle, as another two men yanked Sam from the backseat of the first car.

Steam rose from the damaged cars as the men dragged the struggling Sam towards the SUV which had crushed the driver's side of the first police car.

"Sam, how nice to see you." Tanner smiled as he stepped out of the car to greet their new prisoner. "We have so much to talk about."

"Sam," Linda cried uncontrollably. Her chest heaved with sobs of terror at being alone, as her only link to the world was carried away by the very people who sought to destroy them.

2

Hudich at Work

"The plans are set. The bombs are in play," an Arab spoke, leaning over a map of a European city which was spread out over a table. A large red circle encompassed a railway station. "For an entire month we will instill terror and bring about the destruction of several nations. Our many brothers and sisters, who have flooded Europe over the past century, are only waiting for our signal to bring about one Islamic nation after we crush the infidels."

A group of nine men huddled around a table in the center of a sparsely furnished apartment. Large thick rugs covered every window and a guard rested against the door.

"Are we positive the US Secretary of State will be on the train?" asked another Arab wearing a black head scarf.

"Yes. He, his family, and his security detail will all be arriving. A nice little bonus to our massacre." The Arab leaning on the map smiled. "Fear will spread. No one has the courage to stand in our way."

"Allah has shown us the way. Through their political correctness we have silenced the majority through fear of being called racists and bigots. Now is the perfect time to start the final jihad. Once Europe is ours, we will defeat Israel and the Great Satan the United States of America," an elderly Arab with a long white beard added.

"You don't need to worry about the United States," a deep voice rumbled from the corner. The speaker wore black robes, with a scarf and sunglasses hiding his face from view as he leaned against the wall. "They are destroying themselves. You only need to be patient and they will be ripe for the picking. Give the United States time. There is a 'what can I get for free' mentality taking place that will aid all of us in our goal. The progressive movement compiled with other factors will lead to their own destruction."

"Who are you? Who did you come with? How did you get in here?" another interrupted, casting a glance of protest towards the others as several men in the room drew their weapons.

"I came by myself and I'd put those away before you hurt yourselves. I'm someone who can help you achieve all of your goals. I can give you weapons beyond your wildest dreams and I only ask for a few small favors in return," the dark figure soothed.

"Who is this fool?" an eager-young Arab barked, drawing a long dagger from inside his robes. "Let me kill him before this fool betrays us all. How do we know he is not a spy?"

"If I were a spy, why would I bother with this conversation?" The stranger stood calmly leaning against the wall, watching the others' reactions to his presence.

The elder Muslim held out his hand to stop the impatient Arab's advance. "What kind of weapons?"

The stranger's movements flashed with blinding speed as he retrieved a futuristic gun from his robes and vaporized the young Arab holding the knife. The blade fell to the ground with a clank next to a dark smoking bundle on the floor. "Like these!"

Chaos ruled the room for several moments as the shocked and frightened Arabs scrambled as far away from the stranger as the room would allow.

"That was my brother!" one of the cowering militant Muslims shouted in rage.

"Now, as you can see, I could kill you. *All* of you. But I'm not here to do that. As a matter of fact, I want to help you." The stranger slipped the weapon beneath his robes.

"What is it you want from us?" the elder Arab asked as the others relaxed a bit with the destructive weapon no longer in sight.

"I want the US Secretary of State and his family. Alive. In exchange, I will give you ten weapons like the one I just demonstrated for you." The fully covered outsider resumed his casual position leaning against the wall.

"There's no way!" one Arab shouted.

"It can't be done with our current plans," another added.

The stranger waited as the arguing and squabbling about how in the world they would accomplish this with their present strategy continued.

There seemed to be a strong desire for the weapons, but also skepticism for the man hidden behind the sunglasses. They acted as if they didn't want to help him but didn't know how to get rid of him. They chattered back and forth for several minutes about possible alterations to the plans that might allow them to capture the Secretary of State alive.

"But we are not equipped to pull off a kidnapping like this on such short notice," the old man spoke to the group while glancing at the stranger.

"You don't need to do the kidnapping," the covered man spoke, finally bringing a hush to the room.

"Then how are we supposed to let you have them alive?" questioned the one who had been studying the map.

"I will capture them myself. I just need you to delay your little fireworks display for a few minutes," the stranger said. "All I need is a small amount of time and the weapons are yours, and the Secretary of State and his family are mine."

"Yes, but that could set the United States' sights on us if they think we are holding the Secretary of State," the old Arab stated.

"That is going to happen either way," the stranger pointed out. "But, in this case, you will have some nice weapons to protect yourselves with. And they won't know he's alive. They will think he died in the explosion, along with the others."

"What if we want the Secretary of State?" the dead man's brother barked.

"Like you said, you aren't equipped to make a live capture. I am, but I need a little window of opportunity to accomplish the task. I, too, want the US to think he's dead. That will allow me to achieve a lot of things," the stranger replied.

"And just why do you want him?" the old man asked.

"That is my business. I am not providing information, only offering the weapons. I will give you this one as a down payment if we arrive at an agreement," the stranger stated as he eyed the crowd on the other side of the room. Many of the Muslims' eyes held lust for the weapons, while others reflected rage towards him.

"How much time do you think you will need?" the old man asked.

"Only five minutes!"

"FIVE MINUTES!" the group broke out with laughter and scorn.

"There's no way you can capture the Secretary of State and his family in five minutes," one of the Arabs barked.

"You're a fool if you think you can do this," another stated.

The old Arab put up his hands to bring order to the disruption. "What makes you think you can accomplish such a task in five minutes?"

"I have more skills than you could possibly imagine. I have weapons far greater than the one I am offering you. It must be accomplished in five minutes so that any witnesses to the kidnapping will be killed in the explosion. Like I said, I want the Americans to think that they all perished in the attack."

"Well, maybe we would rather have the better weapons before we strike a deal," the dead man's brother snapped.

"You fail to grasp the fact that I could blow the whistle on this little attack of yours," the stranger stated with a slight edge to his voice. "The way I see it, you aren't in a very good position to bargain at this point."

"Well, maybe we will just kill you now and be done with it," another spat.

"Yes, your dead friend was so successful in his attempt," the man's voice taunted with pleasure. "Any of you other cowards want to step up to the challenge? Now, here is the deal, take it or leave it. I will give you the weapon in my possession, and you will delay your attack for five minutes after the Secretary of State's train arrives. If you do this, I will bring you an additional nine weapons. If you do not agree, I will report the details of this attack and your whereabouts to the proper authorities. Double cross me, and I will wipe out your entire network of cowards throughout the globe."

"We are not cowards, we are soldiers fighting against the great Satan!" one of the Arab's voice trembled as he tried to make his case.

"Yes, attacking unarmed women and children, how brave," the stranger sneered. "So, do we have a deal?"

"May we see the weapon?" the old Arab asked, extending his hand.

"You may." The outsider approached the table causing a few in the group to give way to his presence. He extracted the futuristic gun from his robes and dropped it on the table with a loud thud.

The men in the room took turns holding the weapon, judging its weight as they passed it around the room. When the gun arrived at the brother of the man who had just been killed, he leveled the gun at the stranger, his eyes bloodshot and full of malice.

"Big mistake, giving up your advantage," the man spat.

"Do you honestly think that is my only protection?" the stranger asked calmly.

"Mustafa, what are you doing?" the old man interrupted, trying to defuse the situation as he held out his hand for the gun.

"He's making a case to join his brother," the visitor continued in his cool manner.

"You can't retrieve any weapon before I pull this trigger, sending you to hell for the murder of my brother!" Sweat streamed down the man's forehead.

"True. But you see I don't need weapons to protect myself," the stranger uttered a strange word and the gun flew from Mustafa's hands and back to the stranger, who snagged it out of the air.

The reaction to this new trick resembled the response to the weapon vaporizing Mustafa's brother. Everyone in the room flinched and retreated farther from the stranger.

"What are you?" one questioned.

"Are you sent from Allah?" asked another.

"You are the devil," Mustafa shouted with fear.

The stranger let out a deep menacing laugh. "Call me what you will. I can either help you or destroy you. It's your choice. Do we have an agreement?"

"NO!" Mustafa shouted at the others in the room. "You'll be making a deal with Satan."

"Oh, you people have already made your deal with the devil," the stranger mocked. "What's another one?"

The old man glanced at all of the Arabs in the room and received several nods in response. Only Mustafa and one other shook their heads in disagreement. "We have an agreement. We will delay the explosives until 10:05 tomorrow morning. We will not be held responsible should you fail in your attempt."

"I won't fail," the stranger added as he set the gun back on the table. "I will bring the others here tomorrow night at this same time," he added, and left the men to finish their plans.

A flash of white light and the figure, fully covered in Arab garb and sunglasses, appeared in the center of a great stone hall. Alan, a tall sinister man with dark hair and dressed in a black robe, rushed to greet the man.

"Did they agree?" Alan asked while bowing slightly before the personage.

"Yes," the man responded with a deep voice as he shed his Arabic apparel to reveal Hudich, the dark leader of an evil army. His red-rat eyes seemed to flash with pleasure as a smile spread across his black skull-like face. "Tomorrow morning we will take the Secretary of the United States and his family prisoner."

"Are you sure we can trust them to do what they say?" Alan asked as he straightened.

"No," Hudich grumbled as he strode past Alan and took his seat on the throne on a podium above the main floor. "Their lust for the weapons might keep them in line, but I don't trust them. I have a feeling there are a number of them that might jump the gun on the time."

"What do you want to do about it?" Alan asked as he took up a position to the side of Hudich's throne.

"Put a few Night Shades on the brother of the Arab I killed. Learn his roll, kill him, and have someone else accomplish his task!" Hudich ordered.

"And if others don't hold up their end of the bargain?"

"We will go in two minutes before the five minutes they are supposed to give us. If we use fire to cover our tracks, we should be fine," Hudich pointed out.

"And what if the Arabs do as they said they would?"

"We destroy them no matter what. We can't risk letting that gun fall into the wrong hands. If that old fool somehow tracked it down, he could cause trouble. For too many years we have tried to use him and his people to accomplish our goals. Now is the time to keep them in the dark. Let them try to figure out what we are up to. Oh, we will throw them a few false leads and before they know it—Earth will be ours!"

###

Hudich, dressed in his Arab disguise, stood on the roof of a building across from the Madrid train station. The sun shone down on the warm spring day as a slight breeze ruffled his robes. Alan popped up in the center of the roof and hurried to Hudich's position overlooking the train station.

"Is everything ready?" Hudich's deep voice questioned, not turning from his observations.

"Yes. Mustafa has been taken care of, and our people will carry out his portion of the mission," Alan reported as two Night Shades appeared behind them.

"The train will be in position in a few minutes," Hudich said. "We go in fast. Get what we want and destroy the others. Is everything ready back at your town?"

"Yes," Alan reported. "The cells in the cave are ready for their prisoners."

"And that old fool? Does he suspect anything is about to take place under his nose?" Hudich asked as he turned his head towards Alan.

"No. We don't know what he has been up to for the past two years, but he seems to not be interested in anything taking place in the town. Do you think it was wise ignoring them for so long?"

"Yes. We have been working without their prying eyes as well. It has allowed us to do things without raising an alarm."

Alan pulled a pair of binoculars from under his robes and peered out at the train station. Thousands of people occupied themselves going about their business, traveling to and from work and various other destinations. "Where are the Arabs watching from?"

"From the high rise two blocks back from the station. Tenth floor, third window from the right."

Alan directed the glasses to the location and spotted three Arabs on the balcony of the building. They all peered down at the train station with binoculars of their own, in nervous anticipation. "Do you still plan on waiting after we're gone to see if they hold up their end of the deal?"

"Yes. I have a nice surprise in store for them either way," Hudich's voice carried a dark pleasure in its tone. "Are the Night Shades ready to wipe out the others?"

"Yes. They will all meet the same fate as the people in the train station."

"Excellent. The authorities will never figure out what happened!"

The Secretary of State sat cross legged in a train car, reading the morning paper. His wife sat by his side in the seat next to the window, watching the city zip past. Their two sons knelt in front of the bench opposite them, playing with toy cars. Two security personnel stood in front of the sliding glass doors, while other security officers kept everyone out of this car except for the Secretary's family and staff.

"We should be there in a few minutes," the Secretary's wife commented while peering out the window.

The glass door to the compartment opened and in stepped a speech writer with a stack of papers. He was a young man with short brown hair and bags under his eyes. His disheveled suit gave the appearance of an all-nighter.

The Secretary lowered his paper to glance at the young man, "Did you iron out the final parts of my speech, David?"

"I think we have it, sir," David responded as he approached the Secretary and handed him a few pieces of paper.

The Secretary pushed his reading glasses higher up his nose as he set his newspaper aside and accepted the items from David. The young man fidgeted with his tie as he waited for his boss's approval.

"Why don't you have a seat, David," the Secretary's wife motioned to the bench where her sons played. "Mike, Wesley, move over so David can have a seat!"

"There's no need, ma'am. I've been sitting all night." David managed a weak smile toward the boys.

The car jerked hard toward the window and the power to the car went out. A loud thud echoed through the car as David collided with the window, knocking him out cold. The two boys slid across the floor and the Secretary smashed his wife against the side of the seat. Gasps and shrieks rolled off of their lips at the force that struck the car. The two guards in the hall smacked into the glass windows separating the compartment from the walkway.

"What was that?" asked the Secretary's wife, Sandy.

Before the Secretary could respond a black mist covered all the windows of the car, blocking out the light. It was like being inside a hollowed-out black cloud. Two flashes of green zipped across the hall, flattening the guards at the door.

The door flew open and Hudich stepped through with his hood pulled back, revealing his black skull-like head with red-rat eyes. The Secretary of State and the others screamed in horror as several black-clad figures stormed the car and seized them.

"Mr. Secretary." Hudich smiled, revealing his long canines. "It is a pleasure to meet you."

"Wh—who ar—are you?" the Secretary of State stammered.

His sons wailed with fear as his wife turned ashen with fright, trying to protect the boys. The looks on their faces spoke of entering a surreal house of terror.

"I'm your new master!" Hudich laughed. "Welcome to your worst nightmare!" Hudich turned to one of the black-clad figures. "Take them to the caves!"

"Yes, master," the figure bowed low, and everyone but Hudich disappeared from the car in a flash of light.

The old Arab and his three companions stood on the balcony, staring down on the train stations several blocks away. From their vantage point they could see trains as they arrived and departed the terminals. The station was packed with tourists, business travelers, and shoppers anxious to get to their destinations.

One handed him a pair of binoculars. "Five minutes until we strike!"

"This will be a great victory for Allah." The old Arab accepted the binoculars and put them to his face. "Today we show the infidels that they are at our mercy. It is time for them to bow to Sharia Law or be wiped off the face of the earth!"

"Are we going to give that fool his five minutes?" another asked.

"No, he knew far too much about our operations. Let him die with the others. We have people who can start duplicating the weapon he gave us." The old man lowered his binoculars and checked his watch. "He won't ever know what happened. Besides, I doubt he could have pulled off such a stunt."

A cell phone sitting on the ledge started ringing. One of the men to the right of the old man snatched it up. "What…are you sure…okay?"

"What? Is there a problem?" The old Muslim turned to look at the one with the phone.

"There seems to be something going on in the Secretary's car. All the windows are black. Our spotters can't see him!" the man replied.

"That fool has gone early!" The old man spat, his face flushed with anger. "GIVE THE ORDER!"

"No way," one responded, as the faces of the rest registered bewilderment!

"Yes! GIVE THE ORDER!" the old man demanded, his face changing to a darker shade of red.

The Arab with the phone quickly typed in his message and pressed SEND. A few seconds later a massive blast rocked the city. A ball of roaring hot flame engulfed the train station, sending a shockwave through the city that flattened several buildings across the street from the station. The force of the destruction knocked the Arabs on the balcony to the ground. Screams and car sirens rang out after the deafening blast rolled across the city in all directions.

"What was that?" one asked with surprise.

"Did we ignite an unknown fuel depot?" questioned another. "We didn't have anything that powerful."

"NO, you didn't," a deep voice replied from back within the room. "I supplied the extra power. I needed to make sure all evidence of the Secretary of State's demise appears to have been vaporized." The stranger who offered the vaporizing weapons advanced towards the men.

With panic in their eyes, they scrambled to their feet.

One retrieved an automatic machine gun from under his robes, but before he could level it at the stranger it flew from his hands and over the balcony wall.

The stranger reached up and removed his coverings to reveal Hudich's black skull-like head and red menacing eyes. He flashed a wicked smile, displaying his fangs. "You didn't give me the five minutes I asked for, which means you didn't hold up your end of the bargain! So, you owe me a weapon. Bring it to me!" Hudich extended his hand.

The old Arab trembled as his eyes flicked towards a closed door. "I—it's th—there."

"Get it. Now!" Hudich growled and the old man nodded to another who scrambled to his feet.

The man raced across the room, and as soon as he opened the door the gun slammed into his chest, knocking the wind from him in a loud gasp. He stumbled backwards onto the bed.

The gun zipped into Hudich's outstretched hand. "You really didn't think you could double cross me and get away with it? Did you?" Hudich opened fire, reducing the four Arabs in the room to ashes. Their screams silenced one by one. "That was rather enjoyable. Sending some weak minded fools off to their eternal torment! There will be no reward for them on the other side."

Hudich stepped out of a flash of light and into the chamber where the Zbal had waited to hunt Max four years ago. Alan and several Night Shades bowed to Hudich as he approached the cells that now housed the

Secretary of State and his family. "Welcome to your new home." He chuckled in a low, sinister growl.

The Secretary of State trembled in one cell, while his wife and two boys cowered in the other.

"What the heck are you? What do you want with me?" The Secretary's voice trembled as he found courage to speak. "You won't get away with this!"

"Oh, won't I?" Hudich mocked. "Your people now think you're dead. Vaporized in a blast that killed thousands. They will not be looking for you. You and your family are mine, so I suggest you cooperate in every way or your accommodations may be downgraded. Plus, your family may be forced to suffer for any resistance on your part."

A tear rolled down the Secretary's pale face as he shot a fearful glance towards his family. "What do you want?"

"I want to know how you pulled it off."

"How I pulled what off?" the Secretary shook his head with confusion.

"How you and your party managed to fool the weak minded into electing a president who has no experience and wants to change a free people into a communist-style socialistic state? How you tricked them into giving you control of both houses of congress? You had some help with your deception, and I want to know what it was and where you got it!"

"How we...tricked?" A little light seemed to turn brighter behind the Secretary's eyes. "I think you should set me and my family free." He spoke with a new tone, a soft, convincing melody.

"Yes." Hudich breathed in. "That's what I'm talking about. You're going to tell me where you learned that trick, or life is going to be very unpleasant for all of you. Here no one will hear you or your family's screams!"

3

Evil Spreads

An explosion only a few inches from the tip of Max's wing caused his spacecraft to jerk violently to the left. He forced his ship directly through the fireball in an effort to confuse the enemy on his tail.

"Dang it," he spat as he glanced over his shoulder to see his maneuver hadn't fooled the Koron.

"Max, Max, swing hard to the left," Olik's voice spoke to Max from the earpiece in his helmet.

Max yanked the wheel to the left as a blue laser blast zipped past his ship to collide with the front of his pursuer's craft. The impact blasted the whole front end of the ship away, and the Koron's craft spun out of control before disintegrating into a million pieces.

"Thanks, Olik." Max breathed a sigh of relief.

"Let's get out of here before more of them show up," Olik suggested as he glided his ship even with Max's.

"I won't argue there." Max, a tall sixteen-year-old with wavy brown hair, plunged his spaceship into the atmosphere of Zvezda. Once inside the planet's atmosphere, he let Olik take the lead.

"Let's not mention our little skirmish on this mission to your mother," Olik suggested.

"Hey, but I got three of them," Max chuckled.

"Yes, but we did tell her this was going to be a non-combat operation. I don't think she would have let you come otherwise."

Max smiled to himself as he pictured Olik's face, with his large pale-green head and oversized black eyes, pulling his most stern look. It was an expression Max had seen many times during science or mathematics lessons with him.

"There's the base straight ahead," Olik stated the obvious.

They flew towards a metallic building sitting above the jungle canopy. Max reduced his thrusters and slowed his ship into a gentle hover before dropping it slowly onto the landing platform. As soon as he shut off his engines, he spotted his grandfather and Cindy hurrying towards him. He released the latch sealing his cockpit and then climbed down a ladder on the side of his ship.

"So you had a little fun up there?" Cindy flashed a mischievous grin that made her blue eyes sparkle.

"I wouldn't say fun…" Olik interrupted as he joined them.

"Did you destroy their satellite?" Grandpa asked.

"Yes," Max answered.

"Three of them," Olik added.

"Three?" Grandpa questioned as he rubbed his gray bearded chin, as he always did when his mind seemed to wander with deep thoughts.

"Yes." Olik's alien face showed the concern reflected in Grandpa's.

"What's the big deal?" Cindy questioned, running her hand through her short blond hair. "I'm sure they have more than three of them up there. Which means next time it's my turn to go up."

"Three means they are advancing their agenda quicker than we thought," General Snee burst in with his rough growling voice as he joined the group. He was a large alien with protruding eyes, large nostrils, and small pointed teeth. His egg-shaped head sat on his seven foot muscular frame. "I think we need to take out their communications network. Their numbers are growing and the mark is spreading."

"I'm afraid the general is right," Olik agreed, exchanging a look with Grandpa, whose face had turned to stone as he scratched his chin.

"Mark? What mark?" Max asked glancing at the scar on his palm.

"An evil that is spreading like wildfire throughout the universe. It will soon reach Earth, if it hasn't already. Lines are being drawn and Hudich wants to know whose side you're on," Grandpa said.

"So, Hudich's followers are marking themselves?" Cindy questioned with raised eyebrows. "Won't that make them easy targets for us?"

"Or us for them," Olik interjected.

"Yes, but what about taking out their communications?" the general of the Teeain race asked. His brown skin and his large cat eyes gave Max the impression that the Teeains were a species of tall walking toads.

He kept expecting them to launch some long hidden tongue at a passing insect. Every time he thought he had seen it all another new world left him in wonder.

"I think he's right," Olik agreed. "If we don't do something to hinder their progress they will be able to reach other worlds without the use of a gateway or magic."

"That is obviously why Hudich has given so much attention to this place," Grandpa sighed. "Do you have some maps?"

The general waved them to follow him. As the small group proceeded across the landing platform towards a camouflaged building which rested under some large leafy trees, several troops belonging to the general's race joined then. The general and his men chattered back and forth in a series of clicks and whistles, leaving Max to wonder why they hadn't been given one of Olik's translation devices.

Inside the building several of the general's men worked computers and air traffic equipment. In the center of the room was a table with a glass top. A hologram of some city hovered in the air above the table. On one side of the table were several controls that, when adjusted, moved the map to new locations or zoomed in and rotated the current picture. The general fiddled with the settings and the map changed from a city to a small windowless, moss covered building in the middle of a thick jungle.

The general twisted several knobs, spinning the building around until it came to a stop. The side facing them had a door which suddenly opened, and out scampered a small squad of short hunched-over men with eyes like Olik's. Instead of Olik's green skin, these men had reddish skin that seemed to darken as they moved in and out of the shadows of the jungle.

"This is live?" Cindy asked.

"Obviously, genius," Max smirked.

"Oh shut it!" Cindy tried to hide a smile. "So, what are we looking at?"

"We believe this is the secret hideout of the Smilsums. They have been working with Hudich's people on a secret weapon," Grandpa said.

"They have sworn allegiance to him. If we don't do something to dismantle the pieces, the link will be in place shortly." Olik's face tightened, deep in thought.

"They are very close to achieving their goals," the general interrupted. "I can send my men in to take this bunker."

"I think we should go with them," Olik suggested, turning towards Grandpa.

"I hate to admit it, but I agree," Grandpa said, rubbing his chin as he stared at the hologram in front of him.

"What link? What's so important?" Max asked, his gaze jumping from Grandpa to Olik.

"The link would open up communication lines between worlds. The messages would travel faster than the speed of light. This is the first step in universal travel without a gateway. This could negate the gateway as our upper hand," Olik stated.

"Hudich is searching for more than just a magical way to travel to other worlds. If he can link his followers, he could combine his forces to take over world after world, until they all fall to him," Grandpa added.

"Well, then I guess we'll just have to mess up his plans," Cindy said, flashing a wicked smile.

"So the satellites were pieces to his communication operations?" Max asked.

"Yes," the general stated. "I don't think it's necessary for you to go with my men. They can handle this. There is no reason for you to get further involved. You've helped us enough already."

"I have great confidence in your men." Grandpa bowed his head slightly towards the general. "But I think Olik and I need to have a look at their progress. We have seen it at other sites, but it has been a number of years. We need to see how close they really are."

"Preferably, before your men destroy it," Olik added.

"I understand," the general nodded. "So, how would you like to do this?"

"I think we should go in with your best ground team and take over the bunker. Then we can assess their progress before we destroy it," Grandpa suggested.

"You realize they probably have other bunkers," Olik stated.

"Well, if they're linked, we should be able to locate them as well." Max smiled and raised his eyebrows.

"Gee, you actually made a good point." Cindy winked.

Grandpa chuckled at Cindy's chiding of Max. "What we need from you, General, is for your men to somehow get the enemy out of that bunker so we can go in."

"And we may need their help in getting back out," Olik added.

"Yes, but you are going to get hot." the general smiled. "You will have to wear heat blocking suits which, unfortunately, trap heat in. They use heat trackers to monitor their perimeter, along with video surveillance. You will need to be very careful. We don't know how deep that bunker is underground. There could be thousands of troops stationed there. And if it's as important as we think it is, I'm sure there are other nasty surprises awaiting you."

"That all sounds rather cheery don't you think?" Max smirked.

"Yes." Cindy smiled.

"Just give us a distraction and the supplies we will need," Grandpa said as he shook his head, rolled his eyes, and attempted to suppress a smile.

An hour later they waited in a hanger dressed in their heavy camouflaged suits, with a squad of about forty armed Teeains. Each soldier carried a backpack and an ominously large rifle. Each rifle was the length of earthly muskets, but the hole for the projectile to pass through was big enough for a golf ball-sized bullet.

"The general wasn't kidding about the heat," Cindy complained as she pulled her collar to the side in an attempt to let some cool air in. "With this aluminum-wrapped interior, I feel like a TV dinner inside the oven."

"Yes, but you look like a…" Max started to comment.

"All right, let's not start that," Grandpa interrupted before Max could finish his teasing comment.

"Hey, she doesn't need your help," Max protested.

"I wasn't helping *her*." Grandpa chuckled as Max's jaw dropped open and Cindy laughed out loud.

"Are we ready?" the general asked as he entered the hangar and joined them. "We will drop you and some guides in a canyon about three miles from the bunker. The pilot will keep the ship inside the canyon for almost the entire flight to help avoid detection. The squad will exit about seven miles to the northeast of your drop zone. You have the more difficult terrain to cross, so your head start should put you in position to enter the bunker after they have drawn most of the Smilsums troops away. I'm sure you are going to face some resistance, so be ready." The general let out a few strange clicks and two solders hurried over to join them. "This is Zaat and Kit, they will be your escorts."

They all exchanged names and handshakes.

"Why don't we just use the gateway to get in closer?" Max asked.

"Because we don't know where they've placed all their security devices," Olik stated. "I have the equipment to locate them, so we can either destroy or avoid them all together."

"Yeah." Cindy smiled as if she had known the answer all along.

Max twisted his face up into the goofiest expression and said in his most feminine-sounding voice, "Yeah."

"That's the smartest you've looked in years," Olik jabbed at Max.

"Hey." Max smiled. "Did she bribe all of you to gang up on me or something?"

"Nope, you're just an easy target," Olik chuckled.

Grandpa handed them each a helmet with a glass faceplate that was the same pattern of camouflage as the suit. "All right! Enough fooling around. Let's get going," Grandpa said as he herded them towards the hovercraft sitting in the middle of the hanger.

They all piled into the craft that had an open door on both sides, similar to a helicopter except it was longer, like a plane. Rows of seats lined both walls, with bars running down the center to maintain one's balance if one chose to stand. The hovercraft had three tinted viewing windows positioned along each side. Max and Cindy sat sideways in their seats to watch as the craft floated off the floor of the hangar and out into the forest beyond.

A blur of green zoomed by as the ship rocketed just above the canopy. The slight tilt of the ship here and there indicated a change in course and the increase and decrease of a steady humming gave the feeling of constant speed fluctuations.

"Woo." Cindy smiled and Max laughed as the ship dropped sharply over the face of a cliff, tickling their stomachs.

"I love those drops," Max grinned.

The ship flew through a deep crevice in the forest floor, heading toward a cut in the sheer rock face on the other side. The pilots maneuvered the ship right into the narrow opening in the cliff walls. The steepness of the walls made it impossible for Max and Cindy to see anything except fuzzy walls of rock. Occasionally, Max got a glimpse of a river a few hundred feet below them.

Suddenly the distorted rock walls came into focus, and the vibrations given off by the engines decreased as the ship came to a stop. The craft slowly descended to the bottom of the canyon, where it came to rest on a sandbar next to a raging river.

"Let's go," Grandpa said as he followed the two Teeains out of the ship.

Max, Cindy and Olik hurried out the door. The second they hit the sand the Teeain ship roared to life, climbed back up the canyon, spun around, and flew off. The mist from the river's rapids created a rainbow where the planet's sun penetrated the canyon.

"This way," Kit whispered as he pointed in the direction he wanted them to go.

Zaat took the lead. He entered a thicket of willow-like trees at the back of the sandbar next to the rock wall of the canyon. Inside the shelter of the trees they hiked along a well-used trail. The heat of the day, along with the heavy suit, caused Max to perspire. He constantly fought the urge to run back and jump in the river to cool off as sweat dripped from his nose and down his back. The roar of the river behind them silenced or muffled all other sounds.

The trail curved to the left right up against the cliff face. It ran along the canyon wall for about a quarter mile upriver where it turned into a narrow crack in the mountainside. This split contained a natural rock staircase. The steps were not all the same size or height, but they climbed steadily up the narrow opening. Every once in a while a step would flatten for several dozen feet ahead, like a landing, before abutting the next group of stairs. Some parts of the slit were so narrow it forced Max to turn sideways to get through. His suit brushed the red rock here and there as he went. The pounding of the river grew softer, and the heavy breathing of the group became the dominant sound.

This heat is unbearable, Max thought.

After a grueling climb, the top of the crevice started to draw closer with each step. Zaat brought the group to a halt on a small flat area about ten feet before the exit. "Put on your helmets now."

"This is where we'll need to start scanning for security devices," Kit added.

Max dropped his helmet over his head, which only added to his discomfort from the heat. Now his hot breath bounced back into his face, giving him a slightly suffocating sensation. "This stinks," he mumbled, to which Cindy nodded.

Olik retrieved a round remote control-looking device from a small backpack he had slung across his back. After typing in several commands, two silver antennas extended a few inches from the top. "It looks like the first security sensor is a camera about fifty yards ahead, directly between us and the bunker. It may be pointed directly at our exit point," Olik informed them.

"How long do we have until the Teeains launch the diversion?" Max asked.

Grandpa pushed up his sleeve to check his watch. "Just over twenty minutes."

"I think I should take a look over the rim," Olik stated as he maneuvered to the front of the group. He pulled out a pair of binoculars and crept closer to the top of the canyon. Once there he got on his hands and knees and finally on his stomach, with the top of his helmet barely above the crest. He remained motionless with the glasses stuck to his face for several minutes before he squirmed his way back to them.

"It is watching the crevice we're in, and it appears to be a combination of a heat tracking and motion detector. I don't think we are going to be able to exit this canyon right there without giving ourselves away," Olik said.

Kit and Zaat began clicking back and forth to each other as Kit pointed to a spot a few yards back down the narrow canyon. Everyone's gaze followed his finger to a spot about a dozen feet up and surrounded by thick bushy trees. In addition to the cover which the trees would provide, the canyon wall right next to it appeared to be scalable.

"Either we all go up that way or one of us does and then tries to take out the camera," Zaat spoke in English.

"How far is the bunker from the mouth of the canyon?" Grandpa asked.

"About a mile," Kit answered.

Grandpa lifted his helmet and began rubbing his chin like he always did when he worked on an idea. "Did you detect any other security measures?" He glanced at Olik.

After a few seconds of playing with his gadget, "There are others but they are too far off our direct path to worry about. I only detect the one that could give us away now."

"How much time do you think the diversion will buy us?"

"Maybe fifteen minutes," Zaat replied.

"That's not enough time for us to cross a mile, find out what we want to know, and get back out," Cindy stated the obvious.

"We only need to take out the regular camera. Our suits will hide us from the heat detectors. If only one goes down, they may think it is just a malfunctioning camera," Kit offered.

"True," Olik agreed.

"So, someone is going to have to go up there and disable the camera," Grandpa stated.

"I'll go," Max said eyeing the rock face. "I mean, I'm probably the best climber here and I have that sixth sense."

"Second best," Cindy interrupted. "I'll go."

"In your dreams," Max protested.

"All right," Grandpa raised his voice slightly above a whisper. "Who's better at the invisibility spell?"

Cindy folder her arms across her chest as her lips formed a huge pout. "Max!"

"If I'm going to use an invisibility spell, why do I need to climb up here? Why not just walk right out the easy way, through the opening?" Max asked, waving his hand toward the mouth of the canyon.

"Because my gadget only picks up sensory devices, it doesn't detect trip wires and booby traps. You are going to have to find those for us, and an ideal location for those would be right outside the mouth of the canyon. It will be easier for you to look for them without a camera watching your every move," Olik explained.

"So watch where you step," Grandpa admonished.

"The cameras are straight ahead of the opening to this canyon about fifty yards away. I'm guessing in a tree, so you might have more climbing to do when you get there," Olik stated.

The two Teeains hunched over facing each other and locked hands, giving Max a place to step up. "Get ready," Kit said.

As soon as Max placed his hands on their shoulders and stepped into their hands, they gave a great upward heave, launching Max into the air and out of the canyon. He landed right behind a group of trees and latched onto some lower branches to keep from falling over. Due to the surprise of the short flight, he took a few deep breaths to calm his racing heart. He had only expected them to give him a small boost, not throw him the entire distance.

A quick check of his surroundings revealed a typical forest landscape. Trees and shrubs grew everywhere, but not to the point of restricting passage. His path forward had only a slight incline. The distant roar of the river floated up behind him. Small animals scampered here and there, and the calls of strange birds rang out from the trees and sky.

"*Izginim se*," Max mumbled and disappeared.

He checked the immediate area for any trip wires or traps before rounding the trees to creep towards the spot where the cameras should be. He wanted to be cautious but felt the need to hurry so they could be in position when the diversion happened. After lining himself up in front of the canyon, he weaved his way in the same direction in an effort to locate the security devices. His eyes continually scanned the ground in front of him and the general area for any sign of movement or hidden danger.

Max noticed the farther away from the river he got, the hotter the temperature rose inside his heavy suit. Sweat ran down his body and caused his faceplate to steam up, distorting his vision.

Hushed voices raised the hairs on the back of his neck and froze him in place. His heartbeat pounded in his ears, interfering with his ability to hear clearly. The one thing Max wished the invisibility spell did was hide him from insects. Their ability to follow him by tracking carbon dioxide instead of sight never failed them. Between the muffled roar of the distant river and the bugs flying around his ears and trying to penetrate his helmet, Max couldn't be sure what he had heard.

Swatting his hands around his earholes to chase away the bugs, he started forward once more. He had to force himself to maintain his concentration so as to not lose his invisibility spell before he reached the cameras. The annoying insects and the stifling heat pushed his limits greater than a battle or running. Suddenly the chatter of voices halted him again. *It's only bugs!* Max regained his composure in time to avoid a trip wire running along the bottom of the trees, spreading in a wide circle around the bunker.

Eventually Max spied the cameras in a large leafy tree about ten feet off the forest floor. They sat on the base of a large limb joining the trunk of the tree. Anyone not looking for them would easily miss them, as they rested in the shadows of the tree's canopy, with only the lenses visible from below. Circling the tree, Max found a good spot to climb. He would be out of the camera's direct line of sight. *It would be a lot easier without this heavy suit!*

He placed his foot on a stub about a foot and a half off the ground and wrapped his arms around the trunk before stepping up. Again! Conversations! He waited for several seconds before shaking his head to shoo away the insects trying to crawl inside his ears. Then he ascended the tree until he was even with the cameras.

"Which one is which?" he whispered to himself before realizing the thermal imaging camera had a small screen on the back showing the temperatures of everything out in front of him. *Bingo!* Max unscrewed the wire attached to the other device when some heat signatures on the small screen captured his eye. Lifting his visor for a clearer view, he unwilling gave the pesky insects access to his flesh. He almost lost his balance trying to swipe the little pests away as he scrambled out of the tree so his hands would be free to squash the annoying critters.

He hit the ground hard after jumping the last five feet from the trunk. He swatted and wiped his face several times before closing the face plate once more. "Stupid bugs!" he muttered to himself as he rounded the tree and headed back towards the canyon.

The weird sense he acquired from the spiders poison screamed at him to be cautious. He knew he wasn't alone and he could detect the approach of something very large. It was so big it dominated his thoughts.

Max spotted Grandpa and the others as they exited the canyon, which caused him to pick up his pace. He tried to signal them to stop and forgot about the trip wire he had avoided earlier. His legs caught the wire, dragging Max to the ground. An alarm rang out from unseen speakers, and several Smilsum troops sprang out of the trees above.

Before Max could get to his feet two Smilsum soldiers jumped on top of him, pinning him to the ground. Max caught sight of Grandpa and the others slipping back into the canyon just as the Smilsums flipped him over and yanked of his helmet, and the butt of a gun came crashing down on his forehead. Blackness!

4

Surprise Advances

"He's disabled the camera and is on his way back," Olik said as he went from lying at the opening of the canyon to a kneeling position.

Joe and the others gathered behind Olik as he arose to his feet.

"Are you sure?" Kit asked.

"Yes, he's heading back and he's not invisible," Olik added.

Before they could exit the canyon, an earsplitting ringing echoed through the forest. They hunched at the mouth of the canyon as several concealed Smilsums sprang from the trees to pounce on Max.

Joe's heart leapt into his throat as he ran with Cindy to Max's aid before Kit and Zaat pulled the surprised group back into the safety of the canyon.

"We have to help him," Cindy demanded in a harsh whisper, waving her arm in his direction.

"We will," Zaat stated. "But we need to wait for the distraction to start. That should give us an advantage."

"He's right," Olik agreed. "Besides, I suspect they will conduct a search to make sure he's alone. He's wearing a Teeain suit. They aren't going to believe he's alone."

"Olik, help Kit. I'll hide Zaat. Cindy disappear, climb back up to the mouth of the canyon, and tell us what's happening," Joe ordered.

"*Izginim se,*" Cindy uttered, and vanished.

Joe felt Cindy brush by him and he, Olik, Kit, and Zaat moved back down to where they had been hiding.

"They're discussing something," Cindy whispered back down to them. "There are two of them heading this way!"

###

Sharp pain throbbed in Max's forehead and he couldn't figure out why. Even his eyes ached and he had difficulty opening them. A strange language riddled the air, as shapes started to materialize and were standing over him. *Oh yeah, the Smilsums.* Narrow bearded faces sat on top of overly large frames. They wore black military uniforms with scarves wrapped around their heads.

Max laid on his back in a circle of angry Smilsums. They jabbered back and forth in their strange language and constantly gestured towards him with their weapons. Max used his hands to shade his eyes from the sun so he could get a better look at his captors. As he squinted to see the soldiers, it appeared one of them was speaking to him.

"I...don't understand you," Max said, his head pounding like it was about to split in two.

The one pointing at him signaled for another to come over. They chatted back and forth for a few seconds before the new Smilsum knelt next to Max. "W—who you? What you do here?"

Max received a hard slap that shot pain bouncing through his head.

"Answer!" the Smilsum demanded.

Suddenly, a high-pitched cry, like a scream that teetered on the verge of insanity, echoed through the forest. The Smilsums all jerked in the direction of the call. Max remembered where he was and what he was doing. *The diversion!*

The wail came a second time, but closer. The Smilsums flinched at the noise, their eyes darting back and forth. An uneasy feeling spread through Max's body, as if his blood was draining away. He knew this wasn't the reaction to an alarm but something else. Something more terrifying.

The ground started to shake at quick intervals as if something very large raced in their direction.

###

Joe and Olik helped hide Zaat and Kit with the invisibility spell as two armed Smilsums peered into the canyon from above. They hurried along the top edge on both sides, peeking into the crack. They were on their way back from the front of the cliffs when the spine-tingling screech filled the air.

The two Smilsums at the mouth of the canyon froze. When the second, closer, yell roared, they darted back towards the others surrounding Max.

"What the heck is that?" Cindy asked with a hint of panic in her voice.

Alarm sirens filled the air, adding more disarray to the horrible screaming. Everyone released their invisibility spells and exchanged worried looks.

Joe helped Cindy to her feet as he joined her at the mouth of the canyon. Olik and the others were right behind him.

"It is a Volk," Kit said as the ground began to vibrate beneath their feet. "A giant ravenous monster."

"What are we going to do?" Cindy asked.

"Did the decoy set off the alarm or the Volk?" Olik asked.

"I'm not sure, but we need to get Max out of there," Zaat offered as he swung his rifle off of his back into a ready position.

Another piercing scream launched the Smilsums into a panicked retreat through the trees. Max only had a few seconds to roll under some nearby bushes as the monstrous Volk bounded past him in pursuit of the fleeing Smilsums. A flash of lumpy, muscular, yellow-orange legs darted past Max's position. One enormous man-like foot print covered the ground where Max had lain only seconds earlier.

A moment later the alarm rang out, mixed with Smilsums' cries of horror and the Volk's roars of delight.

Max sprang to his feet to get a better view of the beast as it pursued the frightened Smilsums. To his complete shock the monster snatched up several of the scrambling Smilsums and devoured them in a giant mouthful. The Smilsums weapons bounced harmlessly off the creature's thick yellow-orange muscular skin as they tried to defend themselves. The beast would pick up the fleeing Smilsums with its huge hands and then gulp them down.

"Are you okay?" Grandpa asked from behind Max, prompting him to jump.

"Now is the perfect chance," Kit suggested. "Hurry."

"Do you think we should help them?" Max asked as he tried to pull his eyes away from the gruesome scene. The Smilsums' screams caused his skin to crawl and he wanted it to stop.

"Are you crazy? With that *thing*?" Cindy argued.

"We must go. This could be our only chance," Zaat stated. "They would not try to help us if the situation was reversed."

"But that's not what I'm going to do," Max said, darting toward the massacre with Cindy, Olik, and Grandpa right on his heels. Zaat and Kit followed, but at a distance.

"What's your plan?" Cindy asked as they took shelter behind thick bushes.

"Don't let it catch us." Max managed a weak smile before uttering the invisibility spell and disappearing.

"Great plan." Grandpa rolled his eyes and disappeared, as did Cindy and Olik.

Max worried the invisibility spell might not hide the fact that his heart pounded so loudly in his chest the beast might be able to locate him. He tried to swallow the dry lump in his throat as he circled around the hideous beast pursuing a couple of Smilsums.

The creature was surprisingly quick for its enormous size, standing at least thirty feet tall and scampering about on two legs. It wore some sort of animal skin around its waist, but other than that sparse patches of black hair covered its muscular rough skin. The thing was filthy and gave off a pungent stench in its wake.

As it attempted to grab one of the Smilsums, Max sent a blast of fire onto the creature's back, enabling the Smilsum to avoid certain death. The ground rocked as the monster dropped on its back in an effort to put out the fire. The shock wave knocked Max and the others off their feet.

Max gasped for air as the impact forced the air from his lungs. He almost let out a scream as he caught site of the creature's face for the first time. Its bloodshot yellow pupil-less eyes scanned the area where Max lay concealed behind his magic. Blood and decaying matter covered its foot-long rotting canines, which protruded from the lengthy baboon-like snout. Huge pustules oozed from its wrinkled face as it bounced back up to its feet and continued the chase.

As fast as he could, Max scrambled to his feet and sped after the monster. The beast was an easy target to follow as it towered above the trees, but Max could not locate the fleeing Smilsums. He rounded a small copse of bushy trees as the creature made a grab for another Smilsum.

"*Premakni!*" Grandpa's voice rang out from Max's right, and the spell pushed the Smilsum away from the monster's fatal grip.

"*Prizgaj,*" called Cindy, setting the ground around the Volk ablaze.

The Volk threw back its grotesque head and let out a wail of frustration, using its arms to protect itself from the heat of the fire. Suddenly, the beast leaped several feet into the air and landed well outside the ring of fire. His landing caused the ground to crack beneath his feet and threw everyone to the ground once more.

Before Max could regain his feet, another Smilsum's cry echoed through the forest as he became the latest meal for the Volk. The spine tingling wail of the Volk's latest victim drove Max forward at a greater pace as the beast attempted to corral its next snack.

"*Premakni!*" Max screamed and sent a shockwave into the back of the monster's knees, buckling it.

The sudden momentary loss of its legs forced the Volk to face plant into a group of trees. The impact of its landing dislodged trees and they flew through the air like bowling pins. Loud cracking and thuds accompanied the breaking, falling trees. A raging roar escaped the Volk's lips as it scanned the forest for what had caused its fall, but the soft moan of a Smilsum pinned beneath an uprooted tree grabbed the Volk's attention.

Dirt, spit and blood dripped from the Volk's baboon-like snout as it took two large steps forward to tower over its captive prey. Before it could snatch up its next morsel a perfectly pitched rock struck it in the eye. Two massive hands clamped over its injured eye as it cried out like a hurt child.

Max raced to the pinned Smilsum's aid. "Relax," he said as he began to lift the tree off the trapped man. The expression on the Smilsum's face revealed fear at hearing a disembodied voice. Max cast the spell to reveal himself to the Smilsum he was trying to help, prompting the Smilsum's eyes to grow even wider. Max managed to free the Smilsum from the fallen tree, and was in the process of helping him to his feet when he realized his mistake. The Volk's roar of delight blasted Max with a wave of foul rotting air as the beast towered over them.

"*Oviraj*," Max shouted, throwing his hands in the air with palms up as the Volk tried to smash him and the Smilsum to the ground with its fist. The spell sprang to life just in time as the Volk's hand crunched against the protective shield, driving the invisible bubble shielding Max and the Smilsum a foot into the ground. The Volk's hand broke against the spell and Max collapsed under the weight of the blow.

Before the Volk could recover from its injury, Grandpa and Cindy flattened it to the ground using the *premakni* spell. Then Olik blasted the beast with a weapon he had retrieved from his backpack. The Volk's body convulsed a few moments after being shot and then went still.

Kit and Zaat hustled out of the trees to help Max and the injured Smilsum. Max got up and helped Kit and Zaat drag the injured Smilsum into the cover of some nearby trees. Olik joined them and began examining the Smilsum's leg. The Smilsum's wide eyes reflected surprise at his rescuers. He continually muttered something and didn't show any sign of resisting them.

"What's he saying?" Max asked.

"Thank you," Zaat offered.

"How is he?" Grandpa and Cindy asked, catching up to them.

"His leg is broken but I should be able to stabilize it so he can travel," Olik responded as he dug in his pack.

"How are you?" Grandpa turned to Max. "That was quite a blow you blocked."

"Yeah, nearly drove us into the ground like a stake," Max said as he exhaled in relief. "I've got a bit of a headache and I'm a little light headed, but otherwise I'm all right."

"Really, of all the places for you to be injured, I always thought your rock solid head would be the last," Cindy winked.

"Look who's talking. You could knock down a castle wall with that brick of yours," Max retorted good-naturedly.

"Olik, after you're done with the Smilsum, will you make sure Max doesn't have a concussion?" Grandpa said.

"Just give me..." Olik stopped as he looked past the others.

Everyone whirled around at Olik's reaction to see three Smilsums standing behind them with their guns leveled towards them. They spoke in regular tones as they approached, their eyes darting back and forth at each member of the small company. The continued ringing of the perimeter sirens had hidden the Smilsums' approach.

"They want to know why we risked our lives to save their friend here, and they want to surrender to us," Kit said as he shook his head with disbelief. Everyone's mouths fell open and they stared from Kit to the three Smilsums.

"They saw what you did to the Volk. I think that scared them," Zaat offered.

"Tell them, no one deserves to be eaten," Max said.

Grandpa tried to offer a different response but Kit had already begun translating. His language filled the air with a strange chirping sound. To everyone's surprise, the Smilsums nodded their heads as if agreeing with him and lowered their weapons. They then placed their guns on the ground and raised their hands in surrender.

"It seems you've made some friends," Kit responded.

"They also want to know why we are here," Zaat stated.

"Do you think we should tell them?" Cindy countered.

"I don't think so," Grandpa said, glancing at the others. "We'll take them with us and release them when we leave."

"They may just slow us down and endanger our mission," Olik offered as he finished binding the Smilsum's broken leg. It took a bit of convincing and translation from Kit to get the Smilsum to swallow a painkiller Olik wanted him to take. He and Kit helped the Smilsum to his feet and passed him to two of his friends. "He should be fine to move."

"From the sounds of things our diversion is still taking place, but we have lost a lot of valuable time," Kit stated.

"We need to hurry," Zaat suggested.

"Yes, if they find the body of the Volk or wonder what's happened to it, they will know something is up," Grandpa said.

"Kit, you bring up the rear and keep an eye on the Smilsums. The rest of you follow me."

Zaat led the small group through the trees and back the direction they'd followed to help the Smilsums. They hustled toward their destination with their prisoners in tow. The Smilsums didn't offer any resistance and did their best to maintain the same pattern of movement displayed by the others.

When they reached the spot where Max had deactivated the security sensors, they paused to survey the area. The sirens and sounds of fighting started to diminish with each passing moment, indicating the diversion was almost over. Only the occasional bird or ground rodent moved, making it appear as if the immediate area had calmed down.

"Let's do this," Cindy said.

Max's heart, which had finally relaxed after their ordeal with the Volk, began to beat faster once more. He licked his lips to try to ease their dryness, but his mouth had nothing to offer.

Zaat waved his arm and they scampered from one place of shelter to another in an attempt to remain hidden from any unknown eyes or security devices. After traversing a couple hundred yards of the forest, they spotted their target. Trees and shrubs surrounded the small building, creating the appearance they were devouring the white structure.

Their prisoners, who had remained silent before, began to whisper back and forth to each other rapidly. The closer they got to the building the more agitated the prisoners became.

"What are they saying?" Olik finally whispered.

"I'm not sure. They are using a dialect I don't fully understand now, but they seem to be arguing about something," Kit offered.

"Do you think maybe we should leave them here," Max suggested, and Cindy nodded. "They are unarmed. Kit should be able to handle them until we get back."

"What do you think?" Grandpa asked Kit. "I don't want to leave you by yourself if you are uncomfortable."

The Smilsums continued to chatter back and forth, but now in a more animated manner. Arms flailed and fingers pointed. They seemed unconcerned they were unarmed and surrounded as their voices continued to rise.

"Enough!" Zaat barked, pointing his gun at the Smilsums to bring an end to their discussion.

The Smilsum with the broken leg cleared his throat and raised his hands. He then rattled off something to Zaat.

"He says we must not go in there," Zaat translated.

"Did he say why?" Grandpa asked.

"Yes, but I don't understand the word he used. Did you, Kit?"

"No!" Kit responded and began speaking to the Smilsum. After a few moments: "Something about security or a precaution."

"Ask him if there are troops inside," Olik suggested.

Again the strange conversation went back and forth. "No troops, but he seems to be adamant about us not going in there."

"What do you think?" Olik asked. "It may just be a ploy to keep us out."

"True. I don't think we can fully trust them. They are working for Hudich, even if these Smilsums don't really know it. They have to have some loyalty to their people," Grandpa said.

"I say we go and get this done," Max stated.

"I can handle these Smilsums," Kit offered. "Zaat can lead you the rest of the way."

Everyone exchanged glances. The Smilsums had calmed down and were no longer conversing. Their eyes jumped from face to face as if waiting to see what was going to happen.

Grandpa inhaled a deep breath. "Let's go."

As the group turned to leave, the Smilsums voices rose to a level that could give away their position to any troops in the area. Kit jumped to the front of the prisoners and leveled his weapon at them, bringing about immediate silence. "I've got this covered he said looking over his shoulder at the others."

They left the cover of the trees and headed toward the small building. When they were within fifty yards of the structure the sirens stopped, bringing them to a halt. They stood motionless, listening, as if expecting an attack at any moment. They had just let out a collective exhale.

"Look OUT!" Kit screamed.

Everyone whirled around to see a Smilsum heading toward them with a gun. Max shoved Cindy out of the way before diving in the opposite direction. The Smilsum took aim and fired a shot past the small group and into the building. The impact caused the structure to explode in a huge fireball, raining down hot smoke and debris over the surrounding area.

5

Communications Surprise

Max covered his head to protect himself from the falling pieces of trees, shrubs, and building materials. He coughed hard as smoke penetrated his lungs, stinging his mouth and nostrils. His eyes burned and watered as he rubbed them in an effort to see through the cloudy dust.

"Is everyone okay?" Grandpa coughed, almost tripping over Max.

"Yes," came several responses.

It took several minutes for the smoke to clear. The others removed their helmets and continued to struggle for air, choking and gagging on the thick hot smoke. They managed to make their way back to where Kit had regained control of the Smilsums. Although he appeared to be doing so in a relaxed manner, he carried his gun over his shoulder, enquiring if everyone was okay.

"Why aren't you guarding the prisoners?" Zaat demanded as he continued to brush debris from his suit.

"Because our prisoners just saved your lives," Kit stated.

"What?" Max and Cindy questioned.

"He just tried to blow us up!" Zaat barked.

"Relax. That's what I thought too when I tackled him from behind. He didn't put up a fight and then I checked the settings on the gun. He didn't know how to use it and I had set it to stun. There is no way that setting could have destroyed a building. I think it was a trap," Kit said.

"Well Max, it seems your good deed saved our lives." Grandpa smiled.

"Now what do we do?" Cindy asked, running her fingers through her hair.

It looked like everyone had been playing in a coal pile. Black smudges covered their clothes and faces. They glanced at each other, searching for their next move.

"I think we need to head back to base. Get out of this area before more Smilsums arrive," Zaat suggested.

"What do we do with them?" Olik motioned towards the prisoners.

"Tell them they are free," Grandpa told Kit.

Kit began a conversation with the Smilsums while everyone else prepared to head back to the base.

"What are we going to do about their communications structure? If Hudich is allowed to communicate freely and easily with other worlds, bad things are going to happen," Max said.

"Yes, but this obviously isn't the entrance point to their operations." Cindy waved her hand towards the still smoldering structure.

"Well, we need to regroup and figure out our next move, and I doubt we can do that from here," Grandpa said.

"I agree…" Olik started.

"They want to know why we are here," Kit interrupted.

"I don't think we should tell them that, since we will have to plan another attempt on their communication operations," Zaat stated.

"I think Zaat is right," Grandpa agreed.

"No, you don't understand. They are offering to help us," Kit said. "They've got a pretty good idea what we were up to by where we were trying to go." Kit's gaze jumped to the destroyed building. "They said they want, I'm guessing they are referring to Hudich when they say 'rotting skull-faced demon,' out of their people's lives. They know his people have been here to work on the communications stuff."

"This could be a trap," Olik pointed out.

"Yes, lure us into a situation we can't get out of," Zaat agreed.

"I don't think so. They keep saying something about—it's time for the silent majority to stand up against the radical fringe. A few evil Smilsums are ruling the rest, using fear and brutality," Kit informed them.

"Well, I can agree with that," Zaat said. "It is happening in other worlds and has happened throughout history, where the silent majority has fallen victim to radical groups ruling them with an iron fist."

"I think we should go for it," Max interjected. "I mean, we're here, and with their help it may be the best and only chance we get at this. We obviously don't know how to get into their underground base."

"Dim wit has a point." Cindy smiled.

"Ask them if they can get us into the heart of their communications systems," Grandpa said to Kit, who began chattering away with the Smilsums.

"Yes, this one is a programmer who helped set up the system. He got demoted to military work when an old rival was promoted manager of the operation. He says he knows a few backdoor passwords and can still access the system," Kit interpreted after a few minutes.

"What if we run into more Smilsums?" Cindy asked. "What do we do then?"

"Ask them what kinds of forces are in the facility: guards, checkpoints, other security devices," Olik told Kit.

"Yes, how are we going to deal with any resistance?" Grandpa added.

Once again everyone waited with their eyes glued on the conversation between Kit and the Smilsums. Max wondered if they were going to get the chance to do what they had set out to accomplish.

"They said there will be random guards and workers but if we give them their guns..." Kit started, but a few protests interrupted him. He held up his hands to silence the comments. "Without ammunition, they should be able to cause a diversion."

"How?" Max asked, more loudly than he would have liked. The absence of the wailing sirens allowed his voice to carry. Cindy punched him in the arm with a look that told him to keep it down. Max shot glances in all directions before turning his focus back to Kit.

"Well, we would be high priority prisoners. Especially you, because you are not from this planet. They will be taking us to a top security location, which happens to be very close to the command center," Kit said.

"What about our weapons?" Grandpa asked.

"Conceal what you can carry. We hide the rest here," Zaat said.

"I say we go for it." Cindy grinned in excitement.

"This may be our only chance. Plus, we have inside help." Grandpa tipped his head toward the Smilsums.

Everyone gave a nod of agreement.

"Kit, empty their weapons," Zaat ordered. "Everything you can't hide in your clothes we'll stash under some bushes."

"I'll need one of them to carry my backpack. The equipment we need is inside and it might look suspicious if I'm still wearing it," Olik stated.

They spent the next few minutes deciding what to take and how they would hide some of their weapons in their suits. Kit unloaded the

Smilsums' weapons, which resembled basic firearms that shot metallic projectiles based on a compact explosion. They loaded everything they couldn't carry into a large duffle-type pack which they deposited under some dense foliage. After making sure the Smilsums fully understood the plan, Olik handed over his backpack and they followed the Smilsums out of their place of cover.

One Smilsum, Gor, took the lead, with Max and the others between him and the three remaining Smilsums. One helped the injured Smilsum, while the other pretended to cover the group from behind.

Gor acted as if he was in charge, proceeding through the forest as if he belonged in the area. He took them to the spot where they had captured Max off-guard. They circled around a thick patch of bushes until Gor disappeared into a hidden fold. If Gor hadn't pointed it out, Max would have never guessed there was an entrance.

The inside of the bushes had been hollowed out, and it formed a small room which was barely big enough for all of them to stand. In the dark shade of the blind, one could spy on the entire area through the branches.

"No wonder they caught me," Max muttered.

In the back corner there was a portal with a door in the forest floor. It reminded Max of a hatch to a submarine. It even had a wheel-like locking mechanism in the center.

Gor chatted with Kit in the strange clicking language for several moments.

"He says we will have to climb down several meters to reach the main level of the underground complex. He thinks it would be better if we don't speak for a while. I'll try to pass instructions when I can, otherwise we're just going to have to follow his lead," Kit said.

"This is the last chance to leave before we enter a hornets' nest," Zaat offered.

"I think everyone is settled on going," Grandpa said, and they all nodded their agreement.

Zaat took a deep breath, "Let's get this over with."

Gor twisted the wheel counter clockwise and a loud hiss filled the area when the seal on the door broke. The lid swung upward and a soft whistle of wind came out of the hole as if they were about to enter a ventilation shaft. Gor slid down the outside rails of the ladder. A feat he had performed several times a day.

Max and the others descended the ladder with ease. They had to wait a few minutes for the injured Smilsum to climb down without the use of his leg. Once everyone was down, Gor led them through a round white tube, which reminded Max of a large, very clean, drainage pipe. The width of the tunnel was big enough for them to walk through two by two. The ladder was not the end of their descent underground. The path angled slightly downward, taking them deeper into the planet.

They began passing junctions here and there, and doors started appearing along the tunnel at regular intervals. Even though they hadn't yet passed any other Smilsums, Max's senses kicked into overdrive. He glanced at Cindy to see that she was doing the same thing. These strange powerful senses, produced by the spider's poison two years ago, hadn't lessened. They had both learned to develop and control it better. They also had to learn how to turn that sense off, otherwise it interfered with operations by revealing too much information about their surroundings. On one occasion Max almost got them captured when he mistook a large magical animal for a Night Shade.

Suddenly, Cindy's wide eyes and worried expression reflected what she was feeling upon the approach of a group of Smilsums. Even though Max and the others were posing as prisoners, he knew that while they were deep inside an enemy's fortress, anything could happen. They didn't know the escape routes and could find themselves outnumbered and cornered very easily.

After a few minutes of continuing along in the same direction, voices and thudding boots in the tunnel ahead confirmed what Max had picked up on. Max started to wonder if he should block out his special sense because it only added more strain on his nerves. Plus, he didn't think his little gift was going to help him when there wasn't a handy escape exit nearby. *We must be a half mile from the portal back in the forest!*

The tightness of the tunnel forced them to line up single file along the wall to let the small squad pass by. No one spoke or attempted to ask Gor where he was taking these prisoners, but the expressions on the group's faces indicated a great deal of curiosity. Max tried to avoid direct eye contact in an effort to appear subdued.

Gor held them where they were until the squad had disappeared down the tunnel and the hallway fell silent once more. He chatted with Kit in a low whisper for several moments.

"He says the detention area is around the corner and the command center is a hundred yards past that. Once we pass the detention area, we are going to look suspicious, so after that be ready. If we run into anyone beyond that point, we'll probably be stopped. Plus, we might have to sneak past the prison area. He says there are usually guards," Kit relayed to the group in a low voice.

"Why don't we leave the injured one and another there? If we need to make a run for it, he might only hamper us?" Zaat asked.

"Good point," Grandpa concurred.

After a short exchange between the Smilsums, Kit translated once again. "There is a dispensary in the detention center. They will go ahead and try to create a diversion. They had to have heard of the Volk attack. They will just say he was injured in that, which he was."

"Agreed," Grandpa said as everyone else nodded.

"Everyone ready?" Olik smiled his thin line smile. "Make sure your weapons are set to stun. We don't want to cause a cave in. We don't know how stable this structure is."

"Turn on your senses you two," Grandpa whispered while everyone adjusted their weapons.

"I had to switch it off. It was only adding to the tension." Max smiled.

"Glad I wasn't the only one who thought so," Cindy exhaled.

Gor grunted in his strange language to get everyone's attention and then waved them to follow him. He led them to the turn where he took a peek before proceeding forward. They passed no one, and Gor didn't slow again until they reached the edge of the detention center.

Max could sense several Smilsums—as well as prisoners—while they approached the area, but nothing seemed out of the ordinary. No one acted alarmed or was even aware they were there.

The soft murmur of voices joined the slight whistle of the air current flowing through the tunnel system as they drew near the detention center. Gor brought them to a halt and motioned the injured Smilsum and his aide forward. Max and the others crowded against the wall to let them pass.

The Smilsums' eyes watched as they entered the detention area and disappeared from sight. Even though Max couldn't understand their language, he strained his ears to try and decipher what was happening. His strange senses didn't pick up on anything out of the ordinary.

A slight cough from Gor got their attention and he started forward once more. Suddenly the solid wall to the left gave way to glass windows about twenty yards long. A door to the detention area and dispensary opened in the center of the windows. Gor didn't hesitate, but continued to march straight ahead.

Max chanced a peek into the room. A Smilsum sat at a desk with his head down, buried in paperwork. The injured Smilsum and his aide sat in a corner away from the window, surrounded by three other Smilsums eyeing his wounds. *I think we are going to make it.*

Max's feeling of confidence drained from his body as unrecognizable words from behind them brought the entire group to a halt. Everyone turned to see an extremely large muscular Smilsum blocking the hallway behind them. His huge shoulders almost stretched across the entire hallway. His gruff, loud voice indicated his surprise and displeasure with them being in his hallway.

Gor immediately circled the group to try to talk them out of a bad situation. He chattered back and forth with the hulking Smilsum for several minutes, but the way the large one's voice continued to escalate hinted the situation wasn't going their way.

Max noticed Grandpa's hand at his side waving him backwards, so he took Cindy by the hand and crept backwards a few paces when his head collided with what he thought was a low hanging beam. Max peered over his shoulder to see he had bumped into the elbow of an even larger Smilsum. He and another massive Smilsum stood with their arms folded, blocking passage in that direction. The one Max ran into gave a deep snort as if to strike fear and domination into Max and the others.

Gor seemed to be offering up an excuse as to their presence in the hall, but from the expression on the opposing Smilsum's face, he wasn't buying it. Three additional Smilsums crowded in behind the one speaking with Gor. Max wondered if additional Smilsums had filed in behind him.

"What are we going to do?" Cindy whispered out of the side of her mouth.

The Smilsum directly behind Max gave a loud grunt telling them to keep quiet.

"I'm going to clear a path," Max said with a wink and a raised voice drawing everyone's attention.

"How?" Cindy asked.

"Watch!" Max spun on his heels to face the Smilsums blocking his path and disappeared.

The Smilsums gasped and took a step back with fright. *"Preselim se,"* Max's voice rang out and the Smilsums behind Max and Cindy suddenly parted. They bounced and smacked around like bowling pins as Max shot through the middle of them with tremendous force. He reappeared behind the now flattened Smilsums, gun drawn.

The disturbance created by Max gave the others the time they needed to retrieve their weapons. Blasts echoed through the tunnels, accompanied by hot sparks, bright flashes, and white smoke blinding and
clouding everyone's vision. Stunned Smilsums fell to the ground everywhere, making the hallway more difficult to maneuver. Alarms pierced
the air, raising the tension level of the situation.

Max spun and fired several shots into another group of Smilsums responding to the alarm. Cindy joined him in picking off the new arrivals.

"Forward quickly," Zaat signaled towards Max and Cindy.

"Watch out, they won't be firing to stun in return," Olik warned.

Max and the others began navigating the unconscious Smilsums littering the floor. Max and Cindy kept fighting their way forward, while
Grandpa and the others brought up the rear. Max and Cindy relied
heavily on their strange sense to avoid any direct line of fire from the
enemy, always anticipating when a Smilsum entered the hall ahead or
one waited around a corner.

They brought the group to a halt when the entrance to the command
center appeared through the smoky corridor. Max quickly motioned for
everyone to take up a position against the left wall on the same side as
the entrance.

"Wait here," Cindy ordered.

Before Max could protest Cindy disappeared. His heart raced as he
watched nervously for what he knew was about to happen. The seconds
felt like hours before shots and screams from up ahead rolled out into the
hall. A Smilsum, bent on escaping the unseen assailant, bolted into the
hall where Max sent him off to slumber land. Cindy's high-pitched
scream launched Max forward at an incredible rate.

He rushed through the door so recklessly he almost missed the
warning from his extra sense that caused him to drop and roll out of the
way of the intense gunfire. "*Oviraj*," Max screamed as he scrambled for
cover. The temporary shield gave him enough time to get his bearings
and locate cover behind some metal control stations.

Max attempted to locate Cindy by poking his head around the corner, but the onslaught of enemy fire forced him to take cover. Heavy
smoke choked the air, creating poor visibility, and the defining sirens
drowned out everything but the noise of the weapons' blasts.

Through the open entrance Max caught sight of Grandpa and the
others. Max put out the palm of his hand to tell them to wait. Casting
the invisibility spell, he went around the opposite end of the work station. Blinking lights and spinning radar-like images from the desk com-

bined with the smoke and played tricks on his vision. Several times he ducked or paused, thinking someone had passed nearby. As he moved cautiously through the communications station, he caught his foot on something and went down with a thud.

Max froze with his feet propped up by something on the floor as he lay on his stomach, for fear the Smilsums had heard him hit the ground. A hissing which issued from a cracked pipe in the wall, combined with the sirens, hid the sound of his impact. As Max lifted a leg off the object he felt it move underneath him. His heart leaped into his throat as a rush of adrenaline surged through him. Max scrambled off and turned to see what had tripped him when he spotted Cindy laying in a pool of blood.

Oh no! Max frantically searched for the wound as he flipped Cindy onto her back. Her shallow breath vibrated hair that had fallen over her face, telling Max she was still alive. A dark wet spot on her lower left side sent Max searching for something to stem the bleeding. He fished a jacket out of his suit and stuffed it inside Cindy's suit. Max knew he needed to get her to Olik quickly.

He sprang to his feet, gun drawn. He hurried forward with purpose, weapon at the ready. Max's rock hard determination kept him from worrying about how his advance stirred the smoke in his wake. He located the seven still conscious Smilsums, hiding behind a half wall in the back right corner of the communications center. Max hurtled the wall and was behind the remaining resistance before they could react. Some managed to get a few yards away before Max's spell knocked them flat.

Max hoped that was the last of the Smilsums as he raced back to the entrance to grab the others. "Cindy's been shot," Max screamed. Grandpa and the others darted into the room to take cover from the troops coming up the smoke filled halls.

"What? Where?" Grandpa and Olik demanded, as the others kept troops from crawling up their backs.

"Over here," Max screamed above the sirens and led Grandpa and Olik to the unconscious Cindy. "Is she going to be okay?" Max asked, trying to keep his emotions in check. He had controlled his fear in an effort to get Cindy the help she needed, but now worry grew like a cancer, and he dreaded it would overcome him.

"I've got it. We still have a job to do." Olik began to work on Cindy's injuries.

Grandpa spun Max around. "Go get Gor and Kit. We need a translator," Grandpa ordered.

Max raced to the others holding off a Smilsum advance. Zaat, Kit, Gor, and the other Smilsum fired shots through the broken glass of the entryway, using the wall for cover. The smoky air worked to their advantage as the Smilsums didn't dare rush them without a clear view of the situation. "Kit we need you and Gor to translate for us."

Kit looked to Zaat, "Do you think you can hold them?"

"Yes, but hurry," Zaat replied as he fired a couple of blind shots into the smoke. Several blasts returned, but the wild shots landed well off mark.

Kit explained to Gor what was needed, who relayed the situation to the other Smilsum.

Max led them back to Grandpa, who busied himself at a section of monitors in a direct line on the wall on one side of the entrance. "I just need some simple translations," Grandpa said when they reached him. "What does this say?" Grandpa pointed to what looked like a map of space with several red circles, a couple of yellow circles, and one blue circle around stars or planets.

Kit spoke with Gor, motioning to the spot where Grandpa held his finger. They chatted back and forth for a few seconds. "He says the circles represent worlds where they have established communication systems. Red is for established communications, yellow worlds are hubs, and the blue one is the main communications center."

"That doesn't make sense," Grandpa stated. "This map isn't complete so I'm not sure of these coordinates, but the blue one isn't the world we are on." Grandpa moved his finger to a yellow circle. "Ask him what world this is?"

After a short exchange with Gor, Kit responded, "It's us. Our world."

"Oh no!" Grandpa gasped and the color drained from his face.

"WHAT?" Max questioned.

"That means we are greatly behind the curve and we are in big trouble. The blue circle is *Earth*!"

6

A Surprise Rescue

Linda sat shivering in an empty dumpster with the lid closed. The fresh rain did nothing to whisk away the foul stench of rotting garbage that lingered in the empty container. It only added to her misery. Her teeth danced against each other as she pulled her knees to her chest and wrapped her arms around them in an effort to get warm. Tears rolled down her cheeks as fear and doubt crawled through her mind like darkness, snuffing out any glimmer of hope.

"Sam, what am I to do?" she cried to herself as her exhales created a small mist in the light streaming in through a crack between the lids. She had never felt so completely alone in her life. She didn't know where she was going or what she was doing. She felt like giving up. Letting Tanner capture her. She was tired of running, fed up with this whole cat and mouse game. These people were powerful and usually got their way. She would wind up as a headline of the local newspaper as a mugging gone bad or something. Her family would never know the truth.

Her stomach grumbled to protest her lack of food. She had a little money, but after Sam's capture fear pushed her into this miserable state. She wiped her eyes on her sleeve and rubbed her hands up and down her legs to create friction and generate a little heat.

It was past three in the morning when the rain stopped, but the air remained chilly and damp. A thick fog layer crept over the town, muffling the sound of cars and an occasional barking dog. Linda's clothes had failed to dry out even though her location in the dumpster was out of the rain. She crouched over with her ear turned towards the crack between the two lids, listening for anything moving nearby.

She wished she had Sam's talent to detect things around her and was angry at herself for not suggesting they share their information with each other before his capture. After a few moments of silence, she raised the lid slightly with both hands so she could take a peek. The thick heavy fog made visibility difficult. She could only see twenty to thirty yards in any direction, and even then it was hazy.

"Well, that means they can't see me very well either," she muttered to herself before flipping the lid back quietly, and she climbed out of the foul smelling bin. Her need to get warm and to find some food forced her out into the open.

Spending the last part of her life on the run had cemented certain behaviors into Linda's routine. She immediately jumped into the shadows of the alleyway in which she had been hiding. Her need to keep out of sight had dominated her life for the past several months. Even in the darkness, she paused to look and listen before crossing any well-lit areas, and she always walked on the balls of her feet to help silence her passing.

She traveled a couple of blocks before she spied a small all-night convenience store. The well-lit building appeared to be empty of customers. The clerk sat behind the counter reading a magazine, waiting for his shift to be over. The only car in the parking lot was a distance from the entrance, indicating it belonged to the clerk.

Linda's stomach rumbled at the thought of a meal, but she needed to be sure it was safe before proceeding. No cars had passed for several minutes when she decided she could not stand being cold or hungry any longer. She noticed the store blocked the street lights from the dumpsters on the side of the building. She decided to circle around to this position before risking going out in the open.

She had learned to control her hunger and developed the ability to withstand the cold, but she hadn't quite mastered her nerves. Her pounding heart kept reminding her that Tanner and his men hadn't left the city. They had captured Sam and they knew she was still around as well. They would have eyes everywhere, patient spiders waiting for their dinner to make a mistake and step into the web.

The trip around the building to the dumpster took about ten minutes with all the stopping and checking before moving forward. Still, no one had entered the store and only the occasional car had driven by. Finally, after swallowing the lump in her throat, she left the shelter of the shadows and stepped out onto the sidewalk in front of the store. Her heart pounded and adrenaline prickled the hairs on her arms, back, and neck as she hustled to the door.

The clerk didn't look up from his magazine as the bell rang, announcing her entrance. She hurried away from the glass doors and towards the food aisle. She took a deep breath to calm her nerves and to absorb the warm store air. She found a hot chocolate maker and decided that would help her feel better. As the hot water filled her cup, the front bell rang again, and she almost dropped her cup.

Her heart leapt into her throat, almost choking off her air as she slowly twisted her neck to see who had come in. The rush of fear caused her vision to blur around the edges of her eyes as she caught sight of a short blond woman with very pale skin, dressed in a black rain poncho. "Ouch," Linda gasped as the cup overflowed, spilling scalding water onto her hands. She waved her burned hand through the air in an effort to relieve the painful sensation.

"Are you okay?" the fair woman asked as she passed by down the aisle.

"Yes, just a little hot water." Linda managed a weak smile. Even though her hand hurt, she felt better about the new customer not being one of Tanner's men.

Linda ran her hand under cold water from a small sink on the counter before mixing her hot chocolate. She then began looking for something to eat. The warm sweet liquid spread through her body, chasing away the numbing the cold had left behind. She continued to sip from her cup as she grabbed some snacks off the shelf.

Suddenly, a blaze of light from the front windows filled the small store as screeching tires and slamming doors broke the silence. Three dark SUVs clogged the parking lot out in front of the small store. Linda dropped to a crouch out of instinct. She knew who it was and scrambled towards the back of the store.

The clerk dropped his paper and stared, mouth agape, as a dozen men in trench coats stormed into the store, guns drawn.

"Nobody move!" several screamed as they began searching the store.

"Wh—hat do you wa—ant?" the clerk stammered, raising his arms above his head.

Linda scurried down the aisle, hunched over, and collided with the blond woman, who was staring at the commotion. "Help me. Please," Linda pleaded with tears in her eyes.

The woman gave a wicked smile and held a finger to her lips. "Shh, disappear."

Linda nearly fell over as the woman disappeared right in front of her. Even though she could perform the same feat, the fact a complete stranger just did it shocked her. She barely managed to gain her focus and vanish before the agents spotted her. She felt a hand grab her and pull her into a small opening between two displays.

"What about the back door," Linda whispered, concerning the door only a few yards away.

"No, they have it covered," the woman's voice responded.

No sooner had she commented when the door opened and two agents appeared. One remained in the doorway while the second joined the others at the front of the store after their sweep of the room.

"There's no sign of her," one of the agents reported.

"Are you sure it was her you saw in here?" another asked.

The men chattered back and forth until the bell rang out, silencing them. Through the front door strode Tanner. Even in the nighttime, he wore his sunglasses. "Well?"

"She's not in here," one responded.

"She's in here," Tanner stated. "I know you're in here, Linda. You can't hide. All exits are covered. Don't make me do something drastic to Sam in order for you to see it my way. Come out now and no one will get hurt."

"Wait here," the woman whispered to Linda.

"Oh, she's here," Tanner repeated confidently. "She's just using one of her little tricks."

"You're joking?" a younger agent asked as he glanced towards the empty store.

"Was there just a woman in your store?" Tanner asked the clerk as he walked up to the counter.

"Ah—yes—two," the clerk responded with shock as he too eyed the empty aisles.

Tanner removed his glasses to stare at the clerk. "TWO?"

"Yes, two," the clerk responded with more confidence. "There were two women in here. One was black and the other a pale blond."

Tanner took a quick scan of the small store. The fact his six-foot-five-inch frame towered over the tops of the aisles allowed him to see nearly everyone in sight. "Are you sure?"

"Yes."

"Do you have access to your security tapes?" Tanner asked.

"Yes," the clerk responded as he fumbled with his keys. "The security equipment is just back here." He motioned towards a door behind the counter.

Before Tanner could step around the corner, one of their SUV's crashed through a portion of the windows at the front of the building. Glass and debris exploded inward forcing everyone inside to duck and cover.

"What the…" Several agents responded with looks of shock, while others raced towards the smashed vehicle with guns drawn.

"I have the keys," an agent towards the back of the store said as he held the keys in the air.

"Stay by the exits!" Tanner ordered, pointing to the doors and the newly formed gaping hole in the front of the building. "Don't let anything through. Is that you Linda, or your friend?"

"When I start the fight, get out," the voice whispered to Linda. She felt a hand touch her shoulder and slide down her arm before depositing a cell phone in her hand. "I will call you in fifteen minutes."

"Okay," Linda responded.

"I don't think you've developed that skill, Linda, so it must be your friend." Tanner stated motioning towards the crashed SUV as he stepped away from the counter. "I see your friend is as big of a coward as you. Hiding and running instead of standing and fighting. Cowards!"

"Freeze," A soft voice sounded behind Tanner.

He arched forward as if something jabbed him in the ribs, causing him to raise his hands above his head.

"Don't try anything funny. I am not someone you want to take a chance with," the female voice stated.

"What do you want?" Tanner tried to glance over his shoulder but could only see the terrified drawn face of the store clerk behind him.

"Eyes forward. Tell the clerk to stop the security devices and bring you today's disk."

"Do it," Tanner barked, causing the scared clerk to almost drop his keys before jumping into action. "Do I know you?"

"I doubt it. Back up," the voiced demanded, and Tanner obeyed.

The clerk scrambled into the room and fumbled nervously with the security settings for several minutes before returning with a DVD.

"Place it on the counter," the voice ordered.

No sooner had the clerk dropped it onto the counter, when a heavy whiskey bottle flew off the shelf behind him and crashed down on top of the DVD. The bottle shattered, destroying the disk and spraying whiskey everywhere. The clerk dropped to the floor, whimpering like a whipped dog.

"What's the matter? Too afraid to show yourself?" Tanner taunted his invisible assailant.

"No, I'm not, but I don't want to endanger the people I work for." the voice said smoothly. "Now tell your men to move away from the exits!"

Tanner let out a whistle to get the attention of his men. "Everyone to the front of the store, *NOW*!"

This command received a few puzzled looks and some head scratching, but the agents slowly made their way towards the designated location.

"What about the girl?" one of the agents asked, his head still pivoting in all directions as he searched for their target.

"Is something wrong?" another agent asked, eyeing Tanner with a scowl.

Tanner tilted his head slightly in his assailant's direction and received a sharp poke to the side, which cause him to flinch. "Yes, your hunt for the girl has ended," the woman spoke.

Immediately, all the agents leveled their guns in the direction of the voice and the men started to circle. They blocked the aisles and the front door in an effort to contain the unseen.

"You boys think you can trap me? You've never dealt with anyone like me before," the voice taunted.

Several things happened at once; multiple display items spilled over into the aisle as Linda bumped them in her rush to get out, an agent by Tanner threw a pot of coffee on the invisible assailant behind Tanner and the diversions gave Tanner the chance to land a solid elbow into the chest of the invisible girl and free himself.

"Freeze," several agents screamed at the strange dripping object.

Tanner drew his gun and started to spin around when a loud crack echoed off his arm, causing him to lose hold of his weapon. A grunt issued from his mouth as his knees buckled and he crashed to the floor.

Several shots rang out as a couple of agents attempted to stop the attacking blur of splattering coffee. One waved his gun left then right, trying to keep up, when—WHACK—a large red mark appeared across his forehead before he tumbled to the ground. A high pitched grinding noise filled the store as an entire row of shelves slid up against the wall, pinning three agents against the freezer section.

Another agent got off a shot that caused a beer display to spray foaming suds into the air a second before items started zooming off the shelves, knocking him to the ground.

Two agents who had been guarding the broken windows at the front of the store doubled over and then collapsed to the floor.

Suddenly a strange word rang out and the pale blond woman twirling a black staff appeared, standing over the fallen agents. Linda popped up a dozen feet from the woman, making her way towards the opening.

"FREEZE," the few agents still on their feet yelled, aiming their weapons at the two women.

Tanner chuckled, a dark menacing rumble. "You're not the only one with tricks up their sleeve. And I do know you. There will be no escape for either of you. We want to know who you're working for and we will." He carried his injured arm at his side and used his other hand to retrieve his gun.

The blond woman smiled a mischievous grin. "You actually thought it would be this easy? My employer didn't want me to kill anyone. He didn't say how much of a beating I could dish out."

Tanner laughed again as he stepped down the aisle in front of the woman. "There's nothing you can do I haven't seen before. You're out manned and out gunned."

Screeching tires filled the parking lot as three more black SUVs pulled in and another dozen agents poured out, guns drawn.

"We control the entire city—there is no way out. We will find out who you are and who you work for. Now, lower your weapon or we will be forced to put you down," Tanner commanded.

"There's only one problem you're overlooking." the blond woman continued to flash a beautiful smile.

"What's that?"

"I'm not someone who exists as far as you know, and I know more than tricks." Her staff swung upward in a blur of movement that knocked Tanner's gun up into the air, she spun in a circle and the staff crashed into the side of Tanner's head knocking him out cold. The woman then caught him around the shoulder with the staff to prop him up and snagged the gun out of the air and put it to his head.

"Toss your weapons, including back-ups, over in front of me," she barked as she cocked the trigger. "You, outside, throw your guns in here with the others. Do it now and back away."

The men tossed their weapons into the aisle in front of the woman and then stepped back.

"You too," she ordered a couple of agents who had approached from the back of the building. "I told you, you've never met anyone like me. Linda, do you know how to drive?"

"Y—yes," Linda stammered still shocked by the situation.

"Someone give her the keys to the vehicle in the back," the pale blond ordered, and an agent stepped forward. "Throw them to her," she ordered before the man could get too close to Linda.

The woman dragged her captive towards the hole in the side of the building, with Linda right beside her. Suddenly, several cans of lighter fluid zoomed off the shelf and landed on the pile of guns and then the entire thing burst into flames. The agents stepped back from the flames as the woman flung Tanner to the sidewalk, and she and Linda raced toward the SUV.

"Go start the car," the woman ordered as she bounded into a group of men attempting to block their escape. Her staff twirled like a helicopter blade, delivering a KO at every blow. Whack. Crack. Crash. A half a dozen agents went to dreamland.

Linda dove behind the wheel of the SUV at the back of the parking lot. She fumbled the keys for a second or two before managing to fire up the engine. Suddenly, everything started to shake as if an earthquake had hit the area. The vibrations tickled Linda's hands on the steering wheel of the SUV and spread through her body, raising the small hairs on her neck, arms, and legs. Then all the vehicles except the one Linda was sitting in rose off the ground, flipped upside down, and crashed back to the earth.

"What was that? Who are you?" Linda asked as the blond woman hopped in the car.

"My name is Sky and I'm here to help you."

"How did you do those things?" Linda stammered.

"Later! Get us out of here," Sky ordered as agents began coming out of the small store in an attempt to stop them.

Linda slammed the SUV in reverse and punched the gas. The tires smoked and screamed as she flew backwards into the street before jamming the automatic transmission into drive and speeding away.

"How are we going to get out of here? They will have the city sealed off." Linda moaned.

"Don't worry, we have a way out, but first we're going to get Sam," Sky smiled as Linda's eyes met hers.

"Where are they holding him?"

"In a hotel downtown. Make a left up ahead. We have to hurry. I want to attack them before anyone realizes what is happening. If they think we are running, it should give us an opening to rescue Sam. They will be looking out when they should be looking in. Keep your foot on the gas."

They navigated the almost empty streets without incident. The late hour enabled them to zip through the wet city streets without being seen, except by the occasional vehicle.

"Pull over here," Sky ordered as Linda made another turn, lining the SUV up with a small hotel at the end of the street.

"Is that where they are keeping him?" Linda pulled the car to the side of the road.

"Yes. Leave it running and get out," Sky ordered as she jumped out of the passenger side. The second Linda cleared the SUV, Sky's staff slammed down on the windshield, shattering it.

"Wait in the alley." Sky motioned to a dark road between two buildings. "I'll be back in a few minutes."

"I want to go with you."

"I'm going to do something very dangerous and I want you safe. Wait here. You'll be fine." Sky jumped into the driver's seat and gave the broken window a hard kick knocking the windshield all the way out.

She put the SUV in gear and pressed the gas pedal all the way to the floor. The back end of the SUV fish tailed as it picked up speed and raced down the street towards the hotel. Sky chose the location a little right of center in the building. She brought her left knee up and put her foot on the seat, while holding the pedal all the way to the floor with the other. The vehicle raced towards the small curb separating the parking lot of the hotel from the street.

The tires hit the curb, bouncing the SUV off the ground. It became airborne and flew over the small section of grass before crashing into the back of a truck in the parking lot. The impact flipped the SUV forward. Sky used the extreme force of the crash to spring out of the missing windshield. The whipping of the SUV shot her through the air where she just managed to cast a spell to correct her course. She crashed through a second story window with her arms folded over her head.

The surprised occupants, which included three agents and Sam, jumped as Sky rolled to her feet. Before the agents could react, Sky tore into them with a speed and fury they had never experienced. An array of kicks, elbows, and knees crashed against the men's skulls as they tried to defend themselves, but Sky's skills and speed quickly overcame them. Finally, only Sky and Sam remained conscious in the room.

Sam stood mouth agape, staring at the small pale blond woman who had just wiped out three agents in a matter of seconds. "Who are you? A—and how did you do that?"

"My name is Sky and I'm here to rescue you. We don't have much time so we need to go, NOW!" Sky hurried to the door. Already sirens started to ring out in response to the crash outside the hotel.

"But, how did you know where to find me or who I even am?"

"I've been tracking your situation for almost two years now. I'll explain later. Come on." Sky led him down the back stairs and out into the night.

They had to circle the block to avoid the police and emergency personnel that had arrived on the scene. When they finally found Linda, she threw herself into Sam's arms.

"I thought I wouldn't ever see you again and that Tanner would catch me sooner or later," she cried.

"I figured it was only a matter of time before you joined me and we were never heard from again," Sam hugged her back. After he released her he turned towards Sky. "Now will you tell me who you are and how you found us?"

"I'll explain everything, but now we have to get out of here." Sky pulled her communicator out of her jacket.

"It isn't going to be easy. Tanner will be watching all the exits, especially after what you just did. He will want to get his hands on you even more than us," Linda stated.

"Well, we aren't leaving the city in a manner he knows about," Sky smiled as she extracted a small crystal from another pocket. She floated it through the air towards the back of the alley. As it moved through the air it flashed a small white light. "There's our exit."

Sky led an astonished Sam and Linda through the gateway.

7

Stealing Secrets

Suddenly, five flashes of light disturbed the quiet night in the Nevada desert. After the lights stopped, the starlight revealed five cautious shadows checking to make sure no one had seen them. A car driving down a dirt road several hundred yards to their left caused the group to duck behind some rocks. They waited until the car had climbed a hill and was out of sight before hurrying up the same hill from a different direction.

"Come on!" Larry stressed in a harsh whisper to his friends as he climbed to the top of the small hill. The moonless night hid them from unwanted attention as they moved among the tall sagebrush towards the small compound on the top of a large hill. Larry, a big dark-haired teenager, led the small group towards a section of fence, away from the bright lights placed along the perimeter of the station. He found an area of grass between the sagebrush and laid down on his stomach to observe the area.

Two more boys, Jeff and Brad, dove into spots next to Larry on the ground. While Jo, a girl with pink hair, practically pushed a younger boy, Brian, towards Larry and the others. When they reached the grass, Joe yanked Brian to the ground.

"I don't know why you're being so stubborn," Jo hissed.

"Maybe because I don't want to be here. We're going to get into trouble," Brian stated louder than the others liked.

"Yes, we could. But this is the most fun we've had in years. These little missions for Hudich are awesome," Larry beamed.

"Well, what if I don't want to do things for Hudich?" Brian protested, and received several shushes in response to his higher volume.

"Didn't you say you've had fun on all these trips?" Brad questioned.

"Yeah, while we were doing it."

"Then what are you complaining about?" Jo demanded.

"I think it's cool. You've actually helped set up a highly advanced universal communications system. We are now speaking with all sorts of other worlds, where before we had to travel there to do it. Now we can conserve our time and spend magical energy on other things," Jeff stated.

"Yeah, I wish I had your ability to manipulate people into doing what you want them to," Brad added.

"How can you complain about that?" Larry asked.

"Because how we are getting it is wrong and I feel bad afterwards." Brian moved to a sitting position.

Larry yanked him back down to the ground. "You're going to give us away and then you will be in trouble," he growled.

"Don't touch me!"

Larry felt a shockwave vibrate the ground, pulled his hand away, and raised the palm of his hand as if to say—take it easy. "Just calm down. You should be proud. You're getting information the US military has failed to get for decades. And now we're going after stuff right out of science fiction movies. Just think—intergalactic space travel and space aged weapons."

A faint smile crossed Brian's face, and he laid back on his stomach to observe the compound with the others. They watched as a dark sedan pulled up to a guard shack along the fence to their left. Two armed guards stepped out of the building to inspect the vehicle and its occupants. A soft growl to their right drew their attention as another armed guard, walking an attack dog, approached their area from the right. The animal, acting on an unrecognized scent, tugged his handler in the direction of the concealed group.

"What's the matter? Do you smell something?" The guard tried to reign in the excited canine. "Hold on. Hold on. I'm coming." He turned on a powerful flashlight and began shining it around the area.

"Let's have some fun, shall we?" Larry snickered. "Brad, Jeff, you know what to do."

Brad and Jeff returned Larry's grin before they disappeared. Their footsteps created soft thuds and kicked up small clouds of sand as they ran towards the guard and his dog.

The German Shepherd went ballistic at the invisible intruders. He almost yanked the guard off his feet, charging the fence and barking like mad. A second animal farther back along the fence responded to the first dog's excitement.

He tugged in the direction of the unseen Brad and Jeff as they passed the guards' location and continued to head away from Larry and the others.

"Do you see something?" The guard tried to rein in the out of control canine, his flashlight following the direction the dog indicated. "What is it, some sort of animal?"

The barking dogs had drawn the attention of the guards atop the nearest watch tower on the backside of the compound where bright spot lights sprang to life. They zoomed from the trained animals to the area just outside the fence in an effort to spot whatever had aroused the dogs.

"Let's go," Larry whispered after Brad and Jeff had led the guards far enough away. He, Jo, and Brian raced towards the fence. A few yards before they reached the electric charged obstruction, they cast spells that vaulted them safely over the barrier. The landing forced them all to one knee to maintain their balance before they hustled towards the building in front of them. They kept low to avoid unwanted eyes, and Larry directed them out of the path of any security cameras. They had agreed to go as far as they could without using the invisibility spell, to conserve energy.

They reached their usual entry point, a door in the middle of the building. "Do your thing while we keep watch," Larry ordered, as he and Jo took up positions on the opposite sides of the door.

Brian stepped forward and placed his hands on the door. He closed his eyes and slowed his breathing, going into a state of deep concentration. "There's a guard on the other side of the door," he whispered.

"Really? There's never been one before," Jo responded. "Now how are we going to get in without anyone noticing?"

"Maybe we could lure him out and sneak past him," Larry suggested. "If we're seen or have to fight our way out, we won't be coming back. That won't make Hudich very happy!"

Brian's eyes snapped open and he shot Larry a dirty look. "Let's get out of here." Brian grimaced. Brian hated Hudich. He blamed him for the death of his real parents. The fact Max and the others had failed to get him away from these people had created a certain amount of animosity towards them, also. He didn't trust his stepmother, but under her guidance and that of others, he developed his powers beyond his instructors' tutelage. Although he would never let on, he loved these missions for the opportunities they gave him, both to get away from the others and to test his powers.

"Calm down," Larry hissed. "I'm just saying we will be in trouble in more than one way if we're caught, that's all."

"Okay, what do you suggest we do?" Brian asked, more to see if Larry could come up with an intelligent idea than to actually listen to him. Larry was big and strong but wasn't all that bright. Jo's mental capacity was even less than Larry's. Brian prided himself on how deeply he could think through a problem and come up with a solution. Larry would only see how to use force to resolve things.

"Maybe we could knock him out in a way that will look like an accident?" Larry suggested.

"Yeah, maybe something could fall on him or..." Jo paused.

The roar of a Jeep engine and a flash of headlights prompted them all to cast the disappearing spell. They had to dive out of the way as the vehicle stopped just feet away. A soldier jumped out of the passenger side and pounded on the door. A second later the door opened.

"What is it?"

"Ah, I don't know, but something has the dogs all fired up. This is the fourth time this month," the one from the vehicle stated. "The higher-ups think some sort of animal has decided to build a home nearby. I just need to grab the thermal camera to see if there is anything out there."

Jo gave a soft gasp that caused the man to glance around. "Did you hear something?"

"Nope," the solder behind the door responded.

A moment later the men sped away in the jeep and the three intruders reappeared.

"Crap!" Larry whispered. "Jo, you've got to hurry and get those guys out of there. They will show up on a thermal camera."

Jo gave a short nod and took off towards the fence.

"We better hurry because we're about to lose our advantage," Larry cautioned.

Jo bolted toward the fence at her top speed. She almost bit it twice trying to keep her eyes both on the ground in front of her and on the Jeep speeding towards Brad and Jeff's location. Her mind raced for possible distractions as she realized she wouldn't be able to get to Jeff and Brad ahead of the Jeep. She was sure they would show up on the thermal imaging camera. Although magic could play tricks with the human eye, it couldn't wipe out a heat signature.

She leapt the fence with the aid of a spell. In her effort to hurry, she landed in a patch of sagebrush, which snagged and scratched her exposed skin. She snatched a large branch of the bush as she tried to remain upright but her momentum snapped the branch free and she fell to the desert floor.

"Ouch!" she muttered under her breath as she sprang to her feet and dropped the branch, which caused a small thud. Her eyes moved from a cut across the palm of her hand, to the branch, to the fence.

She hesitated for only a second, then she picked up the branch and heaved it into the electrified fence before she cast the invisibility spell. A shower of sparks and a blue arc flashed, lighting up the whole area as a burnt metal mixed with wood odor floated on the breeze.

"What was that? Something hit the fence," reached Jo's ears as she sprinted towards Brad and Jeff. She forced herself not to call out and hoped she could locate them by following the dogs.

###

The soldier in the passenger side of the Jeep fiddled with the thermal imaging camera as they raced toward the back fence in the area where the handlers and their excited dogs patrolled the perimeter. He had just managed to get the device turned on and was adjusting some of the controls when an eruption of sparks filled the air a short distance behind them.

"What was that?" the driver asked.

"Something hit the fence," responded the passenger as he swung the camera around to that general direction. "What the he..."

"What?"

"Stop the Jeep!" the passenger demanded, swinging the camera from left to right.

The driver stomped on the brake, forcing the passenger to smack into the dash. "What? What did you see?"

"Thanks," said the passenger with a sarcastic look as he recovered and began searching with the camera. "I thought I saw someone running through the sagebrush on the other side of the fence."

"Which way was it moving?"

"In our direction. YES! YES! There!" He showed the driver the definite heat signature of a human running on the other side of the fence. "Get out the spot light! He's heading towards the area of the...hold on. There are two more where the dogs are going crazy!"

While the driver tried to get the spot light on the area, the passenger snatched up the radio and relayed the information to the others. Sirens blared all around as more vehicles and personnel raced to the scene.

"There are three of them," he shouted above the sirens and barking canines pointing to the area a dozen yards beyond the fence.

Several spotlights flooded the area he had indicated, illuminating the dessert.

"Where?"

"I don't see anything."

"They're there, I tell you," the soldier stated, his eyes jumping from the figures on his camera to the empty desert. He watched the three figures meet up in the middle of the sagebrush and then start to run away from the compound. "Hold this right here." He shoved the camera into the driver's hand where he could still see the picture and leapt into the back of the jeep.

"Hey," the driver called to the images on the screen.

The solder loaded the machine gun in the back of the jeep. He cocked and fired the weapon to the left of the figures. The shots rattled along with the other noises, and the desert sand exploded about fifteen yards away from the fence as the bullets slammed into the ground.

"FREEZE!" yelled the soldier as the gunshots echoed over the low hills.

"They stopped," reported the driver and the gun operator let go of the trigger.

"What are they doing now?"

"It looks like they are talking about something."

"We know you're out there!" the gunner called.

Suddenly an entire section of fence twenty yards to the left of the figures exploded inward, creating a large hole in the site's perimeter. All eyes jumped to the commotion in an effort to figure out what had happened.

"What the...they're gone!" the driver reported.

"What? How?" the soldier behind the gun leapt out of the back of the jeep to snatch the thermal camera from the driver. He rotated the device in all directions, even to the spot of the damaged fence. No luck. The figures had vanished.

###

Brian gently placed his hands on the door and closed his eyes. He sent out his instructions through the building's connections. The message passed from door, to frame, to walls, to floor, carrying Brian's command. He remained in this position for a few moments before a click at the latch caused him to step out of the way of the swinging door. On the other side of the door stood the guard, his expression blank as his glazed eyes stared off into nothingness.

Brian and Larry hurried inside, closing the door behind them. Brian touched the soldier's head with his finger, and the guard moved back into a small office off to the side of the main hall. He sat at the desk with a zombie-like stare as Brian and Larry slipped past the security check point.

They maintained their invisibility spell as they crept down the hall to avoid making any unnecessary noise or accidentally bumping into someone coming out of the offices that lined the hall. At the end of the corridor they checked to make sure no one would notice the door to the stairs swinging open before heading into the stairwell. Brian ran along the path he and Larry had travelled several times in the past to get to the creature's cell. Their feet thumped out a faint metallic sound as they shuffled quickly down the metal grating stairs. If they hadn't been there before, Brian would have never suspected the aluminum warehouses on the surface concealed a vast underground structure.

After descending three flights of stairs, a door one story below swung inward, freezing them in their tracks. A guard popped into the stairwell and glanced up and down several times. "I swear I could hear someone coming down the stairs," he stated.

"We need to be on high alert. There are unidentified 'things' about. Plus, we are pretty certain someone has been getting in and out of here over the past couple months," a voice floated in from beyond the open door.

"Well, I don't see anything, but I definitely heard it," the guard re-emphasized as he pulled the door closed behind him.

"We need to be extra careful," Brian whispered to Larry before starting down again at a more cautious pace, gently placing his feet on the steps below him.

"Did you hear that about them suspecting intruders for the past two months?"

"This may be our last trip in here."

"There's no way we are going to get all the information we need to-day. Hudich isn't going to be happy," Larry grimaced.

Brian felt a tingle run up his spine at the idea that had just entered his mind. His lips curled into an invisible smirk. "We could take him out of here!"

"No way!" Larry reached out and just managed to seize Brian's arm. "They aren't looking for two invisible guys, but if their most prized possession disappears, I think they will notice."

"Yeah, but think of how quickly we could proceed if he was in our hands. Hudich never said we couldn't take him. Did he?"

"That's true, and instead of having to worry about getting caught for the couple of hours while we get the information, we would only have to be careful for fifteen or twenty minutes. Plus, think of the praise we would receive." Larry stated.

"Think of the other missions they would trust us with," Brian added.

"Dude…let's break him out of here!"

They continued down the stairs towards the lowest level, taking ex-tra care to hide their footfalls. When they reached the lowest level they paused, and Brian placed his hands on the door the same as before. He waited with his head lowered.

"There is a lot of activity going on," Brian stated, still keeping his eyes shut.

"Probably from Jo and the others."

"Yes, and it's helping us. It seems to be drawing people towards the upper levels. I'm only detecting a handful of people on this floor."

"That might be good for us getting in, but not for getting out."

"WATCH OUT!" Brian barked a little louder than he would have liked as he shoved Larry away from the door. They just managed to clear its path as it flew open.

Two armed soldiers entered the stairwell and paused. They both glanced up the staircase and in the immediate area around them.

"Did you hear something?" the one asked.

"I thought so, but you know how echoes carry in this stairwell," the other responded before they took off at a jog up the stairs, their boots pounding out a metallic rhythm.

"Come on." Brian snagged the door before it could shut, and he and Larry slipped into the lower chamber of the building.

The lighting on this floor was so poor it gave the feeling that they walked the caverns of some kind of dungeon. The desert rock on which the base stood created most of the walls, and the ceiling stood well over ten feet high. Occasional glass walls broke up the airtight rooms, which surrounded a rather dark gymnasium-sized central room. Several work areas and tables filled the center room with table lamps to provide enough light to work by. With the departure of the two soldiers, only three of the work areas seemed to be occupied. A man and two women, each dressed in long white lab coats, busied themselves about their desks.

Brian and Larry skirted along the wall, keeping away from the workers. They had to continually watch their footing to avoid the electrical cords running in every direction. They passed glass room after glass room filled with objects and creatures from other worlds. Brian didn't believe such things existed until two years ago, when he discovered his secret talent was magic. With the aid of his adoptive mother and others, he had now visited strange new places.

They headed for the back corner of the room, the farthest point from the stairwell, where a large dark hallway turned under a rock archway. The lighting went from poor to worse as they entered the tunnel and crept forward. Some twenty yards away a black light revealed lighting strips that had been stuck strategically around a glass enclosure. A deep, heavy breathing replaced the soft electrical hum of the room beyond.

It took several minutes for their eyes to adjust to the lack of light in this area of the compound. A rough scraping noise echoed down the hall as a huge round shape rotated across the reflective strips and two tennis ball-sized eyes appeared through the glass. They hung as if suspended in air, shinning a soft purple in the black light. "I knew you'd be back," a gruff, deep voice rumbled. "I hoped I'd never see you again, but I knew it would happen."

Brian flinched at the tone of the creature's voice. Although very deep and rough, it had a piercing quality to it that stung his ears and nerves. It was as if a sharp fingernail was being scraped down a chalkboard.

The ground shook slightly as the huge alien turned his body towards the glass. In the poor lighting, Brian wondered what it really looked like. He could make out its large size and bulk by noticing where it blocked out the reflective strips, but the black light did little for coloring or definition. The shadows did reveal height and width, which were very large.

"I asked you to leave me alone. I don't want to aid you and your kind," the creature grumbled, causing Larry to back several feet away from the front of the cell. "You are working for the wrong side. I have seen the future. You lose. You cannot conquer the One! When he returns, you will be destroyed."

Larry doubled over, putting his hands over his ears, "Can't you make him shut up!"

"Leave now and never come back," the prisoner grumbled, its voice penetrating their bodies like shock waves.

Brian, not at all happy with the alien speaking, shot a glance towards the main area to make sure no one was coming. He closed his eyes and sent his own command through the ground and into the thing. *SILENCE!* The ground trembled as the creature flinched in an effort to block the command. More shockwaves vibrated the ground as the creature continued to wrestle with the unseen combatant of Brian's magic, trying to free himself.

"We won't be coming back," Brian spoke in a calm voice. "We are taking you with us."

Again the alien jerked back and forth in an attempt to free itself from its invisible bonds, rocking the ground with its movements. A loud thump prompted Brian and Larry to jump several feet back as the creature pushed his face into the glass of his cell. Its massive stone-like face with its large blue tennis ball eyes seemed to be pleading with them.

"Go. Make sure we are okay," Brian whispered to Larry, who bolted back up the short hallway for a peek.

He returned a few seconds later. "We're good."

"Back away from the glass," Brian ordered and the creature obeyed, controlled by Brian's power.

"Once he is free, don't ever let him touch you," Brian spoke to Larry. He then stepped up to the front of the cell and placed the palms of his hands on the glass. Closing his eyes he sent out cords of magic through the cell, probing its secrets, learning how it operated. It only took him a minute or so to fool the manmade electronic system to release the locks without setting off any alarms. A wave of cool air rushed past Brian and Larry, tussling their hair in its wake as the glass door slid open. They wrinkled their noses at the earthy compost odor.

Larry spat as if the smell had invaded his taste buds. "He stinks!"

"Out," Brian ordered, and with a few ground shaking steps the massive alien moved into the hallway, forcing Brian and Larry to back up enough to give it room.

"How are we going to get that out of here?" Larry questioned, quaking at the size of the thing. "There's no way we can sneak him out." Larry waved his arm towards the facility beyond the corridor.

"Yes, this seemed like a good idea before," Brian stated, eyeing the size of the alien in front of them.

"Any more bright ideas?" Larry asked, his voice full of sarcasm.

Suddenly a female worker in a white lab coat strolled around the corner, reading a clipboard full of papers. Brian and Larry didn't see her until she had collided with Larry, sending the papers on her clipboard fluttering through the air. Her eyes jumped from Larry to Brian to the massive Alien. "NO!" she gasped.

"Grab her." Brian pointed to the woman as his heart jumped into his throat.

Her hand grasped a small device on the side of her belt.

Larry, in a state of panic, reacted without thinking and punched the woman right between the eyes, knocking her to the ground. The woman cried out but still managed to trigger an alarm from the device on her belt. Sirens wailed with high-pitched ear splitting rings, and red and white lights flashed, throwing dizzying shadows off the walls and floors.

"What are we going to do?" Larry panicked.

"She's got a gun." Brian pointed as the woman drew a small side arm from the back of her pants.

Larry cast a spell pinning the woman's arm to the ground at her side just as she squeezed the trigger, firing a shot that ricocheted off the walls. Sparks flew as the bullet made contact with rock and the prison glass, barely missing them.

Brian extended his hand and the gun flew from the woman's hand into his.

"Do her! Do her!" Larry barked, his face twisted with rage at being fired upon.

"No." Brian closed his eyes. *Sleep*, his power surged into the woman's mind, which accepted the command. Her eyes rolled back in her head and she passed out.

The thudding of footsteps and the echo of voices mingled with the sirens drifted in from the open room beyond the hall. Larry exchanged a glance with Brian. "That can't be good." Larry rushed around the corner for a peek.

"Come," Brian ordered as he followed Larry. The hulking rock-like alien obeyed with thunderous, heavy footsteps. Brian joined Larry at the corner.

"I say we go invisible and rip these losers apart." Larry breathed heavily with a wicked smile on his face. Flashes of armed soldiers entering the main room appeared and disappeared in the spinning lights.

"Our prisoner doesn't have that ability." Brian watched as soldiers began lining up behind desks and blocking the elevators and the stairs.

"Well, look at the size of him. I'm sure he could absorb a lot of fire power without being hurt. Besides, we could disappear and take a lot of them out before he has to move," Larry said.

"That's not good enough. There will always be more of them around the next corner," Brian hissed as they eyed the preparations for their capture taking place in the room beyond. Brian felt calm for the situation in front of them.

"Maybe we should put him back and take our chances!"

"NO! We're taking him out of here."

"YOU IN THE HALL. COME OUT WITH YOUR HANDS UP," a soldier barked through a megaphone. "WE HAVE YOU SURROUND-ED. THERE IS NO WAY OUT!"

Brian and Larry shot a glance around the area and spotted several cameras lining the hall. Larry launched several fireballs, exploding the devices. "Those weren't here last time."

"They were expecting us," Brian stated.

"Any more bright ideas before I leave you with your new friend?" Larry hissed.

"Ah…" Brian searched for an idea.

"YOU HAVE ONE MINUTE TO COME OUT. OTHERWISE WE WILL BE FORCED TO TAKE YOU DOWN!"

"Maybe you should ask your friend," barked Larry. "Either way, we're going to have to fight our way out of here."

Brian's eyes shifted from Larry to the hulking alien behind them in the corner. The creature's large blue eyes tried to break contact, but Brian's spell held him tight. "Do you know a way out?" he asked the monster.

"Yes," the creature answered after a few seconds of trying to hold back.

"What?" Larry flinched at the sudden piercing pitch of the creature's voice. "How?" Brian asked, his heart rate increasing with excitement.

"FORTY SECONDS." The megaphone announced.

"My ship." The creature's harsh rough voice penetrated their bodies, raising the hairs on their necks and arms.

"Your ship?" Brian asked, his mouth dry with excitement at this news.

"His ship?" asked Larry. "No way, I'm getting into a ship with that thing."

"THIRTY SECONDS!"

"Imagine the technology we could get from his ship," Brian pointed out. "And a pilot who knows how to fly it. Think what people will say if we pull this off."

"Where is it?" Larry asked.

"Well?" Brian asked.

After a moment's hesitation, the gargantuan creature extended his bulky arm and pointed his football-sized finger towards the room behind them. "The ceiling."

Brian and Larry spun back towards the main room and stared at the large saucer shaped ship dangling from the ceiling some twenty feet above them.

8

Confusing a Mind

The perfectly smooth chrome saucer hung from the ceiling above them, reflecting the whirling warning lights, giving off a fun house impression. The ship occupied more than half of the ceiling, only revealing the rafters along the sides and corners of the room. If the alien had not told them what it was, Brian and Larry would have thought it was part of the ceiling's structure or fortification. The large spacecraft blocked the majority of the ceiling lights, making the room darker than it should have been.

"TWENTY SECONDS," the megaphone blared.

"How do we get to it?" Larry questioned. "I think we're still going to have to handle some resistance."

Brian eyed the troops preparing for their advance before focusing on the alien. "How do we get up there?"

"There is a control panel behind the troops that will lower it to the floor. Somehow I don't think you can reach it," the alien stated. He laughed a high pitched laugh that seemed to tease them as its shockwave tortured their nerve endings.

"TEN SECONDS!" This time multiple cracks of metal on metal echoed through the room as the soldiers cocked their weapons.

Brian gritted his teeth as the alien's laughter hit him. His palms were sweaty and his stomach started to do back flips in anticipation. "You need to lower the ship," Brian said.

"No way! You need to lower the ship. I'll distract them," Larry argued.

"I need to stay here with him. You can't control him." Brian motioned to their prisoner.

"You better not hit me with a spell," Larry spat, his brow wrinkled to stress how displeased he was with his assignment. "Give me some sort of distraction to get around them," he added before disappearing.

"TIME'S UP!" Several of the soldiers started to creep across the room, their guns at the ready. The sirens blocked out the sounds of their advance, while the spinning lights created a jumping forward affect. Every few feet one would call out, "CLEAR," as he rounded a desk or passed a doorway.

Brian didn't wait for the soldiers to walk very far. He sent a powerful burst of energy into a row of desks, sending chairs, papers, and desks soaring into the air like an invisible creature had just run through them. As if led by a band conductor, all the guns in the room locked onto the path Brian had just cut through the room. Then he launched a ball of intense light through the path he had just created, keeping it low to the ground.

"FREEZE," several soldiers yelled as they followed the light with their guns, thinking it was someone running between the desks.

Before the spell reached the far wall, Brian increased its size and strength and hurled it out of the swath towards the advancing troops. Screams erupted from the men as several dropped their weapons and covered their heads with their arms when the blast crashed down on them like a tidal wave. The force of the curse flattened those in its path, while its shockwave threw everything nearby in a perfect circle outward. Bodies, desks, and debris flew through the air, colliding with other objects and soldiers in the room.

Gun shots rattled the room as the troops who remained upright opened fire in the direction Brian had hoped. *Another one ought to convince them.* He sent a second energy pulse along the same path, but this time he propelled it into a different section of men, with the same devastating effect.

"Call for back up," shouted one over the cries of the wounded, which created an eerie wail that struck a nerve with Brian. He didn't want to inflict pain on American soldiers. He had dreamed of the praise he would receive if they had pulled this off, but didn't want a body count to do it.

A loud thud vibrated the walls and floor, stopping the soldiers in their tracks. Brian glanced around the room for the source when another earth shaking boom forced him to grab the wall for support. A slow clicking mingled with the other noises as the saucer began moving downward at a snail's pace.

"Who…" the speaker never finished his sentence because a spell flung him violently across the room where he crashed into the wall.

Several cries of pain followed as some unseen force attacked the soldiers, tossing them all over the room. Desks crashed into some, fire erupted around others, and shockwaves cast many about like ragdolls.

"He's going to kill everyone," Brian muttered in horror to himself as he sprang from the hall into the main room. To his surprise not a single solder remained on his feet. "Larry, block the stairs and the elevator," he hollered as he tried to guess how long it would take the alien's ship to reach the ground.

An explosion rocked the ship and a cloud of dust wafted across the room as Larry collapsed the metal stairs inside the stairwell. A second blast destroyed the elevator before Larry hustled back to join Brian. Finally, Larry started blasting all the speakers in an effort to stop the ringing alarms.

Brian coughed several times to clear the dust from his mouth and lungs. "Come," he wheezed and the enormous alien stomped into the main room.

"How do we get inside that thing?" Larry asked.

"Good question." Brian ran his hand through his hair as he tried to spot a door or a ladder. "Where's the door?" he asked the alien.

The alien spoke a few strange words that cut Brian and Larry's nerves again, prompting them to cover their ears. Suddenly an outline of white light created a door a little ways out from the center. The light continued to grow until it swallowed up the shiny chrome as it formed a large opening under the ship. Then a ramp began descending out of the opening.

"Magic?" Brian asked.

"Voice recognition combination," the alien responded.

"Okay, so we have the ship and we can get inside it. How are we going to fly it through several floors of concrete?" Larry asked with a wild expression on his face.

"Well?" Brian indicated the alien should respond to Larry's query.

"My ship has enough firepower to blast us through." The alien's penetrating voice took on a saddened tone.

"Now we're talking." Larry bounced with excitement. "We should blow the whole place up."

"What will happen to the solders?" Brian waved his arm at the unconscious and wounded men and women littering the area.

"They will be consumed by the engines' fire."

"Wicked." Larry's grin reached new levels of derangement.

"N—no," Brian stuttered. His stomach felt as if it would sink into one of his legs and all of his blood follow it. "We can't murder all of these people."

"Why are you worrying about these losers? Didn't they just fire their weapons where they thought you were? They just tried to kill you," Larry spat as he navigated around the desks so he could be ready when the ramp to the craft reached the floor.

"They were doing their jobs." Brian chased after Larry. "They are trying to protect our security here. We are the intruders! We need to figure out how to save these people and the ones on the floors above us."

"It doesn't matter. Only our missions for Hudich matter," Larry barked.

Brian's head spun with pressure as his heart pounded with dread at killing so many innocent people. He spun towards the alien as if seeking answers to the situation. Their eyes met and Brian sensed there was an understanding there when the round boulder-like face furrowed with thought.

"Please," Brian pleaded.

"Move the soldiers into my cell for protection," the alien's torturous voice suggested.

"Larry, come on!" Brian ordered, picking up a machine gun off of the floor.

"No way. The longer we wait, the more time it gives them to get through," Larry stated.

"We're not leaving until all the soldiers are safe in his cell, so I suggest you help me. The sooner we get this done the quicker we can leave." Brian rushed to a group of dazed soldiers trying to get to their feet.

Larry threw up his hands with frustration but followed after him.

"Listen up! We're taking this ship and its pilot out of here. Everyone who can, needs to help get the others into the glass cell. Otherwise you're going to be barbequed when we blast off." Brian held the gun steady.

"GET MOVING NOW! I have no problem cooking you, so move," Larry barked, and fired a few shots into a wall. His face twisted, red with anger.

With Larry threatening to shoot or leave the stragglers to be inciner-ated by the spacecraft's engines, the evacuation of the soldiers into the glass cell went rather quickly. To Brian's great relief, none had been killed. Although no one had escaped injury, the majority assisted the few who were seriously injured into the cell. The alien's spacious cell accommodated the soldiers with plenty of room to spare.

"I'm not going to lock you in, but I suggest you remain inside until we are gone," Brian stated before he and Larry hustled back to the main room where the ship had finished its descent.

The alien remained where Brian had ordered before they ushered the solders to safety. Larry rushed up the ramp and into the ship, leaving Brian and the alien outside.

"What to do about the people on the other floors?" Brian peered around, hoping to find an answer. The rotating alarm lights made it dif-ficult to lock on to anything.

Larry's head popped out of the door. "Come on! And wait till you see inside this thing!"

"The fire alarm," the alien suggested, causing Brian to jump a little.

Brian's eyes immediately focused on the small red box on the wall. He raced across the room and yanked down the lever. Water rained down on them from the fire sprinklers across the ceiling. The alien's saucer shaped craft created an almost fountain like effect as the water spilled off of it in a perfect circle. If not for the sprinklers, Brian would have thought the alarm hadn't worked because Larry had destroyed the loud speakers.

"Go," Brian ordered the alien, as he hustled under the ship and up the ramp.

His jaw dropped when he saw the display of advanced technology. A six foot tall tinted window circled the entire ship a couple of feet above the curve of the ship. The water from the sprinkler system gave the sensation of driving through a car wash. A railing ran around a mas-sive pillar set in the center of the ship, which he had to snatch in order to maintain his balance when the alien climbed the ramp. At almost fifty yards across, the ship housed several rooms inside its circumference. Brian passed sleeping quarters with massive beds, what appeared to be a mess hall or meeting room, and several weapons stores. Dust covered all of the weapons, indicating the soldiers were unable to enter the craft, and the alien had refused to open it.

"I think I've found the cockpit," Larry called from around the bend of the ship.

When Brian finally caught up with Larry, he was sitting in a massive chair where the window extended up the sides of the ship several feet and also over the curve and several feet under it, so that the ground was visible. The chair Larry occupied rested several feet lower than the main floor where there were an additional four chairs, two on each side. In front of the lower chair, a control panel hovered in front of the windshield by some unseen force. There were several strange gadgets along its surface and what appeared to be an oversized steering device.

"This thing is cool." Larry's face beamed with mischievousness. "I'll bet we could wipe out this entire base."

"I'll settle for just getting out of here," Brian said as he stepped down alongside Larry. The ship swayed a little as the alien's large frame meandered around the ship towards them.

"I need that seat," rumbled the alien with his penetrating voice, which caused Larry to jump out of the way. Both Brian and Larry backed away as the alien's large frame lumbered down the step to take up the large pilot's seat.

"Where should we have him take us? Somewhere close to town?" Larry asked.

"Does this thing have a cloaking device?" asked Brian.

"Good question." Larry nodded.

"We can fly your skies without being detected," the alien stated. Larry and Brian cringed again.

"You'd think we would get used to it." Larry's face knotted up with his displeasure at the alien's voice.

"Take us up and head east," Brian ordered.

The alien uttered a strange word and a 3D light green visual display sprang to life above the hovering control panel. Several circular directional, speed, and altitude readouts combined with ship engine stats populated the holographic display. Another couple of strange words were uttered, and several of the instruments jumped with numbers and dials as the ship's engines roared to life. The deep hum of the ship forced cracks to spread through the walls of the building, and the water from the sprinkling system was flung away from the ship as if a gale force wind blew in every direction from the ship.

"Is this thing just going to fly through the concrete floors?" Larry asked.

"No," the alien barked. He extended a football sized finger and tapped a solid light green circle on the graphic display which opened up another hologram display behind the first. This new display had a square border the size of a big screen TV, with cross hairs floating in the center.

The alien then snatched a microphone-like device and held it to his mouth. "If you want to live, get out of the building, NOW!" His harsh voice shook the walls of the structure.

"Why wait, just blast them," Larry complained.

They waited for ten minutes. "Okay," Brian said.

After tapping another circle next to the first, a see through image of the ceiling appeared in the board of the second display. The cross hairs continued to float in the center of the screen. With the touch of a third circle, an additional hum joined the engines and a quick flash of light raced over the ship.

"Shields?" Brian asked.

"Yes," responded the alien. "We don't want debris from the structure to damage the ship." The alien then took hold of a small joystick-like object on the left side of the hovering control panel and squeezed the red trigger on the front. A bright flash of blue blipped across the second hologram and filtered in through the windows as a laser blast blew a massive hole through the complex. Dust and debris permeated the air and a constant blinking of white light, like cameras going off in a football stadium at night, spread over the ship. The force field vaporized chunks of the building and equipment falling from the floor above.

They floated in place while the dust cleared, to reveal that a second laser blast was needed to fully clear their path. Once again a lightshow danced over the ship from the falling objects. Slowly, the alien flew the ship up out of the hole through the center of the complex. Broken mortar, twisted steel, shattered office equipment, fires, and smoke drifted past the window as they passed the various floors of the complex. An occasional flash of light indicated the shield continued to deflect falling debris.

The ship rose above the complex, while the winking lights exploded all around it as ground troops launched an attack. Several of the explosions were strong enough to throw the ship to the side. After a blinding flash engulfed the windshield, rocking the ship backwards, the alien tapped another circle on the front hologram and the area in front of the ship and at a downward angle appeared in the second hologram. The alien grasped the weapons stick and slid the crosshairs over the ground troops.

"JUST SCARE THEM," Brian screamed at the last second.

The alien lowered the crosshairs over to the area just in front of the attackers and pulled the trigger. A blue pulse of light blasted a crater in the ground which was about the size of a house, throwing a massive cloud of dust, dirt, and rock onto the troops behind it.

"Awesome," Larry grinned. "I want to try that."

"NO!" Brian gasped as Larry stretched out his hand and took hold of the weapons trigger. Before Brian could shout out an order, the alien grabbed Larry's arm.

Suddenly, Larry was at peace. He couldn't remember ever feeling this relaxed in his life. A dazzling white light filled his world—both comforting and calming him at the same time.

"Am I dead?" Larry's thoughts seemed vocal as if he didn't have to open his mouth to speak.

"No," answered a strangely familiar voice.

"Who are you? Where am I?" Larry glanced around but only the whiteness could be seen, as if he stood in a room of solid soft white lights.

"My name is Ime and you are on my ship with your companion," the alien answered, and Larry recognized the voice, but the harsh penetrating tone was missing.

"Why can't I see the ship?" A surge of adrenaline flooded through him, replacing the calm. "Are you going to kill me?"

"No. I'm going to show you things. I'm going to show you a possible future. If events do not change, it is the future that will be," Ime spoke.

Suddenly, Larry remembered something from earlier that day. "Is this what you meant by we lose? You've seen it?"

"Yes. Though the future can be changed by events, I have seen a version of the future which showed your destruction."

"My destruction?"

"Not yours personally, but your side's cause. Whether or not you choose to believe this version of future events, or you do something to try and change them, will be up to you."

"How will I know which events to change?" Larry asked.

"I do not have that answer. Nor do I think you can defeat the One. It would be easier to change yourself than figure out which events can change the future."

"What do you mean by that?"

"That is for you to figure out."

Suddenly everything went black. When Larry could see again, he stood in Ime's ship, but they hovered above the earth. An all-out futuristic space battle waged around them. Gigantic space saucers attempted to fend off smaller ships buzzing around them like flies. The larger ship's cannons tried to blast the pests out of the air, while the smaller cannons fired lasers, causing small explosions on the larger cruisers' surfaces. Dog fights flew all about them. Ime's ship appeared to be invisible to the eyes of the others, although he had to constantly maneuver his ship to avoid the steady stream of colorful laser blasts that surrounded them.

It went dark again and when Larry's vision cleared, the ship floated over a huge valley. A battle unlike any he had seen waged in front of him. Bodies of both the living and the dead filled the entire valley. A larger army seemed to be circling a smaller one. Larry recognized Night Shades and other creatures among the more numerous armies pressing in on the smaller force. Hudich's banners flew among them and Larry didn't recognize any flags as part of his world. Magical and technological weapons of every kind hammered at both sides. Airships engaged other airships and flying creatures in the skies above.

"Similar wars are being fought all over the planet and in other worlds," Ime stated.

"Whose side is the United States on? And what countries do these armies belong to?" Larry asked, a strange empty felling spread through him, numbing his body and mind. He didn't care for the horrible scene below.

"The United States has fallen, along with all the other nations of your world. This is a war between good and evil."

"How did the United States fall?"

"A dark society gained control of your country and convinced the people to give up their freedom and let the government take care of them. Convinced that socialism would save them, they spent themselves into oblivion because of the massive entitlement mentality. With the incentives to succeed taken away, exceptionalism and the desire to achieve disappeared. People became lazy and refused to do for themselves. They believed what the government promised, that it could and would take care of them. Those who wished to remain free and self-reliant refused to give up what they worked hard for to those who had grown fat and lazy off the fruit of their labors. Civil war followed."

Larry could not pull his eyes away from the gruesome display below. The emptiness he felt started to change to darkness, and his stomach churned inside his gut, threatening to push its contents up his throat. The vision was so complete that the stench of rotting flesh and decaying bodies stung Larry's noise and taste buds.

"The One cometh!"

A dazzling light filled Larry's sight so that he covered his eyes to shield them from the brightness. When the light faded he caught a brief glimpse of a tall man with reddish brown hair reaching his shoulders, and he was wearing a dark red robe. Another blinding light exploded from his mouth, which started to consume the followers of Hudich.

9

Terrible Loss

"How long has this communications system been operable?" Grandpa shouted, pointing to the circle representing earth.

Kit's conversation with Gor was almost inaudible because of the battle behind them and the hissing and the sirens. "Almost a year."

"A year!" Grandpa's face turned ashen. "We need to…Can he tell us its location on Earth?"

"No, but he can give us the signal type so we can track it," Kit stated after his translation.

Gor sat on a chair in front of a monitor and began typing away at the computer.

"I doubt this is possible since we aren't a hub or the main communications center, but can we disable the system from here?" Grandpa asked.

Another quick word between Kit and Gor, "No, but he says he helped set up the system, and when they were testing it they could ping other locations so that they gave off a tracer beacon. He thinks he could turn the beacon on again, and with the signal type we should be able to pin point the location."

"Excellent," Grandpa sighed as Gor continued to work at the control panel.

"What's happening?" Max joined them.

"How's Cindy?" Grandpa asked with a worried expression. He appeared to have aged several years in the last few moments.

"Stable. Olik says she'll be okay. And the communications center?"

"This isn't the main communications center. It isn't even a hub," Grandpa stated.

"What? Where is it?"

"Earth!"

Max's jaw dropped. They had spent the last year hunting for and trying to destroy the enemy's communications system, only to discover it had been right under their noses.

Before Max could ask why or how, Gor rattled off something to Kit.

"He says the beacon is running. He doesn't think anyone at the center will notice, but he can't guarantee it. He will print off the signal type and beacon frequency for you."

"How could this have happened?" Max shook his head.

"The enemy has been very clever in throwing us off the track," Grandpa said. "Playing us like fools."

"It would be nice to know what they're up to now," Max yelled out of frustration.

"Maybe we can," Kit responded.

"What?" Both Max and Grandpa questioned, leaning closer around Kit and Gor.

"Maybe there is a history of past communications," Kit offered and then started speaking with Gor in the weird click-ish language.

Gor nodded his head and began typing feverishly at the keyboard.

"We need to hurry." Max shot a glance at the battle behind them. "How are we going to get out of this mess? Do you think you can open the gateway down here?"

"I don't have the precise calculations to open the gateway at this location. We are going to have to find another way out," Grandpa frowned. "Go see how Zaat and the others are holding up. We should be ready to leave shortly."

Max rushed back to Olik who was kneeling over a pale, but conscious, Cindy. She groaned and squeezed her eyes tight against the pain as Olik helped her into a sitting position.

"How's she doing?" asked Max.

"I've been shot. How do you think I'm doing?" Cindy complained.

"She'll be ready to move," Olik replied as Max sprang to his feet and raced to the door.

Thick white smoke continued to block the hallways in both directions. Zaat and the other Smilsums fired random shots every few seconds to keep their own army at bay. Max took up a position next to

Zaat against the wall, while returning fire blasted away at the entrance to the command center.

"Are they almost—" Zaat paused as the sirens stopped, "done?" He glanced down both halls as if expecting the enemy to charge them.

Max's senses tingled; something was about to change. "Yes," he swallowed, his eyes trying to focus on anything coming through the swirling smoke. Max put his senses on high alert. He noticed even the soft whistle that had accompanied them on their way in had vanished. Only the hissing pipes from inside the command center and the pounding gun fire echoed through the hallways.

"They're up to something," Max whispered.

No sooner had he finished his sentence when a rushing noise filled the corridor as if a wind storm was pushing its way through the complex. In mere seconds the wind sucked the smoke out of the hallway, taking away their only form of cover.

"That's not good," Zaat stated, spotting something large moving towards them from the direction of the detention center. He fired several shots, which only bounced away from the object. "That's really not good. We may be trapped."

Max raced through the command center, hurdling desks and chairs. He almost knocked Grandpa to the ground . Grandpa caught Max just before he slid into him. "I don't think we're going to get out of here. They're coming," Max shouted.

"We've got everything we need," Kit said, handing a stack of papers to Grandpa.

Grandpa stuffed the material into his pack. "Ask him if there's any other way out of here!"

Kit squawked back and forth with Gor, who gestured to an area in the far left corner of the room.

"He says we could use the ventilation shaft, but he doesn't advise it. They would definitely know where we've gone and they could easily trap us in there." Kit relayed Gor's message.

"We have to hurry," Zaat yelled from the entrance.

"We need something to drive them out. Or make it so that they want to leave." Grandpa furrowed his eyebrows in thought.

"How do you make an army want to leave an underground complex?" Kit stated.

Max and Grandpa's eyes grew wider as they looked at each other, sharing the same thought. "How do you make them want to leave?" they both stated together with knowing looks on their faces.

"What are you thinking?" Kit asked with a raised eyebrow.

"We collapse the compound," Grandpa stated.

"That should make everyone want to leave." Max smiled.

"Olik, we need to bring this complex down," Grandpa hollered. "Kit, have Gor show us how to get into the ventilation system. Max, help Cindy."

Max rushed to Cindy and took over for Olik, who had been holding her in a standing position. Her face was pale and drawn and she held her arm tight against her side. She reminded Max of a person fighting the urge to vomit. Max supported Cindy by placing her arm over his shoulder and gently wrapping an arm around her waist. They crept toward the area where Gor and Kit began removing a section of metal panels from the wall.

"How are you feeling?"

Cindy winced, locked eyes with Max and pursed her lips as if to say, you have to ask.

"Yeah, dumb question." Max chuckled in an attempt to make her feel better.

"Well," Cindy gritted her teeth, "you're good at asking them."

"We need to hurry," Zaat called from the entrance.

Grandpa and Olik scrambled around the room, placing charges at the base of the pillars which supported the massive weight for the underground complex.

"We must seal the air shaft behind us. Otherwise the blast will follow us up the tunnel and kill us," Olik yelled.

"Max, start Cindy up as soon as it's open," Grandpa ordered.

Kit and Gor created a hole about four feet high and three feet wide in the back of the room. Gor chattered with Kit as Max and Cindy joined them at the opening. Afterwards, Gor got on his hands and knees, crawled into the hole, and disappeared.

"He's going up first. He says it's about a five story climb. He also said to be ready, we could run into resistance," Kit told them as he and Max helped Cindy lower herself enough to fit through the wall.

Max followed right after Cindy. He could sense her despair when she leaned against the metal ladder, resting her head against the cold bars. They stood in what appeared to be a large metal pipe with barely enough room for the two of them to stand together. Max tried to see the top, but Gor's bulky frame several feet above them blocked his view. The air was cooler and had a metallic scent to it. Max figured when they sealed the hole it would be almost completely dark inside. Only small shafts of light flickered around Gor's moving body.

"You can do this," Max encouraged, helping Cindy put her hands on the rung a foot above her head. "We are going to have to hustle." He managed a weak smile.

Cindy grunted, putting a foot in a rung above the ground and pushed and pulled herself up. She didn't complain, but her gasps and groans indicated the obvious pain. It took her several seconds to get high enough for Max to start the long climb. He had just gotten off the ground when an explosion rocked the shaft, and a wave of hot dusty air rushed past them. Cindy's foot slipped off its current step and crashed down hard on his hand.

"Ahhh," Max exhaled at the sharp pinch of his fingers between the metal bar and Cindy's weight.

"Sorry," Cindy said as she hauled herself up, freeing Max's hand.

Max raised his hand in the air, squeezing and releasing it into a fist, trying to make sure everything was working. The throbbing made it a difficult task, but all his fingers appeared to be okay.

After he and Cindy had ascended another dozen feet, Grandpa began the climb, followed by Olik.

"Seal the entrance. We have about 15 minutes," Olik shouted to Zaat, while the other two Smilsums entered the air tunnel.

"We need to get as far up as possible," Grandpa barked when he reached Max and Cindy.

Cindy's struggles slowed the group as they tried to get away from the blast zone, which was going to happen below.

"What was that last explosion?" Max asked.

"We needed to give everyone enough time for Zaat and the others to get in the airshaft. Cindy, I know you're in a lot of pain, but you need to move," Grandpa urged, to which Cindy picked up the pace a little.

Heavy breathing and occasional chatter echoed through the cylinder as Max and the others climbed up the long steep tube. Sweat trickled down Max's forehead and dampened his clothing inside the hot suit. His muscles screamed in protest of the sustained stepping and pulling. His fingers hurt and his mouth was dry. He constantly had to wait for Cindy to go up enough rungs for him to continue his climb. He figured by the state of his exhaustion, Cindy must be on the verge of collapse.

Suddenly an incredible force shook and twisted the metal tunnel like a giant playing with an enormous slinky. The blast below rocked the ground violently, and then the whole air vent dropped several feet. Cindy lost her grip and landed on top of Max's shoulders. Max staggered down two rungs with the increased weight. The wall below blasted inward and fire roared up the shaft. A high pitched scream vibrated off the walls when the Smilsum at the bottom of the group absorbed the squelching heat and disappeared. Heat and dust particles choked the tunnel, making it difficult to breathe and see.

"Climb! Hurry! I don't know if or how long the pipe will hold," Olik ordered from below.

The ground quaking event seemed to give new life to Cindy, who began climbing with greater urgency. Max's heart pounded in his ears and sweat stung his eyes as he kept right on her heels. He coughed and gagged on the dust clinging to his already parched mouth. He tried to catch a glimpse of the top of the tunnel around Cindy and Gor, but he could see no end to the thing.

Suddenly, the crunching of metal and a loud pop from somewhere below them assaulted their ear drums. Another wild shake and a shift of the shaft followed. Max tightened his grip on the bar.

"What's happening?" Kit called, fright evident in his voice.

Before anyone could respond, a louder rumble and a crunching of metal pushed Max's heart into his throat.

"The tunnel is caving in! Go! Go! Go!" Zaat screamed, launching everyone into a frantic scramble up the ladder.

Max hustled up the ladder as fast as he could without climbing over Cindy, who had increased her pace but was still struggling. Cindy was like the pacer car on a race track, with everyone backed up behind her ready to speed by.

"Hurry! Hurry!" Kit called from above.

Another terrifying metal-crushing implosion twisted the pipe so violently that parts of the ladder broke away from the wall. The screech of the collapsing pipe pierced Max's eardrum with the sharpness of metal scratching metal. Cindy lost her footing once more. Her swinging legs gave Max a sharp kick in the nose, prompting his eyes to water. Cindy gave a soft groan for a sorry and then clung to the ladder without moving.

"We need to get out of here. NOW!" Zaat cried from below.

Max shook his head to clear the cobwebs. "Cindy. Cindy."

"I can't," Cindy mumbled.

"You must keep going," Grandpa ordered. "Or we're all going to die!"

"Cindy, spread your legs apart," Max said.

"WHAT?"

"Spread your legs and get on my shoulders. You'll just have to pull with your arms," Max said, as the tube began to shiver once more. "Do it!"

Cindy slid her legs apart on the rung just above Max. Max then drove upward until Cindy was sitting on his shoulders. With the added weight of Cindy on him, Max began to climb again. Even with Cindy pulling, Max's muscles began to shake with each step up the ladder. The soles of his feet ached where the bars dug into the center of his feet with the added pressure. Sweat ran down his face and his breathing echoed in his ears.

CRUNCH echoed up the pipe and the pipe shook, followed by a hair-raising scream. The wailing pressed in on Max with the weight of pain he couldn't imagine.

"The Smilsum is pinched in the pipe," yelled Zaat. "I can't..." Another tube rocking, WAAMP, and the screaming stopped, and also silenced Zaat.

"The Smilsum and Zaat are gone! GO! GO! GO!" Olik hollered.

The sudden horrific screams kicked new life into Cindy who began climbing on her own power again. They raced up the tube which continued to pop and jolt as section after section compressed inward from the pressure against the weakened complex. Their heavy breathing echoed in the tunnel and the heat grew to an almost unbearable level. Fear and the gradual increase of light drove them upward.

"You're almost there," Kit called from the opening above.

"You can make it, Cindy," Max encouraged, the feel of cool air from above reaching his face.

CRUNCH! Another section of pipe succumbed to the pressure, shaking the tunnel as if something had hit the outside of the tube with an enormous club.

"HELP!" Olik called his voice full of panic. "My foot is stuck."

"Cindy, Max, keep going!" Grandpa ordered.

Max glanced down to see Olik straining to remove his foot from the twisted metal of the crushed pipe. The sweat pouring out of Max's body turned clammy as fear crawled over his skin. Cindy continued to climb, but Max came to a halt.

Grandpa had dropped onto the crushed section and worked at freeing Olik's leg. Olik's normally thin-line mouth had compacted into a pucker, indicating obvious pain.

The ground shifted, making Max's heart pound against his ribcage.

"Get him out of his boot," Max called, his voice hoarse with dryness.

The pipe shifted and creaked again, causing Max to climb down in an effort to help.

"Good idea. Get your boot off," Grandpa ordered. He and Olik worked at undoing the bindings. "Max, get out of here. NOW!"

Max hesitated a moment, then gradually started back up. Suddenly, light flooded the tunnel as Cindy made it to the top. Max glanced down every few minutes, willing Olik free. *Hurry up! We're almost out!*

"You—are—almost—free," Grandpa's voice rose up the pipe.

Max had just reached the opening when a grating metal grinding froze him in place.

"Joseph, you need to get out of here," Olik moaned through gritted teeth.

Max tried to scream, tried to protest but a lump had strangled his voice box and he glanced down.

"I won't…"

Olik put a hand on Grandpa's shoulder. "Joe, you must leave."

Tears streaked the dirt that covered Grandpa's face as he peered into Olik's large dark eyes. He opened his mouth but before he could respond the cylinder started to collapse. Olik waved his hand upward, catching Grandpa in his final spell and propelled him up the shaft. WAAMP! Another section of the air shaft caved in, and Olik's spell threw Max and Grandpa out of the tunnel and onto the hard dirt.

"OLIK! NO!" Max screamed, scrambling back towards the opening, tears stinging his eyes and running down his cheeks. It felt like he had been kicked in the heart, as if it had exploded. An ominous weight pressed against his chest, making it difficult to breathe.

Cindy crawled over to Max and wrapped her arms around him. Her body shaking with sobs. Joe turned his back on the shaft and placed his hand over his face. Kit lowered his head in respect for his fallen friend.

The ground continued to rumble around them and clouds of dust spiraled upward around them. The collapsing complex launched dirt and debris into the air from every opening in the surface. A final metallic squeal and the top of the airshaft closed, knocking the entire group to the ground. The earth shifted and sunk where the top of the shaft had been.

Max's grief squashed his desire to move. He didn't care what happened. He just wanted the pain in his chest to stop.

Gor started to chatter in a whispered tone to Kit as the rumble of vehicles joined the shifting grounds. The thudding of troops running nearby brought silence to the mourning group.

Max turned his head toward the noise, which sounded about forty yards away behind a group of trees.

"We need to move," Kit hissed.

"Can he take us back to the canyon?" Grandpa asked, his eyes swollen and red.

"We can't leave Olik down there!" Cindy sobbed.

Grandpa squatted in front of her and Max, his face drawn with pain. He wiped a tear off Cindy's cheek. "We will come back for him, but we need to get out of here. I won't leave my friend in this place."

Max discovered his limbs still responded to his commands as he got to his feet and helped Cindy to do the same. The three of them held each other for a second and then made ready to leave.

"How are you feeling," Grandpa asked Cindy, who still held her side and appeared paler than usual.

"I'll help her," Max stated, swinging one of her arms around his shoulders.

The small group hustled into a small patch of trees. Max fought back a flood of tears and glanced back at the crushed shaft. "Goodbye, Olik," he muttered.

"Why don't we just use the gateway?" Cindy asked.

"Good idea. I'm glad someone is thinking straight," Grandpa puffed, pulling out his communicator. His fingers had barely stopped moving when a squadron of Smilsums rushed out of the trees and surrounded them.

After a few strange clicks from one of the soldiers, Kit translated. "He said to drop our weapons and then they want us to move to the center of the clearing."

Everyone tossed their guns in a pile at the feet of the obvious leader, who was giving the orders. Then the small group walked to the center of the clearing, away from the trees, with their hands raised.

The squad of Smilsums worked their way around until they all stood in front of Max and the others with their guns leveled at them. Once again, the leader started to chirp out commands which Kit relayed to the others.

"He wants us to kneel. I think they are going to execute us!" Kit said.

10

Under Surveillance

Max and the others slowly got on their knees. The pain of Olik's death weighed heavy on Max, so much that his body felt as if he carried an extra hundred pounds. His will to fight had taken a serious blow, and he didn't know if he could cast a strong enough blocking spell to save himself or anyone else.

The leader of the Smilsums rattled off a few strange clicks and the soldiers responded by taking aim with their weapons.

"Max you block while I attack!" Grandpa muttered out of the side of his mouth.

Before Max could utter a word a strangely familiar roar caused everyone to look for the source. It happened again, the sound materializing like a ghost out of the air itself. Cindy raised her tear streaked face and a smile actually spread across her face.

Ell sprang out of the gateway into the center of the Smilsums, with Sky riding on his back. The panicked Smilsums stumbled and scrambled over each other in their efforts to flee Ell's snapping razor-sharp teeth. Sky sprang from his back and rendered several Smilsums unconscious with a whirling black staff. Each hard whack brought instant sleep to its victim.

After Ell had chased off the last few Smilsums in the group he trotted to Cindy, who wrapped her arms around his hideous head and cried.

"When you didn't come through, we figured you were in trouble," Sky said, joining the small group. "Where's Olik?"

"He—he didn't make it," Grandpa stammered.

Sky's face dropped. "What?"

Grandpa seemed to be struggling to form words, tears swelling in his eyes.

Max turned his head to hide the tears running down his face in large warm drops. Sky reached out and pulled him and Grandpa into a group hug.

"Let's get out of here! We can talk about it later," Sky said.

"We can't leave him," Max cried, glancing back to the spot of Olik's death.

"We'll need to get the proper tools and equipment to get him out," Grandpa sniffled. "We need to leave now. Cindy needs medical attention."

They helped Cindy through the Gateway and everyone else followed. They took Kit and Gor through, but then reopened it so they could return those two to Kit's base, before sending Ell back to Svet.

After they had attended to Cindy, they related to the others who had been waiting at Grandpa's house the sad tale of what happened to them and to Olik. Max couldn't remember ever feeling so downtrodden. Even when Frank had died two years ago, it wasn't as bad because he was closer to Olik. His father's death was tragic but he was so young when it happened. Somehow Olik's death made it feel as if his father had died all over again, and the world would never be right after this new tragedy.

Max felt the house held a claustrophobic sensation as he sat in the front room with Grandpa, Yelka, and his mother. He stared out the window to avoid everyone's gaze. Somehow, any eye contact seemed to transfer that person's pain and sorrow to him. Even though it was a bright sunny day outside, the world appeared dark through Max's saddened view of things. He didn't want to think anymore. He desired a distraction, needed something to do before the weight of the situation smothered him.

A low rumble vibrated the house, causing Max to finally sit up straight in his chair and look at the others. The pictures on the wall started to sway, and a small vase with flowers on the coffee table slid about four inches before the tremor stopped.

Grandpa had gotten to his feet and slowly raised his arm to point to an area on the far side of town. Max and the others followed the direction of his finger to see a plume of dust rise into the air and then drift away with the breeze.

"What was that," Max's mother asked.

"Do you think Larry and his friends set off some type of explosion?" Max asked.

Sky entered the front door, trailed by two strangers: a black woman and a white man. "What do you think that was?" she asked motioning out the door.

"I don't know. Why don't you take Max and go check it out? He could use something to do," Grandpa suggested.

"Okay. First, this is Sam and Linda. They have a lot of important information for you, Joseph," Sky introduced Grandpa and Max to the people who had accompanied her.

Sky waited for them to exchange handshakes before nodding in the direction of the disturbance. "Come on, Max."

Max and Sky hurried down the steps and out the front gate. They turned right and took the street through the newer neighborhoods. This was the usual route to get to the other side of town without walking through the section controlled by the enemy. At the end of the pavement they made their way along a well-used trail through the sagebrush.

"How are you doing?" Sky asked as they navigated a dry creek bed.

"Okay," Max lied.

"It's all right to be sad. Olik was a great friend. His contributions to our cause will be sorely missed," Sky said.

Max wanted to add a comment but the lump in his throat kept him from speaking. Fresh tears blurred his vision and he turned his head away to wipe them. After a few moments he gained his composure, "Are those people, Sam and Linda, the ones who worked on translating the book Kacha stole from us?"

"Yes. Hopefully, we can use them to track down everyone involved," Sky began, ascending a hill that would give them a view of the entire city and its surroundings.

"I thought we already knew how far it had gone. All the way to the top circles of government," Max stated.

"Yes and no. I believe it goes all the way to the top, but what individuals at the top know is another thing. Some might just be useful idiots, while others are pulling the strings," Sky added.

"I can buy that," Max said.

Before they reached the top of the hill Sky put a hand out, blocking Max's path. "Wait here," she said, before creeping the rest of the way up the hill. Inching closer to the top, she continually lowered herself nearer to the ground. Eventually she was laying flat on her stomach on the top of the hill. After a few minutes she waved Max to follow.

"Do you see anything unusual?" Sky asked as they stared down on the town.

Max's eyes danced over every corner of the small town, looking for any irregularity. He focused his attention on the enemy's side and the fields behind them. Nothing seemed out of place, but the strange tingle in his gut, his sixth sense, told him something was out there. "No, I don't see anything, but I feel it."

"What is your special gift telling you?" Sky turned her head and stared into his eyes with raised eyebrows.

"That there is someone out there. Someone…watching us," Max stated, his brow furrowed with concentration as he tried to find what his senses were telling him.

"So, you don't see it but you detect something? That's interesting. I can tell you no one is watching us from what I see, which means you are picking up something totally different," Sky focused her attention on an area outside of town occupied by the enemy.

"What do you see?" Max finally asked. Because his eyes didn't agree with his feelings.

"I see an invisible ship parked in the field about three hundred yards outside of town."

Max started to laugh, "How do you see an invisible ship?"

"Do you see the hill that holds their underground complex?"

"The one where they kept the Zbal?"

"Yes. Now, if you move about three hundred yards north from that spot you will see a large field with wild grass and sagebrush."

"Okay, still not seeing anything!"

"Notice those three sections where the grass and the sagebrush have been flattened to the ground in perfect rectangular shapes, pushed into the ground a couple of inches. That's where the ship is parked," Sky stated.

"I see what you mean. It does look like something heavy has landed there, but since it's invisible, how can you be sure what it is, is still there?"

"Because if you look at that one section of sagebrush they appear to have a perfect cylinder resting on it," Sky added.

Before Max could comment on this unusual shape of the sagebrush, the back of a ramp descended from the other side of the ship. It appeared to be coming out of nothing. A minute later Brian hurried out of the ship and sprinted towards the town.

"Now do you believe me?" Sky smirked.

Max felt his jaw drop, "Now where do you think they got that?"

"I'm not sure but I am willing to bet it was already somewhere on this planet."

"What makes you think that? And where would they have found it? Better yet, where would Brian have learned to fly it?"

"Think about it. Who possessed the first gateway? The one that your grandfather destroyed?"

"The government," Max said, following Brian with his eyes until he disappeared behind the houses on the enemy's side of town.

A sudden sensation of someone or something following or watching them caused all the hairs on the back of Max's neck to come to attention. He rose up slightly and glanced behind them but couldn't spot anything out of the ordinary. A slight breeze rattled the tops of the sagebrush and prairie grasses, causing him to see movement everywhere.

"What is it?" Sky lifted herself up in reaction to his movements.

"Something is watching us. I can feel it," Max continued to search for the source of his agitation.

Sky grabbed Max's shoulder and pulled him back to the ground as Brian and a small group of people emerged from the town. They hurried along the path Brian had taken, to where the ramp hung suspended in air as if by invisible cords. The wind carried a jumble of voices to them, but nothing they could interpret.

Max and Sky waited as the group disappeared up the ramp.

"Do you still think someone is spying on us?" Sky asked as they remained focused on the spot where something invisible rested.

"Yes."

"Is there more than one?" Sky asked.

"I'm not sure, but for some reason, I can't ignore it. I've been trying to tune it out, but because it is the only thing I can sense, it's like it's screaming at me," Max stated.

"From behind or in front of us?"

"From behind."

"Wait here," Sky ordered and moved over the hill in front of them in a crouched position. She wound her way into a large group of sagebrush and disappeared.

Max couldn't decide whether she was going to take a closer look at what lay hidden in the field in front of them, or if she wanted to search for what he had detected behind them. He lay on the grass wondering how long this would take, when suddenly the group of people emerged down the ramp. They carried someone on a gurney. *Is that Larry?* Max wished he had brought binoculars on this little trip so he could be sure. A group of four transported what he was almost certain was Larry, back into town. After they entered the neighborhood, Brian and another man descended the ramp. Undecipherable bits of their conversation floated up to Max. The tone of the man didn't seem to be a happy one. Brian constantly nodded his head and once or twice he motioned towards the thing behind them.

Two flashes of light caught Max's eye, occurring about ten yards away from Brian and the other man. Hudich and Alan replaced the blips of light and then marched toward the other two.

Max's heart started thumping against his ribs as he glanced around, wondering where Sky was. He worried what might happen if they discovered her trying to get a peek at what was going on. Even with Hudich, the leader of the enemy, only a few hundred yards away—Max's extra sense warned him of other, unwanted, eyes watching him.

He observed the conversation taking place on the ramp before the small group disappeared into the invisible object. "Come on, Sky!" Max whispered to himself as he surveyed the area for any sign of her. The breeze rustling the grasses continued to play tricks with his mind.

Sky appeared suddenly, hunched over on the side of the hill just in front of him, startling him. "You almost scared me to death!" Max gasped, putting his hand over his chest.

She scurried up the last few steps and took up her spot next to him in the grass.

"What did you find?" Max asked.

"You were right. There are two men spying on us." Sky said. "What's going on with the ship?"

"I thought that's where you went. What do you mean two men are spying on us?"

Hudich and the others climbed down the ramp of the invisible ship. Sky put her hand on Max's back and pushed him flatter against the hill top. "Hudich is here!" Sky's voice was a harsh whisper.

"Yes, I thought you knew that. I thought you went to check out the ship. I didn't think you were going to check on my feeling," Max stated.

"Hey, your feelings over the last few years have proven to be pretty accurate," Sky added, her eyes locked on Hudich and the others below. "Now, I'm really curious."

"What, about these men?" Max pressed.

"They're just barely inside the tree line on the side of the mountain. There are two; they looked like military personnel. They have weapons, maps, documents, cameras, video, and other surveillance equipment. They have a little camp set up. I don't know what they are doing, but they are interested in what's going on in this town. And their main target appears to be your grandpa's house," Sky said.

"How long do you think they've been there?" Max watched Alan hurry toward town, away from the others.

"Where do you think he's going?"

"Oh, they carried someone out of the ship on a stretcher. It looked like Larry but I wasn't sure until now. What are we going to do?"

"We're definitely going to have to take a closer look, but we need better gear. I think we should report back to your grandpa and then make plans from there."

"Good idea," Max agreed. They sneaked back down the hill and headed towards Grandpa's house.

"I want to have a closer look," Max stated as they entered the street bordering the trail they had used.

"Me too. I want to know where they got that ship," Sky added.

"No, I want to see the men you found. The ones spying on us," Max corrected.

"Why?" Sky questioned. "I've told you what's going on."

"Because my little voice won't shut down. There is something very weird happening and I want to know what it is," Max reached out and grabbed Sky's arm so they were facing each other. "Please?"

"I don't know," Sky glanced over his shoulder at the tree line on the mountain behind them.

"Again. When have I ever been wrong?" Max grinned.

"Okay," Sky sighed and started marching towards Grandpa's house. "We need to disappear in front of Grandpa's house. Right now we're in sight of their scopes and cameras. So when we hit the front yard, cast your spell."

They hustled up the street to find a pale-faced Cindy waiting on the porch swing as they rounded the fence. She wore a large bandage around her waist and lower abdomen that was visible under her bathrobe.

"Cindy." Sky waved with a smile. "Good to see you up and about."

"Thanks," Cindy responded. "Where have you been? Checking out whatever is out there?"

"What do you mean?" asked Max as he shot Sky a questioning look.

"You don't feel it?" Cindy cocked her head to the side.

"Yes, I just wanted Sky to know I wasn't crazy." Max smiled. "Thanks."

"In fact, we were just about to go and have a look. We will be back in a while," Sky stated before she disappeared.

"See you soon," Max added and cast his spell. "Which way?" Max asked.

"Back towards the hill. We'll head up from there."

It didn't take them very long to reach the hill they had used to spy on Brian and the others. Before they started to climb, Sky described a small creek bed in the side of the mountain, created over the years by snow run off and a natural spring. It was a short distance to the right of the larger deep canyon. "We are heading for that massive boulder about fifty yards into the trees. That will bring us to the left and behind the men. If we use the small creek bed we should get there undetected, as long as you don't make too much noise."

They skirted the hill and navigated through the sagebrush until they reached the creek bed. A small flow of cold-snow runoff tumbled and rolled over the rocks, muffling their footfalls with plops and splashes. The incline of the mountain continued to increase with each step, making sweat form along Max's brow. His heart thumped in his ribcage as he gulped mouthfuls of air in response to the taxing climb.

When they reached the tree line, Max scooped up several handfuls of water from a small waterfall to quench his thirst. "Sky!" he whispered in response to a sharp warning from his senses. All the hairs on the back of his neck stood on edge as some dark presence crept towards them. Max didn't know why, but the urge to step over the small stream and away from the men caused him to act.

"What?" Sky responded in a soft voice.

"Move to the other side of the water. Hurry!" Max emphasized.

The trees and bushes several yards into the forest started to sway. The rushing sound of the wind, mingled with a blood curdling wailing, filled their ears as some unseen force headed in their direction. Trees and bushes toppled over or bent as if some huge invisible creature parted them with its passing. Dirt, leaves, loose twigs, and other debris swirled around and around a semi-tractor-sized tornado-like thing that flattened plant life in its path, without leaving any footprints.

The volume of wind and wailing reached an ear piercing level as the invisible thing stopped on the opposite side of the small creek, about ten yards up from Max and Sky's location. The mass traveled down the bank, breaking trees and bending willows. Max covered his face with his arms as several willow branches smacked him on the head by the unknown creature's passing. Max felt a terror like never before well up inside his chest as the creature went by. The dark presence that floated with it was terrifying and oppressive, and he felt that something very evil had just about touched him. It took all the effort he could muster to hold his ground.

They remained motionless for several minutes after the thing had disappeared back into the forest.

"What was that?" Max asked still frozen in place.

"Something very wicked," Sky stated. "Whatever it was, I didn't notice it before. So, either it just got here or was in a different part of the forest earlier."

"Did you feel it?" Max asked.

"Yes, even without your extra special senses, I could feel how dark and evil it was. Make no mistake, if that thing catches you, it will kill you," Sky stated.

"What do you think we should do?"

"It's up to you. I've seen the men. You're the one whose senses were driving you wild," Sky whispered.

"Yes, but I think that thing was what was setting it off."

"So, you don't want to see the men?"

"Well, while we're here. I might as well take a look."

"Can you still detect that thing?" Sky asked.

"Yes. And…there's more than one," Max informed her as he sent his senses outward to the forest.

Suddenly, Sky appeared out of thin air. "We're behind the men now. It's better we conserve our strength if we need to use it against those things."

Max released his spell as well. "Good point." Max frowned.

"Just let me know if you sense 'it or them' anywhere near us," Sky ordered as she crossed back over the river. "By the way, how did you know it wouldn't cross the river?"

"I'm not sure but something told me it is on some type of leash. There are boundaries it has to obey. And on this side the rope limit is the river."

"Okay, follow me and step where I step. If you sense anything let me know," Sky said, and they proceeded into the trees.

Max followed Sky's lead, circling up and around to the back of the men's location. She indicated a couple of trip wires, which they easily avoided. Max wondered if they were attached to some type of explosive or just an alarm system. His senses detected the strange-unseen creatures checking their marked boundaries. The sixth sense created by the venom of Pajek, the zombie spider, told him there were at least two creatures out there.

They crept forward at a snail's pace. Sky's eyes continued to scan the forest ahead of them. Max felt his way, trying to keep track of the strange creatures' movements. Every once in a while, he would freeze when a warning would go off inside his skin, and then it would die down as the creatures moved towards them before turning away.

Soon the crackle of a static-laced radio conversation broke the silence. Sky guided Max into a group of trees ten yards behind the small lookout post. A camouflaged covering protected the setup from the elements, with a canvas tent set up nearby. They had all the equipment of a major spying operation: satellite uplinks, spy scopes, radio equipment, weapons, laptops, and food provisions. From the look of things it appeared they had been there for some time.

Max listened intently now that they were close enough to hear the conversation. There were three of them: one laying in the grass under the shade of a tree, while the other two worked under the camouflaged tarp.

"Okay," the one responded into the radio. "They want us to go check out what Max and Sky were looking at."

Max shot a glance at Sky whose expression seemed to ask the same question, *they know our names?*

"I never thought things would get this weird when we were assigned to this project," the other responded, putting a pair of binoculars up to his face and gazing down on the town.

"Me either. I mean this stuff is right out of the twilight zone or X files. Magic, aliens, you name it."

A steady uneasy churning started in the pit of Max's stomach and the more he heard, the more it started to rage inside his gut. *How did they find out about all of this?*

In answer to Max's silent question one of the men responded. "To think this all started with the hunt for a killer."

"I thought it began with a top secret project back in DC." the other questioned.

"Yes and no. We think we can trace that project back here, but it's kind of sketchy. There are definite connections, but this happened with a tip two years ago about a killer who vanished in Mr. Rigdon's house and has never been heard of again. A killer who ate his victims. He just disappeared in this massive ball of light."

"How do you know?"

"I've seen the footage from the surveillance cameras. They found the spy equipment shortly thereafter and disposed of them, but we saw enough to warrant all this."

"So this killer just vanished in a ball of light?"

"Well, we think so. The footage didn't show him disappearing, but others came out of it and went back into it. We assume wherever it goes, that's where we will find him."

Max's head spun with this new information. He had forgotten all about the cameras and listening devices the FBI installed on the third floor the day Uncle Frank died. *How could we be so stupid*, Max cursed himself. It was foolish to think the FBI wouldn't want to investigate further. This proved they still think Grandpa is hiding Uncle Frank.

One of the men pulled out his cell phone and dialed a number. "No, we can't see anything from our location," he stated. "Max and Sky should have reported to Joe by now. You need to hustle over there and find out what's going on!" The man paused before responding again. "We'll try to find out all we can from our location, but we don't want the others to know we're here either. See what you can find out on your end, and we'll do the same." With that he hung up and stowed the phone in his jacket.

"So, they want us to check out whatever happened over there." The other nodded in the direction of the invisible craft.

"Too bad we can't send these THINGS down there," the other stated as he rolled his eyes. "I don't trust them and they…make me very nervous."

"We won't be sending them anywhere at the moment." The one who had been resting in the shade finally spoke up. "They're here for our protection and we're completely safe from them."

"So you say?" the scared one responded. "How do you know how safe they are? How do you know we can maintain control of them?"

"Because I set them free," the one in the shade responded, with a fire in his eyes. "I'm the one who unlocked their secret. We're perfectly safe. They obey all my orders. Watch," the man said jumping to his feet. He muttered a few enchantments.

Immediately, Max's senses screamed inside his mind that danger was coming. He stretched out his arm and tugged on Sky's shirt as she concentrated on the man. Their eyes met and he jerked his head sharply in the direction they had come from.

Sky nodded her understanding and waved him back with her hand as she started to move.

Max stepped backwards onto a dried twig, which created a loud snap. All eyes fell on him and Sky, and suddenly the forest erupted behind Max, throwing him and Sky several feet in the direction of the men. A screech of madness shattered the silence of the forest, cracking trees and crushing plant life, when the creatures spotted Max and Sky.

11

On the Loose

A second roar of wild rage sent a wave of putrid heat rushing over Max. It seemed to absorb all the light from the forest. Max had the distinct impression the grim reaper himself had arrived to collect their souls.

Before Max could think, Sky dragged him to his feet and pulled him through the center of the camp. Max barely had time to register the shocked faces of the men as they raced past them down the hill. A scream of terror followed by a disturbingly loud crunch propelled Max's heart against his ribcage and sent a chill up his spin. Additional roars from other parts of the forest grew in volume, joined by two additional short-lived screams and crunches.

"How close are they?" Sky yelled over her shoulder, sprinting down the hill, taking huge leaping strides.

"Thirty yards and closing fast. What are we going to do?" Max scrambled to keep up.

"I'm not sure. These things are not like anything I have ever encountered before. I don't know what's going to affect them. Feel free to try anything," Sky barked, and created a wall of fire hundreds of yards long between them and their pursuers.

Max glanced back to see if the barrier would hold, but the invisible things seemed to consume the fire. First one huge hole in the fire appeared, and then another and another, before the entire wall went out. Their calls increased in volume and intensity, as if Sky's magic excited and enraged them at the same time.

"It didn't work!" Max hurtled a large patch of sagebrush. He darted through the trees, following Sky's lead as she veered left out of their downhill sprint. His extra sense screamed inside his head, warning of the oncoming danger. Out of the corner of his eye, shadows started to appear in small flickers before covering trees and bushes. The evil that chased after them started to block out the light of the world.

"Head for the stream. Maybe their boundary is still in place, but I doubt it. I'm sure the death of their handler released his hold over them," Sky informed him.

Max's heart thumped in his chest, and his lungs burned as he forced himself to sprint at top speed. Trees cracked and smashed to the forest floor behind him, propelling the two of them forward. The air carried a rushing of wind like a freight train plowing through the forest, gaining on them every second. Max's special sense warned him of the danger about to swallow him.

"Don't stop," Sky called as they jumped the small stream.

Max's foot caught on a root and he stumbled forward, but Sky's incredible reflexes helped her catch him by the arm, keeping him from falling. A spray of water rained down on them as the creatures crossed the river.

"Head for the canyon," Max yelled through large gulps of air. "I have an idea." Max hoped they could reach the canyon, a hundred yards ahead of them, before they were destroyed.

"Share it now," Sky barked as they scrambled over several large boulders.

"To jump in," Max rasped as the dryness in his throat burned with the effort to speak. His muscles begged him to stop, as sweat ran down his back and forehead.

A roar in Max's ear and a wave of rotting heat, like the smell of decaying flesh, stung his nose, telling him time was running out. They dashed up a deer trail through the sparse pine trees.

Max didn't know why, but his sixth sense made him tackle Sky, dragging her to the left, sending them both rolling down a steep incline. A sound like a high speed car wreck echoed through the forest, followed by cries of rage. The side of the hill dished out a harsh beating as they bumped and bounced over rocks and small bushes.

After their tumble slowed they sprang to their feet and dashed towards the canyon, while the sound like a rushing freight train continued to build again as if a tornado pursued them.

"Use the *preselim se* spell when you fall," Max ordered, as the canyon floor appeared ahead of them.

"Don't go to Grandpa's in case they can follow," Sky stressed.

"We can't leave the planet. What if when we come back we're still falling in the canyon and hit the bottom?" Max stated as they reached the edge of the canyon, with the creatures barreling down on them.

"Go to...to protest camp." Sky and Max dove over the edge.

Max's heart pushed up into his throat, and his stomach flipped over while they sped towards the rocks at the bottom of the canyon a couple hundred yards below. Max stretched out his arm and took hold of Sky's hand as they continued to drop. Their eyes met and they cast the spell.

They landed with a hard crash on top of five unsuspecting protesters in the middle of a shocked, screaming crowd.

"That was fun." Max held his side, climbing off the pile, rubbing his ribs.

"Sorry." Sky bounced to her feet in a ready position, scanning the area for any sign of the things that hunted them.

"What are you doing, man? You look like plants for the 'one percenters,'" one of the protesters shouted at them.

"Yeah," a rough looking woman added.

"You can't come into our domain and start knocking people around," a rather large dirty man barked.

He tried to shove Max, who reacted on instinct. Max quickly swung his arms in an upward circle, catching the man by the wrist and elbow of one arm. He twisted the wrist downward and applied pressure against the back of the guy's elbow, driving him face down onto the ground, sweeping the occupier's leg with his foot. "I suggest you keep your hands off me! We didn't mean to hurt anyone. It was an accident."

"You're breaking his arm." The man's friend rushed forward to help but Sky lowered to the ground, kicking his legs out from under him. Groaning, he hit the ground hard.

The crowd had now created a circle around the small skirmish and began chanting foul words at Max and Sky. They shouted things like, "one percent creeps, capitalism losers, go back to your mansions, give us our due."

"We need to hurry," Sky stressed in Max's ear. "We aren't safe here."

Max scanned the area, suddenly remembering the things that were chasing them, but only the angry protesters filled his view. Instead of the smell of hot decaying breath, only sweat and unclean body odor floated on the air; shouting replaced the roar of rushing wind.

"The creatures?" Max questioned, releasing his hold on the man.

"No, something else. I don't think those things followed us or they would have caught us already and turned this place into a slaughterhouse." Sky's eyes danced from one ornery face to another. "We have to hurry."

Max followed Sky, forcing their way through the jeering people. At first the protesters tried to block their path, but after Sky jabbed a couple in the throat, dropping them to their knees and silencing their voices, the others let them through. The insults continued to follow Max and Sky while they hustled through the camp.

"Who are we hiding from?" Max asked as they passed out of the protesters and down a side street.

Sky led him into a building with a glass entryway where she peered back at the dirty site they had just left.

"What are you looking for?" Max started, watching the crowd, half expecting to see a Night Shade emerge from among the people.

"There are controllers in that crowd," Sky stated, suddenly dropping down into a crouch, pulling Max with her.

Max spotted a tall pale man with white hair glancing at the building where they had taken refuge. He wore a blank face that almost looked petrified, as if no emotion had ever crossed its surface. Something seemed odd about the man. He wore the same style of clothes as the others, but Max's special sense told him there was more to the man than one could see.

"What's a controller?"

"They control this weak-minded crowd of useful idiots with magic. I discovered them while I was hunting for what happened to the book and those who translated it. I didn't confront them but kept out of their way." Sky eyed the man.

"Is he human?" asked Max, noticing the strange abnormally chalky-white look of his skin.

"I think he is human on the outside. I can't say what's on the inside. So he probably was human once, but whether that same individual occupies that body, I can't say. They are wicked and powerful," Sky said.

"Why do they control these people?"

"They influence the weak-minded. Those in power want total control of everyone. They want to enslave people and elevate themselves. Who in his right mind would ever give up freedom for supposed comfort? Once they have lulled you into dependency and false security, they control you. When they control your food and way of life, they can get you do all sorts of evil things, like slaughter people," Sky answered.

"So what you are saying is, whoever has the book is doing this? What are they doing, building an army?"

"I'm not sure. Originally, I thought this was a ploy of Hudich's, but now after our run-in with those creatures on the mountain, I'm not so sure. Yes, now I think it has something to do with the book. Building an army is exactly what they are doing. Every day more are joining their cause, thinking they are going to get something for free. Nothing in life is free. Anything worth having is worth working and fighting for. Socialism and Communism only lead to slavery and destruction." Sky smiled weakly

Max watched as a shorter, almost ghost-white man joined the first, his face frozen in the same manner as the other's face. Even though their lips barely moved, they appeared to be having a conversation about Max and Sky, as one gestured to the spot Max and Sky had fallen on top of the protesters. After a few minutes, the new one gestured toward the building in which they had taken refuge.

"What are we waiting for?" Max questioned.

"Well, I'm curious," Sky stated, still inspecting the odd-looking men.

"About?"

"If these things are truly something brought about by magic unlocked from the book, those who possess it have made more progress than we thought. I'm sure our new friends back at Grandpa's can answer some of these questions. I just want to see if they try to contact anyone."

"That might mean getting a little closer," Max suggested.

"Or creating some sort of magical event that would prompt them to contact those who are in charge," Sky winked.

"Should we tell Grandpa what we are up to? Cindy probably heard the commotion on the mountain and I bet they're worried," Max said.

"Good idea. Send him a message."

"What, exactly, do you want me to tell him?" Max questioned. "I mean, how long are we going to be and what are we going to be doing?"

"Tell him we got a lead on the book and that we should be back tonight. Oh, and tell him about the things on the mountain. They're loose, and who knows what they are going to do. Better have them keep their eyes open."

"Good thinking. You're right, they should be ready for them." Max took out his communicator, a futuristic device that allowed him to use the gateway to send messages in their world and other worlds. His fingers tapped out a note which he sent to his Grandfather.

In a matter of seconds Grandpa responded to Max's call.

"There's big trouble. We have to go back! Those things left the mountain and have entered the town." Max felt the color drain from his face and his head started to spin with worry.

"We have to move!" Sky grabbed Max's shoulder and pulled him away from the window and deeper into the building as they spotted the pale men coming toward them from across the street.

They hustled through the building until they found an empty hallway and cast their spells.

Max and Sky touched down on the street in front of Grandpa's house into total chaos. Spells exploded all around them, and high pitched screams broke through the noise of several freight trains barreling through town, crushing everything in their path. A crowd had gathered inside the fence around Grandpa's house, and people were fleeing in their direction.

A loud warning inside Max's body caused him to dive into Sky, pushing them out of the way of a spell which zoomed up the street into the tornado coming toward them from the other direction. The curse slammed into the thing, freezing it in place as if a small hurricane raged inside a glass silo.

Max's jaw dropped, but before he could register what happened, Sky snagged him by the back of the shirt and dragged him inside the fence. After she closed the gate Max spotted Hudich storming up the street, looking more terrible than ever. He shot another spell at the thing, destroying it in an explosion of sparks and burning debris.

"JOE," Hudich roared in his deep voice. His red eyes were shining as if a fire blazed inside them. "What sort of magic is this you've unleashed on us?"

Grandpa hopped down the porch steps and hurried toward the fence where he met Hudich, Alan, and a small group of their cohorts. "If it isn't the pot calling the kettle black," Grandpa barked back through the fence. "Trying to blame us for your work."

"We wouldn't harm our own. These things destroyed several of our houses and devoured six people. Why would we do that to our own people?" Alan spat with venom.

"As you can plainly see, we were attacked too." Grandpa motioned to the crowd of people standing in his yard. "So by your same logic, why would we unleash this on our own people? We thought you had brought these things."

"Max," Sky whispered into his ear with her hand cupped over it. "Grab Cindy and your mother and meet me upstairs, NOW."

Max flashed Sky a questioning look. He wanted to see what was going to happen and, with Hudich standing on the other side of the fence, he didn't think he should leave.

Sky jerked her head toward the house with a stern look in her eyes, prompting Max to obey. The look on her face told him it was serious.

Max weaved through the crowd until he found his mother and Cindy. He struggled to stifle a snort as Cindy gave him the same expression he had used on Sky, when he explained to Cindy what he wanted.

"What is so important?" Max demanded once they were all inside the house.

"We need to hide that stuff up in the forest before Hudich decides to do some poking around. This could be a link to the book. Information we don't want him to have." Sky led them upstairs to the gateway.

Sky's plan was simple. Max's mother would operate the gateway, while the three of them chucked all the equipment through the opening.

"What about the dead bodies?" asked Max as they stepped out of the gateway into the forest where they had almost been caught by the strange monsters.

"Bodies?" Cindy crinkled her nose.

"And they aren't going to be pretty," Max informed her, remembering the spine-tingling crunching that followed the men's screams when they died.

"Gather everything. We'll worry about the bodies last," Sky ordered.

They dashed back and forth through the camp picking up, papers, computers, cameras, and a variety of other devices. A sharp intake of air from Cindy told Max she had found one of the bodies—or what was left of it. Max had noticed it while collecting the camping equipment. It wasn't so much a body as red splatter on the trees and bushes.

A roar rattled the forest to the right of the camp. They all exchanged glances.

"Hurry!" Sky set them in motion again.

###

"I think one of your followers accidentally let something loose they had no control over," Joe argued with Hudich and Alan through the fence. "It wouldn't be the first time."

"What do you take me for, *Old* Man? I know what my followers are capable of and what creatures we have control over. I have never seen this thing before," Hudich growled in his deep voice, pointing his finger at Joe through the fence. "We didn't have one of these things, let alone two of them. And how would we have gotten them here?"

"Well, they didn't appear to be things of substance. I figured you had created them from magic." Joe almost flinched, saying these last words. Even though he wanted to convince Hudich that some rogue individual on their side had made the beasts, he didn't want to give away the fact they were, indeed, created magically. He could sense Hudich was slowly putting the pieces together. It wouldn't take him long to connect these strange things with the book.

"You know very well that…"

A roar on the mountain side interrupted Hudich, and all eyes looked toward the mountain.

"What has been going on here?" Hudich mumbled under his breath.

"That's precisely what I want to know." Joe tried to continue his charade. "What have your people been doing? Just an hour ago a rumble vibrated the whole town and now these things appear and attack us."

Hudich's head jerked around at Joe, and then he found Brian in the crowd for one brief moment before returning to Joe. "Perhaps you are right." Hudich's voice changed to a more agreeable tone.

"*What?*" Joe couldn't hide the shock from his question.

"It's none of your concern, *Old* Man. Alan, get everyone out of here. I'll be back in a moment." Hudich disappeared in a flash of light.

Max, Cindy, and Sky rushed back and forth, hauling camping supplies and equipment to the gateway. Thunder like a freight train continued to grow as another invisible beast headed in their direction.

"We need to hurry," Both Max and Cindy stated, and their eyes met after a serious warning from their special senses.

"Gather up all these loose papers while I do a quick double check." Sky motioned toward a rather large paper trail that looked like a bomb had scattered them.

"We don't have a lot of time," Cindy warned as she and Max began cleaning up the papers littering the forest floor.

Papers not only covered the ground but were stuck in branches and bushes, some of which were quite a ways in the air. Several of the trees only needed a good shake to release their collection of papers, while Max had to climb others to get at the documents.

Sky returned to help them in grabbing the scattered files and other small items. "I think that's everything. Let's take one last sweep of the area."

They hustled around the camp, looking for any missed items, when a roar only a hundred yards away demanded their attention. Max peered around and noticed Sky waving him back toward the gateway. That's when he saw the cell phone. It dangled from a branch about ten feet off the ground, hooked by a length of camouflaged clothing that had been shredded by something.

"There's a cell phone," Max pointed towards the item and headed for it when a flash of light to his left caught his attention. His warning signal went into overdrive when Hudich appeared only a dozen feet from Max, his back toward him. Max's heart, which had already been pumping quickly, went into overdrive. It pounded in his ears, muffling all other sounds. He swallowed against the dryness in his mouth as his eyes moved from Hudich to the cell phone hanging about six feet above him.

A roar from the oncoming monster indicated it would soon be on top of the camp. The beast, like a rushing freight train, knocked over trees and was coming fast. Max knew he couldn't climb the tree in time and Hudich was sure to hear him. Slowly, he extended his shaking hand toward the cell phone and concentrated. *Pridi*! The cell phone, along with the torn piece of clothing, zipped out of the tree and into Max's hand.

Hudich twitched, sensing something, but the approaching beast held his attention. His cape flapped in the rushing wind as he clinched his fists.

Max slipped the cell phone into his pocket. He took one last look at Hudich before he turned to see the concerned expressions on Sky and Cindy's faces. They both seemed to breathe a collective sigh of relief and Max opened his eyes wide as if to answer with an, *I know*. They all started tiptoeing toward the gateway. Max knew they had to hurry. His warning system screamed about the extremely close danger. He wanted to run to the gateway. He swallowed his fear, locked it away and crept forward toward safety.

"Where did you come from?" Hudich mumbled to himself in his deep voice as the small hurricane drew nearer.

Cindy put her hands in the gateway and was in the process of pushing herself up when the cell phone rang. Max clamped his hands over his pocket, trying to silence the device. Even with the noise of the approaching freight train, the ringing caught Hudich's attention. Hudich glanced back over his shoulder and his eyes met Max's.

12

Strange Events

Everything seemed to happen in slow motion. Hudich cast a spell which stopped the magical creature's approach, and Max broke into a sprint towards the gateway.

"Max," Hudich yelled in a long drawn out breath, sending several spells after the fleeing Max.

Max's extra sense saved him from the first few curses. He was able to dive and duck out of their paths. Finally the speed of Hudich's attack was too much for Max, and a spell slammed into his back, launching him face down into the ground. Pine needles and dirt filled his mouth, nose, and eyes as his face slid along the forest floor for several feet.

"What's going on here, Max?" Hudich growled, storming toward Max, firing spells all around him to keep him pinned to the ground.

A crack, like the breaking of a large branch, filled the air. Hudich's feet were knocked out from under him, and he flew up in the air and landed flat on his back. Sky appeared over him and cast a spell which hammered into Hudich, sinking him into the ground several inches.

Water streamed down Max's face as he tried to blink the dirt out of his eyes. He coughed and spat as he jumped to his feet in an effort to locate the gateway. A blurry Sky stood over Hudich for one moment and then went soaring into the air several dozen feet above the ground. The force of Hudich's spell smashed her through tree branches and bushes before she crashed into the ground.

Max hurled several *prizgaj's* and *premakni's* at Hudich, who swatted them away like annoying flies. Hudich's counter spell hammered Max in the gut, doubling him over. His extra sense warned him to drop to his stomach while another curse zoomed over his head, knocking over a small tree.

Cindy, still recovering from her wound, couldn't stand it and threw an attack. Cindy's spell caught Hudich off guard. He didn't appear to realize she had been waiting just inside the entrance to the gateway. The blast knocked him backwards several yards, but he maintained his balance, blocked a spell from Max, and then Sky.

Before Cindy could gather enough strength to try again, Hudich located her and hammered her back into the gateway. Cindy's small distraction allowed both Max and Sky to move a little closer to the gateway while they continued to fight for their lives.

Hudich resembled a ninja master, dueling with Sky and Max at the same time, blocking their attacks with ease, while landing blows here and there. Max knew they were slowly losing ground and if he didn't come up with something soon, they were going to die.

"You can't win," Hudich taunted as if in answer to Max's thoughts.

Hudich's spells were forcing Max and Sky away from the gateway. Sky spread her arms wide and swung her hands around until they clapped. Trees and bushes in a wide circle around Hudich uprooted and collapsed on him like an imploding bubble. This new tactic forced Hudich to go on the defensive. Trees slammed into him from multiple directions.

The new clearing created by Sky's spell opened up Max's view to the caged creature with the fury of a storm, located a hundred yards behind Hudich.

Hudich threw off the trees and other debris, launching objects in all directions. A fire of rage danced in his red rat eyes. He sent a massive curse at Sky. Even though she threw up a blocking spell, Hudich's curse drove Sky and her invisible wall backwards several yards. Sky's feet dug small ruts in the ground as she braced against the blow.

Max made his choice; thrusting both arms out from his chest he screamed, "*Premakni!*" Max's spell sped through the forest and smashed into the invisible cage holding the strange monster captive. The plan worked when the force of the spell destroyed the cell, releasing the beast.

Sky saw what Max had done and fired off multiple spells to hold Hudich's attention. Max cast a number of his own. Hudich blocked their volley and was preparing to respond when the thing, which had closed the distance between them, screamed its insane roar.

Hudich almost fell over as he scrambled away from the invisible beast in surprise. Max bolted for the gateway, but Sky sent several more spells at Hudich before she joined Max. With Hudich's attention on the strange thing, Sky's attack flattened Hudich face forward into the ground.

As Max helped Sky into the gateway, he caught sight of Hudich lifted high off the ground by the magical creature. His heart raced with both fear and anticipation, expecting the horrible crunch that would end Hudich's life. Hudich roared with pain when one of his legs bent in an awkward position, but then a shockwave erupted from Hudich which destroyed the beast in a shower of sparks. Hudich dropped to the ground and the force of his spell knocked Max and Sky back in and through the Gateway, where Max's mother quickly shut it down.

Grandpa and the others waited in the yard and watched Alan escort his people down the street. The roars on the mountain, joined by the sounds of a battle, captured everyone's attention. The crowd inside the fence moved to the side of the yard where they could get a better view of the mountain. Brightly colored explosive lights winked at them from just inside the tree line.

"What do you think is going on up there?" one of the group asked Grandpa, his eyes glued on the mountainside.

"I'm not sure. I think Hudich went after another creature, but there are other things, or people, up there also." Grandpa rubbed his chin thoughtfully.

"What should we do?" Mrs. Anderson asked from close by.

"Wait here," Grandpa stated, putting his hand up to keep anyone from leaving.

"So, you…"

Hudich's roar of pain echoed off the mountain, making everyone fidget and glance at one another, wondering what had just happened. A flash of light brighter than anything they had seen so far was followed by what sounded like a sonic boom vibrating the ground. Then silence followed.

"What's happened?" others in the crowd questioned.

A battered and bleeding Hudich appeared on the other side of the fence. His chest heaved with large deep breaths and his eyes burned a darker red. "What have you been up to, Old Man?" he hissed through clenched teeth.

"What are you talking about?" Grandpa asked in surprise.

"Up there on the mountain. You've unlocked powers you can't control," he stated.

"We have done…"

"Don't lie to me! You have the book. You've been experimenting," Hudich roared with such force that the protective spells around the yard sparked and crackled here and there. "I just witnessed that brat, Max, and his friends, covering up your activities. They were lucky this time. Next time I catch them out like that they won't get away from me. We are coming for your people." Hudich waved his arm over the crowd. "We are coming soon and you will all be destroyed." He glared at Grandpa for another few moments before vanishing in a flash of light.

After waiting for a few minutes, Grandpa turned to the crowd. "I think you can all go home now."

As everyone started heading for home, Linda and Sam met Grandpa on the porch.

"What was that?" Linda asked with wide eyes.

"That was Hudich. Someone your people overlooked in their desire for power and to unlock the secrets of the book. We don't want him to know we don't have the book. So, whatever Max and Sky were doing up on the hill might have given us a little more time to get it back. That book in his hands could be devastating for everyone."

Suddenly, Cindy's mother appeared in the doorway, "You've got to come see this."

Grandpa nodded for Linda and Sam to follow. "Come on."

Grandpa's jaw dropped when he saw the mess scattered across the entire third floor. There were papers, surveillance equipment and camping gear everywhere. Yelka knelt in front of a very pale Cindy, with the others standing over her. Cindy appeared to be in pain, but conscious.

"How is she?" Grandpa asked, joining the others.

"I'm okay. Just a little shaken up." Cindy smiled.

"What happened?"

"She took the full force of a spell from Hudich, trying to help me and Sky," Max stated.

"What were you doing?" Grandpa's face lined with concern.

"Don't worry," Sky spoke up with a smile. "I've seen that look before. We weren't trying to take any unnecessary risks."

Max and Sky explained all that had happened from the time they went to check on the strange noise on the other side of town. They told them about Larry and the invisible ship. They then went into Max's feelings of being watched, which led them to the men who appeared to be spying on Grandpa's house. They added how the creatures were with the men on the mountain, and how a couple of them escaped from the men and the strange boundaries controlling them.

"So, when Hudich showed up, I figured we had better get all the stuff from that camp before Hudich discovered it," Sky finished.

"We didn't realize there was another one of those things up there until we had already started picking up the equipment. That's when Hudich showed up. If this stupid phone hadn't rang, we probably would have made it out of there without him detecting us." Max held out the cell phone.

Grandpa took a deep breath, "Good thinking. What do these things mean?"

"That we've been under observation ever since Frank's death," Cindy spoke up.

"That's what I thought," Max agreed.

"There has to be more to it. If these agents had some kind of control over these beasts, there are more dangerous men trying to figure out what is going on here," Grandpa added.

"Hey," Max said, snapping his fingers. "I just remembered something. There is one of them among us."

"That's right," Sky added. "They were in radio contact with someone who is posing as one of us. They wanted to know what Max and I had found out on the other side of town."

"Grandpa, did anyone show up to find out about the noise before these creatures went on their rampage?" Max questioned.

"I don't know."

"Yes," Cindy struggled to sit up. "Remember, I was on the porch. It wasn't just one person but a small group of them."

"Can you think who they were?" Sky asked.

"There was Mr. Taylor, Mike Wick, Mr. and Mrs. Hanson and that Phil...I can't recall his last name," Cindy said.

"Phil McCormik?" Grandpa asked.

"Yes, that's him."

"We need to watch all of those people very closely," Sky stated.

"What's going on here," Sam interrupted, spreading his arms wide with his palms showing. "Don't get me wrong. We're grateful to you for getting us out of that mess with Tanner. Now, we've seen some pretty strange stuff over the past year, but these things here make our experiences pale by comparison."

"Yes, I can see where you would be confused. But you see, you are part of some very important clues for us," Grandpa said. "It might be better if you tell us what you have been up to for the last year or so, and then we will be able to answer all of your questions. I suggest we move to the kitchen where we can all be a little more comfortable."

Downstairs, Sam and Linda began telling the others how they were hired to work on translating sections of a mysterious text. They explained how there were others, and they all worked on separate pieces and worked alone. "Once we started to unlock the secrets of the writings, people started to disappear," Sam stated.

"They were very strict. It was almost like being in prison. They watched us eat and had cameras in our dormitories. If we ever had time together, everyone would always get called away," Linda added.

"How did you manage to communicate privately?" Yelka sang the question.

"Well, when we all figured out we were translating from the same book, we started passing notes. The higher ups weren't interested in the language per say, but the power in the book and the spells," Sam stated. "There were a few of them who were involved in learning everything. They were the ones who detected what the rest of us had learned and could do."

"And reported our skills to the higher ups," Linda added.

"How did you get out?" Grandpa asked.

"We all had different skills. After we witnessed one of the translators, who was learning everything, use their new powers to read the mind of another linguist, we knew we were in danger. Apparently, he had discovered something horrible and destroyed it before they could get their hands on it. They ruined his mind but eventually got what they wanted."

"That's when we banded together and used our new skills to break out," Linda finished.

"And you've been on the run ever since?" Sky stated more than asked.

"Now, please tell us what these things mean," Linda begged.

"It started way before you or I were born," Grandpa said. "But, I will start with my job as a young man working for the government."

"Will he ever get better?" Larry's teary-eyed mother asked, holding the hand of her comatose son. She had been sitting beside his bed for the last two days, ever since Brian and Larry had brought back the alien and his ship.

"I don't know. It's been almost three days and nobody seems to know what's wrong with him. All of his vital signs are normal." Alan tried to comfort his wife, but the dark circles under his eyes and his drawn face showed his concern.

"What did the alien do to my baby?" she sobbed. "Why isn't Hudich forcing him to do something about what he did?"

"We've been over this. We can't trust him. He may do worse things. He doesn't want anyone to touch the alien, and we need him for our plans," Alan stated.

"Well, Brian can control him. Why doesn't he get answers out of that monster?"

"I told you. The only thing Brian could get out of him was that Larry's eyes were being opened." Alan sighed.

"Well at least Hudich is letting you stay here until you renew your strength and leave," she managed a weak smile.

"He has put me in charge of getting information out of the Secretary of State. We've had him and his family for weeks now. They are beginning to realize that the world thinks they are dead and there is no escape. It's time we start turning the screws," Alan informed her.

"Why not let Brian just get it out of them? What does Hudich think they know anyway?"

"We're not sure. They have gotten hold of powerful magic, and Hudich wants to know where it came from. It's strong enough to fool a weak-minded country and get them to give up their freedoms. Only a strong enchantment can influence free people to willingly become slaves."

A moan from Larry drew their attention. His head rolled back and forth and his legs kicked a few times. Then his eyes snapped open.

"He's awake," his mother cried with a smile.

"Son, can you hear me?" Alan asked.

Larry's eyes met his father's. "I have seen the One!"

Hudich paced around the spaceship as Brian used his magic to garner information from the alien. Several engineers stood around writing down the information. Everyone except Hudich wore earplugs to lessen the harsh nerve-scratching voice of the alien.

Hudich's breaths came in deep grunts as he pondered the many things gnawing at his thoughts. What were the old fool and his people up to on the mountain? It wasn't like them to mess with dark magic. *Yes, it was dark magic, and powerful too.* He had been certain the book had fallen into the hands of others until the other day. Now, he wasn't sure what to make of these strange events.

The conversation happening nearby with the alien barely even registered against the things bothering him. This part of his plan had been accelerated by Brian's decision to capture the alien. As long as the old fool and his people didn't draw unwanted eyes to their small town, this project should be accomplished ahead of schedule. Any unwanted intruders would be dealt with, he would see to that.

Alan came running up the ramp, drawing him out of his thoughts. "Larry is awake," he said, unable to contain his relief.

"Did he say anything?"

"Yes, but it was confusing. He said he had seen the One. Do you know what he is talking about? The One?"

"I have heard several prophesies over the years about a One, who will bring to pass many great things. He will be unstoppable in battle and no one can match his power. Some events give credence to these old wives' tales. But there is no one will stop us. They are just foolish imaginations of weak minds," Hudich grumbled. "Did he say anything else?"

"He asked about what had happened and how long he had been out. Normal stuff for someone who has been asleep for three days. The doctor examined him and everything seems to be okay." Alan smiled.

"Good, because we have a lot of work to do. Get several Night Shades to keep everyone away from this ship," Hudich ordered as he nodded for Alan to follow. He marched down the ramp and back toward town.

"And if they have to use force?" Alan raised his eyebrows.

"Dead men can't tell anyone anything. What little they might have seen will disappear with them," Hudich stated.

"Missing individuals could bring even more attention to us."

"Dump the bodies in some city far from here."

They walked into the neighborhood and up the street. Hudich led Alan into the cave that housed supplies and the prison which had held the Zbal that Larry used to hunt Max. They proceeded through the storage area and past the place with various torture devices. In the back room torchlight flickered off the walls, and the four prisoners cowered, each in a different cell.

Hudich went straight towards the Secretary of State and squatted on his haunches to be at eyelevel with the Secretary. "It's nice to see you again." Hudich smiled a devilish grin. "I'm sorry I haven't been back to see you earlier, but I have several projects that required my attention. Now that you and your family have gotten used to your new home, we are going to find out what you know."

"I…I d—don't know anything," the Secretary of State stammered. "You won't get away with this."

"Oh, but I will, I promise. I also promise you will tell me everything you know. You'll see. I have no problem harming your loved ones." Hudich glanced towards the Secretary's wife and son in the other cells. "And we have ways of inflicting pain that you can't even imagine."

Even in the poor light, the Secretary's face was drawn and his eyes reflected his horror. "Please, don't hurt my family."

"I won't be hurting your family, you will be. You are the one who controls their pain. All that is required is cooperation, and they will not suffer…too much." Hudich laughed a deep menacing chuckle.

"W—what do you want to know?" the Secretary stuttered as his eyes bounced back and forth from Hudich to the terrified, tear-stained faces of his wife and sons.

"I have watched the history of your country from its inception. I want to know how an unqualified communist came to power. How was he able to gain control of the media and the weak minded? Although I don't consider many men to be great, your country has had some exceptional leaders as far as your race goes. This bumbling fool in the White House isn't one of them. How did he do it? I detect some powerful magic at work here. I want to know where it came from. Where did you people learn it?"

"M—magic. I don't know anything about magic," the Secretary wailed, tears forming along the bottoms of his eyes.

"It's amazing how they all think they know nothing," Alan added with a wicked grin.

"It seems we need to provide a little demonstration to jog his memory." Hudich stood. He snapped his fingers and a spark preceded the crack. A couple of seconds later several flashes of light brought a number of Night Shades and the Krick into the world inside the cave.

The black-hooded Night Shades hissed their evil laughs as they hustled around the cave. Two brought a rolling table from the other room, while others dragged the terrified, screaming boy from his cell. His screams didn't match the wail of his mother as she tried to squeeze herself through the bars to help him.

"Please don't do this," the Secretary hollered.

The Krick, an extremely pale skinny creature, had almost transparent skin. His eyes were a milky white as if he had cataracts over both eyes. His extremely long lanky arms appeared to be made of only skin and bone. He wore tattered pants tied with a cord. Probably the most disturbing feature of the Krick was his mouth. It was a perfect circle lined with hooked teeth. A long dagger like tongue licked out of the opening as the Night Shades strapped the boy to the table.

"I want to introduce you to a friend of mine. What his name is I can't tell you. We call him the Krick. He has an unquenchable thirst for blood. And don't worry, Mom, you will get your turn on the table. His razor sharp tongue will make an incision, and his teeth allow him to hold onto his victim tightly. Now for the more frightening part," Hudich smiled a wicked grin. "His tongue also deposits eggs into the blood stream of his victims. As the embryos develop, they cause all sorts of problems. Some of which can be corrected, others cannot, I am afraid. They will eventually cause severe vomiting and are released from their host in the bile."

"Wait...wait, I'll tell you everything I know." The panicked Secretary caved.

"I know you will, but there's a lesson to be learned here," Hudich answered, and then waved for the Krick to have at the boy.

"NOOO," the Secretary and his wife screamed as the Krick locked onto the boy's stomach.

13

The Quarantine Zone

Tanner stormed into his office in DC. The dark circles under his eyes, from the lack of sleep, matched his foul temper. He slammed his door shut with such force the blinds on the door fell to the floor with a loud crash. His blood pounded in his temples with such furry that his gentle massaging didn't ease his headache. He thought he had finally wrapped this whole chase business up—and then she showed up.

The blond woman infuriated him. *She's the one I've been looking for*. Plus, no one ever made a fool of Tanner and lived to tell about it, and he would make sure it never happened again. He had made it his mission in life to destroy her, but first he had to find her. Taking several deep breaths, he tried to focus. He needed to start the search for this elusive woman. Several in his detail got a good look at the woman, so they needed to get a composite picture of her drawn and distributed to everyone under his command.

Before he could reach for his phone, the door to his office opened with an irritating grating noise as the broken shades scraped along the floor. "What's our next move?" asked an agent, dressed in a black suit, eyeing the broken blinds.

"Get me a sketch artist. I want pictures from everyone who saw the blond woman. Then get all the video from the hotel and convenience store that wasn't destroyed. Locating the woman is our top priority. Hack into the FBI, CIA, and Homeland Security databases if necessary."

"I'm on it," the agent stated.

"Let me know the minute you find anything," Tanner ordered.

"What are you going to tell the higher-ups?" the agent asked. "They thought this trip was supposed to have tied off all the loose ends."

"Nothing. Until we know more about this woman, as far as they know we took care of everything. Either they know something they haven't told us, or she is someone they are completely unaware of, and I want to know which it is. I..." Over the shoulder of the agent standing in the doorway, Tanner noticed two men dressed in dark suits stepping into the reception area. He didn't recognize them. The men locked eyes with Tanner and headed straight for him.

"Who are they?" the subordinate in his doorway asked, looking behind him.

"I don't know. Get to work on that other thing while I see what's up," Tanner said, and the agent departed as the men stepped into his office.

"Tanner?" one man asked.

"Yes, who wants to know?" Tanner asked with an edge to his voice.

"I'm agent Tyson and this is agent Jones. We're from the FBI." The agents flashed their badges. "And we were told to share some information with you."

"What kind of information?" Tanner raised an eyebrow.

Stepping over the blinds on the floor, the agents closed the door behind them and walked closer to Tanner's desk. "We were also told you were an expert at handling situations outside the norm. We were informed you had just recently finished up your last project and needed something else to do."

"Apparently you have friends in high places because we were told to bring this to your attention," the other agent added.

"What's the job?" Tanner circled the desk and sat down on the chair. He folded his hands behind his head and leaned back in the chair, putting his feet up on the desk in an effort to appear disinterested. He didn't like people from other agencies. They usually had attitudes and he wanted to put them in their place. At this moment only the woman interested him.

"A special division, we'll say they belong to the FBI, has been assigned to watch some people in a small town. These people seem to have some...ah...strange abilities?"

"Abilities? And what's the job?" Tanner repeated.

"I'm not sure we can explain. It is something you will have to see," one said.

"How you handle the job would be left up to your discretion," the other added.

"My discretion? And what exactly are these abilities? Are we talking ninjas or what?" Tanner said with sarcasm.

"Cute," one of the agents said to show his displeasure with Tanner's lack of seriousness.

"Your pay would be triple your current salary, and anything you need would be at your disposal," the other added, trying to sweeten the pot.

Tanner took a deep sigh. "What can you tell me?"

"We can tell you it coincides with your last project."

"In what way?" This statement sparked Tanner's interest.

"The abilities or skills these people possess are along the lines of what you have worked with in the past," one said.

"But far more advanced," the other added.

This statement brought Tanner's feet to the floor and he leaned forward on his desk. "What's the set up? Do you have pictures? Maps?"

One of the agents pulled a manila folder out of the inside of his jacket and tossed it onto the desk. Several documents and loose photographs slid out of the folder and spread across its surface.

Tanner collected the loose items into the folder by pushing them back in like shuffled cards. He then opened the folder and started to browse the contents. "So, why haven't I heard about this project before and why do you need me now?"

"Contrary to your belief, Tanner, you aren't as high up on the chain as you'd like to think. Oh, you have your uses, but you're only told what you need to know." The agent jabbed at Tanner's ego.

"But I'm the most important link in that chain, because I don't FAIL. So, someone must have fallen on their face somewhere if you've come to me." Tanner eyed the cocky agent.

"If you must know," the other jumped in to break the tension between the two. "We had an accident with our crew."

"An accident?"

"They're dead," the testy one stated. "So, now you've entered a situation where we need you to know something."

"Killed by these people?"

"No. They were killed by one of our…experiments," the easy-going one stated.

"And what does that mean?" Tanner leaned back and returned his hands behind his head in an effort to show he wasn't interested in this new assignment without being given all the details.

"Do you know who the handlers are, Tanner?" asked the agent who was impressed with himself.

"Aren't they supposed to be over the experiments? In control of them? And under the direct control of the society? They are who sent me on my little hunt over the last year or so," Tanner said.

"Well, one was assisting an observation team stationed on the mountain above the town of these people. He took some…pets with him and they turned on them, killing our crew," the calmer agent said.

"Do these people know they were being watched?" Tanner leaned forward once more and went back to flipping through the photographs and documents inside the folder.

"Well…"

"So, yes," Tanner interjected, shooting the men a look of disgust.

"The pets have been destroyed and the equipment has disappeared," the calmer one stated. "We do, however, have a man on the inside. We've been in contact, so all is good there. We can arrange a meeting."

"How long have these people been under observation?" Tanner paused on every picture to study it a moment.

"Over two years. Originally, they were suspected of harboring a murderer. The FBI managed to place some cameras and listening devices in the main house of interest a few years ago. They were only in place for a few hours, but they showed us things we didn't think were possible. We believe these people may be the source of the book. Their leader is an elderly gentleman who once worked for the government. He was involved in some top secret projects, but all the information on it seems to have been destroyed."

Tanner flipped over a photograph and his heart jumped with excitement. There on the photo in front of him was the blond woman who had thwarted his effort to capture the final two translators. "Is there any other information you think I should know?" Tanner changed his tone to a more pleasant one.

"I take it you want the assignment?"

"You actually haven't told me what my assignment is."

"Observe and gather information on the town's occupants before capturing them for interrogation," the calm agent stated.

"We need to know what they are doing, how they got their abilities or technology, and to then eliminate them as a possible threat to the society," the other agent added.

"It sounds interesting." Tanner smiled. "And I'm not busy at the moment. What else haven't you told me?"

"Everything we know is in those files. I wouldn't underestimate these people. Things exist in that town that are more deadly than you can imagine. Two years ago something, I don't know what to call it, took over the town. No one could go in or they died instantly."

"And I have my usual discretion?"

"What part of 'eliminate the threat' didn't you understand?"

Two days later a squad of camouflaged soldiers crept into the area of the camp where Max, Cindy, and Sky had gathered up all the equipment. With their machine guns at the ready, they checked every inch of the forest in and around the camp. In addition to scouting the area, they placed trip wires and cameras around a wide perimeter of the site.

Finally, after lookouts were in place, the leader met up with a couple of soldiers in the center of the former camp. He activated the headset with the microphone resting on a thin wire in front of his mouth. "The area is secure," he spoke into the device.

Tanner and another agent hiked down into the camp from a higher position up the mountain. They stepped over the wire that a guard at the upper boundary of the perimeter had pointed out to them.

"I don't like this location," Tanner muttered, spotting the captain conversing with a few members of his command.

"Me either. If the people we're after know about it, I would expect them to keep an eye on it," his companion added.

"So, where would you suggest we go?" Tanner asked with raised eyebrows. He already knew where he wanted to be, but he wanted to know if his best pupil, Agent Smith, knew the answer.

"Somewhere down in the town. An empty house or inside our informant's house," Smith stated.

"Very good. The only problem is: how are we going to accomplish that? According to the documents, everyone down there is in on whatever is going on here. I think we'll need the assistance of Vic."

"The area is secure," the captain informed Tanner and Agent Smith when they joined the small gathering of soldiers.

"Did you find anything?" Tanner asked.

"Three large blood stains, but other than that, nothing. Should we set up camp?"

"No. We need to find a different location for base camp. This one will be on their radar." Tanner pulled a pen and small notepad out of his jacket and jotted down an address. He then tore off the piece of paper and handed it to the Captain. "I need your best man to find a safe way into this house."

"Jones," the Captain called, and a medium height soldier hustled to join them. The Captain passed him the address. "Find a secure route to this address, a way inside, and don't be seen."

"Do you have a map?" the soldier asked, to which Agent Smith pulled one out of his jacket and gave it to the soldier.

The soldier dropped his pack and most of his gear, saluted, and hastened away with his weapon.

"Thompson," the Captain called again, and a different soldier appeared.

"Sir," Thompson saluted.

"Find us a different base camp. One where we can operate safely and a lot closer to the town," the Captain ordered.

"Yes, sir." The soldier saluted again and hurried away.

"Oh, we're going to get along just fine." Tanner smiled at the Captain.

He led Agent Smith to an area where Grandpa's house could be seen through the trees. He produced a set of binoculars from inside his coat and zoomed in on his target.

"So, what are we going to do first?" Smith asked. "Go after the woman?"

"No, we'll leave her for Vic. I think we need to take out their leader. Chop off the head of the enemy and they will be in disarray."

"The old man?"

"Precisely."

"So, they've unlocked the power of the book," Yelka said in her sing-song voice, eyes wide, shaking her head. "Those fools don't know what they've done."

The small group of Grandpa, Yelka, Sky, Max, his mother, Cindy, her parents, Linda, and Sam stood around the third floor, discussing all the events going on around them.

"Yes, and apparently they've been watching us for the past two plus years," Grandpa added with a frown. "So, it seems we have more to worry about than we thought."

"And Hudich's plans are farther reaching and farther along than we expected. Where did they get that ship?" Sky asked.

"We need to come up with some serious plans to get answers and counter Hudich and this group with the book," Cindy's father stated.

"And we need to make sure Hudich doesn't know we don't have the book. We got lucky today," Max said.

Grandpa took out his flashing communicator and his brow furrowed even deeper, as if a shadow passed over him. He walked to the control panel and fired up the gateway.

"What is it?" Everyone exchanged questioning glances as several of Olik's people carrying some strange equipment came through the gateway.

A lump swelled within Max's chest, one he had suppressed over the last day due to events occupying his attention, pushing tears up into his eyes. The pain in his heart made it difficult to breath. Olik had been his friend and teacher. Max hadn't expected him to die. Somehow he had expected Olik to be there forever.

Grandpa closed the gateway to have a brief conversation with them before starting it back up. After they disappeared he shut it off again.

"Going to get his body?" Yelka wiped her eyes on a hanky before blowing her nose.

Grandpa nodded.

Everyone in the room felt the weight of losing their friend, except Sam and Linda who had shocked looks on their faces. They weren't used to seeing aliens and monsters like everyone else.

"So." Sky slapped her hands on her thighs in an effort to ease the sorrow. "We need to figure out what Hudich is doing with a spaceship and get our hands on the book. If that's possible. Is there anything you two can add about where you escaped from?" Sky turned to Sam and Linda.

"We don't know where we worked. As part of our contract they picked us up at a military base in Virginia. We flew in a windowless plane and got off inside a large hangar. They kept us indoors for the entirety of our stay. We managed to escape when they were shipping us out," Sam stated.

"That was in Phoenix," Linda added.

"We think we were on our way to be killed." Sam exchanged a glance with Linda. "We knew at that moment we had to escape. We used what we had learned to jump from a moving truck safely, and have been on the run ever since."

"There were fifteen of us originally. We are the last two," Sam continued.

"You were never outside? So, you were like in prison?" Cindy asked with surprise.

"Well, that's not totally true. We had a garden and a workout area that was in the center of several large buildings," Linda said, as if looking back into her memories.

"Yelka," Grandpa said with a sly smile as he gazed at her.

"I'm on it," Yelka sang. "I need you two to come with me. We're going to help you remember everything."

Sam and Linda looked at Yelka and then traded worried expressions.

"Don't worry. It's harmless, nothing to worry about." Grandpa chuckled.

"One of you can watch while I help the other. If you feel uncomfortable with what I'm doing, you can stop the session." Yelka smiled.

Sam exhaled a deep breath and then nodded for Linda to join him as they followed Yelka out of the room.

"So, where do we start? Or do we wait and see if Yelka can get us a lead?" Max asked.

"We have lots of small leads but nothing substantial," Cindy's father stated.

"We should start going through all of this equipment and documentation," Max's mother motioned.

"That's a good idea. We need to see what information we can garner from this stuff. The path to these people might be in this very pile of papers. We might be able to track them down with the right piece of information," Grandpa suggested.

Max sighed as if he wanted something more exciting to do than comb through the items from the camp.

"Don't worry, I have some leads you can help me on later," Sky winked.

"And me?" Cindy piped up.

"Of course."

###

Two days later Tanner and Agent Smith had a cozy little lookout post in the attic of the man's house. They had drilled several small holes in the roof and placed all sorts of observation devices gathering round the clock data on all the comings and goings surrounding Grandpa's house.

Tanner's mood always turned sour anytime he caught sight of Sky. He wanted to take that woman down and couldn't wait for the opportunity to exact his revenge on her. Even the warnings from the inside man about how lethal she was, didn't deter him. He had Vic, his own little pet, a product of these experiments from the strange book. Tanner chose Vic and trained him to be the ultimate predator. He had only tested him once, with crushing results.

"Are you still thinking the old man?" Smith asked, watching Grandpa walk towards the elementary school on one of the monitors in front of them.

"Yes. As soon as we have the frequencies we should be able to finalize our plans to grab him. By the way, how long are they going to take? We've been set up for three hours now," Tanner scowled.

"They said any time now," Agent Smith added as he checked his smart phone for a message that hadn't arrived. "Are you going to use Vic to capture him?"

"Won't be necessary. Vic will be for the question and answer session before I turn him on to that witch!" Tanner spat.

"He might destroy this whole town," Smith chuckled.

"I don't have a problem with that."

"Me…" The sudden buzz from his cell phone drew his attention. "Great, we've got them." Smith eyed his cell phone as he typed several codes into a laptop computer. Instantly the soft sound of distant voices began to flow through a set of speakers attached to the laptop.

The voices were quiet and hard to make out, as if the people speaking were far away or whispering.

"Can we pump up their range?" Tanner leaned an ear towards the speakers.

"Oh yeah." Smith smiled as he punched several more commands into a software program on the computer. The voices, which had been hushed and hard to make out, still had a faraway sound, but were now easy to hear.

"Who would have ever thought the deaths of those idiots could have accomplished something they had struggled for years to do. How much easier could it be than to have the people you want to monitor, willingly carry the listening devices into their own house?"

14

Hitching the Wrong Ride

Max remained next to Cindy and his mother, a few paces behind Grandpa and Yelka, observing the funeral procession make its way down the isle of the dome-shaped galactic church. They stood at the back of the chapel, waiting for the service to begin. Olik's coffin glided along about three feet off the floor as an alien maneuvered it into position at the front of the building. A priest directed the mourners to be seated and then began to offer words of comfort. Max put an arm around his mother and held Cindy's hand with his other hand.

Olik's translation devices enabled Max and the others to understand what was being said at the funeral. The topics of the service surprised and comforted Max. He had to release Cindy's hand several times to wipe the tears running down his cheeks. Several speakers gave an account of Olik's life and accomplishments. Olik's wife, whom Max had never met, spoke of seeing her husband again in the next life, and how they and their children would be a family once more.

Even though the sense of loss weighed heavily on Max, thoughts of seeing his friend again gave him peace. Somehow, with all the crazy things he had experienced over the last several years, he knew it was going to happen. He didn't doubt it for a minute.

After the funeral, Grandpa introduced Max and the others to Olik's family. Max noticed the women of Olik's race had softer features. Their cheek bones were not as pronounced and their lips, although very fine, were a little fuller than their male counterparts. They also had longer, thicker eyelashes. Olik had a young son and a daughter about Max and Cindy's age.

"Olik talked about you all the time." His wife shook their hands.

"He was a good friend and teacher." Max fought to hold back the tears.

"Thank you; I only hope Lita will be as useful to the cause." She managed a weak thin line smile that reminded Max of Olik.

"Lita?" Cindy questioned.

Olik's daughter stepped forward and introduced herself to everyone. "I will be replacing my father," Lita said in a soft voice.

Max, Cindy, and the others shot a glance at Grandpa. Max didn't understand how Grandpa could ask more from Olik's wife. She had just lost her husband. How could Grandpa expect her to put her daughter in danger?

"Oh, this wasn't Joseph's decision. Olik had been training her to be his replacement just as Joseph has been teaching Max. A lot of the things and information you have gotten from Olik actually came from her," Olik's wife stated, as if reading their thoughts.

"In fact, I am planning on sending her with you, Cindy and Sky, on your next mission. I think it will be a great way for you to get to know each other," Grandpa stated.

"I don't doubt your skills," Max backpedaled, noticing Lita with her hands on her hips in a scornful manner. "I was...ah...thinking of your family."

"He's not that bright." Cindy elbowed Max in the ribs. "It will be nice to have you. We need more women to keep the not-so-intelligent ones up to speed."

They spent the next hour visiting Olik's family and others involved in the effort behind the scenes. They met several scientists and technicians who were responsible for building a lot of the high-tech gadgets they used. They also ate some of the strangest food Max had ever seen. Some of it was delicious but Max didn't know, and wasn't sure he wanted to know, where it came from or what it was.

"I didn't know Olik believed in God," Max stated as they exited the gateway onto the third floor of Grandpa's house.

"Me either," Cindy added.

"What made you think that?" Grandpa questioned.

"Well, he's a scientist. I just thought all of them believed in evolution," Cindy added and Max nodded.

"So you thought he subscribed to the big-bang theory?" Grandpa chuckled. "Look at the world around you and the intricate order of things. What are the odds of that happening by chance? Think of the bumble bee and all of the life it sustains. All of that life would have never existed if it took it millions of years to figure out it had to pollinate all forms of plant life."

"That makes sense," Max stated.

"If a bomb went off in a printing press do you think it would create a dictionary?" Sky smiled.

"When you put it like that, it does seem unfathomable," Cindy said.

"So who did create all these worlds?" Max asked.

"Can you think of no one? That's something you need to find out before it's too late," Max's mother said.

"So, you're saying He's real?" Cindy questioned.

"Of course He is," Grandpa stated.

Suddenly, Martin bounced into the third floor room with a huge smile painted on his face. "So, are we going?"

"Going?" Max crinkled his nose and shot his mother a sideways glance.

"But, it was…"

Cindy's mother elbowed her in the side as the smile on Martin's face started to fade. "But, I thought it was…"

"Of course you're going, Martin, and a few more will be joining you," Max's mother stated. "Lita, Olik's daughter, will be coming along and so will Mike, Jenny, and Tim."

"That doesn't sound like a date," Cindy protested, putting a hand on her side to block her mother's second elbow.

Max had been looking forward to his and Cindy's official first date since getting his driver's license a few weeks ago. Disappointment passed over Max like a shadow, not being able to do something normal with Cindy, alone. They had been planning this date for over a week, and now it was just another trip to the drive-in. "So, what are we seeing?" Max forced a smile.

"I thought we were going to that superhero movie," Martin said with excitement.

"You two better go change." Max's mother indicated Max and Cindy's dress clothes they wore to the funeral. "Lita will be coming along in a few minutes."

"She wants to come today?" Cindy questioned.

"Her mother thinks it will be good for her to get away for a little bit. Plus, you can get to know her better," Yelka said.

"But will she like a 'human' movie?" Max raised his eyebrows.

"Don't you like alien movies?" Grandpa chuckled.

"Ah, yeah." Max still didn't think she would enjoy it, because all the alien movies he'd watched were human made.

"I'll meet you downstairs in fifteen minutes," Cindy said.

"Yes, you better hurry. Clarksville is a good hour away, and the movie starts in about an hour and a half," Max's mother called after Max and Cindy as they hustled down the stairs.

Downstairs, everyone waited for Lita to join them. They were going to take Aunt Donna's minivan loaded with plenty of blankets and chairs so they could sit outside in the warm summer air. A cooler loaded with drinks and plenty of snacks had been loaded into the back of the van.

When Lita came down the stairs, she was wearing a baggy sweat-shirt with the hood pulled up over her head. "I hope you don't mind if I join you?" she said.

"We're happy to have you." Cindy looped her arm through Lita's. "We need to even out the number of boys to girls. With four boys and only two girls, they might have been as smart as us, but now it's not even close."

Lita smiled that familiar Olik thin line smile which seemed to light-en everyone's spirits. For one short moment, it seemed Olik was still with them.

A frantic knocking on the front door drew everyone's attention. Max's mother opened the door to reveal a worried Mrs. Johnson at the door. Her eyes were red and puffy and her hair disheveled. "Henry is missing!" she exclaimed in a shrill voice. "He should have been home hours ago. I can't reach him at the office or on his cell phone."

Henry was Mrs. Johnson's husband, who worked at the power sta-tion located fifteen miles outside of town. The Johnson's were a younger well-liked couple without children. Henry helped Grandpa with a lot of home projects to protect the neighborhood and teach magic lessons.

Max's mother put an arm around the distraught woman's shoulder and guided her into the front room. "Are you sure he didn't run an er-rand to Clarksville? He may be in a bad area for wireless. You know how unreliable service is coming from there."

"No, he called me and told me he was on his way home around 2:30 this afternoon." She sniffed.

All eyes glanced at the clock on the wall, which now read 6:00 pm.

"I'll get everyone on it." Grandpa moved to his feet and headed for the front door.

"Do you need our help?" Cindy asked.

"No, you kids get going. Have fun." Max's mother waved them toward the door.

"Come on. If we get there early, we can get a better parking spot for the movie," Max said, opening the front door to let everyone pass by.

The small group piled into Max's aunt's new minivan and headed towards Clarksville. The trip lasted just over an hour, and with a restroom stop, they arrived at the drive-in with only a little time left before the start of the feature.

With the pleasant evening air, the drive-in was almost completely full. Max parked the vehicle a few rows from the back where everyone spilled out with lawn chairs and blankets. A small portable radio provided the sound to the theater. The group formed a line in the front of the van, with Max at one end next to Cindy and Lita.

They were having a good time until Max noticed that Martin and Mike, who had gone to the restroom, had failed to return after almost twenty minutes. Max found himself constantly looking over his shoulder toward the restroom.

"Do you think something is wrong?" Cindy asked. "I don't feel anything."

"Me neither, but that doesn't mean something hasn't happened," Max stated.

"They have been gone a long time," Lita commented.

"If they're not back in ten minutes, I'll go look for them," Max stated, casting a glance in the direction of the concession stand.

"Can you…" Cindy started to whisper before sitting very erect and cocking her head to the side as if she was listening to something.

"I feel it too," Max said in a low voice. "And it's coming fast…"

Max threw himself forward onto the hard blacktop, while Cindy flipped her chair backwards, pulling Lita with her. They barely avoided tranquilizer darts that zipped over their heads and stuck in the plastic arm of Jenny's chair, causing her to jump.

"Get in the van," Max ordered, scrambling to his feet and diving into Jenny, knocking her out of the path of several more darts.

Cindy rolled on top of Lita and then pulled her into a roll to avoid additional darts, which stuck into the grill of the van. Suddenly, Cindy stopped and reversed direction to avoid another couple blasts.

Max opened the door and then dropped into a crouch as a dart cracked the passenger side window. He went to help Jenny, but she had fallen asleep with a dart in her backside.

"I think they're reloading," Cindy called while she and Lita dragged an unconscious Tim to the van.

Max hauled Jenny into a back seat and then helped Cindy and Lita get Tim inside.

"They're coming." Cindy's head jerked back and forth in an effort to spot their attackers.

Max hopped out of the van, not wanting to be trapped inside. He just cleared the door when Cindy spun on her heels. Her spell caught a man dressed in black clothes and threw him into the windshield of the car behind him.

Suddenly, rapid gun fire rang out all around the drive-in, followed by screams and the roar of engines. People scrambled into their vehicles, while others raced for the exits on foot, pulling loved ones with them.

Lita extracted her own futuristic weapon from inside her sweatshirt, and several bright blue flashes immobilized another couple of armed black-clad men. The sudden bright flashes created even more panic among the crowd when those caught up in the traffic jam at the exit started to abandon their cars.

"Stick with Lita," Max ordered Cindy.

"Where are you going?" Cindy called after Max as he hustled away in a crouch.

Max heard Cindy cast several more spells, and out of the corner of his eye he saw more blasts from Lita's weapon zip across the drive-in. The overwhelming urge to dive compelled Max onto the pavement as the popping of automatic weapons rang out. A sharp pain exploded in Max's lower leg where a bullet made contact. Max gritted his teeth and rolled behind an empty car. He grasped his leg with both hands, expecting to have to stop the bleeding, when he discovered there wasn't a wound.

"They're using rubber bullets?" Max questioned out loud as a stream of bullets pinged the car he was hiding behind. "This is going to be easy." Max breathed and used the *izginim se* spell to disappear.

Crawling on his hands and knees, he put another car between him and his attackers. Taking a deep breath, he focused all of his concentration on the car he had been hiding behind. *Premakni* echoed in his mind. The power of his spell picked the car off the ground and flung it toward the men shooting at him.

"LOOK OUT!" a voice hollered over the screams and car alarms, seconds before the crunch of metal as the car crashed down on top of another, sending broken glass in all directions.

Max sprang up and raced away from the vehicle he had taken cover behind in an effort to get behind whoever was attempting to capture them. *I hope Cindy and Lita are okay.* The occasional wink of blue light indicated that Lita was still active. Before he ducked under the fence he spotted a man flying through the air, and Cindy's voice rising above the chaos.

While Max darted around the outside fence, he patted his empty pants pocket to find disappointment, picturing his communicator sitting in the cubby hole on the van's dash. He released his invisibility spell to maintain energy. If it wasn't for his extra sense, the result of Payek's venom, Max would have run headfirst into a group of black-clad snipers. Instead, he swung through several patches of sagebrush behind the group of four men, where he stopped to listen for a second.

"I don't see him," one spoke into a radio.

"He was just there a minute ago, before that car tried to kill us," answered another.

"He did that!" the one in front of him barked. "WE need to be careful."

"HE DID THAT? WHAT ARE WE DEALING WITH HERE?" someone else replied frantically.

"Just dart him and hurry." The order was given as wailing police sirens started to drown out the panicked crowd.

Max took a quick scan of the area in search of a weapon, when his eyes locked onto a night stick on the belt of one of the men in front of him. His heart slammed against his chest at what he was contemplating.

"We've got the girls and you're not going to believe this. One of them…isn't human!"

Max heart jumped into his throat, but the fear of losing Cindy, Lita, and the others propelled him forward. *"Pridi,"* he yelled with such force that the night stick ripped free of the man's belt. Max caught the weapon out of the air, cleared a patch of sagebrush, and landed in the center of the men.

Two quick strokes and the stick crashed onto the back of two of the men's skulls, knocking them out cold. Max dropped into a squat, kicked out his leg, and spun—sweeping the legs out from under another. *"Premakni."* Max launched the fourth into the fence. *"Zakluci."* He added, and the fence closed around the man, entangling him in the twisted metal.

The other was on his feet. Before the man could extract a pistol he had at his side, Max broke his arm with the nightstick. The man grunted through clenched teeth as his other fist caught Max square in the face. Stars popped in front of Max's eyes and blood gushed from his nose. He staggered backwards and tripped over one of the unconscious men.

Roll, Max's senses told him as the other man advanced towards him. Obeying his instinct, Max turned over rapidly, and a dart meant for him struck the man advancing towards him. Max followed the man's eyes to the other who had fired the dart, right before the one who had punched him fell face forward. Snatching up a fallen machinegun, Max whirled around and squeezed the trigger. His shots hit their mark, causing the man to double over and retreat to safety.

"He's behind the fence," crackled through a radio on the ground next to one of the unconscious men.

"Leave him; we've got the others. The police are here. Round up the men," came through the speaker.

Flashing lights grew brighter and the sirens increased in volume as the police arrived on the scene.

Max made a split-second decision to stick with his friends even though his radio, which meant help, sat in the van only fifty yards away. He cast the invisibility spell and waited. In a matter of seconds, two black SUVs skidded to a halt. Several men piled out and gathered up the unconscious men. Max took advantage of the fact they had to help free one man from the fence and sneaked into the back of one of the vehicles.

His heart stopped when his knee collided with a box in the back of the SUV, creating a loud pop. All heads turned in his direction while Max held his breath, maintaining his uncomfortable position in midair. The return of the man who had been caught in the fence broke the silence, and Max settled into the tight space between the back door and the last row of seats.

The SUV pealed out as the last passenger jumped in and slammed the door. Max had to brace himself to keep from bouncing around like a pinball as the vehicle raced across the uneven prairie.

"Go to night vision," one of the men ordered, and the driver killed the headlights. A green screen materialized across the inside of the windshield, giving the world a green tint but increasing visibility to noonday.

Through the tinted windows, Max noticed several more black four-wheel drives racing across the ground. Every once in a while the SUV would hit a large mound or patch of sagebrush that would send it airborne for a few seconds.

"Did you secure the packages?" rattled through the radio.

"All but one. The older boy."

"That will do. We were able to capture our other target. Bring them to the camp."

"Yes, sir."

By the position of the mountains in the distance, Max figured they were heading farther away from Grandpa's town. Suddenly the road turned smooth as the tires let out a screech upon hitting black top. The engine roared with greater intensity as the driver pressed the throttle to the floor.

After a few hours of driving, Max needed to conserve energy. Holding the invisibility spell for this long depleted his strength. He decided to lay as flat as he could and release his spell. Finally, when he couldn't hold his breath any longer after he reappeared, he figured they hadn't noticed him. Drowsiness overwhelmed him, but he knew if he fell asleep he didn't stand a chance of getting them out of this mess.

Max's spirits continued to darken as the SUV put more miles between them and Grandpa's town. *We must escape before we are locked away somewhere.* Max wracked his brain for an idea. He didn't want to wreck the vehicles for fear of hurting the others and also leaving them without transportation. He needed a way to stop them and handle their captors.

The sky started to change from black to a dark blue. Stars began to disappear, and Max concluded they were out of time. Gathering his strength, he disappeared again and took a long look at his fellow occupants. All but the driver had their heads slumped over, asleep. A total of five men rode along with him.

Through the tinted windows, Max counted two more SUVs and what looked like a black moving truck. He was in the second vehicle from the front. Closing his eyes, he sent a wave of magic out the front of the car and into the one in the front of the line. A quick search with his magic told him none of the others were in the front vehicle. Now, he focused on the large truck bringing up the rear. The presence of magic bounced back to him, causing his heart beat to go a little faster, thinking he had found his friends. Then another surge of magic appeared, something Max didn't recognize. It seemed to block Max's magic. One minute he felt he was reading his friends, and then it was as if they were gone.

A mischievous smile spread across Max's face as an idea began to grow inside his mind. He noted how close the vehicles were traveling together and remembered the technique used by the police against a fleeing suspect. *Premakni!* Max's spell slammed the gas pedal to the floor, propelling his vehicle into the back of the one just in front of them. Another quick spell jerked the steering wheel, sending the front SUV spinning out of control before it started rolling over and over in a huge cloud of dust, flying metal, and desert plant life debris.

Max's SUV started to swerve back and forth with loud chirps as the tires tried to hold on to the road. All the passengers bolted upright with fear and surprise.

Premakni! Max commanded, spinning towards the back doors of the vehicle. The doors couldn't withstand Max's blast and exploded outward, colliding with the windshield of the SUV behind them. In an effort to avoid the flying doors, the driver overcorrected and the car flipped end over end into the ditch. The large truck and Max's SUV slammed on the brakes, trying to figure out what was happening.

While still holding on to the invisibility spell, Max leaped from the back of the SUV the second the vehicle came to a stop. He knew time was against him and he had to free the others before his energy gave out. He reached the large truck as the passengers stepped clear of the vehicle. Max seized the strap to the automatic weapon the man had slung around his back and caught the surprised man in the face with a hard punch that sent him to the pavement. Leveling the weapon and cocking it at the same time, Max released a volley of bullets in front of the surprised men who had climbed out of the two vehicles still on the road.

"Everybody out in the street where I can see you! And toss your weapons into the ditch slowly," Max screamed as loudly and with as much aggression as he could muster. In a backwards skip, Max positioned himself behind the large truck and where he could still see all of the men at the same time.

"*Pridi,*" Max barked with a scowl as one of the men moved a little too quickly for his liking, and the man's sidearm flew out of his hand and landed at Max's feet. With a hard kick, Max sent the pistol off into the ditch.

"Can I at least check on my men?" asked the driver of the SUV Max had hidden in, after all the men had disarmed themselves and stepped to the center of the two lane highway.

"After you open this door," Max stated. "Who has the keys?"

"I do," answered one of the men. "B—but I'm n—not opening t— that." The man's face went pale and his eyes grew wide.

"Open the door!" Max ordered, waving him towards the back of the truck with the machine gun before returning its aim at the group.

"You don't want to be doing that!" the driver of his SUV said.

"Let my friends out. NOW!" Max barked.

"Don't say I didn't warn you," the man stated, and the entire group took several paces back while exchanging worried looks.

With trembling hands the man with the keys extracted them from his pocket. They rattled violently as he tried to locate the one to the door. He took a few steps towards Max and then held up a single silver key. "This one. The only silver one on the chain opens the door. I'm not going to let it out!" He then tossed them at Max's feet.

Max squatted while continuing to aim the weapon at the men. He snatched up the keys with his free hand. "Is the key to drive the truck also on this chain?"

"Yes, it's the one with the black rubber head, b—but you aren't going to live long enough to drive away if you open that door."

In the excitement of the situation, Max tried to use his magic to ascertain any danger, but he couldn't detect anything. It was as if there wasn't any magic in the area besides his own.

"Move over there where I can see you." Max pointed the gun at a spot where he would still be able to see them and unlock the back of the truck at the same time.

"Don't say we didn't warn you. There is…something back there we can't handle. The one who can is in that vehicle." The man pointed to the SUV that had cart-wheeled off the road after Max had sent the back door into its windshield. The group shuffled to the area Max had indicated but, again, they crept a little farther away from the truck.

Once Max was satisfied, he approached the back of the truck and slid the key into the lock. Giving the key a hard turn created a soft click. A deafening roar was followed by an incredible force which threw Max twenty feet down the road as the doors to the back of the truck exploded outward.

15

Dwindling Numbers

The impact with the pavement knocked the wind out of Max. It took all of his concentration to maintain his focus and not blackout when a hulking eight-foot beast-like man stepped out of the truck onto the highway. Balls of massive muscles covered the thing's body from head to toe. It gave the impression some artist chiseled this massive deformed man from a huge pale pink stone. Round bulbous lumps covered its face, only giving way to a mouth of rotten teeth and black marble eyes. He wore what appeared to be torn, stretched out sweatpants. To Max's surprise there appeared to be a warped distorted tattoo of a samurai warrior welding a sword across the beast's chest.

The truck rose about two feet when the weight of the enormous man stepped clear of the truck. His eyes gave off a white flash, locking on to Max. A wicked smile spread across the stone-like face as he lifted his clinched fists high in the air and then like a giant whip-slammed them onto the pavement. The crushing force rolled through the ground, shattering the road, and the pavement became like water with a wave rolling its length.

Max tried to scramble out of the way of this shockwave, but his struggle to regain his breath impeded his escape. The swell tossed Max off the road, impacting him with the base of a thick tangle of sagebrush. Sharp branches scratched and cut him everywhere. He leaped to his feet as the beast strode towards him. Its long legs closing the distance faster than Max had imagined.

The thought of his helpless friends trapped in the back of the large truck with this thing stifled Max's fear, propelling him into action.

"*Premakni*," he screamed, but what happened next surprised Max. The spell hit the hulking monster square in the chest, causing the thing to hesitate for a moment. The creature's skin stretched and boiled as the hulk of a man increased in size, both width and height.

"*Prizgaj!*"

Fire erupted all around the advancing terror, but then changed to waves of heat that drifted into the body of the stone man. Again, it increased in stature. The thing laughed a playfully wicked-giggle, like a child who'd discovered a tasty treat. Its eyes flashed brighter with excitement and its feet vibrated the ground, increasing its speed.

Max bolted onto the prairie. Using a short blast of magic against the ground, he hurtled a barbed wire fence about twenty yards off the highway. *You have to outsmart it! You can't use spells against it...* Max's senses told him the creature was tracking his magic and it was fully locked onto him. Even if he felt safe enough to use the transportation spell, he wouldn't leave the others out here in the middle of nowhere.

His lungs burned while he sprinted around sagebrush and up a small sandy slope. His feet sunk several inches into the soft sand, hindering his speed. The harsh breathing of his pursuer and his keen sense warned of the closing danger.

Max's heart jumped against his ribs and it felt like his blood had turned to ice, lowering his body temperature. The back of his calves burned into a hard frozen knot as the beast grabbed his leg. A piercing scream echoed over the prairie when the beast grabbed Max, then quickly yanked its hand off of Max's leg in pain, as if it had lost its fingers.

Waving his arms downward in a circle to the sides of his body and up behind him, Max used a spell to spray sand into the eyes and mouth of the shocked beast.

The playful laugh of the stone man changed to a guttural roar of rage when the sand stung his eyes and filled his mouth. It coughed and rubbed its basketball-sized fist against its eyes to clear the small painful particles.

Max reached the summit, then turned in a circling pattern back towards the vehicles. He used the steepness of the hill to his advantage and covered two or three yards per leap down the hill. He spotted the men retrieving their weapons and helping the others in the crashed vehicles. To his surprise, they seemed to be ignoring the back of the truck. *What has happened to them?* Fear for his friends propelled him forward. *Preselim se truck.* The spell transported him to the back of the truck in an instant.

Peering into the back of the truck, Max's stomach did a back flip. "Cindy." He felt nauseated at the thought he had hitched a ride with the wrong group. "STUPID! STUPID! STUPID!" Max scolded himself and slammed his fists on the bed of the truck.

Ground shaking thuds warned him of the hulk still pursuing him. Max spun on his heels with gritted teeth and a scrunched expression, to face his enemy. He launched a vicious spell of scorching flame up the hill and encompassing the beast. Max held the spell for as long as he could before it fizzled out, and he staggered backwards to support himself on the back of the truck, his strength almost gone.

The fire continued to rage for another few minutes until finally the body of the creature siphoned it off. Its skin bubbled and stretched like an infestation of insects had tunneled under its surface. After consuming all of the flames, the creature's body almost doubled in size since its first appearance. Its features grew more distorted, groaning with delight as if Max had fed it life sustaining energy.

Once again its eyes locked on Max and winked a bright light, and a crooked smile eased across its face. A harsh playful laugh rolled off its lips, then it started forward with large earth-rocking steps.

Max tried to swallow to relieve the dryness in his throat. His eyes darted around for a way to escape; he was too tired to fight or run. Suddenly he patted his pocket to feel the keys he had taken from the driver to let the beast out. A ray of hope sparked inside his mind. He yanked the keys out of his pocket as the creature stepped over the barbed wire fence.

"*Gori*," Max lifted the barbered wire fence out of the ground, tripping the thing.

Its fall shook the ground, forcing Max to grab the truck in order to remain upright. His energy almost gone, he used the last of it to wrap the raging beast in the sharp wire. With one last jerk of his hands and another spell, he tightened the trap. "Thanks, Hudich," he gasped, in reference to an incident almost two years ago when Hudich tied Kacha in a similar fence.

Max leaned against the truck and made his way to the driver's side of the truck. As he climbed into the cab he spotted the men starting to organize. Heavily armed, they raced toward the truck. Max's hand trembled with exertion as he forced the key into the ignition and started the truck.

"FREEZE!"
"STOP!"
"GET OUT OF THE TRUCK!"

Max cranked the wheel and put the truck into gear. He floored the pedal just before the men opened fire. Max ducked as low as he could in the cab of the truck, circling the road. The windshield shattered and metal split where bullets pierced the vehicle all along the driver's side. The truck swerved off the road, almost tossing Max out of his seat as it bounced through several patches of sagebrush before finally ending up back on the road. Max released the wheel, letting the vehicle straighten out before changing gears and gaining speed. As he accelerated the wind blasted him in the face, forcing him to squint and his eyes to water.

In the passenger side mirror, Max caught site of the two SUVs whipping around and giving chase. Max ripped through the gears as fast as he could, but the weight of the truck kept him from gaining the necessary speed to outrun the smaller SUVs. The distance between them started to decrease, and gunfire erupted all around Max's vehicle.

A bullet tore through a back tire, shredding it off the vehicle. Max struggled to keep the crippled truck on the road, turning the wheel back and forth, swerving left and right, trying to maintain control. When another bullet took out another rear tire, Max screamed, *"Preselim se Grandpa's!"*

An exhausted Max touched down in the street next to the front gate to Grandpa's house. He rested with his hands on his knees, gulping in large deep breaths. Before Max could regain his energy his mother, along with Yelka, his aunt Donna, Cindy's and the others' parents, rushed out of the house towards him.

"Oh Max." His mother's call had that subtle hint of relief and worry at the same time.

Before they reached him a chorus of questions preceded them. "Where are the others? What happened?"

Their drawn expressions, combined with the dark circles under their eyes, told Max they had spent the night in a sleepless state of concern. When Max straightened to meet them, his mother's arms wrapped him in a tight hug. His eyes moved over the others' faces as he rested his tired chin on his mother's shoulder. Both Cindy's mother and Aunt Donna's eyes were puffy and red. Max pushed himself away, spotting the van parked on the street next to the house.

"How did the van get here?" Max asked.

"Forget the van," Cindy's father interrupted. "What happened? Where are the others? We got a call from the police telling us there was some sort of violent attack at the drive-in. Wanting us to account for our family members and to come and pick up the van. We didn't know what to tell them, so we said everyone was accounted for, and I drove your mother over to pick up the van. So you tell us what happened."

"Maybe we should get off the street first?" Yelka advised, casting a wary glance around the neighborhood and using her arms to direct them back into Grandpa's yard.

Once everyone was inside the house, Sam and Linda joined them in the front room. Max explained the events at the drive-in. How they noticed Martin and Mike's failure to return, and then the attack. He told them about his little adventure and how he had hitched a ride with the wrong group. "I thought they were in the larger truck, but inside was this massive creature with a samurai tattoo on its chest."

Linda, who had been listening from the entryway, exchanged a quick glance with Sam. "What did this tattoo look like?"

All eyes turned to Linda.

"Ah...it was really distorted as if it had been stretched by the beast and it grew more so. Every time I used magic on the thing, it seemed to absorb the magic and used it to grow stronger. It actually grew taller and thicker right before my eyes."

"Yes, but what did the picture itself look like?" Sam asked.

"It was a man dressed in black robes with red trim, holding a sword over his head with the blade angled behind his back." Max's face screwed up with concentration, trying to picture the warped tattoo in his mind.

Linda gasped and put her hands over her mouth.

"Did it have a green dragon patch on the right side of its robes?" Sam pressed.

"Um, now that I think about it, that's what it was."

"Why?" Cindy's father asked.

"Just before we escaped, there was a rumor surrounding one of our co-workers who tried to leave. I thought it was just a joke, until now. It had to do with something he was working on. The word was he had unlocked a way for them to control anyone who had developed 'special talents,'" Sam used his hands to make quotes in the air around the last two words. "It was also supposed to make you stronger and cause some kind of transformation."

"That's an understatement," Max added.

"If that's Jake's tattoo, then the rumor is true," Linda stated with wide eyes.

"Another rumor." Sam swallowed and glanced around the room, "Is that the others who were captured, like Linda and I, fell victims to this experiment."

"Not my child." Martin's mother broke out into tears.

Yelka put a reassuring arm around Aunt Donna, and the feeling in the room grew dark and thick as if they had stepped into a room that was too small to hold them all, and the light began to drain away.

"Anyway," Max continued, telling the others how he had managed to escape. "I don't know if that thing," he shot a look to Sam and Linda, "Can track me or not."

"What do you think?" Max's mother asked while looking at Yelka.

"Hey, where's Grandpa?" Max questioned.

"That's another problem," his mother stated.

"After we got the call, we sent him through the gateway. We haven't heard from him since." Yelka frowned.

All the Arab terrorists in the underground complex cast wary looks at the cloaked figure that towered over them and roamed the halls with their leaders. He commanded fear whenever he appeared—every few weeks. At first there were those who attempted to prove their power over this non-believer, but their deaths were quick and terrifying. They called him the sword of death after he single-handedly destroyed an entire terrorist cell that tried to capture the special complex they now occupied. Even his well-dressed companion commanded respect. Fear of being hunted by this demon, and the weapons and technology he gave them, kept them from fleeing to other terrorist cells. What he provided would advance their cause more quickly. For the most part, the regular soldiers tried to stay out of his way and let their leaders work with him.

"Here are the latest transmissions." One of the militants handed a stack of papers to Hudich, who passed them to Alan.

"We still don't know what they mean?" another Arab questioned.

"World domination," Alan stated with a wicked smile.

"I have a new project for you," a deep voice rumbled out of the covered face of the demon as he dropped some blue prints on a table in the center of the room. He wore sunglasses over the only area not wrapped behind the scarf. "These are just part of the framework for the project. I, or my friend, will check on your progress often and bring you additions to these plans."

"The men…ah…grow impatient. They wish to strike at the heart of the infidels. If we could carry out an attack." The Muslim radical across the table swallowed and shot a nervous glance at the Arab next to him. "The men will be less restless."

"No," the tall figure barked, commanding attention. "You can continue your silly holy war after you build this. An attack now could draw unwanted attention to this complex. Build this new item and you will have the upper hand against all enemies. First you will need to create some way to conceal your efforts from satellites, a camouflaged cover of some type."

"What is it we are going to build?" one of the Arabs asked.

"You will know when you build it. It will give you dominance!" Hudich held out his hand and Alan gave him a thick manila folder which Hudich passed to the man. "You need to transmit this data as soon as possible."

The Arabs accepted the commands and then escorted Hudich and Alan back to the surface. They offered their best efforts and sincere departing words, but they were always happy to see Hudich go.

Alan followed Hudich into the forest, away from the camp. They weaved their way through the thick jungle. Alan attempted to speak but Hudich gave a sharp grunt to silence him. It wasn't until they were another thirty yards deeper that he allowed Alan to speak. "We were being watched," Hudich stated.

"I don't trust these people." Alan glanced over his shoulder.

"They are useful and necessary at this time."

"And when they are no longer useful or they do something stupid, which they are known to do?"

"I will dispose of them."

They both cast their spells and transported themselves away.

"How are things progressing?" The man in the suit, Mr. Toms, picked up a beaker filled with a reddish liquid off the table in the center of the room and eyed its contents. The florescent lights caused the particles inside the beaker to wink, making the liquid appear to be made of glitter. He was a tall, muscular, black man with a shaved head and hardened features. A scar ran from his cheek bone down to his jaw line on the right side of his face.

"We've found something very curious I think you should have a look at," the elderly man in the white lab coat said while resting on the stool next to the table.

Around the spacious lab, scientists busied themselves with various experiments. It contained all the most modern equipment for performing extensive research.

"Oh?" Mr. Toms asked in a deep voice as he raised an eyebrow. "A problem?"

"Not a problem, but something we can't explain." The scientist set his glasses on the table and rubbed his eyes.

"With the alien?"

"No, we've kept her…well all of them, heavily sedated and lowered their body temps. They have no idea where they are. They are so doped up, I don't think they can tell a dream from reality. The problem is with the virus, or at least, when we tried to administer it to the others."

"Is it not working on them?" The man put down the beaker to stare at the scientist. "I thought you said they all had varying degrees of magic."

"They do. Actually stronger than any of the others we started with, especially the blond girl. Even the alien has magic, but we didn't inject her per your orders."

"Then what's the problem? I hope it isn't bad news. You know how the group hates bad news."

"I don't think it's bad news. More like something we can't explain." The scientist put his glasses back on.

"A change in the virus?"

"Not exactly. It is growing in all the subjects. The rate of growth seems to be proportional to their magical abilities. They are going to be powerful weapons for us in our quest to achieve world domination."

"Then what is it?" the man demanded.

"The blond girl's body will not accept the virus," the scientist stated.

"Does her magic protect her? I thought that was one of the reasons we heavily sedated them. Then they couldn't fight it."

"No, her blood attacks it."

"Like an anti-virus?"

"No, her blood really attacks it. It won't even let the virus enter her blood stream. Her blood forces its way into the syringe, killing the virus.

We can't even apply enough pressure to get the virus out of the needle. We've actually broken a dozen needles," the scientist stated.

"That is interesting. You have my attention. Have you examined her blood?"

"Yes. It contains proteins we have never seen and is almost black in color when drawn. At first we thought maybe we had another alien, but we checked her records. She was born prematurely in Madison, WI. She has all kinds of blood work records we've accessed. So, we don't know if her magic changed her or something else did."

"Could she be infected with something else? She has been places we have only dreamed about," the agent stated.

"What do you mean?" the scientist questioned.

"I thought you were smart. She was caught with an alien. What do you think I mean."

"Sorry. I guess you're right. I'm just really tired and not thinking clearly. It could be another virus, possibly. Would you like to see what happens when we try to infect her? I have footage," the scientist offered.

"No, I want to see it with my own eyes. Set her up. I will administer the virus to her personally," the man in the suit stated.

Mr. Toms followed the doctor through the well-lit compound. The place had the look and feel of a futuristic hospital. Airtight rooms made of glass lined the halls on both sides of the hallway. Doctors and scientists moved about the halls, carrying out top secret experiments and medical procedures.

"Nice to see our money is going to good use," Mr. Toms commented as they passed a room where a man controlled mechanical arms in an isolated box to perform a dangerous experiment where he released some kind of gas for a group of rats to inhale. A second after they breathed in the chemical, they began to fight amongst themselves.

"In here." The doctor typed a combination on an electronic keypad, and two glass doors opened to their right. "You can hang your jacket on the rack." He motioned to a stand in the corner. He then pulled some rubber gloves from a dispenser on the counter. After tossing a pair to Mr. Toms he slid on the other pair.

He went to a stainless-steel temperature-controlled storage cabinet and took out a small vial with a clear liquid inside. After grabbing a new syringe, he led Mr. Toms into a cold dark room where Cindy lay unconscious under a blanket on the table. All the latest medical equipment monitored her every vital statistic: heart rate, brain waves, temperature, oxygen levels and blood pressure. IVs dripped nutrients and anesthesia into her blood stream.

"How long have we had her and the others?" Mr. Toms asked.

"About a week," the doctor answered while filling the syringe with the virus from the vial. "Watch the heart monitor." The doctor touched the IV with the needle and Cindy's heart rate went from sixty beats per minute up to one hundred ten. Where the IV went into her arm, a dark reddish-black liquid made its way up the tube.

"Interesting." Mr. Toms accepted the syringe from the Doctor.

"Her heart rate will do the same thing if you just touch the needle to her skin," the doctor said.

They stood watching her for a moment until her heart rate returned to normal, and the dark color in her IV disappeared. Even in her sedated state, her eyes flickered back and forth rapidly beneath her eyelids, as if an unpleasant dream played in her mind.

Mr. Toms held the needle above his head like he was about to stab a victim with a knife.

"Wait." The doctor held out a hand to stop Mr. Toms. "If you are going to do it that way, let me strap her down tight." The doctor moved around the bed and secured the arm and leg bindings which Mr. Toms had failed to notice under the blanket. He then stepped behind Cindy's head and put his arms on her shoulders. "Okay."

Again, Mr. Toms raised the needle above his head and swung down towards Cindy's upper arm. Before the needle made contact with Cindy's skin, her back arched and her chest jerked upward, tugging at the restraints. The needle sliced across Cindy's skin, bending sideways and cutting a deep three-inch gash. Her dark blood attacked the needle, swarming around it like some kind of aggressive liquid insect and caused the wound to close and seal itself.

Cindy's whole body shifted toward Mr. Toms and her arm flipped violently toward him as the needle slit her arm. The needle bounced off Cindy's arm and stuck into Mr. Tom's side. The force of the stab injected the contents of the syringe into his body.

"Ughhh," Mr. Toms gasped and staggered backwards, knocking over some of the equipment monitoring Cindy's vital signs. He pulled the equipment on top of himself as his eyes rolled into the back of his head, and he thrashed about on the floor.

The doctor yanked an emergency cord above Cindy's bed, sounding an alarm. Cindy settled into a relaxed state while other medical staff arrived to help Mr. Toms.

16

Mind Control

Joe sat in the chair, struggling to stay awake as the bright penetrating light obscured his vision. He felt confused, not knowing why someone had woken him out of the best night's sleep he had ever had.

"What is the machine on the third floor of your house," a soft female voice asked.

"It's just extra storage space," Joe mumbled, with drool running down his chin.

"You know that's not true. You've been holding on to a secret. A secret you've wanted to share for such a long time. The burden of keeping it has made you so tired. It is very heavy." The voice sounded comforting, as if it could relieve his exhaustion. "Imagine life without that burdensome load."

"What secret?" Joe mumbled, his head collapsing onto his chest, snoring softly.

Behind a two-way mirror facing Joe, Tanner and Agent Smith sat with a short round woman. Tanner slammed his fist down on the arm of his chair. "We've been at this for over a week and we're getting nowhere. How are things progressing with the others at the hospital?"

"The alien is safely sedated. Three have been given the virus successfully which has taken hold as anticipated. Yesterday there was an accident with the blond girl involving Mr. Toms," Agent Smith reported.

"What kind of accident?" Tanner asked with interest.

"Apparently, he tried to force the virus into the blond girl and stuck himself with his own needle," Agent Smith stated.

"Is he infected?"

"No, the needle cut the blond girl and her blood destroyed the virus. He doesn't seem to have suffered any adverse effects. Wasn't he your mentor?"

"Yes. He isn't one to make mistakes and if he does, he eliminates them," Tanner said.

"What do you want to do?" Agent Smith nodded toward the slumbering man in the chair.

"Take him back to his room," Tanner ordered the woman.

"Yes, sir," she responded and hustled out of the room.

"Maybe we could find a way to use the girl. Sleep deprivation and truth serum is getting us nowhere with the old man. We can't use other forms of torture because that would mean waking him up, which would give him the full use of his magic," Agent Smith said.

"I like the idea. If they can't use her, why shouldn't we. Have them transport her here," Tanner ordered.

"Where do we start?" Max asked Sky while he, his mother, Sky, Yelka, Sam, Linda, and the others sat around Grandpa's kitchen, discussing their options.

"Someone among us has to be passing information to these agents," Max's mother replied. "How else would they know to attack you at the drive-in and then take Grandpa right from under our noses?"

"They're watching us. And they're close," Cindy's father noted.

"That doesn't mean they're holding them nearby," Sam said. "They have vast resources at their disposal. I doubt Joseph or the kids are anywhere near here."

"Where would you suggest we look?" Mike's father questioned, leaning on the table. Desperation lined his face.

"I wish we knew. We didn't know where we were," Linda said as she met everyone's eyes.

"What help can we expect?" Donna asked, eyeing Yelka.

"We are on our own. Tracking Hudich's activities have stretched us thin. I have sent out for help but we can't expect any for a couple of weeks. Fenster and others are busy trying to dismantle Hudich's technological advances. I can track these men but it will take time," Yelka said.

"I say it's time to stop being the hunted and start being the hunters and attack them." Sky smiled a mischievous grin.

"That could start a war," Cindy's mother said.

"We are already at war. And we are outnumbered. It's time to start changing the odds," Sky stated.

"I agree," Max said.

"You're not thinking clearly about this." Max's mother put a hand on his shoulder.

"But I am thinking clearly. If we start making it difficult for them to accomplish their designs, reveal them to the world, they will have to stick their necks out to swat us. Then we could chop the head off," Max said.

"It might work," Yelka mused.

"How do you want to do it?" Cindy's father rubbed his hands as if he was eager to join the hunt.

"Yelka will have to run the gateway because we will need to jump from place to place quickly and often," Sky stated. "Not to mention giving our victims a one-way ticket to Pekel."

"You two might get caught in the net," Max's mother pointed out.

"So, I get another trip to Pekel. I've been there before and you can always come get me," Max grinned.

"We need others to find the mole and keep an eye on our friends on the other side of town," Max suggested.

"Linda and I can find the mole," Sam voiced. "We know how they work. I think we would be able to spot them better than any of you."

"That's a good idea," Yelka said.

"I think Jim should help. I'm willing to bet these are the same people who are after you. That makes you a target as well. That could be the mistake they make to reveal themselves," Sky said.

"Good thinking," Cindy's dad agreed.

"Now, no offense to anyone else, but I think it should be only Max and I doing the hitting and running," Sky stated. "He's had the most training and has the greatest mastery of magic."

"We'll keep an eye on our friends," Cindy's mother stated, putting a calming hand on her husband's shoulder. "We won't let you down."

"Where do you want to start?" Max's mother asked.

"At the protest camp," Sky stated.

A loud crash of shattering glass and a hard object bouncing along the floor drew everyone's attention. Max and Sky flew through the house to see that a rock had been thrown through the front window. Max caught sight of Larry and his gang racing away on their bikes.

Max bounded out the front door and down the steps. "Larry, you *loser*," Max shouted.

When he returned, everyone else had made it to the front room to investigate the damage.

"What do you make of this?" Sky tossed the stone to Max.

He rolled it around and on one side and read what was written, "Who's the One?"

Something was wrong. Cindy couldn't move. She felt incased in cement and she couldn't make her mind focus. She was so tired. The few times she had managed to open her eyes, nothing looked familiar.

She wondered if she had been in an accident. She knew she was in a bed with medical equipment, and doctors and nurses were continually checking on her progress. She struggled to remember what had happened. Was it a car accident? Did she survive a battle? Were Max, Grandpa, and the others okay?

What happened to me?

You were taken captive. A thought, almost a voice answered her.

Am I dead? She wondered at hearing the deep male voice.

No, you are heavily sedated. The voice came again.

Why? Am I hurt?

To prevent you from using your magic.

What about the others?

They are here.

Where is here? Cindy asked.

On a secret base in the Nevada desert.

How are you able to communicate with me? Do you know magic?

No. I can hear your voice inside my head. It must be your magic. I am compelled to answer you. The voice replied.

How did this happen? I could never do this before.

I don't know but please make it stop.

What is your name? Cindy asked.

They call me Mr. Toms.

Who are you? Who do you work for?

I work for a secret society who are involved in a plot to overthrow the United States' economy and bring about a new world government. I get things done.

This is the strangest dream ever! Cindy thought before she fell asleep.

###

Cindy tried to open her eyes but she was so tired. The needles in her arm hurt and her backside ached. She wanted to stand but her muscles wouldn't respond. She couldn't seem to escape this dream-like state.

People chatted back and forth around her but she couldn't make out the words. *What are they saying?* She attempted to scream but only a soft groan rumbled in her throat. *Listen to me! What's wrong with me?*

I told you. You are heavily sedated. You've been taken captive.

Who is this?

Mr. Toms.

Are you a figment of my imagination?

No.

Am I dead? Cindy asked.

No.

Cindy was so confused. She wished she could think clearly. Even her thoughts felt like they were hard to form, as if she could only grasp pieces of them at a time. It was comparable to watching a movie through fog, only parts of the picture could be seen here and there.

If she had been in a serious accident, where were her parents, Max, and the others? Were they okay? Why hadn't they come? Would she know if they had?

Help me?

What do you want?

To wake.

I'm coming.

Do you know where I am?

Yes.

Who are you?

Mr. Toms.

I'm so tired. Cindy's thoughts started to scatter and she drifted off to sleep.

"Wake up," a deep voice spoke softly in Cindy's ear.

She felt annoyed at being awakened out of such a deep sleep. Something was different however. Her thoughts were clearer and not as disjointed. She opened her eyes to see a large, bald, black man standing over her.

"Where am I? Who are you?" she asked.

"I am Mr. Toms. You are in a top secret facility in the Nevada desert," Mr. Toms repeated.

"How did I get here?"

"Some of our agents captured you and your friends at the drive-in," Toms said.

Cindy peered up into Mr. Tom's eyes and noticed his pupils were a milky white and he had a blank stare. He stood like a statue, unmoving, appearing to be under a strange spell. Cindy scooted to the other side of the bed and tugged at the restraints binding her arms and legs to the bed.

"Where are Max and the others?"

"Max got away. The others are here."

"What do you want with us?" she asked in a high voice, her eyes roaming around the room. She spotted an unconscious doctor face down on the floor.

"We want to know where you got your powers. How we can eliminate your threat to our society. Our plans are for a new World Government where we rule the lower class and control their lives," Mr. Toms stated without emotions.

"*Raztrgaj*," Cindy commanded and the straps on her arms and legs burst, tearing in half. She turned her attention to Mr. Toms, ready for a fight, but he remained motionless, not noticing her actions.

"Why are you just standing there?" Cindy leaned closer to him for a better inspection of the man.

"You told me to help you and so here I am," Mr. Toms rattled off.

Cindy didn't catch it before but his voice had a kind of mono-robot-tone to it. "I told you to help me? And you, who brought me here, obeyed me?"

"Yes."

"You're kidding, right. This is some kind of experiment, isn't it?" Cindy started scanning the room for any hint at what might really be happening.

Suddenly, a nurse walked into the room while reading a clipboard. As her foot snagged on the unconscious man on the floor, she glanced down with a confused look. "Oh, you're awake. I didn't think that was supposed..." Her eyes jumped back and forth between Cindy and Mr. Toms. "Sorry, ah, sir. But what happened to the doctor?"

Cindy was at a loss for words. Mr. Toms continued his dead stare as if he hadn't heard the nurse's question. *What's going on?*

You told me to wake you so I obeyed your wishes. Mr. Tom's thoughts answered in her head.

"Shall I bring help?" The nurse fidgeted leaning toward the door.

How can I hear your thoughts? Did you do this to me?

I do not understand the question.

"I'm going for help." The nurse's voice trembled as she jumped through the doorway.

"No," Cindy shouted, still confused by the situation and the anesthesia. "Stop her!"

The speed at which Mr. Toms sprang into action shocked Cindy. He chased down the frightened nurse in the adjacent room. He grabbed her by the hair of her head, yanked her backwards off her feet, and dragged her screaming into the room.

"Let her go," Cindy ordered to which Mr. Toms released her.

The woman scrambled away from Mr. Toms to a corner of the room and cowered like a beaten dog. Her wide eyes streaked with tears and her chest heaved with each breath.

"Unhook me," Cindy ordered. She didn't understand why Mr. Toms seemed to be carrying out her orders, but she was going to take advantage of it.

Mr. Toms removed the needles from her arms, silenced the machines, and helped her out of the bed. The moment he finished this task he resumed his statuesque pose.

"Tell me what's happened since they brought me here." she ordered, and Mr. Toms complied.

He explained about the operation to take them at the drive-in, about failing to capture Max, and how Max had hitched a ride with the wrong trucks in his effort to rescue them. She learned all the details about the others and the kidnapping of Grandpa who was being held at a different location. What terrified her was the information about the virus and how all but Lita had been injected with it.

"Is there a cure?" she asked, gazing into Mr. Toms glossed over eyes.

"I don't know," he responded in his robot-like manner.

"Why didn't they give it to me?"

Mr. Toms explained the way Cindy's blood attacked the virus and no matter what they tried they couldn't get her body to accept it. He told her what happened when he attempted to administer it to her himself.

"So." Cindy paused, her heart racing with a mixture of fear and excitement. The events surrounding Payek were the scariest of her life. Before Sky showed up to rescue her, Max, and Ell, she thought they were going to become part of Payek's living dead. That she would lose herself to the great zombie-like spider. Then the strange effects of the spider's poison, both good and bad. The extra special senses she and Max now had saved them from danger several times.

Now she had this strange control over a man who accidentally stabbed himself with a needle contaminated with her blood. "So, you must do whatever I say?"

"I don't understand the question."

"Twirl in a circle like a ballerina," Cindy ordered, and Mr. Toms raised his arms above his head and danced in a circle. "Cool." Cindy grinned mischievously.

She hopped out of the bed and the cold floor sent a chill through her bare feet. "Find me some clothes."

Mr. Toms spun on his heels and headed out the door. Cindy's eyes met the nurse's, whose pale tear-streaked face held a confused expression. The doctor groaned and rolled onto his back, his chest rising and falling with each breath.

The nurse rose up and peered into the next room through the glass window. Mr. Toms had gone elsewhere in search of clothing for Cindy. The nurse met Cindy's gaze once more before she bolted for the exit.

"*Zakluci*," Cindy commanded, and the door locked before the nurse could open it.

"Please. He'll kill me," the nurse cried pounding a fist on the glass door.

"Not while I'm in charge," Cindy stated pulling a cover off the bed to keep warm while they waited for Mr. Tom's return.

The doctor stirred some more and Cindy told the nurse to tend to him. She paced back and forth in front of the door, wanting Mr. Toms to hurry. *What's taking so long?*

I had to find where they had put your stuff.

Bring the others' stuff too.

"Where do you think you are going to go?" the doctor asked. He had regained consciousness and was sitting up against the wall, with the nurse checking a lump on the back of his head.

"Well, with Mr. Toms' help, I'm sure we can get out of here," Cindy stated while continuing to walk back and forth, chewing on her fingernails.

"Mr. Toms won't help you," the doctor almost laughed.

"Who do you think gave you that knot on your head?" Cindy asked. "Plus, I'm pretty sure there was a good reason you kept me sedated. You're afraid of me." Cindy stooped so she could be at eye level with him. She created a flame that burned about an inch above the palm of her hand, causing the jaws of both the doctor and the nurse to drop. "Now, I'm going to ask you a question and you better hope you have a positive answer for me. Is there a cure for the virus you gave my friends?"

Before the doctor could answer, the door opened and in walked Mr. Toms with an arm load of clothes.

"Put them on the bed," she ordered and he did as she told him. The doctor's face stretched longer, his eyes and mouth growing wider with shock.

"Now, my question," Cindy continued.

"I—I don't k—know," the doctor stammered.

"So, you are administering a virus you don't have a cure for." Cindy's face crinkled with disgust.

"We just d—do as we're told," the doctor tried to explain. "But your blood might hold the cure. It attacks the virus and destroys it. Rather quickly I might add."

Cindy glanced at Mr. Toms, and the thought of having control over more human beings and extra voices in her head didn't appeal to her. She didn't want to be a human version of the horrible creature whose poison still coursed through her veins. "What does this virus do to them?"

The doctor's explanation didn't help Cindy's mood. Her mind raced with the two possibilities, and both ended with her friends as mindless zombies under the control of others. *But they wouldn't mutate under my control.* Then she noticed the dead stare and slight drool on Mr. Toms's face. *Can I release him? Do I have magic or what?*

As she tied her shoes, her curiosity grew. *Could she let go? Could she bring it back?* She wanted to know how to discover the extent of this new power. Her heart pounded with excitement and her palms grew sweaty. This could blow up in her face. What if she managed to release him and couldn't regain control? She needed him to get out and to help the others.

"Bind them," Cindy ordered, making her choice.

After Mr. Toms had secured the nurse and the doctor by tying their hands and legs with cords, Cindy took up a position next to the door. She had Mr. Toms stand behind the bed to give her a chance to flee if it didn't work. Closing her eyes, she reached out with her new sense. Guiding it along the ground, she could feel all the objects in the room, touching them, becoming one with them. She penetrated Mr. Toms, reaching inside his brain, seeing his memories, detecting his fears. Then, deep inside his mind, she found the connection between them. *I release you!*

She opened her eyes and watched Mr. Toms who stood quiet for a few moments then shook his head like mosquitoes buzzed outside his ears. When his head stopped, his eyes grew clear. "What's going on here?" His eyes went from the empty bed, to the doctor and nurse, and then to Cindy.

Cindy opened the door, slipped through into the other room, and then locked the door behind her. Mr. Toms extracted a handgun out of the inside of his coat and raced to the door.

Taking a few deep breaths to calm her nerves, Cindy reached out again. Working quicker this time, she dove into Mr. Toms mind. His blood responding to her touch, carrying her message into his brain, Cindy restored the connection.

"Put the gun away," Cindy ordered as she entered the room.

The eyes of the doctor and the nurse showed their wonder at what had just happened.

"He didn't even know he had been under your control," the nurse said.

She could barely contain the rush of adrenaline. With this new found magic, although very disturbing, they had the possibility of placing their own spy into the heart of the enemy.

Cindy went to a cabinet and started digging through the contents. She felt sick at what she was about to do. She didn't want this, but time was running out. Now they could have the upper hand. Still, she worried about losing herself and becoming a monster. She hurried back to others.

"Yes, as I suspect no one would know. He will be an excellent spy for us," Cindy said, with a syringe in her hand. "Neither will you."

"What?" the faces of the nurse and doctor drained of color, and they struggled against their bonds.

Cindy stabbed the needle into her arm and drew a little blood into the plastic container. "We'll see how well you like being the victim. Don't worry. I will release you after you've helped us escape."

Taking her blood, she injected it into the doctor and then the nurse. They both twitched and kicked for a few moments before succumbing to the poison in Cindy's blood.

Can you hear me? Cindy thought.
Yes!

17

The Hunt Begins

Max and Sky crept through the camp, always keeping away from open light sources. The early morning hour helped to hide their movements. The occasional sound of conversation or music floated past them as they zigzagged through the tent village. The smell of body odor and urine stung Max's nose, and he wondered how people could stand to live in these conditions.

Sky threw out the palm of her hand, telling Max to stop where he was. Max huddled behind a small dome tent, barely able to fit behind the structure. The snoring occupant slept on, unaware of their presence. Max sent out his senses. Even though Sky was in the lead, Max didn't want anything to catch them by surprise. He detected one target in the center of the park, but there were more magical camp controllers behind them. They were far enough away to not worry about at the moment.

Several cars at a traffic light pointing towards the park turned as the light changed, their headlights swinging over the park and then disappearing. Sky's hand dropped when the park turned dark once more, and they continued to weave through the maze of campers. They worked their way into a thick patch of trees where they could see in all directions and still have good cover.

"Is our target in the camp?" Sky asked.

"Yes, in the center, and there is something else," Max said, casting a glance in the direction they had come. "Something different." He closed his eyes. "And there are several of them. They are tracking us."

Sky hopped around Max to check the area they had just come from. Her sharp eyes penetrated the darkness. "Dogs?"

At the far edge of the park a pack of four legged animals moved about with their noses against the ground. They followed the same path Max and Sky had created traversing through the park.

"They aren't dogs." Max glanced over his shoulder. His senses prickled his fear like never before. "Or they aren't anymore."

"Some kind of magical mutation. These idiots have no idea what they are playing with. It will consume them. We're going to need a change of plans." Sky slid her sword out from under the back of her jacket.

"Where were you hiding that?" Max asked, surprised by its length.

"You haven't learned all that much in five years, have you?" Sky teased.

"Yes, I have." Max smiled in the darkness while waving a silver futuristic gun for Sky to see.

"Good boy," Sky stated, turning back to the strange animals tracking them. "They are following our magic. Probably sent here after our last visit."

"This can still work. When we take out those things, whoever or whatever is controlling them is bound to notice," Max suggested. "I'll handle those things. You get what we came for. Besides, I think we should introduce the world to these things."

Max sprang from the trees and sent a shockwave of magic towards the beasts, giving them an obvious trail to follow. With the beasts locked on him, Max bolted from Sky, angling away from the strange dogs.

A high-pitched howl, almost a scream, broke out across the camp, which sent chills through the air. Several additional howls answered the first and the animals broke into sprints, sensing their prey was on the move.

Max cast the *premakni* spell as he scrambled between the tents, flipping them over, arousing the occupants, and awakening the camp from its slumber. Confused people emerged from the tents into the path of the rampaging beasts. Shouts of anger turned to screams of panic as the protestors caught sight of the strange creatures. The beasts didn't distinguish between people who accidentally got in their way and the magic they pursued.

A woman's frantic cry for help stopped Max's flight. He wheeled around and raced into the heart of the pack. He threw up the blocking spell as two of the monsters leaped towards him with their extra-large canines exposed, ready to clamp down on their victim in a death grip.

The beasts hit the invisible wall with a bone-crunching impact. The wounded beasts crumpled to the street.

"*Premakni! Premakni!*" Max compressed the life out of the animals between his spell and the hard street. The size of the beasts shocked Max. They were the size of bears and looked like hairless werewolves that hadn't finished their transformation. It was as if someone had assembled them out of deformed twisted features: teeth, eyes and limbs. Pus and a blood-like substance ran and oozed from cracked skin.

"*Pridi,*" Max screamed, yanking a third beast off an injured woman. The creature zoomed through the air towards Max, but before it reached him Max cast the *premakni* spell, sending the beast out into the street to collide with a dump truck.

Max's senses warned of an immediate danger closing fast. "*Preselim se, Parku,*" Max flashed across the park as two beasts attacked. Max touched down a hundred yards away from where he had been.

People screamed and fled in all directions as police cars arrived on the scene with sirens blaring and lights flashing. One of the beasts went down in a hail of bullets as it hurtled itself at a group of police officers. The final two creatures disappeared into the crowd and didn't appear interested in Max or his magic. *Were they called off the hunt?* Max questioned to himself.

Max rushed forward in an effort to follow one of the beasts, thinking it might lead him to their master. The screams from the frightened crowd grew louder wherever the things raced, showing Max their path of retreat. Sending his senses ahead of him, Max locked on to one of the targets. Even after they sprinted past the crowd, into the side streets away from the park, Max could feel them.

Soon, Max lost ground and the stitch in his side wasn't helping him catch up. *Preselim se, beastu*, he thought and transported himself almost on top of a creature. He landed a yard behind the four-legged monster. To his relief, the creature continued on its current course, not realizing he was there.

The thing trotted down a dark alley where it disappeared into an open garage door. Max paused in the shadows, debating whether or not to risk following an unknown monster into its lair. Max's heart almost stopped as the second surviving beast jogged by only two feet away from where he stood. Max leaped back and flattened himself against the wall.

Before he could get over the shock of having the beast run past without seeing him, the door closed. He had made up his mind to find a way in when Sky popped out of nowhere next to him.

"You almost gave me a heart attack." Max laid back against the wall, putting his hand over his heart. He took a few deep breaths to calm himself.

"Well, I can't let you go in there by yourself," Sky whispered.

"I thought you were going after those strange dudes?"

"I was, but when you started that commotion, they headed this way. They entered through a different door. I was just searching for a way in when I saw you," Sky said.

"Why would they flee? And why didn't those things notice me? I mean, I practically landed on one and the other almost ran me over," Max stated.

"I don't know. I think they are worried."

"About?"

"I almost had the target, when you destroyed a couple of those beasts. They might think they are outmatched, or…" Sky paused.

"Or what?"

"They are setting us up for a trap," Sky said.

"Well, we wouldn't want to disappoint them, let's spring it," Max grinned.

"I'm so proud," Sky stated. "I have taught you well. But first we need to find a way in. Send Yelka a message to get ready."

Max took out his communicator and typed in the message. "Okay, how do you want to do this?"

"Are we here to make a statement or what?" Sky asked.

"You're right," Max stood and pulled out his weapon. He adjusted its force, pointed it at the garage door, and pulled the trigger. A flash of red light zipped across the alleyway and slammed into the metal door. The door exploded into a shower of tiny, hot, metal sparks that flew in all directions.

"That should get their attention," Sky said. "What's beyond the door?"

Max closed his eyes and sent out his magic senses again. It moved through the alley and through the newly created hole. "Nothing magical on the first floor," Max advised. "That doesn't mean there won't be any resistance."

"Oh, the possibility of more fun." Sky hurried to the opening with Max on her heels.

They ducked through the shattered garage door opening into almost total darkness. Even after Max's eyes adjusted, the blackness limited his vision. Sky appeared as a dark apparition gliding along in front of him. Faint light filtered in from what appeared to be windows covered with a thin film of some kind.

CRACK! Pain and lights popped in front of Max's eyes and a falling sensation overcame him. Someone seemed to be calling out to him from a great distance. He didn't recognize the person's voice and he didn't seem to know his name, but still he spoke to Max.

He struggled to open his eyes, but an extremely bright light hurt, and he blinked rapidly in an effort to take in his surroundings. He lay on the floor in a white room, with a massive mirror covering an entire wall. His head pounded from a large bump on the back.

"Are you listening?" a voice asked through a speaker situated in the top corner of the room.

Max put a hand over his eyes to shield them from the intensity of the light and sat up, leaning on the opposite arm. His head throbbed from the effort. "Are you talking to me?" he asked, trying to look into the mirror.

"What are you doing in our warehouse?" the voice asked.

Max's eyes searched every inch of the floor, "Ah...I saw an opening and decided to investigate. I was just curious." He climbed to his feet. He went to the mirror and used it for support as the blood rushed to his brain, creating a twirling sensation as if the room spun.

"You are trespassing on government property," the voice stated.

"Which government?" Max placed his finger on the glass to see it touching the reflection, confirming it was a two way mirror.

"The United States Government. And the things happening inside this building are top secret. You neither have permission to be here nor proper clearance. You are facing felony charges. That's which government." the voice lectured.

"Oh, I thought it might be the imposters trying to gain power and control by other means, than the actual voice of the people. Can I get some aspirin? I've got a terrible headache. Compliments of a security officer, I'm sure."

"You're facing several years in federal prison, so I suggest you bear with the headache and answer the questions," the voice stated.

"Come on. How long are you going to pretend you don't know?" Max pressed his cheek against the cool mirror.

"Know what?" the voice asked.

"Well, I don't carry ID when I'm out snooping, but I'm positive you've searched your databases for my picture. If you have access to the best facial recognition software, which I'm sure you do, you know who I am and where I'm from.

"And your point?"

"Well, you have to wonder what I'm doing so far away from home. You even have to worry how safe you are behind this mirror." Max turned his face towards them and smiled.

"You have no idea who or what you are dealing with. We can make you disappear if we so choose," the voice said.

"Unfortunately, I can't have that. I have a mission to accomplish," Max informed them.

"What is your mission?"

"Well, I'm hunting."

"Hunting what?"

"You, of course." Max smiled mischievously, taunting the people behind the mirror.

"Well, from where I'm sitting, you're not doing a very good job," the voice fired back.

"That's what you think. Maybe this was all part of my plan. I have you right where I want you." Max walked around the room looking high and low, taking in all the details. He sent his senses into the room beyond the mirror to see what he was facing. He detected magic but it wasn't in the room behind the mirror.

"You're funny. For someone who's in your situation, you don't seem to realize the level of trouble you are in."

"Actually, I'm in an excellent situation." Max ran his fingers over the wall, away from the mirror, and acted unconcerned about the people beyond the mirror. "I know there isn't anyone currently on your side of the mirror that can handle me."

Laughter from multiple voices came through the speaker. "You should be a comedian, kid. We have some of the highest trained personnel in the world at our disposal but you, a kid from a small town, are going to take us down."

Max stopped his inspection and faced the mirror once more. "Oh, I'm definitely not talking to the right people. You really don't know who I am, do you? Otherwise, you would have brought some more muscle. Apparently, I haven't had the effect I was hoping for. I guess I'm just going to have to go bigger. You grunts let me know when someone worth talking to arrives."

The door opened and a massive man in a black suit entered the room. He stood almost a foot taller than Max, and the tightness of his suit jacket revealed his cord-like muscles.

"Okay, here's your chance to prove how outmatched you have us, kid," the voice from the speaker mocked. "We'll see how cooperative you are after your little chat with our friend there."

"Him." Max rolled his eyes. "That's all you got?" Max doubled over with laughter. "And you guys thought I was funny?" Max struggled to breathe through his fits of laughter.

"Knock that smile off his face," the voice commanded.

The man took off his jacket and then cracked all his knuckles. Max continued to laugh with tears leaking out of his eyes. In three long strides the man towered over Max. As he reached down to snatch Max off the floor, Max sprang upward. "*Premakni*," Max called as he landed an upper cut to the large man's chin. The power of the spell impacted on the man's jaw with such force it lifted him off the ground and threw him flat on his back.

"I told you," Max said with a smile, turning towards the mirror.

He waited for a few minutes but the voice never responded.

"It's about time," Max said.

"Hey, I wanted to watch the show," Sky's voice came through the speakers.

"Nice." Max smirked. He joined Sky in the control room, dragging the large man with him.

"Secret Service." Sky handed Max an ID from one of their captives.

"As in—the guys who protect our government officials?" Max questioned.

"You tell me. You forget, I'm not from around these parts. I'm not familiar with your government's agencies," Sky said.

"Well, the Secret Service protects Presidents, current and past, as well as other government officials. I have a feeling we're going to draw some serious attention from people in very high places." Max took a deep breath and opened his eyes wide.

"Are you a little nervous?"

"Yep!" Max smiled.

"Good, I'd be worried if you weren't." Sky nodded. "People without fear usually make mistakes."

"Do we want to take any of these men back home for questioning?" Max asked.

"I don't think so. They may or may not know anything. I'll see what we can get right here. If we take down a couple of these mutants, or whatever they are, we are going to be found by people with answers." Sky winked.

"So, where to next?"

"You tell me. I can't detect the targets like you can," Sky said, as she squatted in front of the prisoners. "Okay, gentlemen. I need some help. If you provide me with the information we need, I won't be forced to do something unpleasant."

Max closed his eyes and inhaled a deep calming breath, and as he slowly released it, he cast his web. He searched the building for other sources of magic. He could sense all forms of life, although it used a lot of energy to do so. He discovered a year ago, if he only sought magic targets, he could conserve his strength. He had shared this discovery with Cindy and Yelka. Yelka explained magical beings used the magic of the earth, so all were connected this way. Max and Cindy's new ability took advantage of what the earth already contained, so little effort was required.

Max's eyes snapped open. "They are aware of us."

"What?" Sky rose to a standing position.

"I found them. And when I did, I let them know we are here," Max said.

"Did you do that on purpose or…?"

"No, they just sensed my magic. They are coming."

"Call Yelka. Have them get ready. If they are coming to us, it should be fairly straight forward," Sky stated. "Now." Sky spun back towards the men and clapped her hands together with a loud crack. "You gentlemen are going to be bait."

"Do you want to do this here?" Max asked.

"No. There is a larger space, like a warehouse. I think that would be a better spot. Plus there are additional exits. Here, if something goes wrong, we could be trapped," Sky advised.

"We need to hurry," Max warned.

They used magic to transport the men from the observation room to the middle of the warehouse where Max had melted the door, allowing them to enter.

They were in the process of tying the men together in a circle when Max grabbed Sky's arm. "Wait, I have an idea. Let's use them like a web with the net," Max suggested.

"How much time do we have?"

"Not much."

They spread the men in a circle on the floor and tied them together with ropes laid out around and between them. While Max checked how secure the men's wrists were, Sky opened a few side doors to help them see the darkened warehouse better. The room consisted of a large cement floor with several bay doors. Steel beams all around the room supported the floors two stories above them.

The lights sprang to life, and Max squinted against the instant intensity of the bulbs. Two figures stepped out onto a catwalk one floor above the main floor, while Max and Sky circled around, placing the secured men between them and the newcomers.

The figures moved along the catwalk until they reached a set of stairs and started their descent. One was a man dressed in a business suit, and the other was one of the pale white-eyed things from the park.

"So, Max Rigdon has decided to pay us a visit," the man sneered when he reached the last step.

Max's mouth fell open and he took a couple steps back as the man and the creature strolled towards them. He wanted to speak but couldn't find the words. He glanced to Sky, who maintained her focus on the two figures, then back to the man across from him.

"I see you recognize how much trouble you are in," said the man with silver hair and an aged face. "You may think you can get out of this mess but you are wrong." He waved a hand in the air, and more of the pale-faced things appeared on the catwalks all around them. There were twenty to thirty others.

"I think he underestimates us." Sky flashed her beautiful smile.

"I don't know who you are, but I will," the man said. "You obviously don't know who I am. Why don't you tell her, Max."

Max regained his composure and gritted his teeth. "It doesn't matter who you are or how much power you think you have. You have friends of mine, and I really don't like you or what you and your ideology have done to my country. You and your people have turned a lot of us into an entitlement society so you can gain votes. Preaching your redistribution crap as you rack up massive debts. Turning everyone against each other. Even an idiot knows you can't spend your way out of debt."

"You've got a big mouth for a sixteen-year-old kid. We are trying to make everyone equal…"

"NO! Well, yes, you are trying to make everyone equally miserable except you and your ruling class." Max's blood boiled with the thought of these people trying to destroy his country and take away the citizen's freedom.

Now Sky starred at her pupil. "Okay, Max, who is this loser?"

"Don't raise your voice to me! I'm the Vice President of the United States!"

18

A New Zombie Queen

Cindy paced around the room, pondering her options based on her newly acquired subjects' answers about what she faced in the vast secret complex hidden in the middle of the Nevada desert. Her biggest concern, besides how to release the others, was how to stop the virus. According to the information from the doctor, her blood might contain the cure, although the prospect of controlling her friends turned her stomach. "I wonder if Yelka can help." she muttered to herself.

"Can we get to Lita without being seen?" she asked, facing Mr. Toms, the doctor, and the nurse, who stood motionless with glazed eyes.

Her newfound power repulsed her, while at the same time pumping exciting adrenaline through her veins, giving her a heightened sense of pleasure. Her mind swam with the possibilities of her domination and the increase in magical powers. *STOP IT! WHAT ARE YOU THINKING!*

She shook off the wave of euphoria and forced her mind back to the task at hand.

"So, Lita isn't infected?" Cindy asked for the fourth or fifth time.

"No," all three answered.

Again, the satisfaction of control teased her ego. Even though they didn't know Lita was the alien's name, her connection to them allowed them to understand her in a way no one ever had before. *How far is she from here?* she asked with her thoughts.

"In a temperature controlled room one floor down," they answered in monotone unison.

"Would it be easier…?"

Voices from the adjacent room sent Cindy diving into bed. "Act normal," she commanded as she slipped under the covers.

To Cindy's horror, her new subjects didn't grasp her meaning and continued to stand like zombies. Her heart raced as two men in lab coats crossed in front of the window on the side of her room heading to her door.

"Talk about something," she commanded, but still didn't get the desired response.

The door opened and Cindy lay back in the bed and closed her eyes.

"This is the one whose blood rejected and destroyed the virus," one said, as if he hadn't noticed the strange group starring off into space.

"This is the one Tanner wants," the other stated. "He said to keep her seda... Oh, Mr. Toms, are you performing tests?" he asked in a surprised, nervous tone.

"Yes," the doctor answered after Cindy's command.

"I'm trying something new." Mr. Toms obeyed the thoughts Cindy put into his head.

"Well, we've got orders to transport her," the second man stated, glancing at the other.

"Tell Tanner, he'll have to wait until I'm finished," Mr. Toms grumbled, raising his voice to Cindy's desired level.

"Ah...I better get him on the phone." A worker took out a cell phone.

Cindy panicked. She didn't know who had the greater authority here, Toms or this Tanner. *GET THEM*, she ordered and her slaves attacked the two new arrivals. They latched on to the two unsuspecting men with vise like grips, dragging the men to the ground.

The men kicked and squirmed in an effort to free themselves, but Cindy's magic coursed through her subject's veins, giving them power and strength. Cindy's heart beat with excitement as she felt her magic overpower the helpless victims. She hopped out of the bed and hovered over the men, a grin painted across her face. "I didn't want to have to resort to this." Cindy's chest heaved, taking in large gulps of air as if she had participated in the struggle. Once again she retrieved a needle, drew a small amount of her blood and injected it into the two terrified men.

The surge of power coursed through her body, tickling her brain with a soothing wave of euphoria. The degree to which she could sense her blood traveling through her victims' bodies was beyond her imagination. She could see inside their thoughts as they tried to hide themselves and lock her out of their minds. It was like a small war waged inside their consciousness, a fight that lasted but a brief moment before Cindy's magic conquered their will to resist her.

"That's better," Cindy soothed. "Now, who is this Tanner?"

No one spoke, but a flood of information downloaded into Cindy's brain. She discovered that not only had she, Lita, and a few others been taken prisoner, but Grandpa had also been captured about the same time. The detail to which she knew every aspect of these people's lives was astounding. It was as if their memories were part of her own. She knew their successes, their failures, their relationships, all in clear vivid pictures that would spring to life on the movie screen of her mind.

She dove into the darkest corners of Mr. Toms's life as he held the deepest secrets. She witnessed murders, wars, interrogations, and secret meetings. She stood with him in the oval office, at the headquarters of the CIA, and in rooms with power hungry men sitting around ornate tables, planning to overthrow the governments of the world and install a new world order, beginning with the United States. A system where they would control every aspect of everyone's life.

Her excitement peaked as a particular furtive meeting played out for her viewing. Mr. Toms wasn't an active participant, but an observer. His job would be to carry out orders to put their secret plans into motion. In this scene an overweight man, who seemed out of place with the powerful men in the room, brought a leather bound book and some video tapes which he placed in front of the men. Mr. Toms stepped forward and handed the man a briefcase. The man checked the contents to verify it was full of money.

Satisfied, the heavyset man wished the others good luck, and Mr. Toms escorted him out of the room. He later killed the man by injecting him with a toxin before he could leave the building. Mr. Toms returned the money to the high powered men in the conference room. They were watching the videos and discussing what all these things meant.

Next, Cindy sat in a room viewing another episode of Mr. Toms's memories. The secret group discussed plans on overthrowing the freedom of the United States and gaining world domination with the power they had gleaned from the book. They revealed how the book increased their abilities to control the weak-minded and bring about a mob mentality. This knowledge prompted Cindy to do a deeper search into Toms's past.

She discovered the formation of a dark society going all the way to Grandpa's building of the original gateway for the government. Although Toms wasn't a part of this original group, he learned its origins when he was brought on board to take care of the darker deeds of the group. This original society had captured a creature using the first gateway, which helped them learn a few magical skills. Through the mistreatment of the creature, it passed away before they could achieve a greater mastery of magic. Over the years the group struggled to control and gain new skills. They created a team to investigate all manner of unexplained events around the world.

With a little luck and their ever increasing skills, they managed to put one of their own in the White House. They had set up people all over the globe to topple governments and create confusion. They were very close to accomplishing their designs.

Cindy jumped through different memories, learning locations and operations. She saw Sam, Linda, and others translating the pages of the book in their prison-like complex. The sheer numbers and the reach of this dark society astounded Cindy.

Next, she concentrated on the task at hand. In seconds she knew the building she was in as if she had walked its halls everyday of her life. She discovered where they were keeping Lita, Martin, and the others. She accessed codes to doors, and where cameras and security checkpoints were positioned.

She gathered information on this Tanner and where they held Grandpa. She uncovered the identity of the traitor in their town and the position from which they kept tabs on all events happening around Grandpa's house.

The more Cindy learned about this horrendous scheme to control all life on planet earth, the greater grew the rage against them. While those at the top of this dark society planned on living like kings and controlling others, the rest of the world would be nothing but slaves living in poverty. They wanted to decide everything for everybody. To wipe out those who opposed them, their plans involved accusing and blaming others for the things they did in order to keep their real goals in the dark. Their magical powers had helped them control the mainstream media to the point where they could spin their agenda and lies any way they wanted.

"We need to get moving." Cindy pulled herself out of Toms's memories. "So, they were going to take me to this Tanner."

Cindy climbed back into the bed and under the covers. "Take me to Lita," she ordered, and her slaves complied.

Cindy pretended to be in a comatose state while her slaves wheeled her out into the main hall. With her eyes barely open, she noticed how odd it looked with five people moving her cart at the same time. She used her thoughts to have only the doctor and the nurse push the cart while the other three acted as escorts.

After they had passed several rooms on their way towards the elevators, Cindy decided to probe for more information. *How many prisoners are at this location? Why are they here?*

The questions flooded her mind with information from all five of her subjects, each with a unique perspective of the operations of the complex. Once again the scale of this dark society's reach and their resources blew Cindy away. She learned this facility held more than a hundred prisoners, weapons, biological agents, and viruses.

The wheels of her bed continued to click along as they headed for the elevators. Occasionally voices sounded as they passed an open door or others in the hall. No one questioned them, in fact it appeared most feared Toms and hurried along their way.

So, these people have been monitoring us and now they've decided to go after our people! Cindy realized her knuckles turned white with her vice like grip on the bars of her bed and her jaw hurt from clenching her teeth. *Their well-oiled machine is about to blow an engine!*

Get some weapons! Cindy commanded the three agents. *Meet us in Lita's room!*

Mr. Toms and the other two men in lab coats peeled off, heading towards a stash of weapons. Cindy could actually see what they saw if she closed her eyes and looked into their minds. While she, the doctor, and the nurse traveled down one floor in the elevator, the other three collected automatic weapons and plenty of ammo.

The elevator doors opened and they ran into a couple of guards who blocked their path.

"Where are you taking this prisoner?" they asked.

"We have orders from Tanner," the doctor responded with what Cindy put into his thoughts.

"So why have you brought her down here?" one of the guards asked. "No one is allowed on this floor without the proper permission. We weren't notified of your coming."

"Oh, we don't have time for this." Cindy hopped out of bed and stuck a needle into the arm of one guard.

The other guard staggered backwards and drew his gun, pointing it at everyone while fumbling along the wall with his other hand, he triggered the alarm. "Freeze! Mark, move back! What did you inject him with?" he yelled as sirens blared at a deafening level.

Mark, the guard who had been injected, remained motionless for a few minutes while Cindy broke down his mind. Then he climbed to his feet and moved to his unsuspecting friend.

Cindy raised her hands above her head and stepped away from the elevator, keeping the other guard's attention on her. Mark attacked his friend, forcing the gun upward into the air, where several shots fired during the ensuing struggle. Cindy leaped forward and injected more blood into the second guard, and a moment later she controlled another life. The rush of magic and adrenaline reached a new high, providing great pleasure in her growing power.

Take me to Lita! Guards watch our backs! She commanded, and her subjects carried out her wishes. *Protect us! Bring me more...* Cindy stopped, horrified by her growing hunger. She wanted to get her friends and escape. *Plus, destroy this operation. Bring this dark society to naught, forever.*

She raced through the hall ahead of her zombie-like companions. She no longer needed them to guide her as she knew the complex inside and out. She paused to type in the security code to Lita's door, when the report of gunfire reached her ears. She momentarily dropped into Toms's mind to see him and the others surprising a rush of armed guards trying to climb into the elevator on the floor above. *Bite them! Bring them to me!* A dark Cindy reared its head. "NO." Cindy fought to control her emotions.

Her breath formed small wispy clouds upon entering the ice-cold chamber where they had placed Lita. Her lungs hurt as she struggled to draw in the icy air. Everything she touched burned her skin, causing intense pain, and turning the contacted area black. *What is happening?* Cindy tried to hurry, but her joints ached and her movements slowed as she dashed back and forth. She adjusted the temperature and inserted an IV into Lita's arm with the proper drugs to counter the sleep agents that had put her under. Cindy's level of knowledge astounded her. In the last hour she had gained more education than the average person learned over a lifetime. She had become a doctor, a scientist, a nurse, and a special agent.

"Come on, Lita," she muttered as the temperature in the room reached seventy-four degrees. Soon the IV drip had pumped the necessary medication into Lita's body.

First, Lita's eyes twitched beneath her large saucer-like lids. Then her chest rose up and down when she started to take in more air. Her eyes blinked open.

"Lita," Cindy said.

At first, Lita's thin mouth opened but no words came out, and she moved her limbs as if restoring life to her body. "Ci...Cindy?"

"Yes, it's me." Cindy smiled and actually fought to hold back tears as a lump grew in her throat.

"What happened? What did they do to us? To *YOU*?"

"They tranquilized us at the movie theater and have had us heavily sedated ever since. But we're getting out of here." Cindy sniffed and wiped her eyes.

"Are you sure that's *all* they did to you? You look...a...two shades from dead," Lita said, her black round eyes studying Cindy's face.

Cindy glanced around the room for a mirror but already knew there wasn't one in this section of the complex. "It must be the drugs," Cindy offered, but an ominous shadow started to spread through her. Was it a result of what she was doing?

Cindy unstrapped Lita from the bed and helped her to her feet. She had to hold her upright for a few minutes while the feeling in Lita's legs returned.

"Cindy!" Lita warned as the zombie-like doctor and nurse staggered into the room with their blank stares. The rattling of gunfire floated in the open door with them.

The doctor and the nurse both hissed and their heads spun around as if searching for an invisible attacker. In Cindy's mind she felt their pain caused by the cool air on their skin and in their lungs.

What's happening? Cindy flashed through the minds of her subjects to get an idea of their situation. The guards had prevented anyone from entering their floor. Several dead bodies lay across the floor just outside of the elevator. One floor up Toms and the other two had taken control and bodies lay everywhere. Some had bullet wounds, but others had bite marks that showed strange signs of decay. One of the other men had been shot but remained mobile with a severe limp, dragging his wounded leg with each step. Somehow, in his coma-like state, he was able to function with this injury.

"It's okay. Ah, there are two things going on here. First, I have my own little army. I don't have time to explain. Second, we need to get the others and help them. They have been infected with a magical virus," Cindy informed her.

"How did...you have a what?" Lita shook her head with confusion and took a few wobbly steps on her own.

Cindy noticed Lita's hospital gown hanging down to her thighs. "You can't run around very well in that. Bring her some clothes," Cindy ordered, and the doctor and nurse left the room.

"Why? How?"

"Later. The others are in temperature controlled rooms on this floor too. I don't know how we are going... Never mind, I know everything," Cindy stated.

"Do you know where your communicator is?" Lita asked.

"I forgot about that. Give me a second," Cindy stated, dropping into the minds of her victims. Only Toms's held information about her communicator taken from the drive-in. "It's not in this facility. It's where they are keeping Grandpa."

"Joseph has been captured, too?"

"Yes, the same night we were taken, but he's at another location."

"How do you know all these things?"

"It's probably better you don't know." Cindy felt mortified at herself for what she was doing. Horrified—but exhilarated. "I'll explain later." Somehow Cindy needed to repress her new and highly addictive hunger. Shame at turning people into her own puppets and reading their minds and emotions wasn't right with her. *I hope we can get out of here without me having to control more people. Lita can protect me. Keep me from sinking lower.*

The doctor and nurse returned with clothes that were much too big for Lita, who had to tie the belt around her slender waist to keep the pants from falling off. "It's better than what I had. So, where are the others?"

"This floor. Come on." Cindy nodded towards the exit and then sprinted for the door. She raced down several hallways, navigating them like she had years of experience walking the premises. "We have to hurry, more troops are heading this way," Cindy stated, when she noticed neither Lita nor any of her subjects were behind her.

She paused in the empty hallway for a few moments before heading back to find Lita. She found her walking on shaky legs, holding on to the wall for support. "Are you okay?"

"I don't have any energy," Lita frowned.

"You haven't eaten for several days." Cindy checked Lita's charts in her memories. "I'll be right back." She dashed to the nearest wheelchair stored in a room not far away. *I haven't eaten either. But, I'm not even hungry.* She wondered if her new magical powers sustained her running. *I'm not even breathing hard.*

She returned to Lita and helped her into the chair before speeding off to get the others. *Bring food!* She commanded the doctor and nurse in her mind.

The other three were all in the same room. They slept in temperature-controlled, individually sealed, tube-like beds. Although the room itself was warmer than Lita's, it still bit Cindy's skin. Cindy checked their faces through the glass windows on the lids. What she saw terrified her. All had strange growths on their skin, as if it boiled underneath and the bubbles had worked their way to the surface. Nothing in Cindy's memories told her how to help them. She did know the cold chambers were slowing the spread of the virus that was taking over. Once the process was completed, they would be slaves to a person Cindy couldn't see, even in Toms's mind.

"Should we get them out of there?" Lita asked, joining Cindy to peer down at Martin and the others.

"NO! The cold is controlling the spread of what they infected them with. We need to keep them in these beds until we can get real help." The condition of her friends stoked the rage inside Cindy.

"How are we going to move them?"

"First, we're going to give them all a taste of their own medicine," Cindy snarled, a flame burning behind her eyes.

"What can we do?"

"Wait here!" Cindy ordered. "The doctor and nurse are bringing you some food." Cindy's voice sounded different in her own ears. It had a familiar soft pleasing ring to it, almost soothing.

"Are you okay?" Lita asked. "You look like you're getting worse."

"I'm fine. I'm getting stronger. I'll be back with help." Cindy hustled out the door and toward the elevators. *Meet me at the elevators*, she commanded Toms and the other two on the floor above.

When she reached the guards on her floor, they continued to monitor the elevator and the stairwell. Muffled voices from the staircase reached her, indicating a small group of confused guards trying to assess the situation.

"I need help. I've been shot," one of the guards cried, obeying Cindy's will. "Toms has lost his mind. He's helping the intruders."

"Can you get to us?" one of the men behind the door called.

"I think so," he responded, lying down in front of the door. Then he pushed the door open a crack and the men on the other side pulled him through.

A few seconds later a rush of magic and knowledge flooded Cindy's body, elevating her sensation of power and excitement. She smiled to herself at the plan to send her man out with a syringe of her blood. Her new group of soldiers marched out of the stairwell and down to the room with her friends.

Maybe I can cure them? The doctor seemed to think so. You could know their darkest secrets. You could know everything. You can take control of this complex. Take down this dark society with your own army. They tried to control you. Cindy's thoughts pleased her.

Cindy entered the room where Lita waited by the three temperature-controlled tubes containing their friends. Lita's eyes grew wider than Cindy thought possible, and she actually sprang sideways to put a bed between her and Cindy.

"What's wrong?" Cindy soothed with a soft pleasant voice.

"Cindy? Is that you?" Lita's alien features reflected shock and confusion.

"Of course it's me. I was just here a minute ago."

"You look diff... Cindy behind you!" Lita pointed to the group of guards coming through the door.

"It's okay." Cindy put her hands up to try to calm Lita's fears. "They are here to help us."

"How? You're controlling them. How?"

"They are mine," Cindy heard herself say, but couldn't believe she said it.

"Cindy, you're ch—changing. You look like...you're dying. You have no color in your skin."

"I'm getting stronger," Cindy responded. "You don't understand. I'm going to free us. I can stop them. I know their secrets." Cindy tried to circle the bed separating her from Lita.

"I think you need to stop. You are even acting scary." Lita scurried around another bed, always keeping away from Cindy.

"Why do you fear me? I can get us out of here. I can help you see." Cindy smiled as the guards started to close off Lita's options for retreat. "We can be one, you and I."

"What are you doing?" Lita started to cry. Tears rolled down her smooth, pale, alien face. *"Premakni,"* she called, blasting the closest guard out of her way.

"Mmm, a magical creature." Cindy hungered. "You will help me get stronger. We can conquer these people."

Lita managed to cast a few more spells in her defense, but in her weakened state her energy failed her, and she slumped against the wall. "No, Cindy."

Cindy's soldiers lifted Lita off the ground and placed her on a table. The doctor handed Cindy a syringe with which she extracted a small amount of her blood.

"It will be over soon. Everything will be all right," Cindy said holding the needle out in front of her.

19

Strange Revelations

"You two are in way over your head. We have the muscle and we know how to use it," the Vice President said, gaining some control of his temper. "You have some skills but you are outnumbered." He continued moving towards them with his tall pale-faced companion.

"Skills." Sky laughed. "Your skills are no match for us. We can take you now."

"Perhaps you are speaking of your so called leverage." The Vice President motioned to the men tied on the floor.

"They mean nothing to him," Max whispered under his breath, his muscles tensing in anticipation of a fight.

Even the men in the circle sensed what Max thought. Their eyes were wide with fear as they struggled against their bindings. Muffled pleas for help hovered above the circle as they screamed and tried to beg for mercy through their gags.

"Perhaps you have forgotten the United States doesn't negotiate with terrorists." The Vice President nodded and all of the pale-faced creatures stretched forth their hands. Lightning sparked and zipped through the air. The white-hot fire shot from their fingers and into the heads of the men in the circle.

Max and Sky threw up blocking spells to keep the lightning bolts from touching them. Max closed his eyes against the piercing brightness of the lights. He blinked rapidly to clear the shadows left behind when it stopped. Once his sight returned, the scene before him turned his stomach. All the men in the circle slumped against the ropes that held them tight, steam rising from their heads.

"As you can see, you have no cards to play and you are over-matched," the Vice President spoke confidently.

"There's nothing more I like to do than tear down a little man with an over inflated ego," Sky smirked mischievously.

"All of them?" Max questioned.

"All of them," Sky answered. "Especially the cocky old man who's going to wet himself when he sees what we have in store for him." Sky spoke loud enough for everyone to hear and her eyes bored into the Vice President's, who actually took a step back. "He's yours, the rest are mine!"

"Kill them," the Vice President screamed in a high shrill voice as he bolted for a door behind him.

"*Zapri!*"

Max sealed the door tight before the Vice President could escape. Max dove out of the way of several bolts of lightning which rained down towards him and Sky from the pale-faced army.

Sparks and fire erupted all over the warehouse, and the air grew cloudy with white smoke and the smell of electricity.

"*Pridi!*" Max yanked one of the tall figures off the skywalk and drove him head first into the center of the dead men. The creature crumpled from the impact of his fall.

Holding her swords, which glowed with an inner fire, Sky spun and dodged the lances of her attackers. Her blades slashed through steel with a nerve-grating pitch as she cut through support beams and brackets. Red-hot potholes exploded in her wake while she continued to dance out of the way of the enemy's fire.

Max tried to spin away from a blinding burst of lightning and collided headfirst with a pole, almost knocking himself out. As he staggered backwards in a dizzy haze of darkening pain, a searing fire bubbled the skin on his back and he screamed out. Throwing his hands high over his head and arching his back away from the pain, he launched his own fire. *Prizgaj!*

His spell engulfed his attacker, who wailed and screamed in an effort to escape Max's deadly net. As the creature searched for an escape from its coming demise, it collided with another, igniting its clothing as well.

"Max! Duck!" Sky yelled, and Max dropped to the floor as one of her swords flew spinning over his head and into the chest of the thing who had accompanied the Vice President.

The burning from Max's back made his head swim, combined with the stench of burned flesh, he fought the urge to vomit. Only his adrenaline gave him enough focus to keep moving to avoid being killed. A crunching, grating metal sound caught his attention due to Sky cutting half the supports to the catwalk. Chunks of cement and dust pelted them as the damaged catwalk broke free of the wall in several locations. Most of the pale beings tried to maintain their balance instead of keeping up their attack.

Max raced to the center of the room. Leaping over the bodies of the dead agents, he reached the center of their trap. "Sky, let's go!"

"*Pridi*," he yelled and swept up the Vice President and pulled him into the circle.

Sky raced into the center of the circle and started pulling in all the wan zombie-appearing people with her. Her magic circled the room like a huge lasso. When all of the creatures entered the edges of the net they had created, Sky slashed the holding rope.

Max caught Sky by the hand. "*Preseliva se, up!*" The spell transported Max and Sky upwards ahead of the rising net and through the gateway. They made it through seconds ahead of the others.

Max and Sky landed in a ball and rolled to their feet. They scrambled out of the way of the massive pile of bodies and rope trailing after them. The knot of dead soldiers, pale-faced creatures, and the Vice President of the United States of America pushed Max and Sky right up to the edge of the force field.

"Change the gateway to Pekel," Max and Sky screamed.

Yelka worked frantically at the control panel, making the necessary adjustments to change the opening, which caused the gateway to flash brighter for a second.

"*Premakni*," Max and Sky called while thrusting their arms outward towards the tangle of bodies. Their spells propelled the group back through the gateway and into Pekel.

Yelka shut down the gateway and turned off the force field.

"Take care of Max and call the others. I'll get them some supplies." Sky rushed from the room.

"Take off your shirt and lay on the floor," Yelka ordered, hustling from the room as well.

Max winced and gasped at the intensity of his injuries. Now that his adrenaline level returned to normal and his anxiousness from battle dissipated, his burned back pained him at every move.

A moment later Yelka returned with her version of a first aid kit. She began by floating her hands over Max's back, uttering a healing spell which removed the blisters and closed the broken skin. Then she applied a special salve of her own making from various healing plants gathered throughout other worlds. "You're going to have another strange scar, due to that spider venom in your blood. Why did Sky go to get the others?"

Max exhaled in relief, "You won't believe who we snared in our little trap that just got sent to Pekel."

"Who?"

"The Vice President of the United States," Max said, getting up off the floor.

"That does require everyone's input." Yelka's eyes grew wide as she pulled out her communicator and started sending messages.

Max hurried to his room to get a new shirt. After he changed his clothes and got some water he returned to a crowded third floor. His mother, aunt, Cindy's parents, Yelka, and Sky had already started discussing what kidnapping the Vice President of the United States meant.

"So this conspiracy to take over the world goes all the way to the top of our government," Cindy's father mused. "I say we use him as leverage to get our people back."

A serious exchange of ideas went back and forth as they discussed how best to use the Vice President, with everyone adding their thoughts and opinions.

"Well, if we keep him, he will have to stay in Pekel. We still don't know who is passing information to these people. It would be very difficult to hide the Vice President of the United States here," Max offered.

"I agree. Plus, a day or two in Pekel and I'm sure he'll be a lot more willing to help us with any information we need," Sky said.

They finally agreed to keep the Vice President in Pekel, and all but Yelka would take supplies through the gateway to their new prisoners. Max ran down to the hidden weapons room on the second floor and collected more guns for the others. A half hour later they stood inside the force field, fully armed with supplies for their captives.

They dropped out of the gateway into a small field surrounded by a thick, tangled forest. Dark-gray clouds hovered low over the forest floor and released a steady sheet of rain. The thick cloud cover changed the landscape's colors to a dull gray version of a natural forest.

"Oh…" Cindy's mother covered her mouth with her hand and rushed to a stand of trees to vomit.

There on the floor of the valley were the mangled bodies of the dead soldiers. It appeared something large had taken advantage of the easy meal and consumed most of them. Only scattered body parts remained in the red-stained grass.

"Where are the others?" Cindy's father asked while Sky circled the soaked field, searching for signs of their flight.

"We have to hurry," she said, joining the group after several minutes. "Of course, they left in a rush, and for good reason. Whatever did this is chasing them. Keep your weapons ready. Max, bring up the rear and keep your eyes open."

Sky led the group into the thick arms of the forest, which tugged on clothing and scratched exposed skin at every turn. Every ten yards they crossed a section of knocked over trees and crushed foliage.

"I take it whatever is chasing them caused this damage?" Cindy's mother asked.

"Yes," Sky answered.

The wind rocked the trees, rustling the leaves, and keeping the group members on their toes. Even in the chilly damp air, sweat started to join the rainwater running down Max's face. His heart beat with nervousness and with the strenuous hike, which involved fighting through thick brush and then climbing over the downed trees.

After an hour of hiking, the wind took on a strange howling noise. With each passing minute, the wail continued to increase in volume. It started to raise goose pimples on Max's neck and arms with the realization it was some kind of living thing making that horrible sound.

"I don't want to meet whatever that is," Max's mother stated as Max helped her over a large fallen tree.

"I'm afraid it's unavoidable," Max stated.

"Why's that?" Cindy's mother asked as he helped her after his mother.

"That's what's chasing the VP."

"He's right," Sky answered. "We need to hurry. It may already have them."

They pushed harder through the jungle-like forest to emerge at the base of a massive rock mountain with cracks and crevices lining its steep rise. About a half mile along the face of the mountain, a huge, hideous, beast dug with its long sharp claws at a crack in the rock.

Everyone hopped back into the cover of the trees to avoid catching the attention of the creature. The monster clawed and bit at the rock, trying to get at whatever had taken refuge in the cavity. Its rage seemed to grow with each failed attempt to snatch its meal. It stood about thirty feet tall on its hind legs. Sparse, coarse hair grew like spines all over its flesh, and its eyes bulged from its dinosaur-like head. Its paws seemed multipurpose, allowing it to grab and dig with all fours. A long spiked tail snapped against the stone mountain like thunder, and its roar, a deep growl, vibrated the ground on which they stood.

"I say we waste this thing," Cindy's dad said. "Go for full power."

"We have to be careful with that. We must wait about fifteen minutes between shots at that setting while the power source recharges," Max advised.

"What do you think?" Max's mother asked Sky.

"We need to find a safe place to hide in case we fail to kill it on the first attack. We have no idea what that thing is capable of," Sky said. "Remember, we don't have the use of any magic here."

"There." Cindy's mother pointed to a small narrow canyon about half the distance between them and the beast.

"That thing will *spot* us for sure," Max's mother stated, eyeing the distance.

"We'll make our way through the trees until we only have to jump the small gap between the trees and the canyon." Sky led them back into the forest.

Once again they struggled through the dense vegetation, all the while the ground continued to tremble more and more because of the monster's attack on the rock face. After another few minutes of weaving through the trees and pushing away the thick underbrush, they poked their heads out of the trees. The beast appeared more frightening from this vantage point than the previous one.

Sky turned to Max and waved him forward, and he hustled to join her. "Take up a position behind the rock and I'll send the others across. Don't miss if it should turn and see us." Sky put her hand on his back which caused him to flinch. "Sorry, forgot about the burn. Go!"

Max leaped from the cover and dashed to a large boulder about halfway across the gap between the trees and the canyon. Once he had set up a defensive stance with his weapon aimed at the creature, Sky sent the others. One by one they crossed the distance until Sky joined Max behind the boulder.

"So how do you really want to do this?" Max asked.

"Well, unless Olik isn't the genius I always knew him to be, this isn't a fair fight." Sky winked as she adjusted the weapon to full power, and Max did the same. "When it turns, aim for its chest, anywhere else might not stop it."

"How are you going to get it to turn?"

"Do you think a rock would do the trick?" Sky tossed a small stone in the air and caught it.

"Not the way it's focused on its prey. It's pulling all kinds of rocks on top of itself right now," Max said.

"You're right." Sky drew out the broad sword that was her favorite weapon. "Shoot it in the chest. Be patient until you get a clear shot and *don't* miss."

"Wait!" Max tried to stop her but she sprang around the boulder and bounced towards the beast.

"What's she doing?" the others cried from the mouth of the canyon.

"Just get ready," Max advised them, and they all activated their weapons.

Sky shot cat-like over and around rocks and fallen trees, closing the distance between her and the beast, still scratching and clawing to obtain its quarry. Max leveled the sights where the beast's chest should be when it turned towards him.

With the beast distracted by the meal hiding in the crevice, Sky made it right next to the beast's hind legs. She appeared to be studying the monster, searching for a weak spot. With her sword still held tight in her hands she spun back to Max, forcing him to shield his eyes from the glare. Sky glanced up as the sun appeared through the clouds. She stretched out her blade and rolled it back and forth to see the sun's reflection.

She sped towards a large boulder, closer to the cliff face, and hopped on top of it. Then with the blade of her sword, she reflected the sun so it flashed into the bulging eyes of the beast.

At first it continued to dig furiously, only blinking off the small annoyance, but then it paused, the strange phenomenon registering in its brain. The beast acted curious at first, cocking its head to the side and watching the dazzling light. Its rage seemed to have passed as it reached for the strange light. Sky stuck her sword all the way through the beast's paw.

It roared with pain and fury, yanking its hand free of the strange light with the sting. Sky sprang off the rock and the beast realized an easier meal was out in the open. To Max's horror, the beast didn't turn its chest directly towards him, but dropped at an angle on to its front legs.

Although the thing covered a lot of ground with each thunderous step, Sky was too quick and agile for it. Every time it tried to snatch her with its paws, Sky managed to avoid its foot long claws and stick her sword into the beast's flesh. Once, twice, it tried to bite her but jerked its head back with a wicked howl.

Max kept waiting for a clear shot while Sky continued to lead the beast in his direction. Besides the cat and mouse game, which made the monster bounce and snap back in response to Sky's strikes, Max never got a good shot.

"Lay on your back," Sky yelled as she raced towards him. "When he steps over you, shoot him!"

Max found a spot between several stones where he wouldn't be crushed accidentally if the thing stepped on him. A few seconds later, Sky landed on the rock behind his hiding spot. She slowed to ensure the beast would pass directly over the spot, then at the last second leaped over Max and away from the creature.

The ground shook with each heavy step of the beast, vibrating Max and the rocks around him. Rain water forced him to blink rapidly to keep it out of his eyes. He held the gun at the ready as the monster's head, then its shoulders, moved over him. The thing stunk like decay and urine. Its overpowering scent threatened to suffocate Max when it stopped before he got the shot he wanted.

A menacing cry raised the hairs on Max's body. Several loud booms sounded as Max's mother and the others, unaware of Sky's plan, opened fire on the beast. The force of the blasts rocked the beast sideways, but it remained upright and then countered. It sprang at the opening, forcing Max's mother and Cindy's parents to retreat deeper into the gap.

Max gulped fresh air when the monster moved and no longer covered him where he lay. Max went to sit up but the beast's tail slammed down on him, pinning him to the ground. Several of its spiny hairs pierced Max's flesh, causing him to cry out. The beast's tail slid back and forth, rubbing Max like a cheese grater.

Sky's voice seemed to call to him from a great distance. "GET READY AGAIN!"

Max couldn't see anything that was happening. He thought he heard a couple more blasts mingled with the roars of the creature. Suddenly, the beast's tail lifted away, releasing Max, but before he had a chance to catch his breath, Sky stood over him. Her sword flashed white hot as the monster attempted to snatch her with its razor-sharp teeth. This time, instead of hurrying away, Sky gave ground a little at a time, leading the beast exactly where she wanted it.

Once again the thick, stifling odor choked Max's lungs, and the beast finally crept into position. Max fought the urge to fire too soon. Time froze in his unbearable prison under the body of the hideous beast. Finally, the thing's chest hovered directly above Max's position. Max extended his arms, putting the barrel of the gun on the monster's chest, and he pulled the trigger. A white hot blast blew a two-foot wide hole through the center of the beast.

A flood of sticky, rank fluids rushed out of the opening, bathing Max in slimy goo. The monster collapsed on top of Max, trapping him under its body. Max struggled to slide his face into a position between two rocks where he could breathe so the weight of the thing and its body fluids wouldn't drown him.

Max had to remain in that sickening position for another twenty minutes while Sky and the others blasted and cut and pushed the dead creature off of him.

"Are you okay?" Max's mother asked, inspecting him.

Despite his painful injuries, Max flailed his arms and used grass and leaves to wipe the horrible smelling stuff off him.

Sky doubled over with laughter at the sight of Max's squirming, as though spiders were crawling up and down his back. Even Max's mother cracked a smile in reaction to Max's hysterical dance.

"It's not funny." Max laughed. "That was so gross."

"I didn't know you could bust a move," Sky roared.

"Cindy would be impressed." Max's mother chuckled.

"Cindy." Max stopped his protest. "Let's see what we can do to help her."

Max continued to pull leaves and grass from the forest to wipe off the smelly gunk as they went to join Cindy's parents. Sky had sent them after the Vice President and the pale-faced creatures. They navigated the rocks at a modest pace, when Cindy's mother called to them from out in front of the split the monster had attempted to penetrate.

She practically sprinted towards them, breathing heavily from the effort, "We've got the Vice President and the other men."

"Men?" Max and Sky questioned and glanced at each other.

They all hustled after her to where Jim held the Vice President and the others at gun point.

"What does this mean?" Max asked Sky, staring down at the men with the Vice President.

"I don't know." Sky shook her head.

20

A Call for Help

Brian sat in the copilot's seat next to the alien, just like when he and Larry escaped with the extra-terrestrial from the secret military base. Larry's mother occupied the seat her son had used on that trip.

"Please, don't make me do this." The alien's sharp high-pitched voice broke the silence.

"Make him do it," Larry's mother hissed to Brian. "Let's go get my husband."

"But, you will bring pain and suffering to millions," the being stated.

"Take us up," Brian commanded, and his magic gripped the alien in its chains, forcing it to obey.

Its large fingers moved over the controls and the three dimensional display sprang to life. After a few more adjustments, the saucer hummed to life and the ship lifted away from the ground. Brian watched through the windshield as the craft rose several hundred feet above the small town. Then the windshield rotated around the saucer and stopped, with only blue sky and a few clouds filling the window.

"Please," the alien begged.

"Shut up!" Larry's mother barked, covering her ears in reaction to its piercing voice. "Order him to be silent!" Her face crinkled with rage and disdain for the pilot.

"Take us where we want to go," Brian ordered smugly. Although he didn't enjoy the cutting voice of the alien, he disliked Larry's mother even more. If the alien annoyed her when it spoke, he wouldn't stop it.

The g-forces sucked him back into his seat when the alien punched the throttle. The blue sky turned darker and darker with each passing second. Suddenly, stars started to appear in the black sky as they zoomed out of the atmosphere and into space.

"I have need of some highly trained men for a mission deep inside the United States. This is a chance to hit a top secret American military site," Hudich's deep voice spoke from under his disguise to the radical Islamic leaders. They were inside the secret bunker located deep in the thick vegetation of the Philippine jungle.

Hudich stood at a table with Alan and the three Arab leaders. A small fan stirred the humid air, yet sweat formed along the men's foreheads.

"How many men are we talking about?" their leader asked. "We don't have enough men now to work on the plans you gave us."

"I thought you had connections to other secret organizations." Hudich's grumblings hinted at his annoyance. "This mission will provide us with the materials necessary to help you achieve your fondest dreams."

"*Nuclear* capabilities?" asked another of the militant Muslims.

"And the technology to deliver it?" questioned the first.

"I can deliver whatever you want," Hudich said, "But what you are building here is greater than any nuclear weapon. With this technology, you can strike at the heart of your enemy and there is nothing they can do about it."

"The great Satan, the United States of America?"

"Israel?"

"Yes, you could bring about your global Islamic state." Hudich whetted their appetite.

"How will you get our men inside the United States?" asked the head Arab. "How do you plan to transport them out of here?"

"Leave that to me. I will also supply them with advanced weapons." Hudich produced a chrome-colored futuristic assault weapon from under his robes. He pointed the weapon at the small fan and vaporized it in a shower of tiny white sparks. "You will have the advantage against your enemies."

Staring at the weapon, the Arab's eyes swam with a hunger for power. They chattered back and forth in Arabic for a few minutes before one of the men hustled out of the room.

"You will have your men," the older one replied.

A short time later, Hudich and Alan led a group of thirty men into the thick jungle, away from the secret construction site. They entered a small clearing where the men glanced around with confusion.

"How are we traveling?"

"What are we doing here?"

"Where are our weapons?"

"What's our target?"

"You will be given everything when we get to our destination." Alan smiled.

"But how are we going to get there? Magic?" the group of men laughed at the strange man whom they neither trusted nor wanted to work with.

"This is a pipe dream," another spat.

Hudich took out the gun and disintegrated a tree at the edge of the clearing. A small cluster of ash and cloud floated with the sparks in the air, causing the militants to gasp with shock.

"Now, form a circle around us and hold hands with the men on either side of you, forming a chain around us," Hudich ordered. He and Alan took up a position at the center of the clearing.

The reluctant Arabs, now fearful of the two, but lusting for the weapon in Hudich's hand, did as instructed.

In a bright flash of light, Hudich and Alan transported the group of terrorists to a hillside in a remote desert location. The only source of light was a small group of buildings surrounded by a tall fence, located in a valley a few hundred feet below their location. The men acted like rodents evading a hawk as they cowered at the sudden change of scenery and going from day to night. They gasped and some actually let out panicked shrieks.

"Relax," Hudich grumbled. "You are inside the United States of America and our target is that secret military base." He pointed to the complex below. "Alan."

With the mention of his name, Alan disappeared for a moment in a flash of light. A minute later, he reappeared with a wooden crate. He flipped open the lid to reveal a case of futuristic assault rifles like Hudich had demonstrated. After a short instructional, Alan handed out the weapons.

"Feel free to kill everyone in the base," Hudich encouraged, to the great delight of the Arabs.

They spoke with each other in Arabic as they judged the power of the weapons, feeling the gun's weight in their hands. They acted excited at the prospect of taking down a US military base.

Before leading the men down the hill, Hudich used a spell to trick the security cameras so they displayed the same empty image. They hurried to a section of fence that wasn't as well lit as most areas. They paused for a moment to take in their surroundings.

"No guards," Alan commented at the empty grounds.

Hudich studied the complex with renewed interest. "You're sure this is the correct information we extracted from the Secretary of State?"

"Yes," Alan replied. "He indicated this location held the secret to their success."

"There is indeed magic here," Hudich stated, "But something is wrong. I think they've lost control or something else unexpected has happened."

"My Lord?" Alan questioned.

"I sense an ancient magic, but not the same type of magic that brought that idiot into power."

"Do you want to call off the attack?" Alan questioned.

"No, but we'll send these fools in first. I don't like this disturbing revelation. We need to be cautious."

"Is it that dangerous?" Alan swallowed hard.

"Yes. It has the power to consume everything in its path. Be very careful." Hudich warned.

Hudich used another spell to disable the alarms and short out the electrified fence. The small group hurried into the compound.

Lita struggled against the arms holding her in place. Her hands groped at everything within reach of her small range of motion. "Cindy! No!" she screamed, her fingers grasping a hose. She shook violently as Cindy moved the needle towards her skin. Lita managed to pop the hose out of its bindings, releasing freezing cold gas into the air.

Cindy's soldiers moaned with pain and their skin turned a black and blue color like diseased flesh. They released their hold to escape the burning cold. Lita swung the hose around and drove a hissing Cindy back before she could inject her blood.

Cindy opened her mouth wide and a high-pitched cry issued forth. Her twisted face took on a nonhuman look and her eyes had changed to resemble those of a doll's, all black marble. Her hair appeared to be charged with static electricity, sticking out like quills.

Lita kept them at bay with the cold air issuing from the hose. While holding them back with one hand, she unfastened the tank with the other so she could move about and retain her only form of defense.

With her weapon in tow, she reached the temperature control panel and set it as low as it could go. The vents around the room immediately began pumping chilly air into the room.

"Why are you fighting me?" Cindy spoke in a smooth seductive voice.

"Because you're not yourself. They've poisoned you somehow," Lita called. "You're changing."

In a matter of minutes, the room had dropped to a temperature that affected Cindy and her followers' skin and movements. They shrieked and wailed at the biting cold air on their bodies and in their lungs as they breathed. The cold air even caused Lita discomfort as she pulled the sheets off the bed and wrapped them around her.

"You won't be going anywhere," Cindy stated in a sweet calming manner as the frigid air forced them out of the room. Lita glanced around the room for anything that could aid her and the others in their dilemma. *Are you your father's daughter or what*, she thought with a thin smile as she spotted all the electronic equipment around the room.

Cindy didn't understand what was happening. Why was Lita fighting her? Didn't she know the power they could achieve together? They could take down all of their enemies with this newfound magic.

A painful spasm started in her brain and shot a jolt down her back that almost caused her to drop her blood intended for Lita. A cold, like fire, burned her beautiful, pale skin and the bite from the icy air turned her flesh black.

Cindy opened her mouth but the scream that flowed out of it wasn't her. It felt like a combination of all the anguish of her children combined. She must stay away from the cold and protect her children from its sting. *Why is Lita hurting me?*

Soon the stinging air grew to an unbearable level, driving Cindy and her followers out into the warm air of the hall. Cindy watched her prey…her friend…through the glass window. Somewhere deep inside a twinge of guilt and sorrow nagged at her brain, but then a flood of information from her subject's memories and emotions increased her pleasure.

Bring everyone to me! She commanded and her people went to work. *Your time will come. I will cut the power.* She lusted after the lost power and knowledge she could obtain from Lita, but she had other things to do. *This tasty morsel can wait.*

Cindy walked the halls of her new kingdom without fear. She ascended the stairs to the next level where Mr. Toms and a few others held several people at gun point who were not infected by Cindy's blood. He had four bullet holes in his chest which oozed a black blood-like liquid. Cindy put her hand on his chest and she delved into the cellular level of her most powerful servant. Searching out his wounds, she commanded his body to repair itself. His pain was hers and she wanted it to stop. By healing her children, she grew stronger.

We've been sealed in. They aim to trap us here, Toms's voice spoke inside her head.

They won't be able to stop us, Cindy responded as she held up a syringe full of her blood. *Prepare them.*

Cindy's subjects brought out the prisoners, one by one, for her to inject her will into their veins. There was no stopping her. The thrill of each new store of information and memories heightened her senses beyond anything she had ever felt before. The warning voice telling her what she was doing was wrong soon fell silent. She had to make them pay for what they had done to her and to discover their secret plans.

There is great magic here, stolen from that man in Mr. Toms's memory. A book! The book? An image of the book joined a memory that seemed a hundred years old. In it her friends Max, Grandpa, and others sat around the table looking at the same book. *Max, Grandpa, help me*, a part of her cried. *They stole our book! A book that is within your reach, with great magic for you to claim.* The new Cindy smiled at the rush of this possibility.

Bits and pieces of new spells flashed through Cindy's mind after she absorbed the lives of her new subjects. *Bring me all the texts. The fools above won't hold me here! And turn up the heat. After I control this new magic, we will crush all resistance and spread our kingdom. There is none who can stop us. This pitiful little society will fall to my power. They will send more but I know how to protect us from their weapons. We will claim them and they will become one with us.*

Lita continued to check the hall beyond the windows, fearing Cindy's return. She breathed warm air into her cupped hands and rubbed life into her cold fingers. It had been over an hour since Cindy left, and no one seemed to be on her floor. *Perhaps she has forgotten me?*

She studied all of the electronic pieces she had taken from various computers and equipment in the room. She needed something to fuse her creation together. She shot another peek at the window and then the line of nitrogen tanks before she decided to walk around a bit for warmth. She peeked through the windows at her friends in their frozen state, and decided against opening the cryogenic chambers holding them. She didn't want more Cindys running around.

Lita frowned to herself after a search of the room didn't turn up anything that could be used to make the tools necessary to complete her project. She would have to make a trip out into the other rooms, and she needed to hurry before Cindy remembered her. She would have to avoid being seen by any of Cindy's zombies. Alerting them was akin to telling Cindy.

She went to the door to get a glimpse into the hall when she spotted the security camera in the hallway. *I guess it's time to hack the system. The more eyes I have the better.*

Lita went to the only computer she hadn't stolen parts from and turned it on. She jumped into DOS mode to avoid the regular operating system. Her thin pale fingers flew over the keyboard, diving deeper into the machine language, down to the ones and zeros. In a short time she had reworked the operating system and obtained access to all of the old files and programs.

"Now, to get into your security system," She muttered to herself. "Perhaps with the use of the cameras I'll be able to find what I need and get out and back as fast as possible before I'm discovered."

After Cindy took control of the entire floor she used her extensive knowledge of the structure to gain uncontested access to the floors above. After cutting into an air shaft used to remove toxic fumes created by the various experiments in several labs, they made their way to the floor above. Cindy waited until all of her children had reached the next floor before she attacked. A wave of Cindy's subjects swept over the occupants on the level above. With their attention focused on the elevators and staircases, Cindy's army overpowered them while she spread her control by injecting more of her blood into the recently captured people.

The new high created the desire for more power and more knowledge. Now Cindy had knowledge of military secrets and tactics. She trained her thoughts and her army on the control center of the whole operation that was two floors above. She gained possession of an arsenal of manmade weapons of all kinds, including chemical and biological agents. *These will be a last resort. They will rob you of knowledge and magic. These creatures are more appetizing when they are full of life for me to feed on.*

Proceeding from floor to floor, she set different groups of subjects to a variety of tasks: some captured more victims, while others began searching computers and files for all the information from the book. Others even started taking over the security and defense systems to the entire complex. *We must prepare for a fight and how best to expand my kingdom. Those inside this society know there is trouble here, but they are unsure about the extent of the problem.* She smiled to herself. *Let them come like yummy flies to the spider.*

"Sir, we have a problem at the facility." Agent Smith rushed into Tanner's makeshift office at their temporary facility.

"Just a second," Tanner spoke into his cell phone and then pressed the mute button. "We might have a bigger problem. What do you have?"

"We don't know what it is, but we've lost control of the operations center. It may be an outbreak of some kind. We received reports of people going crazy and attacking others. Someone reported Toms walking around like some kind of zombie. A guard claimed to have shot him twice in the chest and he just kept coming. Didn't even try to avoid the guard or take cover after receiving fire. Then there were reports of losing contact with some floors and now, nothing. There isn't any communications at all."

"There has to be someone on the inside. Call everyone's number we have there," Tanner ordered.

"Do you want to send in troops?"

"Negative. Set up a perimeter and don't let anybody out. If necessary, torch them."

"What do you have?" Smith asked, nodding to Tanner's phone.

"The Vice President has disappeared."

Smith's mouth fell open.

"He, a squad of commandos, and about twenty experiments—all gone," Tanner said, shocked.

"What's going on around here?" Smith asked.

"Get us the quickest transportation to the facility. Instruct the doctor to keep Mr. Rigdon heavily sedated, and get me all the data of anything going on back in his town," Tanner ordered.

"Got it." Smith dashed from the room.

Tanner unmuted the phone. "We're on it."

Lita flipped through the security cameras of the entire facility on her computer screen. After she found herself through the camera in her room, she checked the floor she was on for any signs of movement. She was relieved to find that level and the two floors above appeared to be empty. When she finally found all the workers and security to the facility, she couldn't wrap her brain around what she was seeing.

The people marched around like robots. Some of them moved with ease, while others appeared to be malfunctioning in their gait. Even their appearances had mutated. Their skin had turned a pale green color while their eyes were almost solid white. She gasped and almost fell out of her chair when she focused on Cindy.

Cindy was not the same girl she had met almost a week ago. She looked like a zombie queen out of a horror movie. Her skin was deathly white and her features were sunken looking like she was only skin and bone, as if something had sucked all the fat and muscle out of her body.

"I've got to get help," Lita muttered with fear. She rushed to one of the nitro tanks and snatched it up before heading into the hall.

Even though the cameras didn't show anyone in the hall she navigated carefully, expecting danger around every corner. Holding the nitro tank at the ready, she checked corners and behind all doors. Time seemed to freeze during the journey through the halls and the walk seemed to last forever. She couldn't remember ever being so scared in all her life. Losing one's will would be a form of personal hell. Did they realize what had happened to them—prisoners inside their own minds without control of their own actions?

She found the room with the necessary tools and collected the items she would need before running back towards the room with the others. A high-pitched cry propelled her forward blindly. Another scream joined the first and she glanced back to see one of the transformed humans, with its strange staggering type-movements, giving chase.

When she rounded the corner she spotted a second one hurrying towards her from the other direction. Carrying the heavy tank limited Lita's speed, and she pushed herself to make the door before being caught between the two creatures. She ducked under the one closing from the front when she turned into the room. Its vice-like fingers latched on to her arm and pulled her arm toward its opened mouth as if trying to bite her. Lita screamed and swung the tank around into the side of the thing's head, dislocating its neck, but still it held on. While the other closed the distance, Lita released the cold air into the hallway, unable to aim with one arm in the grip of the zombie.

The creature roared its pain and attempted to pull Lita out of the cold air where the other once-human waited to help it. Lita used the tank to knock the creature off its feet and pulled it deeper into the cold air where it finally released its lock on her arm. Lita almost fell into the room as the sudden freedom caused her to stagger forward. Before the cold air dispersed from the room, she regained her balance and sealed the door.

The creatures slammed their fists against the thick protective glass in a futile attempt to gain entrance. Lita hurried to the computer to see more of Cindy's things heading her way on the security screens. "I don't have much time."

Spreading the tools across the table, she went to work connecting computer boards and circuits with a soldering gun. She hooked the new computer up to one of the spare screens and keyboards from the ones she had dismantled.

The pounding on the window continued to grow as more and more of Cindy's zombies arrived. A few of them brought equipment and cracked open the control panel on the outside door. Lita found it difficult to focus on them and her task at the same time. *HURRY!*

Her fingers tapped out commands on her knew computer, writing a program to create the operating system and program it for her desired task.

Screams penetrated the room when the door to the room opened a few inches while fingers and hands tried to force their way through. A prompt flashed on Lita's screen just as the zombies pried the door open enough for Cindy's soldiers to enter the room one at a time.

Lita typed her message into the machine, hit the enter key, then grabbed a nitro container to prepare for her final stand.

21

Hide and Seek

"They're just men," Max's mother stated. "I thought they were some kind of weird creatures."

"How dare you endanger my life! I am the Vice President of the United States," the Vice President hollered. "I demand you take me back, NOW!"

The mysterious men seemed dazed and confused, not comprehending what was going on. They mumbled incoherent sentences and their arms jerked about at random intervals as if they attempted to swat invisible flies.

"You better watch it." Max smiled while shaking his head.

"You have no idea how *much* trouble you people are in," the Vice President continued to rage.

"Don't say I didn't warn you." Max chuckled while everyone but Sky eyed him curiously.

"What are you talking about?" Max's mother asked when Sky jumped in the face of the Vice President.

"What are you laughing at…?"

Before Cindy's father could finish his question, Sky jabbed the Vice President in the throat. He fell backwards while clasping his neck with both hands, gasping for air.

"That!" Max laughed. "You don't *ever* yell at Sky!"

"*You* have no idea how much trouble you are in." Sky smiled. "No one knows where you are. This could be your permanent place of residence. And in case you hadn't noticed by the monster trying to make lunch out of you, you aren't on earth anymore. So, if you ever want to leave this place, you better make me very happy."

"How am I supposed to do that?" he wheezed.

"By answering all my questions truthfully. Now, we brought you and your...men some supplies. I suggest you camp here and try not to draw any attention to yourselves. If you haven't noticed, the neighbors aren't very friendly here. And your companions seem a little out of sorts to let them wander about on their own."

"What's happening to them?" Cindy's mom nodded at the men, who appeared to be slowly transforming before their eyes.

Their skin, which had been a pale white, now had patches of color spreading on their bare arms, neck, and face. Pigment started to return to their eyes, taking away the albino look. Their faces, which had been stretched and taut, bubbled with features.

"I'm not sure," Max's mother responded.

"Pekel must be affecting their magic." Max shrugged his shoulders as if he was unsure of his idea.

"Forget them," the Vice President hollered while not daring to anger Sky by showing her up. "What do you want to know so I can get out of here?"

"Not just yet. Do you think we would trust an answer from a politician? A man who has made a living out of lying to the masses. No, I think you need a little time here in this lovely place to convince you that we control your life," Sky stated.

Max's communicator started vibrating with a message. He dug it out of his pocket and read the information. "Yelka received a signal from Lita. We've got to go!" Max's voice took on an abnormally high octave due to his excitement. Relief began spreading through him, nibbling at the dark shadow that had clung to him because of the loss of his friends. The guilt of not being able to help them had consumed his thoughts. Max's fingers typed instructions for Yelka to open the gateway nearby.

"Did she say anything about Cindy, the others?" Cindy's mother asked anxiously.

"No. Just that we have to hurry. There's trouble." Max tucked his communicator back in his pocket and took out his crystal. He waved it through the air and it flashed the location of the gateway. "There!" He pointed.

"Well, I suggest you ponder about how truthful you want to be when we return." Sky slapped the Vice President on the cheek playfully several times.

Everyone dumped the equipment they had brought on to the ground next to the Vice President and the evolving men. Then they all hurried through the gateway.

Yelka didn't bother to turn off the gateway or the force field when they stepped through. Instead, a brighter intensity from the gateway indicated she changed its location. She moved as close to the gateway as she could. "Take the weapons, they're in trouble. You are going into a hot zone," she yelled, with her hands cupped around her mouth like a megaphone, to be heard above the humming equipment.

"Barbara, Rachel, wait here. They may need medical assistance when we bring them back through," Sky ordered, drawing her sword. "I'll go first. Max, Jim, look before you leap." Sky hopped through the gateway.

Max poked his head through the gateway to see Sky spinning around a medical room with strange metal tube-like beds. Her sword flashed red, beheading men and women with every swipe of her blade.

"Help Lita. Aim for their heads," Sky instructed as she cut a swath through a swarm of attackers.

Max pulled his head back to the third floor of Grandpa's house. "Lita is in a corner to the left. Sky said to shoot the attackers in the head," Max told Cindy's father as he cocked his weapon and leaped through the gateway.

Max landed in the middle of a full-scale battle. Sky continued to separate the strange people from their heads with her white hot blade, while Lita sprayed a cloudy mist at the things, driving them back in shrieks of pain and anger. Max raised his weapon and blasted two of the strange humans right between the eyes. Seconds later, Cindy's father joined the fight.

Right in the middle of the struggle, the creatures just gave up like someone flipped a switch. They acted like robots, all turning in unison and making their way toward the door. They didn't run or rush to escape the slaughter. No one spoke. There wasn't a call of retreat or any indication how they all knew to leave at that moment, but they exited the room and faced them from the hall.

'Where's Cindy?" her father asked Lita, while Sky positioned herself in front of the door.

"I don't know but…but she controls all this. They hate the cold; it freezes their skin and hurts them." Lita started to cry from relief as she waved at the dead in the room and those watching them from the hall. "They were given some kind of virus. I think this has something to do with it. Look at the others." Lita pointed to the bed-like chambers.

Max and Jim raced to the chambers to peer through the glass windows at the strange change taking place to Martin and the others. Sky backed away from the door, holding her sword at the ready, to take a peek.

"We need to get them to Yelka right away," Sky urged.

"She's right," Jim stated, his face pale with fear. "What did they do to my daughter?"

"I don't know, but she's taking on another form. She's been injecting her blood into everyone and then she controls them," Lita replied.

Max and Sky exchanged a quick glance.

"Jim, take Lita. Have Rachel operate the gateway. We need Yelka to tell us how to move Martin and the others," Sky ordered.

"What about Cindy?" he asked, not wanting to leave.

"Let's deal with one thing at a time. We don't even know where Cindy is at the moment. Let's take care of those we can," Sky's tone softened.

Cindy's father nodded, and then he helped Lita into the gateway with the aid of his crystal.

"She's injecting her blood?" Max stated as if he had bitten into something bitter.

"I've seen this before," Sky said. "When I rescued you from the spider two years ago. These people act just like the spider's zombies. I had to behead those creatures to stop them as well."

"How could they have triggered that part of her? And why would she keep doing it?" Max glanced at the disturbing scene on the other side of the glass. His stomach started to spin, creating a sinking feeling. The thought of his best friend turning into a zombie spider gave him horrific chills. He bent over and picked up a syringe full of Cindy's blood and eyed it with fear. "I wonder if it would hurt me? I mean, I have the same poison flowing through my veins."

"I don't know. But I don't think you should try it. I can feel her magic and it has grown very strong. You might have the same blood, but you don't have her power."

Max peered at the zombie-like people watching them without really seeing. Their eyes stared straight ahead and didn't follow Max or Sky moving about the room.

"What are we going to do?"

"Let's get the others out of here first and then we'll help Cindy. I don't think we have to worry about anything worse happening to her. She does have an army."

Yelka hopped out of the gateway, along with Cindy's father. Her eyes swept over the battlefield and her face twisted into a grim expression. She actually gasped and jumped back a little at the sight of the people on the other side of the glass. "Why are they just staring?"

Sky glanced at Max and he shrugged his shoulders. He knew Sky was hesitant to share what they both believed with Cindy's father. "Ah…we think Cindy is controlling them."

"What?" Yelka sang in a higher octave than normal.

"First, what can we do for them?" Max interrupted, motioning to Martin and the others in the strange chambers.

Yelka peeked at Martin and then the others through the windows, noting distorted features and their strange growths, which appeared to be consuming them. Then she read the charts and checked the electronic monitors controlling their vital signs. "It appears their comas have been induced and their body temperatures lowered to control the spread of the virus," she said.

"What kind of virus?" Max asked.

"A magical virus. It is taking control of them physically and mentally. It appears it was given to them specifically. They wanted to see the results when given to someone who already has magical powers." Yelka held up a chart. "It says they gave it to non-magic people, but they didn't write down the results. At least not on these charts."

"How do we get them out of here?" Sky asked.

"We take the beds." Yelka frowned.

Cindy let out a terrifying scream that echoed through the halls. Pain racked her body, and she flinched and jerked against the overpowering anguish. The sensations flooded through her like her head was being separated from her body. Flashing through the minds of her subjects, she found the source of her agony. A woman and others killed her children. The woman's blade brought death and pain with each stroke.

Sky, Max, Cindy cried from a small corner of her mind and ordered her subjects to withdraw into the hall. *Why are you hurting me? You're causing me pain. You are my friends. Why would you do this to me? You should be helping me. I'm taking down this society, it's what we want.*

Why won't you join me? We can be so much more than we are. Cindy watched her friends through the glass and an overwhelming sadness crept through her, as if she would never see her friends again. They had grown apart and no longer wanted the same things. They didn't want to be with her. She tried to cry but no tears would come.

If you're not with me, you are against me. Anger coursed through her, replacing her sorrow. *I can make you comply.*

In another corner of her vision, Cindy spied several men dressed in nonmilitary gear rushing across the gap between the fence and her compound. *More. Bring them to me!* she ordered, and a section of her army went to intercept the newcomers.

Cindy took control of the entire complex. She had access to weapons, communications, and security controls. Her subjects worked to satisfy her every demand. They secured the area and captured any stragglers attempting to hide their knowledge from her. They acted like bees taking care of their queen.

She devoured all the spells and magic to be found in any of her army. There were some with a variety of skills she didn't have before, which she absorbed and fused to make her own. She chose an auditorium as her lair because of its almost impenetrable construction. Her knowledge of the complex told her there were very few bombs capable of penetrating this safe haven. They wouldn't dare detonate a weapon that powerful on American soil. *It would raise too many questions,* she soothed. *This society fears the masses they seek to control. They don't yet have the strength to seal the world's fate. Not everyone is as weak-minded as they believe.*

And now I will know all their secrets. I will do what they could not. Everyone will be united. She slid her fingers over the old leather bound book sitting on the desk in her new place of dwelling, walking in a circle around it. She flipped open the cover and discovered she could read the strange writing on the pages.

Bring me all who try to enter our home! Set a trap for those men who entered the compound on foot. I will hide you with my magic.

###

Hudich and Alan led the group of terrorists across the compound. No alarm sounded and no visible signs of life were revealed. When they reached the closest building, they all huddled in an area out of the bright lights shining down on the area.

"Are you sure this is the place?" questioned one of the Arabs.

"This is the place, but something is wrong," Hudich grumbled. He could feel a power stronger than he had ever sensed before. "We need to be very careful." He placed his hands on the building next to him and closed his eyes for several moments. "There isn't anyone in the area behind this wall," he said with his palms still flat against the building. The wall around his hands turned a white-hot color and it started to spread. The smell of burning metal floated on the air while a round hole the size of a door melted away.

The terrorists gasped and spoke rapidly in their language at what they had just witnessed.

Hudich and Alan ducked into the hole, with the Arabs in a tight knot behind them. They entered a dark, empty storage room with shelves stretching from the floor to the ceiling. A faint light entered through cracks around a pair of double doors on the other side of the room.

"What are we after?" questioned one of the militants following them.

"Weapons for you and a book for me," Hudich said, leading them across the room.

"What is in this book?" another asked.

"Things you couldn't possibly understand." Hudich paused and leaned against the doors to send out his feelers. After several minutes he stepped back and stared at the doors.

"What is it?" Alan asked this time.

"I'm not sure. Something or someone is blocking me. I can feel a strong magic, but it won't let me in and gives me false images. The magic is very old and extremely powerful," Hudich said.

"Do you want to go back?" Alan peered at the doors as if expecting them to swing open and consume them.

"No, two can play this game. We must become one with this place. Use our magic to conceal our passing. We are going to play a very dangerous game. One mistake could be fatal to our plans. Be ready to make a quick escape, if necessary," Hudich warned.

"And the others?" Alan asked with reference to their terrorists friends.

"Bait," Hudich whispered. "Get ready to check the building. Kill anyone who gets in your way." Hudich raised his voice for the Arabs to hear. "They are Americans, so strike hard."

"Allahu Akbar," the Arabs said to one another, preparing for battle.

"Fools," Alan muttered under his breath as they exited the room for the hallways beyond.

They remained in a tight unit, checking the halls in both directions for any signs of security. No alarm sounded and no one moved in the hall. No noise of any kind reached their ears from the structure itself. Nothing indicated anyone was around or alerted to their presence.

"No one's home," Alan said.

"Don't be fooled. They know we're here," Hudich acknowledged. "That way." Hudich pointed down the hallway to the left. "We need to find the stairs. This structure goes deep underground."

The Jihadists crept down the hall with their weapons clutched at the ready. Their heads rotated every which way as if they knew something was wrong. Even without any magic, the feeling of imminent danger permeated the structure. It crawled under their skin and entered their lungs when they breathed.

The group reached the end of the hall and turned to the right. They passed doors and darkened windows on both sides of the hall, but still no resistance. The temperature increased as they proceeded deeper into the complex, creating a stifling effect.

"Stop!" Hudich whispered, prompting everyone to freeze before they crossed in front of another set of double doors on the right wall.

The men crouched a little lower and raised their weapons in preparation for battle. Their breathing seemed abnormally loud in the empty hall. The leader glanced to Hudich, who stood tall in the center of the group, seeking instructions.

"Send out someone to scout around," Hudich responded.

The leader glanced at another and rattled something off in Arabic. The second man scuttled to the head of the group and advanced up the hall. He inched his way to the double doors where he took a peek inside. He glanced back at the group, shaking his head, and then continued past.

"Go," Hudich commanded and the group followed after the first.

The scout checked every window he passed before moving on. When he reached a door with 'Stairs' written in white letters across the front, he gave a soft whistle and said something in Arabic while nodding towards the door.

"He's found the stairs," reported the head Arab.

As they crossed in front of the double doors, the doors exploded outward and a wave of attackers poured into the hall. The terrorists fired their weapons into the throng with almost no effect. Cindy's subjects swallowed them up by their sheer numbers. The Arabs kicked and screamed while the zombies pumped Cindy's blood into their veins.

Hudich vanished and sprang out of the rush. The force of the attack bounced him off the wall, but he kept his concentration and hid himself with magic. Alan tried to use the disappearing spell to escape, but the push slammed him to the floor. Before they could inject him with blood, he engulfed himself in a magical fire that incinerated the syringe and ignited his attackers. Until his fire consumed their fingers they refused to let go, and more attempted to join their injured brothers and sisters.

As a last resort Alan cast the transportation spell, which ripped him out of their clutches and carried him out of the building.

Hudich used his magic to indicate to them no one was there, that he was a part of the building, one with them. He watched as those he brought with him succumbed to the power that lived inside this place. The last survivor at the end of the hall tried to help his friends, but the group conquered him as well.

Hudich envied this power and coveted it. This could be the ultimate weapon. A universe full of his slaves to control and dispose of at his pleasure. He would risk everything to have it, so he waited. It would take patience but it would be his.

A flood of a strange language flowed through Cindy's mind. It wasn't anything she had ever learned, but she understood it perfectly. *Terrorists on US soil? Here? How?* Cindy dove into their memories and the dark world of extreme Islam. These men treated women as possessions and loved death more than life. Cindy had never encountered souls so devoid of compassion for other human beings in her life. There was no remorse for murdering infidels, or children, or innocents they felt disgraced the family honor.

Cindy witnessed a secret base in the jungle on a remote island in the Philippines. There were several aspects to this secret base. It housed a high-tech communications center and a vast covered area where construction of multiple top secret weapons and other things were underway. Her new subjects worked on these projects for a strange-clothed man that hid his identity and would show up with instructions from time to time.

He always wore dark glasses and scarves over his head to hide his face. This man caused fear and loathing in all the Muslims there. In other memories this strange man appeared with another man who looked familiar. *Alan! Who is your friend? Hudich!*

Cindy jumped back to the plans to try to figure out what they were building. Hudich hadn't given them complete designs in order to keep the big picture from them, which frustrated her new subjects. They hoped it was a destructive weapon, but it was very large.

Then Cindy followed Hudich and Alan into the jungle where Hudich had his subjects hold hands. In a flash of light he transported them to her base. Cindy tracked them to the battle. *So, Alan got away but Hudich is here. He is playing hide and seek. I will find you, and your magic will be mine.*

We must protect the book. Build a trap around it, she ordered.

Max, Sky, Yelka, and Cindy's father prepared all the chambers so they could maintain low temperatures during transport to Grandpa's house. This required reattaching the tanks Lita had removed to defend herself from Cindy's people. They wheeled the chambers in front of the gateway, and together they lifted the first heavy chamber through the gateway.

The people outside the glass remained motionless with their blank stares. They stood so still they could have been statues.

"What are they doing?" Yelka wondered, continuing to glance in their direction.

"I think Cindy sees what they see," Sky suggested, as they pushed the next chamber into position. "She is watching us."

"What do you think has happened to her?" Yelka asked with a puzzled look. Her eyebrows raised on her tan face.

Sky shot a look at Max and then Cindy's father.

"You two think something, so let's hear it," Cindy's father said. "It's obviously not good, but let's hear what it is, and maybe we can figure out how to help her."

"We think she's becoming like the spider on Svet," Max said. "She's been injecting her blood into everyone."

"And look at them," Sky said. "If they aren't zombies, I don't know what is. The only way we can stop them is the same way I had to do it two years ago."

"Okay, so how do we help…?"

The people in the hall started shifting around and organizing into a human wall. They lined up several rows deep all the way across the hall. Then several rows of troops armed with strange weapons positioned themselves behind this human wall.

"We have to hurry," Sky ordered, and they all worked to pick a chamber off the ground and push it through the gateway.

The sense of urgency increased as Cindy's troops advanced through the door before they could retrieve the last bed. Max and Cindy's father hustled to wheel the one remaining chamber to the gateway. Sky slowed the progression of the human wall by removing heads left and right.

As the troops at the back of the wall forced their way through the opening, they fired loaded darts into the room. Sky whirled and ducked to avoid the small projectiles, continuing to hack into their structure. Yelka threw up a protective spell that shielded her from the objects.

"Forget the bed. Into the gateway," Sky yelled, while more and more darts flew all around the room.

The group rushed for freedom and dove into the gateway. They landed in a pile on the third floor and Sky sprang to her feet. "Turn off the gateway," she screamed, as multiple darts struck Max and Cindy's father through the still open portal.

22

Cindy's Funhouse

"I'm hit." Cindy's father crumbled to the floor.

"Me too," Max added, trying to yank out every dart he could reach. A surge of heat rushed to the areas where the darts had punctured his skin.

"What's happened?" Cindy's mother rushed to help her husband after the force field disappeared. She rolled him onto his stomach so she could tug the darts from his back and legs.

Yelka, Max's mother, and Lita aided Max in removing the darts he couldn't reach.

Sky nudged Cindy's mother aside and bound Cindy's father's hands behind his back and tied his legs tight.

"What are you doing? He's injured. Maybe poisoned," Cindy's mother protested with a shocked expression.

"He's contaminated and will not be himself in a few minutes," Sky said.

"But what's wrong with him?" Tears streamed down Cindy's mother's face. "And where's Cindy?"

Sky jumped in front of Max's face and locked eyes with him. "How are you feeling? Tell me the truth."

Max lost eye contact for a moment while his mother stripped his shirt off of him and Yelka began examining the wounds.

"Ahh," Max gasped as Yelka began to feel the injuries with her fingers.

"They are hard as if a small stone has been placed under his skin," Yelka informed them.

"They burn like crazy," Max moaned. "But so far I'm okay," he answered with a grimace.

"What's going on?" Cindy's mother had lifted her husband's shirt to reveal a different type of wound compared to Max's. Instead of round hard lumps, Cindy's father's were black and cracked, as if the skin was dying. A bloody puss oozed from the puncture wounds.

"You have to admit it, the girl is thinking," Sky said.

"What do you mean?" Yelka asked as she moved to Cindy's father who let out a hair-raising yell. Everyone jumped as the wail froze their blood.

"That last attack was genius. She knew she couldn't reach us otherwise," Sky said.

"Yeah." Max cringed away from his mother's probing of his wounds.

"What's happening to him?" Cindy's mother asked.

Max and Sky told Cindy's mother and Max's mother their theory about Cindy and what was happening to Cindy's father.

"What would make her do these things?" Cindy's mother asked, as her husband started to squirm against his bonds. He didn't speak or even roll over onto his back. His movements were lethargic and his struggles half-hearted.

"I think she might have had good intentions to start with but got in over her head." Sky tried to offer.

"I agree," Lita piped in, drawing everyone's attention. "She actually rescued me at first and acted fairly normal, but the more she passed her blood to others, that's when she started to change." Lita gave everyone the details of the events leading up to her call for help.

"How are we going to help her? My husband?" Cindy's mother sobbed, motioning to her zombie like husband on the floor.

"I think Cindy might have revealed the solution," Sky said.

"How?" Max lowered his shirt.

"You!" Sky said.

"What?" everyone questioned.

"Well, not just you. You can enter her lair. Her blood won't hurt you," Sky stated.

"How are painful round knots under my skin not hurting me?" Max complained.

"Okay, it won't influence you. You have the same poison in your blood. Her blood won't work on you," Sky said.

"And it won't work on Ell." Yelka's face reflected her understanding. "And Ell can penetrate her mind."

###

Daddy, Cindy cried in a corner of her mind. He was there but it wasn't him. She had access to his knowledge and his memories, but he wasn't the same man who had raised her. She craved his comfort and wanted him to wrap his protective arms around her. *Daddy, please help me.*

Yes, he responded in a trance-like fashion.

Help me? She pleaded again.

What would you have me do?

I need you to get me out of this prison. I want to be free.

I can't move.

Why won't you help me? Cindy could only see the floor through his eyes and hear voices in the background, but she could tell he couldn't move. His small view of the floor reminded her of someplace she knew that was far away.

Daddy, help me! Cindy submerged herself in her father's memories. She found some comfort in the scenes of her as a little girl with her father. How he had protected her and comforted her when she was sad or scared.

Daddy, talk to me! Why won't you come to me? A rage started burning inside her while frustration started to build. *You aren't my real father. You are a shell of him. Leave me alone! If you can't help me, I don't want you.* She thought bitterly.

###

"They still have weapons." Max pointed out when the small group made plans to help Cindy.

"Yes, but you'll be with Ell, and you both have that extra sense." Sky winked.

"You don't think there's another way," Max's mother protested. "Yelka, what do you think?"

"I'm afraid I agree with Sky. I don't know another way we can help her." Yelka frowned.

"There has to be a way to limit the amount of resistance they run into," Lita said. "Somehow use the gateway to remove some of her subjects."

"That's a good idea," Max said. "We lure some of them into the gateway and send them off to Pekel. They are part of the organization we are trying to take down, anyways. Plus you can't use magic in Pekel. It might actually limit Cindy's powers because it will sever her connection to them."

"Agh…what's going on here," Cindy's father suddenly spoke causing everyone to jump.

"Oh Jim. Oh Jim, what happened to you?" Cindy's mother helped him roll onto his back.

"How long have I been out and why am I all tied up," he grumbled.

Sky stooped over and cut his bounds. "Do you remember anything?"

"The last thing I remember was trying to get Martin and the others through the gateway. Then everything seems fuzzy as if I was in a dream, but it was one of those dreams where you can't see anything clearly. I thought I heard Cindy talking to me but when I answered, it wasn't me." He sat up and winced against his wounds. "What happened to me?" He reached around his back to feel the bandages.

"You took several darts loaded with Cindy's blood. You became a—a—a zombie," Cindy's mother said.

"If she can release her subjects, it should help bring her back. Ell has his work cut out for him. He's going to have to talk Cindy into releasing her subjects and relinquishing her power over them," Yelka said.

"Well, let's get started by taking care of some of the resistance. I say we dump them with the others," Sky added.

"We're going to have quite a collection on Pekel." Max half laughed.

"It'll be good for them." Sky smiled.

For the next hour they managed to transport thirty to forty of Cindy's subjects to Pekel. The operation of luring them into the gateway and then using a spell to push them back into Pekel worked three times before Cindy's subjects evacuated the area around the room. This allowed them to move the last bed without interference.

With the freedom to move around the room which held the temperature controlled beds, they fortified it and turned on the air conditioner. As a result of being stuck like a pin cushion by Cindy's subjects, Max donned some body armor while they brought Ell from Svet. They decided to keep Cindy's father back at Grandpa's, fearing that close proximity to Cindy could make him susceptible to her powers.

As they explained to Ell the circumstances around Cindy and what they needed him to do, he acted like a concerned parent eager to protect his injured child. Ell's bond with Cindy had been cemented in place from their adventure with the Zeenosees almost five years ago. Cindy had saved his life, and in return he helped Max and Grandpa rescue her. Although his appearance as a grotesque monster would frighten the average person, he had become a beloved member of the family. The size of a medium-sized elephant with rows of razor sharp teeth, he was a great asset. His ability to communicate through touch made him the best candidate to break into Cindy's mind.

First we have to find her and we might have to fight a small army to do it, Max informed him.

Anything to help Cindy, Ell responded.

You two will be on your own once you pass through the doorway, Sky informed them. *If she managed to get me under her power, you would not be able to reach her.*

They placed a thick tarp over Ell's back to help protect him from darts, and Max carried an unusual automatic weapon. He placed a hand on Ell's neck so they could communicate as they navigated the complex in search of Cindy.

"You might be able to ride him some of the way, I advise you to take advantage of that. You'll have a better angle to shoot from," Sky stated. "When you shoot, aim for the head." She handed Max a two-way radio. "Keep me informed."

"Got it." Max took a deep breath. Even though he knew Cindy's blood wouldn't affect him, a swarm of her subjects could tear him apart. Besides, who knows what kinds of creatures and weapons were stored in this facility. They had unleashed some magical creatures on the world, which meant they had more than physical weapons.

You ready? Ell asked, glancing backwards into Max's eyes.

Let's go get her. Use your senses. She has total control of this place. Who knows how she will react to us.

She really is in great danger of losing herself.

Yes. Max frowned and they entered the hall. A wall of heat slammed Max and Ell in the face, and they gasped for air.

As soon as they turned the corner, Max spotted the security camera in the upper corner of the hallway. Cindy knew they were there. Max took the lead and held his weapon ready. A complex like this would definitely have a service elevator to move larger objects between floors, but he didn't like the idea of being trapped in an elevator. While Cindy's army could corner them on the stairs, somehow Max thought the stairs would feel a little more open. He wondered if Ell could even fit into the stairwell.

They made an initial sweep and the floor appeared to be empty. Max reported this condition to Sky.

"She's clever, so stay on your toes," Sky ordered.

To Max's disappointment, there was no way Ell was going to fit into the stairwell by the main elevators. He put his hand on Ell's nose, *We need to find the service elevator or another set of stairs.*

It's hot in here, Ell panted.

I'm sorry. Sweat ran down Max's back and face, the extra armor increasing his discomfort from the heat. He could only imagine how unbearable it was for Ell with his thick fur coat. *Cindy turned up the heat. The cold bothers them.*

Maybe we should see if we can cool things off.

If we stumble across the heating and cooling equipment before we find Cindy, I say we do that very thing.

What if I can't get to any of the other floors?

Oh, I'm sure we'll find a way. This complex is huge, and they had to move equipment and supplies down here. It would be impossible without some way to get equipment between two different levels.

The floor was a lot larger than Max had imagined, with hallways continuing to turn left then right, and then straighten out again. Almost a half hour after they left the room, they found a dimly lit room the size of a basketball court. The room held a couple of large glass chambers where scientists could conduct experiments on deadly compounds and viruses by using electronic arms or by reaching in through the side with rubber gloves. There appeared to be garage doors on the far side of the room, but Max couldn't be sure in the poor light.

The greatest discovery for Max and Ell was a stainless steel wash area measuring twenty by twenty feet, with a four inch rim and several drains in the floor. Max smiled when he spotted the hose on the wall.

He touched Ell's side and told him to step into the basin. After he watered Ell down he doused himself in the cool water. The refreshing soak seemed to lift their spirits, and they left puddles of water in their wake as they moved toward the large doors.

We may have found our way up. Get ready, who knows what's be-hind these doors, Max thought before he pushed the button that opened the large steel door. He extended his finger and paused, holding it an inch away from the control.

He reached back and touched Ell's nose, *Do you feel anything?*

There is something right behind that door. I can't tell what. It is as if something is trying to block my senses.

I'm getting the same impression. I think Cindy is trying to hide what's behind this door.

That means there is a trap waiting for us beyond this door. More of her zombies or something else?

I think it's a zombie but it might not be human. Let's back up to the center of the room and I will open the door from there. That way we will be able to react before whatever is behind this door is on top of us.

Good idea.

Her powers have grown if she can hide things from us at a distance.

Yes. Who knows what she knows now if she can read all these people's minds. She might know spells I can't counter. Are you ready?

Yes.

"*Premakni,*" Max whispered, thrusting his hand toward the control panel. The spell pressed the open button and the large garage-like doors started to open.

Shadows danced all over the floor as the door rose higher and higher, but still nothing visible greeted them—only a large flat platform beyond. Screeching and wailing, almost like chatter in a crowd, drifted into the room when the door finished opening. Through the doorway they could see a spiraling ramp on each side of the platform, which disappeared to the left and right. On the left it climbed upward and to the right, downward.

They waited motionless, listening to the chatter continue, with shadows flashing across the platform floor. Max swallowed the dryness in his throat as his heart threw itself against his chest. He gripped the weapon with one hand and touched Ell with the other. *They're on the ceiling!*

They crept forward, their eyes fixed on the upper ceiling of the doorway. With each step the clicking and chirping increased in volume and frequency. Max wiped sweat and water off his face with his forearm to keep it from stinging his eyes and blurring his vision.

Max inched forward to see several winged creatures hanging from the ceiling. At first he thought they were bats, but these were something else. They were so black he couldn't make out any definite features except their blood red eyes containing vertical slits. They looked like living shadows, creatures without real substance, hanging upside down from the ceiling.

"Crap!" Max muttered when one of the creatures locked eyes with him.

A cry escaped the thing's mouth that raised the hair on the back of Max's neck and arms. The creature's mouth, which was full of barracuda-like teeth, just materialized out of the center of the shadowy mass.

Its signal triggered a wave of horrifying answers, and a flood of shadows zoomed through the garage door toward Max and Ell. The strange flying shadows were so thick the room became pitch black. Sharp razor like claws tore at Max and Ell's flesh, and painful bites penetrated Ell's fur and Max's clothing.

Ell snapped his bear trap jaws down, trying to devour the flying menaces, but they slid through the gaps in his teeth like liquid, to re-form and continue their assault. He jumped and twirled in an effort to twist his way out of their painful attack.

Max received a worse beating because he didn't have Ell's thick fur to shield him from the nasty teeth and claws of the black nightmares. Blood ran from several open wounds and the number continued to grow. "*Premakni!*" Max screamed while rolling his hands like a wave through the air. The spell flung the swarm off him, and Ell and slammed them into the ceiling and walls, but with no real effect. The second the spell's blast dissipated they attacked anew, as if receiving no damage to their liquid, shadowy-like bodies.

A second before they were on top of Max and Ell again, Max threw up a wall of fire which divided the darting creatures, forcing them to dive away from the consuming flames. They flashed their barracuda teeth and chattered their high, screeching protest, momentarily retreating.

To Max's disappointment, the creatures which had been burned by the fire dropped to the floor in soupy black puddles, and after cooling off they re-formed, rising up out of the puddles to reengage in the fight. Because the fire seemed to drive them away the best, Max cast the spell again, building a tornado of fire around him and Ell. Max could feel his energy waning and the spells had added to the already unbearable heat in the building. He pushed his fire outward and drove the creatures as far away as he could in order to catch his breath.

Max hunched over, breathing hard, resting on his knees when Ell bumped into him.

Look in the basin, Ell spoke to his mind.

Max's eyes locked on to several cracked solid bodies of the winged creatures lying in a puddle of water Max had created when he cooled himself and Ell off with the water.

Of course! Going from high heat to suddenly cool can break a liquid structure!

Get the hose, I can burn them, Ell stated.

The next wave of biting and ripping landed before Max could reach the nozzle. Ignoring the cuts and gashes all over his body, Max turned on the water. "*Premakni!*" Max screamed and drove the vicious nightmares off of him and Ell.

Max found the trigger to the spray nozzle and prepared himself. Ell waited until the creatures were almost on top of them and then he threw up a net of fire which he wrapped around the flying attackers. He closed off all possible routes of escape and started to close the trap. Sizzling, black liquid-like tar dropped out of the shrinking ball of fire. The second they hit the floor Max sprayed them with cold water, hardening their shells and destroying the bodies of the winged beasts. Their shrieks of madness turned to cries of pain and then silence.

Max breathed hard in the heat, staring at the steaming broken forms which littered the floor. Blood ran down his face and arms, and multiple tears covered his clothing. After a minute of regaining his strength, he walked over to Ell whose face oozed dark blood from several bite wounds. *Are you okay?*

Yes. Nasty little things, weren't they?

A loud roar echoed from the ramps beyond the open bay door.

I don't think Cindy is done with us yet! Max spun toward the noise.

That sounds a lot bigger than these things.

Max swung himself onto Ell's back. *Which direction do you think that came…?*

The roar reached them again, closer this time.

Below us.

Then let's climb.

Ell sprang through the open bay door and turned on to the ramp leading up when a beast larger and scarier than Ell emerged from the depths. The thing almost filled the entire tunnel while it rumbled forward, right on their heels. Its claws clicked on the cement as it ran. It appeared to be a massive, deformed, bald bear. Foot-long canines protruded from its gaping maw, and its muscular torso wore a broken and blistered skin.

If not for its enormous frame, which hindered its movements in the tight tunnel, it would have overtaken them. Instead, Ell managed to maintain a safe distance, circling the spiraling tunnel, climbing to the higher floors.

I think it's driving us into a trap. Ell suggested.

I could kill it or collapse the tunnel, but then we are corned with no route of escape.

When they reached the next platform, Max pointed his weapon at the closed bay doors and blasted an opening in one of them. *Into the hole!*

Ell dove through the opening into a storage room that was the same size and dimensions as the one below. Except this room held rows of warehouse-type shelves stretching from the floor to the ceiling. They raced down the center isle towards a door on the other side, while the beast behind them widened the hole with its massive claws. The shredding metal created a nails-on-the-chalkboard sound that vibrated the room.

The fact the beast didn't fit through the hole or in the narrow isle between the shelves seemed to enrage it. Its roars of madness chased the hairs up Max's back. A loud pop and then another sound of metal and concrete breaking rocked the room. A rumble, like the coming of a terrible storm, prompted Max to look back. The beast had collapsed the back two rows of shelves and they collided with the next, dislodging them from their bindings and creating a domino effect.

Faster! Max urged as the falling structures started to gain on them.

Ell smashed through the closed door and kept running, when the entire wall behind them crashed down in a cloud of dust and shattered concrete. The roars of the beast on the other side of the rubble barely penetrated the clog created by the cave-in. Supplies, bricks, steel, and various objects sealed it away from the area Max and Ell occupied.

Max held his weapon tight as the dust started to clear. He coughed several times in an effort to clear his lungs of the debris cloud. Dust and other particles stuck to his wet clothes and skin, giving him and Ell a chalky appearance. The rumble of the beast on the other side of the destruction told the story of an enraged hunter whose prey had eluded it.

Max gagged and spit the gritty air from his mouth. Ell sneezed and wagged his large tongue, also struggling for air. As Ell panted, his large tongue flashed with small items stuck all over it.

After placing a hand on Ell, *I don't think it's coming through any time soon. Let's see if we can find some water.*

Good idea, Ell agreed.

Max's eyes watered in an effort to rid them of dust while they moved away from the cave in. Both he and Ell continued to choke on the thick air, even after they had left the area affected by the dust cloud.

There. Max pointed to a water cooler bottle resting against the wall behind a security counter. He hustled forward and, using the dispenser, he filled a paper cup to rinse his mouth out before drinking some. Then he lifted the large plastic bottle out of its holder and flipped it upright. He hauled it around the desk to Ell, and with his knife he cut a larger opening. As Max pushed the water to him, Ell seemed preoccupied with something.

Ell stood with his head cocked backwards, looking at something behind him. He didn't move for several moments. Max's heart increased its pace. Max put a hand on Ell's shoulder. *What is it?*

There's something else out there. Can you feel it?

Ell's tone was so ominous Max sent out his magic through the floors and walls, expecting to find some new nightmare Cindy had sent after them. What he found was even more terrifying. The shock from what he discovered caused him to instantly pull his magic back.

What did you find? Ell asked.

Hudich is here.

23

The Race to Cindy

Hudich kept in the shadows, using his magic to stay hidden from Cindy's eyes. He took the form of one of her soldiers. He ventured deep into Cindy's lair, cautious not to be too aggressive, blending with Cindy's magic, and becoming a part of her domain. He told her he was her friend and part of her army, letting her see through his eyes but not revealing his mind to her. He lied to her, telling her she had already learned all she could from him.

He continued to use the invisibility spell while moving through the halls. He didn't want them to let her see him with physical eyes, as she might realize she hadn't really captured him. The deeper he penetrated her lair, the more cautious he became. She had installed trip wires set to inject an unsuspecting victim with her blood. Hoards of foot soldiers waited to obey her will and bring fresh minds and bodies under her control.

She is powerful, but she is new to this type of magic, he told himself. He knew if he waited and she learned to control her newfound capabilities, he would never get another chance to gain control of her.

"Hudich, I know you are here. I have the book and know its secrets," a soft seductive female voice spoke over the intercom speakers, running through the entire complex. "You can't hide from me. I can unleash spells that are more horrible than you can even imagine. They can destroy the body and enslave the soul. Kacha only scratched the surface of the power held within the book's pages."

A lust for greater magic swelled within Hudich's breast as the pleasing female voice confirmed his suspicions. He suspected the US government had gotten the book in order to dupe the majority of its citizens into voting a foolish incompetent into The Oval Office. *They couldn't have deceived so many without a powerful magic source.*

"Why hide from me, when together we could become more powerful than if we are separate," the soft voice continued. "Think about it. Together we could rule the universe. I'll give you a little time to think about it. After that, I will unleash things that will terrify even you."

"Max and Ell, I know you are here as well. I want you to join me, too. Imagine our minds as one. Please come to me," Cindy's strange soothing voice spoke.

So, I can capture the book and destroy Max at the same time. This should be fun! Hudich proceeded with even more caution, due to Cindy's warning.

When Cindy finished her announcement, Max stared at Ell with his mouth wide open. It amazed him how much Cindy sounded like Payek from two years ago. She did confirm what he and Ell had just detected, Hudich was in the building.

Ell put his foot on Max, almost knocking him over. *She just gave us away. Hudich now knows we are here. We will have to watch out for more than just Cindy's soldiers now.*

I can't believe how much she has changed. She wants to consume Hudich's mind. I wouldn't even want a small peek into that dark place. Worse, she's read that evil book and is threatening to unleash unspeakable things. They won't discriminate between Hudich and us, Max thought.

She needs our help before she sinks to a depth from which there is no return. We need to figure out her location, and fast.

How do we do that, this complex is huge. She could be anywhere. We need a map of this place. Maybe that will help us determine where she is.

You and I can find her, we have the ability. We will have to penetrate her magic and locate her.

I think only one of us should search for her and the other should keep watch, Max suggested.

Good idea. We should find a safe place to operate.

Max sped to a security desk a short way down the hall, with Ell right behind him. On a wall behind the desk was a layout of the floor. Max floated his finger over the map as he scanned the various rooms. "There." He tapped the room with his finger. "It's temperature controlled and there's only one way in. We can turn down the thermostat, which should hold off her friends."

They hurried to the room they had found on the map. Max immediately went to the control panel and set the temperature to thirty-two degrees. They noticed the change in the air almost immediately. Max jammed a chair under the door handle and joined Ell.

After he placed a hand on his neck, *I think you should be the one to find her. You are the one who will be able to penetrate her mind so if something happens to me, you can keep going.*

Max blew warm air over his hands and rubbed them together. He could already see his breath in the cold air. He took up a position where he would have a clean shot at the door, while Ell lowered himself to the ground and closed his eyes.

###

Cindy watched Max and Ell slip through the trap intended to drive them toward her. Through the eyes of her servants monitoring the security cameras, she knew everything that was happening in her lair. Now they had entered a room on the floor below her and adjusted the temperature. *They call themselves my friends, when they hide from me and cause me pain. That room won't protect them. I know a spell that will bring them into my fold.* Cindy patted the leather-bound book affectionately.

First I must deal with Hudich. He is the greater threat to my kingdom. I need to make him reveal himself. She flipped the book open to a page with crudely drawn sketches of people holding their heads and screaming as if being tortured by something.

Ah, the haunting spell, this should mess with Hudich's mind. Cindy smiled wickedly. *Duhovi najdi Hudicha!*

A wailing, as if the damned in Hell had arrived, filled the halls of the complex, followed by the rushing of wind. Transparent distorted figures materialized all around the room before making their way into the halls to begin their hunt for Hudich. Whispers of doom mingled with the moaning and the blowing wind.

Others of her servants relayed information of a massive force assembling around the perimeter of the complex. Dozens of helicopters, carrying a vast contingent of armed troops, dropped their loads just outside the fence. More forces driving military vehicles created a cloud of dust as they zoomed up the dirt road to the complex.

Ah, more memories and knowledge. Cindy hungered for those things like a starving person desired food. She jumped into the minds of a group of scientists working on a bomb inside a lab.

How's it coming? she asked, even though she knew the answer. A part of her held to the old tradition of conversation with her subjects, even though they never answered. They only executed her will. The plans and the complex equations flashed through her mind, telling her that her test project was ready. *I wanted to use the first one on Hudich. Build another*, she ordered the scientists.

She flashed into the mind of Mr. Toms and other trained soldiers. *It's ready. Take it to the surface and deploy it.*

Colonel Jackson stepped out of a helicopter and walked to the fence. "Tear it down."

All around the perimeter fence, troops wrapped cables around support posts and then attached the other ends to vehicles. Engines roared around the fence as tires flipped dirt and rocks everywhere, ripping the structure down.

With the fence gone, troops took up strategic positions around the area. Several snipers set up on a small hill overlooking the complex, while others made ready in jeeps and other military vehicles. Several helicopters circled the area from above.

"What do we have here? Any eyes on the inside? Hostages?" the colonel asked.

"Unknown, sir. All we know is we've lost communications," a captain reported. "They do a lot of top secret research here, sir. It could be some chemical or biological agent got loose, but all of our security and detection devices have been deactivated. The only biological agent that could do that sort of thing walks on two legs, sir."

"Send in a squad," the colonel ordered.

"Shall I have them suit up just in case, sir?"

"Do it."

The captain barked out orders for a team in chemical suits to make a general sweep of the complex. In a matter of minutes, a squad of a dozen men wearing yellow hazmat suits and carrying detection devices, jogged across the distance from the fence to the outlying buildings.

Before the men reached their destination, the doors to another building opened, and Mr. Toms and a group of soldiers emerged, carrying an object covered with a tarp. A gust of wind whipped up a dirt devil, causing the tarp to flap in the rushing air, but it didn't reveal its hidden contents. A soldier bringing up the rear hauled a metal frame of some sort, which appeared to have legs. The group went about their business as if they didn't care about the army around the perimeter, or the troops in the open only a hundred yards away.

"Tell the squad to hold up and get me a bull horn," the colonel ordered at the sight of military personal exiting a building in the center of the compound.

The captain gave the order through a radio and the men in the hazmat suits stopped in the open area and took up defensive positions. A soldier brought a megaphone to the captain, who in turn gave it the colonel.

The colonel put the device in front of his mouth and spoke into it. "This is Colonel Jackson of the United States. We are here to take control of this facility. You need to stop what you are doing and put your hands in the air so we can identify you."

Cindy's soldiers continued to execute her orders as if nothing else existed around them. They reached a spot in the center of the compound, and the man who had been in the rear put the stand on the ground. The others lowered the object onto the stand and removed the tarp to reveal a bomb.

"*Freeze*," the colonel screamed into the megaphone at the sight of the weapon.

Cindy's subjects ignored the colonel's command and adjusted the bomb so that the weapon stood vertically. Mr. Toms stepped forward and began programming the weapon.

"Take them out now," the colonel ordered, and the snipers opened fire on the group.

The projectiles struck their targets in the chest, knocking the zombie-like men to the ground and breaking their limbs. Everyone waited for a few moments to verify the targets were down.

"Tell the bomb crew to contin..." the colonel didn't finish his sentence.

All of Cindy's wounded subjects struggled to their feet.

"What the heck," the captain spat with a stunned expression.

Mr. Toms activated the weapon before another round of fire tore through the group.

"Pull them *out*," the colonel ordered, and the captain relayed the message.

The group in the hazmat suits turned and sprinted towards the perimeter when the device went off. A loud pop echoed over the complex and a reddish cloud shot into the air and rolled over the entire area.

"It's a chemical weapon," the colonel yelled when the mist reached them. The shockwave transported the agent through the air in a miles wide circle.

Troops tried to cover their faces in an attempt to avoid breathing the chemical in but succumbed to the haze from the weapon. The men in the hazmat suits tried to rush to the aid of their fellow soldiers but to no avail. The toxin overcame all the soldiers sent to assess the situation, in mere moments. Their eyes became a milky white and took on a glazed look, but otherwise they appeared fine.

One of the circling helicopters managed to swerve out of the path of the rising red cloud, while three others dropped like stones after the cloud enveloped them. Seconds before they crashed to the earth, the pilots regained control and flew them upward. They hovered for a few seconds and then they rotated in the direction of the one copter that had escaped Cindy's control.

"What's going on with them?" asked one of the soldiers, watching the three helicopters engage the fourth. Even though the one had a lead, surprise and the skill at which Cindy guided her puppets was too much for him. The helicopter exploded in a ball of flames and black smoke before chunks of flaming metal and debris dropped to the ground.

"What the…what do you think it was?" asked one of the soldiers in the suits.

"We…ah…I think we've got bigger problems," stated a third as he noticed the perimeter. Every soldier around the complex stared at them with blank expressions. They didn't raise their weapons in a threatening manner, just marched towards them, closing the circle.

"What do we do?" asked one of the men.

"I don't…" the highest ranking officer panicked. "They're on…our side. Aren't they?"

"Not anymore," another hollered and he opened fire, cutting through a section of oncoming zombies. The others attacked as well, mowing down large sections of Cindy's subjects, only to be dumbfounded when they staggered to their feet, broken but undeterred in their mission.

"Everyone fire into the middle. When they are down we'll make a break for it," one suggested, and they all blasted a section about twenty yards across of the tightening noose, creating a break in the chain.

"Run," another shouted, and the group sprinted for the opening. Before they could gain their freedom the helicopters appeared. They hovered in front of the soldiers, exploding the dirt yards ahead of their escape, stopping them in their tracks. Their momentary pause was all the time needed for Cindy's subjects to crash upon them like a storm. The men kicked and screamed as Cindy's army ripped them out of their hazmat suits and prepared them for injection.

I must reach Cindy before Max. Hudich smiled to himself as he continued to be one with Cindy's magic. *This could be an excellent opportunity to get the book and rid myself of that old fool's replacement.*

He held his invisibility spell steady to avoid being seen by Cindy's subjects, which really meant being spotted by Cindy. He moved only when her magic allowed, as it ebbed and flowed through the building, searching for him. *She is very powerful. I must be quick before my strength fails me.* His prolonged use of multiple spells started to zap his energy, and the weaker he grew the greater the possibility of detection.

"Hudich!" a voice whispered at the corner of his senses.

"Hudich. We will have you," another small voice joined the first.

Hudich glanced up and down the hall for the speakers. *She found me?*

"Hudich, we see you."

"If we see you so does she," the ghost-like voices continued.

Remain focused! She's trying to trick you. Clever girl. It's just a spell. He waited in a corner as a wave of soldiers wandered by his location. None of them turned or gave any indication they knew he was there. *If she knows where I am, they would have attacked.*

"She does know where you are. You're walking into a trap," the soft whispering voices continued.

"We're telling her where you are. She sees you. We see you. You can't hide from the dead," another voice spoke.

Out of the corner of his eye a white mist flashed by; his head jerked in its direction. He stared down the hall as more of Cindy's subjects staggering by.

"You can't escape the dead. We know your secrets, Hudich."

Another flash of a ghost-like figure moved at the edges of his vision, just out of focus.

Ignore them. You have a job to do. Hudich continued to be one with Cindy's senses, a part of the building, its furniture, its walls, and its doors. He slipped from his spot in the corner and kept pace with a group of soldiers in hazmat suits.

"You can't ignore us. We know your location. She will have you. We will have you. You will be one of us, soon."

Max gripped the gun tighter when a group of Cindy's soldiers walked in front of the large window showing the hall. They didn't go to the door but stopped in front of the window and faced him. Even though their eyes stayed forward, it didn't appear as if they were looking at anything in particular.

He glanced at Ell, who was in deep concentration, before watching a cloud of his warm breath float through the air. A soft whisper caught his attention, snapping his head toward a corner of the room where he thought it had come from.

Then another voice behind him prompted him to whirl around, aiming the gun in the general direction. Soon, there were soft murmurs all around him, increasing his heart rate, raising the hairs on the back of his neck.

It was as if the room was full of ghosts. He checked Ell. *Still in deep concentration.*

After a few minutes the unrecognizable voices grew clearer.

"Hudich, we see you."

"She sees you. She will have you," the spectral-like voices taunted. "The dead know all. Join us, Hudich."

"But, I'm not Hudich." Max couldn't help himself. He wanted the spine-chilling voices to stop, but they only increased their eerie calls.

Soon, ghost-like figures and mists jumped at the edges of his visual field. "She's unleashed something. Some kind of spell. It's just an illusion. She's trying to flush Hudich out."

The color drained from Max's face, and he turned his focus back to Cindy's subjects to see them standing in the doorway. They hadn't entered the room but appeared to be preparing to do so. Max realized the temperature in the room had increased because he could no longer make clouds with his breath.

He hustled over to the thermostat and tried to adjust the device but without success. No matter what he did, it appeared Cindy had locked him out of the system. The ghostly voices continued their spooky taunts directed at Hudich, and the see-through shadows danced just out of his direct line of sight.

Max took a deep breath, preparing for the coming attack. "Cindy, did you forget the new spells we learned over the last two years?" Max muttered to himself as he swung the gun over his shoulder.

More of Cindy's subjects crowded the hallway, creating a log jam which would make it impossible for Max and Ell to pass. They continued standing with their zombie-like gaze into nowhere.

Max positioned himself in the direct path of the entrance and about ten yards back from the door. He tried to swallow against the dryness in his mouth and wiped his sweaty hands on his pants. *Hurry Ell.*

"Why are you fighting me, Max?" Cindy spoke in a soft calm voice that issued from the speaker system and reminded Max of Payek two years ago.

"Why are you attacking us?" Max countered.

"I want you to join me. Be one with me," she spoke.

"I thought we were already on the same side."

"But we could be so much more." Cindy soothed. "So much more powerful than we are now."

"You mean you could be so much more. We would just be your slaves. No thank you," Max fired back. The doors to the room flew open and a wave of zombies rushed in.

Max thrust his arms forward, "*Snezi!*" A rush of biting wind and a snow storm slammed into the oncoming attackers, freezing their skin.

Moans and shrieks at being caught in the sudden surge of frigid cold air, stopped Cindy's subjects. Arms and legs flailed as a mad scramble for the hall commenced. Cindy's soldiers fought and climbed over the top of each other to clear the exit.

A rage at Cindy's transformation surged through Max, helping him hold on to the spell. He threw out such a storm that snow drifts started to grow around the corners of the hall. The wind chased Cindy's subjects out of the halls and into adjacent rooms in an effort to stop the flesh killing cold.

Max dropped to his knees when he finally released the spell. His chest heaved in and out, trying to catch his breath. Although the spell drove Cindy's subjects away, the ghostly figures continued their bone chilling taunts, floating just out of focus.

Ell pressed his head against Max's back. *I know where she is. She's in an auditorium on the floor above us. She sits on a stage surrounded by her subjects and other dangers. Hudich is getting close to her. She lures him with the book. Cindy is in a very dark place very near a point of no return. I fear if she takes Hudich she will be lost forever. If Hudich gets hold of the book, he will destroy her.*

24

A Violent Reunion

Then we need to reach her before Hudich does. If she's in an auditorium with a stage, there may be access from below. Do you think you can get us directly under her?

Yes. We need to hurry.

Max held on to Ell's head and Ell helped Max to his feet.

Can you walk? Ell asked.

No. Max took a deep breath. *I can run. It will be easier to run than to expend more magic.*

They raced through the doors and out into the hall where they tramped through large puddles of water created by the heat in the building and by Max's spell. Ell took the lead, navigating the halls with the use of his senses. A swarm of Cindy's subjects gathered behind them where they had dashed through the halls after hiding from the storm.

Ell acted like a massive bowling ball, racing ahead. He smashed into Cindy's subjects like a charging bull, smashing and knocking them out of the way.

Max, still trying to recover from the sustained use of his last spell, gulped large mouthfuls of air in the stifling heat. Sweat streamed down his forehead, stinging his eyes and leaving a salty taste in his mouth.

Ell crashed through a set of double doors into a darkened room. He spun and faced the door after Max caught up to him. The hair bristled along his neck as he bared his teeth to the attackers pursuing them.

In one fluid motion Max swung the weapon off his shoulder and opened fired. He aimed high, squeezing the trigger, releasing Cindy's subjects from her hold on them in the only way he knew how.

"NO!" Cindy's strange new voice screamed through the speaker system. "Argh!" She sounded like she was in pain.

After mowing down more than a dozen subjects, the rest of them fell back, taking refuge in the adjacent rooms.

We are below the auditorium, Ell stated as Max put his hand on Ell's side.

Max ran his hand along the wall while keeping an eye on the hall. When his hand felt the light switches, he flicked them on. They stood in a large room with a high ceiling, which sat under the stage. It appeared to be originally used for lifting and lowering scenery and stage settings, but now it was a storage room for basic office equipment. There were chairs and desks and other types of office furniture littered around the space. Ropes and pulleys ran from the ceiling above to the floor.

After Cindy's subjects retreated, the ghosts with their whispers directed at Hudich returned. Max figured it was just a distraction to flush Hudich out, because they didn't seem to realize he and Ell were not Hudich. They flashed at the corners of their eyes and whispered about Cindy having *him*.

Walking around the room under what Max figured was the stage above him, he studied the ceiling. He noticed several pins holding the stage in place and a system of wheels and gears that hinted at the possibility of lowering the structure. He checked the room and spotted a rolling ladder in the corner.

Rushing to Ell, he placed a hand on his side. *We need to drop the ceiling. Help me clear all this stuff out of the way.*

Ell turned into a bulldozer; lowering his head, he smashed, crushed, and pushed desks out of the way. Max picked up the broken fragments and threw them in a pile so he would be able to push the ladder around the room without interference.

"Max, what are you doing?" Cindy's strange soothing voice questioned through the speakers.

Max shot a glance at the halls to see Cindy's subjects remained out of range. *She's going to do something.*

We have to hurry. I think Cindy is going to attack with greater firepower, Max told Ell.

"How's it going?" Sky's voice crackled through the radio, nearly giving Max a heart attack.

Max almost dropped the radio in his rush to respond. "We're okay. Can't talk at the moment."

"Okay, just worried, I've heard gunfire."

"Talk when I can." Max tucked the radio back in his vest.

"I don't want to hurt you, Max and Ell, but I can't let you do what you're planning," Cindy said.

Max pushed the ladder under the first pin he came to and hustled up the ladder, while Ell continued to clear the area. A large bolt latch secured the stage to the auditorium above. It took a lot of effort for Max to rotate the latch and slide the bolt free.

"Don't force me to *kill* you," Cindy stated, her voice soft but with an edge to it.

She is very powerful, Hudich thought to himself, listening to Cindy speaking to Max and Ell. *She has turned on her friends, which makes her even more dangerous. I can no longer manipulate her by harming them.*

The ghosts continued their taunts all around him, but he ignored them, seeing them for the distraction they were. He waited against the wall, still under the cloak of his magic. The room he wanted was across the hall. He only needed an escort to take him inside.

After a couple of minutes, several of Cindy's children entered the room, with Hudich right behind them. The sight that met his eyes shocked even him. He stood in an aisle of a large auditorium. The entire structure had been set up like a giant spider's web. A figure he barely recognized as Cindy sat on a crystal-like structure in the center of a stage. Razor wire ran all through the auditorium in a web-like pattern. The book sat on a table a few feet from Cindy's perch.

"You want this, don't you?" Cindy's twisted arm reached out and caressed the book. "I know you are here, Hudich. You've hidden yourself from my eyes well, but I know you are in the room. You can't totally conceal your presence from me. I know we've been enemies in the past but, together, we would be so much more powerful. I know you've come for the book. I know its secrets and I have mastery of its power. Soon, everyone on Earth will be one. True peace will come to Earth, with me as its master. You could help me spread my kingdom throughout the universe. Join me!"

"As your slave? I don't think so. I will have the book and you will be dead." Hudich sent his voice from another area of the room.

"I'm sorry to hear that. It would have been so much easier if you came willingly. Oh, but I must tell you, you will never again leave this

place. If you disturb even one wire, you will be mine and then I will take all of your followers. Your organization will be mine. You will be a valuable weapon in my collection."

"We shall see." Hudich chuckled, bouncing his voice off a different wall. "You are powerful, but inexperienced. I have lived longer and faced greater threats than you." Hudich could sense this last statement might not be true. He had never seen anyone take total control of so many in so short of time. It was very old magic. *Older than him. Perhaps older than the book.*

He observed Cindy's subjects moving around the outskirts of her elaborate web. There wasn't a soul between the edge of the web and Cindy. The web didn't just form a large circle, it created a structure which stretched from floor to ceiling like an enormous three-dimensional object. Cindy's chair and the table actually sat above the ground, supported by thousands of threads.

"Come to me. Join me," Cindy tempted in her most flattering voice.

"I will come, but only to kill you." Hudich let his voice be heard from his current location. "Every maze has a solution. I will come."

"Take your best shot. If you use magic, you will be mine."

As one of Cindy's subjects passed his location, Hudich shoved him into the web and vacated his hiding spot. The second the subject made contact with the wiry web the strings sprang to life. It was like a giant invisible spider snatched the man out of the air and wrapped him so tightly in the web-like wire, cuts formed along any exposed skin. Millions of robot-like spiders the size of a fist popped out of the air and swarmed the victim, injecting him with hundreds of mechanical fangs.

"There will be the same type of reaction to the use of any spells against me," Cindy said with confidence. "My defenses are sound."

"What if my spell just destroys everything in this room but me?" Hudich tested.

"If you are so confident in your powers, why don't you give it a try," Cindy taunted.

Max slid down the handrails and pushed the ladder over to the next pin. A growl from Ell stopped him before he could climb the stairs again. Cindy's subjects lined the halls, carrying an array of weapons.

"Block the door," Max yelled. He used all the energy he had to cast a spell. His magic lifted a good portion of the destroyed desks and shelves and dropped them in front of the doors.

Ell following Max's lead and began adding to the pile. Ell jammed the mess into the doorway when Cindy's subjects opened fire. Bullets penetrated the wood and other debris blocking the doorway. Ell and Max jumped behind the wall to shield themselves from the barrage of bullets.

What are we going to do? Ell asked. *We need to hurry. Hudich is in the auditorium as well.*

We can't let them pin us down or occupy our time, Max said. He dropped his hand and prepared his weapon while casting the shield spell. Racing in front of the pile, he held down the trigger. Bullets ricocheted off his shield while he ripped through the barrier and into Cindy's subjects.

Max's wild shooting only caused a slight pause in the surge from Cindy's subjects. More and more bullets shredded the barrier, sending wood splinters and chunks of laminate flying away from the pile. The top of the pile gave way first, and pieces of shattered furniture started rolling off the top like lava from an erupting volcano.

Max's eyes scanned the room for a possible solution. When his eyes came to rest on a fire extinguisher, he didn't hesitate. He yanked the red cylinder off the wall and once again using the shield spell, he raced back to Ell.

We need to just wipe them out, Max said with disgust. *I don't think we will be able to accomplish what we need to otherwise.*

I agree.

When the barricade fails, I will toss the fire extinguisher into the entrance and shoot it. This should give us some time to knock out the pins.

If they...

Before Ell could finish his sentence, the gunfire stopped. A creaking sound replaced the sudden silence before the pile started to slide back into the room. The scraping of the pile grated off the walls.

Get back!

After the explosion, don't worry about me, just take out the pins holding up the stage!

They scooted all the way against the wall as arms reached in between a narrow gap in the blockage and the door frame. The pile shifted again, and a single subject of Cindy's squeezed through the tight gap.

Boom! Max fired, releasing him from Cindy's spell.

Boom! Boom! Boom! Max created a blockade in the tight opening.

One long hard surge pushed the pile several yards into the room. Max tossed the fire extinguisher into the center of the opening but immediately lost sight of it in the crowd. Aiming high he held down the trigger and waved the automatic weapon back and forth, releasing several waves of Cindy's children from her control.

Max continued to fire until he emptied the clip. He released the empty case onto the floor and struggled to get a new one out of his jacket. His slight delay gave Cindy's army the opening they needed to pour into the room. A flash of fur and a brisk wind spun Max in a circle when Ell sprang forward. His jaws snapped shut like a steel trap as he ripped his way through the swarm of zombies.

Ell pushed the fight back into the hall and out of sight. Max glanced at the hall and then at the ladder and made his choice. He rushed up the ladder and fought to release the second catch. After he rotated the bolt to open, he hammered the butt of the gun against the bolt until it released.

He hustled down the ladder and pushed it underneath the next pin. He had just started up when gunfire rang out in the hall, drawing his attention. "Ell," he muttered, then shot up the ladder. With renewed urgency, he released the third pin. His heart raced and the heat caused him to sweat profusely. After wiping his eyes, he counted eight more pins. "This is taking too long."

Still no sign of Ell, and the gunfire continued while he struggled with the fourth pin. "COME ON!" he screamed, pounding it free with the butt of the gun once more. Each new pin was harder to release than the one before. The weight of the shifting platform pinched the next pin tighter in place.

With each passing moment his concern for Ell grew. Even if he managed to get Cindy down to this level, he couldn't speak to her mind like Ell could. Ell was key to the plan to save his best friend. Releasing the eighth pin, he realized the area had grown quiet. He decided to take out the ninth pin before going in search of Ell. This pin was wedged so tightly, Max's hands slipped off the bolt and slammed his knuckles into a wooden support beam. "Ahhh," he growled and swung the gun like a baseball bat, flipping the bolt to the position needed to remove the pin.

A muffled rumble, like someone struggling to speak, drew Max's attention. The entire room was full of Cindy's soldiers. Near the door they carried a tightly bound Ell. It appeared they had wrapped him in a cocoon, with only his nose and eyes showing. Their eyes met and Max didn't hesitate. He swung the gun several times, knocking out the ninth pin.

Cindy's subjects scrambled up the ladder toward him. *"Premakni,"* Max screamed, flinging them back down the stairs, knocking each other over like dominos.

Max climbed onto the top railing of the push ladder, while Cindy's soldiers regained their balance and climbed back up the ladder after him. Max stood with his legs bent, eyeing the final pin ten feet away. As the zombies reached the top of the ladder, Max inhaled a deep breath and jumped, *"Preselim se pinu."*

He twisted his body with the gun held like a baseball bat as the spell launched him through the air. Upon reaching the final pin, he swung the gun around and unlocked the bolt, before he landed on top of a tight knot of Cindy's people. Max screamed as he struggled to keep Cindy's subjects at bay.

Before Cindy's subjects could secure him, Max rolled onto his back, pointed the weapon at the final pin, and pulled the trigger. The bullets exploded into the pin and its casing, destroying the final lock holding the floor up. A loud pop echoed off the walls when the floor shifted and dropped about a foot.

Hudich dodged and maneuvered around Cindy's subjects, seeking a solution to Cindy's maze. He inspected the mass of web-like wires which filled the entire room. He didn't see them at first, but after he threw Cindy's robot into the structure and witnessed the response, Hudich could now see the tiny mechanical spiders. They used the shadows of the web to make it look like they were a part of the network. Their bodies the same color as the web itself.

I must become a spider to walk on the web, Hudich thought. *Be a natural occupant of the structure. Use the web, not trigger it.*

Hudich found a hole in the center of the web that resembled a tunnel leading in a straight line down to Cindy. No wires crossed this four-foot wide circle. It was as if an invisible drainage pipe had been built in the middle. Distorted and twisted, Cindy sat upon her throne at the end of the tunnel.

This could be a trap. Hudich slid onto the web, using the wires like a spider would. With his hands and feet he walked across the lines, lightly as a spider, without alerting its host to his presence. He kept his weight distributed across multiple strands at all times, avoiding the mistake of most spider's victims of vibrating a particular strand.

He managed to descend several yards into the hole when an enormous pop rattled the entire web. The structure shook hard and from every direction, but the electronic spiders remained inactive. Hudich had just regained his nerves when Cindy's platform dropped a foot into the floor. The sudden jolt knocked many of the small spiders out of the webbing and onto the floor. They hit the floor but did not attack. The tunnel became tighter and twisted. At the end of the shaft Cindy hissed, her head spinning in all directions.

Another loud crack rang out, snapping through the web like a whip. Cindy's platform jerked downward another foot before stopping, almost knocking her out of her chair.

"Man the wheel," she hissed.

Arms seized Max everywhere, twisting and scratching his skin. Cindy's voice rang out with rage and panic. "Man the wheel."

All of Cindy's subjects dropped Max and Ell to the floor and rushed to secure the gears from lowering Cindy's throne any deeper. Max sprang to his feet, the gun still in his hand. Pressing the weapon to his hip, he leveled it at just above their shoulders and pulled the trigger. Rotating his hips back and forth, he decreased the number of Cindy's army by several dozen. A large number of bodies littered the floor, creating a small pile.

Even after the last one fell, Max continued to fire at the gears and wheels, destroying the mechanism. Chains and wheels broke and snapped, releasing the floor which dropped like an out of control elevator.

Max's heart dropped with it as his eyes focused on Ell. *"Premakni,"* he screamed, sliding Ell out of the way before he dove clear of the crashing structure. The stage landed at a slanted awkward angle due to the pile of bodies which were next to the crank. The pile held a corner of the stage off the ground.

The sight that met Max's eyes terrified him. Cindy's face and body appeared stretched and elongated, and her eyes were like great orbs without pupils. Instead of her even white smile, there were large fangs protruding from her upper lip.

She rose from her throne like a pale ghost and her eyes locked on Max. "Max," her voice turned back to its seductive tone. "Come to join me."

"NO!" Max barked. "I've come to help you."

"I don't need your help. You need mine. Soon you will understand. It will all be over in seconds. She snapped her fingers and millions of mechanical spiders dropped out of her web, racing toward Max on their short legs.

Max sent out a spell that scattered the spiders like leaves in the wind. As soon as they landed and righted themselves they returned to the chase. Max scrambled backward into a corner of the room, away from the speedy machines. Everything he threw at the devices barely slowed their pursuit.

"Argh," Max howled when several of the small creatures tried to inject him with their syringe-like fangs, while trying to wrap him in their wiry webs. But this proved to be their undoing as Max's blood actually shot back up the incisors, protecting him against their toxin. The small vials boiled in a war between Max's blood and the toxin, before finally exploding all over the small machines, short-circuiting them.

Max tore at the strong sticky wire to keep from being immobilized, knowing he would be useless to his friends if he failed. The fact his blood destroyed the small creatures, kept them from securing him with their webs.

Max jumped up and down on as many as he could, crushing them with his boots, breaking their small legs and bodies. Even though they died attacking him and caused Max physical pain with their needles, numerous spiders swarmed all over him.

"No," Cindy hissed while Max and his blood destroyed spider after spider.

A loud growl rolled through the room where Ell struggled with his bonds, drawing Cindy's attention. His eyes captured hers as if he wanted her to focus on him.

"If you will not join me, Ell will," Cindy stated, flexing her jaws. She strolled toward Ell, eyeing him in his secure state. "You will be mine."

Blood issued from cuts all over Max's body as he fought to keep the mass of mechanical spiders at bay. In his peripheral vision, Cindy hovered over Ell. He wanted to help Ell, but it was all he could do to fight the robotic army.

Then Hudich appeared on the platform, dark and terrible.

25

A Battle of Minds

Max cast a spell that flung the spiders away from him, attracting Hudich's attention.

"Max," he hissed with an evil grin.

Max's senses warned him of the danger in the air, and he threw up a blocking spell just in time. Hudich's spell smashed into Max, driving him backwards across the floor. Their magic acted like a magnet to the mechanical spiders, and they attacked again, but this time they also had their sights set on Hudich.

The mass of mechanical spiders forced Hudich to protect himself from them. Bites from the tiny pests meant his demise.

Max seized the opportunity of a distracted Hudich and launched an offensive. Several of his spells landed, knocking Hudich around the room. Max didn't let up, even though his spells had only a small effect on Hudich, they also destroyed many of the mechanical spiders.

###

Cindy stood over Ell while Max struggled with her tiny mechanical army. Confusion at Max's resistance to their venom troubled her, but at the moment she craved Ell, wanting to add him to her army. "You will be a powerful asset. We will be joined forever, my friend."

She knelt next to Ell and opened her elongated mouth and sank her teeth into Ell's leg. Pain exploded in her jaw like biting cold when she tried to inject her venom and a voice spoke deep inside her mind.

How dare you speak to me, Cindy raged with confusion. Her subjects never spoke to her. She owned their thoughts and controlled their actions. It infuriated her that one of her children dared to speak to her.

Cindy. I'm here for you.

Silence. Who are you? Show me your thoughts, Cindy ordered. *Report!*

I am not one of your people. I am your friend. I've come to help you. Ell spoke to her mind.

I don't need any help. I control all. All shall bow before me and become one. I will create the perfect universe where everyone is equal and does their part.

That's a lot of work, controlling the universe. Wouldn't you rather take a break and get away, run with the sun on your face, Cindy? Ell replied.

Silence! I command you to be quiet. How dare you interfere with my utopia. If you won't join us, I will be forced to eliminate you.

You haven't been successful at destroying me so far. What makes you think you can do it now? I think you don't want to lose me. You want me to help you. You want me to take you away from all of this. Don't you want to go home? Ell continued.

Home? This is...my home. I live here. There is no other...home, Cindy's thoughts took on a confused pattern.

No, this is a military installation. The people here took you away from your parents and friends. Don't you remember? They captured you at the drive-in. Ell tried to bring Cindy to the surface. He could sense she had put up a protective wall around herself. It was as if she desired to hide from the fact she had turned into something evil, something she detested. He wanted to avoid opening that wound and bringing her world crashing down. A distraught Cindy might not be strong enough to do the things she needed to do, to fight her way back.

I haven't lived here...all my life? Lies! Lies! Lies! You are here to steal my power and my children from me. You want it for yourself. Cindy hissed.

You have friends and parents who love you. Another life—with responsibilities. You helped rescue your friends from this place. You sacrificed yourself for them. They sent me to get you. To take you home.

Home?

Yes, let me take you home. Let this place go. You will feel light and free, able to run and play, Ell tempted.

But who are you. How do I know you can help me? You may be here to destroy me and my children.

I am your friend. We have been on many adventures and enjoyed days in the sun and nights under the stars. You have saved my life. Now it's my turn to save yours, Ell stated.

I...saved you? You're just trying to trick me so you can kill me and my children. If you are here to help, tell me who you are! Cindy demanded.

How about I show you who I am and then you tell me my name, Ell offered. *See if you remember our times together. I will let you see my memories of us.*

Cindy saw herself standing in a jungle, staring at something. Her face wore a curious expression as she inched her way forward. She stretched forth her hand and touched a massive foot. She jerked her hand back with raised eyebrows before placing her hand back on the foot.

The scene changed and she sat on the ground eating a melon-like fruit. She peeled off a couple of pieces of hard shell, which had already been cracked, scooped out the meaty flesh with her hand, and devoured it. After eating the entire fruit, she slept against a tree.

A flash and she sat soaking wet on a hard stone floor in a cave with the roar of crashing water filling her ears. A constant mist permeated the air as she wrapped her arms around her knees and shivered uncontrollably. A short time later she leaped through the back of a waterfall out into the night air.

The vision changed again and she flew through the air with her arms bound to her sides. She continued to climb higher and higher into the air until she landed on a hovercraft. The Zeenosees dropped her into a cage beneath their ship and she clung to the bars of a cell, watching something happening on the ground below. She screamed to stop a horrible crime.

The next memory showed her and Max sitting on a rock shelf, surrounded by a deep pit on all sides. They wandered around trying to figure out a way across the canyon. Finally, after some debate, Max raced towards the edge and she cast a spell which threw him over the bottomless pit. Max extended a ramp to let her across and the two of them battled Marko, before using spells to fling him across the canyon. The prison zipped back and forth before it stopped and Marko dropped into the hole.

Max, Cindy thought.

Yes, Max is here to help take you home.

Before she could respond another vision spread in full color across her mind. In the reflection of a large revolving mirror, she stood with her arms wrapped around a huge hideous monster. It had long shaggy fur like a dog, but it was roughly the size of mid-sized elephant with rows of razor sharp teeth and a big bulbous nose.

Ell. Ell help me! Cindy pleaded.

There you are. I knew you were in there somewhere.

GET OUT OF MY HEAD! I DON'T WANT TO GO. I WILL RULE THE WORLD.

Wouldn't you like to go for a ride through the tall grass on Svet? Ell suggested and prodded another memory into her mind.

She and Max lay on the grass under the stars on Svet. They leaned against the large furry body of Ell while wrapped in blankets. They laughed and joked back and forth, having a good time.

Come with me and we can run and play, Ell said.

How do I come with you? Cindy asked.

You need to trust me.

What do you want me to do? Cindy questioned. *LEAVE ME ALONE!*

Help me. Cindy fought an inner battle of wills.

I will help you. The first step is going to be the hardest. You will need to fight as hard as you can. You need to let just one person go, Ell said. *Just one.*

NO! I'm trying to build my empire. How am I supposed to do that without everyone's help? I need to destroy this secret society! Cindy hissed.

Another vision opened to Cindy's mind. She, Max, and others strolled around Svet, showing Ell where to find food. They walked through the tall grass with the wind on their faces on a cool fall day. *Wouldn't you like more days like this?*

Yes. But it is so hard.

Maybe we could look at this from a whole new angle, Ell suggested.

How so?

Maybe we can eliminate someone who annoys you. Someone whose memories are not pleasant to look at. A person who is very bad. Do you really want that type of individual with you? How could you have a perfect society with such people sucking the life out of others? Doesn't a person like that make everyone weaker? An individual that just makes your skin crawl.

A flood of memories zipped through Ell's mind. His connection allowed him to see what Cindy saw. The memories paraded so quickly Ell had trouble making anything out. It was a blur of color and sound before it stopped.

"The old bat won't miss a thing," a man's voice stated as he filled out and signed a check as the name on the account, a Tina Madsen. He entered a Jared Madsen for the payee and the amount well over ten thousand dollars. After he put the check in his pocket he went out of the bedroom into a tiny front room where an old woman watched T.V. He kissed her on the cheek. "Later, Grandma."

Next, he stood over a woman, waving a clenched fist in the air. The woman cried, trying to stop blood from flowing out of her nose. "Don't you ever talk back to me again," the man screamed.

What a horrible man, Ell thought.

Yes.

Do you really want to associate with someone like that? He should be in prison, not a part of any civilized group. Why would you want to be connected with him? I say we let him go.

He is a disgusting man, isn't he?

Yes, let him go.

I want to. Cindy struggled.

Ell could feel Cindy trembling, and her thoughts hinted at fear of the unknown. The disruption of her new world frightened her. She didn't think she would feel normal anymore. It seemed she had only ever had this life—as if it was the sum of her whole existence.

I will stay with you to the end, Ell said. *Let him go.*

L—leave me, Cindy commanded.

It seemed like there was an audible click and Ell discerned a change. The man's memories were still there but only a small part of Cindy's, and they were no longer so clear or sharp. Cindy's heartbeat increased and her breathing became erratic.

Ell took her to memories of everyone back on Svet enjoying a beautiful day, helping her to feel the warm sun on her face and smell the wildflowers. He showed her a perfect day with friends and family.

How do you feel?

Scared. A storm of emotions and conflicts raged inside Cindy. Somehow there was a peace with letting go of that individual, but at the same time, some pain. A very real and sharp ache began inside her mind, which hinted at not being whole or normal.

But isn't it better to be rid of that despicable human being?

Y—yes.

Let's find another. We can turn it into a game of dump the losers. How many Larrys can we get out of your life!

Fewer Larrys sounds nice. Cindy trembled.

Ell helped Cindy locate and release another three people with undesirable qualities. After each separation Cindy felt lighter, almost like a heavy load lifted off her shoulders. Somehow the peace and relief started to outweigh the pain and the emptiness.

###

Hudich roared as he fought Max and the tiny mechanical spiders with magical webs, which tried to ensnare him by shooting strands of the sticky substance through the air like streamers on New Year's Eve. Sparks and fire exploded all around him as he cast an array of counter spells to block and destroy everything trying to bring him down. Still, the sheer ferocity and number of attacks forced him to keep backing away to a spot where the wall shielded his back.

Max fired everything he had at Hudich, trying to keep him off balance. Helping force Hudich into a corner, he spotted the book on the floor behind Cindy and Hudich.

"*Pridi*," Max called, and the book flew through the air and into his hands.

A shockwave like an exploding bomb ripped through the room, flattening Max and pushing him across the floor. Hudich stood tall and menacing in the corner. Burning pieces of the web floated around the room, while malfunctioning spiders jerked or sputtered, lacking purpose.

Max sprang to his feet and zipped out the door just as another explosion blew him into the hall. Hudich tried to stop him from getting away. Max rolled to his feet and sprinted through the complex.

Every time Max turned a corner the area behind him disintegrated in a cloud of smoke and debris. His plan to lead Hudich away from Ell and Cindy seemed to be working. *Do I lead him back to Sky, to help? No. Think!*

###

I feel so empty, like I'm dying, Cindy thought after she released number seventeen.

You are doing so well. You are so brave. We need to do this so you can go home. I will never leave you, Ell thought.

Look at this Larry. Ell located another candidate in Cindy's memories. It was a woman who verbally abused and belittled anyone she ever came in contact with. *She's just a big ball of sunshine, isn't she?*

Cindy actually laughed at Ell's comment and a warm feeling spread through her. *Yes, she is.*

Once again they went in search of a new 'Larry,' and images flashed across their minds. Almost all of Cindy's subjects had horrible things in their past they wouldn't want people to know, so it was fairly easy to spot the undesirables.

Stop! Cindy shouted in her mind. *And this is me, Cindy,* she added so Ell would listen to her. *Max is in trouble and we need to do something with these people.*

Do you see Sky? Ell asked.

Yes.

Do you think you will be all right if you use your powers to control the people still under your command to round up those you've released and escort them to Sky? And can you send others to help Max? Ell asked.

Yes, I think so. As long as you stay with me, Cindy said, her nervousness touching Ell's senses.

I won't leave you, no matter what. I will keep feeding you memories.

Sky paced back and forth in the room which had held Martin and the others in their hyperbolic chambers. It felt like Cindy had forgotten about her or else Max and Ell required Cindy's full attention. The short conversations with Max didn't relieve her concerns. She hated being in a situation where she couldn't risk turning her skills over to Cindy to control. This would prove fatal for Max and Ell.

The sound of boots marching in the hall drew her attention. The thump, thump reached her before the actual bodies creating the noise. Soon, a group of people with their arms over their heads, escorted by some of Cindy's subjects, appeared in the hall. When they reached the door the group stopped. The prisoners acted confused and they appeared to be under their own control. Their movements were smooth and their eyes didn't hold the blank stare of the others.

One of Cindy's minions approached the window and held up a hand written note with one hand while knocking with the other.

Sky stepped toward the glass, holding tightly to the handle of her sword. Her gaze continued to jump back and forth from the note to the door. When she got close enough to read the crude handwriting, her mouth dropped.

Sky, transport these people to Pekel. More to come.
Cindy

"It's working," Sky breathed with a surge of excitement. "They've had to have reached her."

Sky took out her communicator and told Yelka what was about to happen. After she arranged things with Yelka she went and put a chair in front of the gateway.   Then she hurried to the door and hit the open button. Even though the situation felt legitimate and that it wasn't a trap, she kept on her toes and wasn't about to let her guard down.

"Okay, line up in front of the chair," Sky ordered as the group entered the room. Cindy's subjects remained in the hall, which was what Sky preferred.

Sky moved to the person at the front and pointed her sword at the individual. "Climb up on the chair and then step up and forward."

"What?" questioned the person at the front.

"Just do it!" Sky ordered.

A woman got up on the chair and took a giant step forward and disappeared, to the shock of the others in the room. The man directly behind the woman backed into the people behind him.

"Where did she go? You're going to kill us!" gasped the group.

"She is fine. Keep moving or you won't be," Sky threatened, putting the tip of her sword in the center of the man's chest. "GO!"

The weary, confused people didn't dare tempt Sky and they started entering the gateway. No sooner had the last person in the line vanished through the gateway, when Cindy's subjects closest to the door lost their glazed vacant look, and a new batch of Cindy's soldiers arrived to push them into the room.

More pounding on the window caught Sky's attention as another of Cindy's subjects held another note against the window. Sky sidled towards the glass, keeping her weapon ready and pointed at the new arrivals.

Max is in trouble.

Cindy

Below the words Sky noticed a crudely drawn map. Sky pulled out her communicator and sent an urgent message. A few moments later, Lita stepped out of the gateway, brandishing a heavy-duty weapon.

###

"You *can't* escape *me*, Max," Hudich roared, firing spell after spell, destroying hallways and offices in an attempt to get what he came for. "The book will be *mine*."

Sweat streamed down Max's face, and he gulped air in an effort to relieve the stitch in his side. He fired reckless counter attacks as he raced at full speed through the building. To his relief, Cindy's subjects let him pass unhindered and attacked Hudich with all sorts of modern weapons.

These small roadblocks only slightly delayed Hudich's advance. His powers were greater than any manmade weapon or small amounts of magic Cindy's subjects possessed. It didn't appear Cindy could channel her spells through her soldiers. His fire turned Cindy's subjects to ash, releasing them from Cindy's power while helping to free Cindy at the same time.

Max found the hall littered with rubble where he and Ell had entered. An opening to the previously blocked room indicated the beast had tunneled through. Max slowed his pace. The last thing he wanted to do was to run recklessly into that ravenous bear-like creature.

Fearful of Hudich overtaking him prompted him to duck into the hole the creature had dug. The opening sat at the top of the pile which had blocked the creature from this section of the complex. Inside the hole, Max had access to the ceiling of this floor. He climbed up into the crawlspace between the ceiling and the floor above. After moving down the section where the wall below supported the ceiling, he found an opening between the boards that formed a wall, and dropped the book inside.

He hustled backward out of the opening and down the pile just when Hudich rounded the corner ahead of him.

"Max, there's nowhere left to run," Hudich roared. "Where's the book?"

"Someplace safe!"

###

Max is in trouble, Cindy stated. *We need to help him with all I have. I need to inject Hudich with my blood. No other weapons will stop him.*

NO!

What? Why not? Cindy questioned.

I am afraid for you. I may not be able to bring you back if you take him as a subject. He is full of evil. It would take you to a darker place than you were before.

Hey, I read that vile book. I know its secrets and you brought me out of that.

But you haven't practiced those secrets. You yourself were not bad. You know some evil things but you didn't use them. With Hudich, I'm not sure you will just be able to take him. He will fight back, which means he might have access to your mind.

But if I don't help Max, he may die. I am willing to give my life for his, Cindy offered.

If you do this, I will stay with you until the end.

Max felt it before it happened and threw up a blocking spell. Hudich's curse ricocheted off Max's shield and crashed into the pile of rubble, disintegrating bricks and sheetrock. Max countered again when the second attack came, harder this time, forcing him to step back to maintain his balance.

"Your powers have increased, I see," Hudich's deep voice roared. His red rat eyes burned with a flame as he fired off another curse.

Max waved his arm, flinging the curse away in a shower of sparks. He attempted to go on the offensive and sent a volley of spells at Hudich, which he flicked away like annoying flies. Max tried to brace himself, sensing what was coming, and cast the blocking spell.

Hudich unleashed a fury of curses that hammered at Max's defenses, driving him to his knees. Each new assault erupted closer and closer to Max's skin until one reached its mark.

Max covered his head with his arms while a burning heat scorched his skin, causing him to cry out. Suddenly, an invisible vice-like grip clamped down on his body and yanked him across the room where Hudich caught him under one of his clawed feet.

"You cannot win. You are going to bring me the book, or I will make your death more painful than you can possibly imagine." Hudich pushed down on Max's chest with his foot, grinding his claws into Max's clothes and flesh.

"*Premakni*," Max screamed, catching Hudich off guard and throwing him into the ceiling. He rolled away, but before he could climb to his feet a burning erupted at every nerve ending, feeling like Hudich had dipped him into boiling water.

Hudich flipped him through the air and smashed him into the floor on his back before stepping on him again. "You're going to regret…"

Max detected something in the room. He wondered if the entire racket had roused the creature's curiosity. Then he spotted them. Rows and rows of Cindy's subjects filled the halls from both directions. They carried an array of dart guns and leveled them at Hudich.

"Cindy, NO!" Max screamed, causing Hudich to press down even harder with his foot, forcing the air from his lungs.

Hudich shielded himself from the first wave of darts filled with Cindy's blood, stopping them dead in the air, crashing them into an invisible wall. He tried to lower his shield to counter, but more of the tiny projectiles sought him out. He swung his arms like a windmill to knock down each new attack, but they forced him to release his hold on Max.

Max rolled away from Hudich, but a lull in the battle allowed Hudich to track him down once more and pin him with his foot. Hudich countered and flattened several rows of Cindy's subjects. A moment later, they were back on their feet and firing more of the tiny darts.

From under Hudich's powerful leg Max attempted to join the fight, but Hudich slammed him with a spell. Max struggled on the edge of consciousness, the world became a blurry haze of Hudich, Zombies, and a floor covered in tiny syringe-like darts.

Ell's words played at the front of Max's mind, *I fear that if she takes Hudich she will be lost forever.* Then an idea popped into his head. He snatched up a needle and put his plan in motion.

Hudich roared, blasting back the surge of Cindy's subjects in their efforts to take him.

Max stabbed Hudich in the leg with a needle, drawing his immediate attention.

"NO," Hudich gasped, his face lined with an expression of fear. "She won't control me!" his voice sounded fearful.

"She won't. It's *my* blood!" Max injected the needle's contents into Hudich's leg.

Hudich clamped his hands around his leg just above the area Max had stuck with the needle as if trying to stop Max's blood from spreading through his body. "You should have used Cindy's blood. She was strong enough to take me. You *are* not!"

Hudich went ridged standing straight up and then falling over. When he hit the ground, Max blacked out!

26

Sky's Battle

Max took Hudich! Cindy thought with fear.

What? How? Ell asked.

Max injected Hudich with his blood. They are both down, Cindy stressed. *Sky is almost there. Plus, more troops are arriving at the compound.*

Let Sky help Max. We need to hurry. The best way for you to help Max is to release your prisoners. Send them all to the gateway!

Somehow, knowing Max was in trouble and needed her help gave Cindy the strength to release her control of the people so Lita could ship them off to Pekel. She controlled each new wave of freed individuals with the ones behind them.

###

Sky raced through the halls of the complex, checking the crudely drawn map to verify her path. It wasn't necessary at first because every time she passed a group of Cindy's subjects on their way to the gateway, they would point the direction she should go. She followed the same course Max and Ell had taken on their way in, but instead of facing the obstacles they fought through, she met empty destroyed halls, rooms, and labs.

She walked across the tops of fallen shelves where she entered the room where the creature had caused the cave-in. She used the metal support beams of the broken and damaged shelves to walk across the destruction without slipping into holes everywhere. About halfway across the area, a low growl caught her attention.

Through the large hole at the top of a cave in, a flash of movement blocked the opening. *Max!* She knew he lay on the other side of the hole and shot forward. Her cat-like balance enabled her to run at full speed across the narrow poles of the shelves.

Sky sprang through the opening to see a defensive line of Cindy's subjects being torn to bits by a mutated, massive, bald bear. Its claws and teeth ripped through Cindy's soldiers, who attempted to fight back with automatic weapons, which only enraged the beast. On the floor behind the helpless zombies lay Max, and off to the side of the mound created by the destruction was Hudich.

Sky didn't know if this creature wanted Max or if it was only attacking anything that moved, but even still the massive beast could trample him to death. Sky drew her sword and sprang into action. She slashed the beast across its hind legs, causing them to buckle under its massive weight.

The mutated bear roared with rage and pain, dragging itself around by its massive, muscular front arms. Even with malfunctioning hind legs, the mobility of the creature surprised Sky, forcing her to retreat from its sharp front claws.

It struck out, trying to snatch Sky, but she stuck her sword right though its huge paw, ripping the blade out of her hand. The wounded creature whipped its stuck paw back and forth trying to get the thorn out of its flesh. It howled with pain, slicing open its own mouth while biting the blade, trying to release itself from the sharp object.

Sky took out one of Olik's specials from her jacket, turned the setting to high, and released the beast from its misery. A flash of bright light entered its massive head and then the thing fell lifeless to the floor.

Not taking a second glance at the poor hideous creature, Sky bolted to Max. She checked for a pulse and exhaled a sigh of relief when she felt his heart still pumping blood through his veins.

"Come on, Max. Wake up," she spoke softly, patting his cheeks.

No matter what Sky tried, she couldn't rouse him. The only thing giving her comfort was the fact she could feel his heart beating. She glanced around to notice several of Cindy's subjects standing with their blank stares. *Cindy must want to know what's happening.*

"Help me get them back to the gateway. Max and—Hudich. We want them both," Sky pleaded out loud, hoping Cindy could hear her.

Several of Cindy's subjects stepped forward and lifted Max and Hudich off the ground. After pulling her sword out of the dead beast's paw, Sky escorted them back to the gateway where not only Lita waited, but Jax and Fenster were there as well. "Good, I could use your help. I'll get Cindy to draw me a map to her and Ell, while you take Max and Hudich through the gateway. When you come back, we'll go get her and Ell."

"Okay." Fenster nodded toward Jax. They retrieved Max from Cindy's subjects and took him through the gateway. After a few minutes they returned for Hudich, while one of Cindy's subjects drew another crude map.

"We won't have any problems from these zombies, but Cindy said more troops are arriving. Come on, she and Ell may need our help to get out." Sky bolted through the door with Fenster and Jax right on her heels.

"Glad you guys could pull yourselves away from your projects," Sky stated.

"Yelka sent word there was big trouble here and you needed help," Fenster said in his deep voice as they raced through the halls.

"So, we know where Cindy and Ell are. What about Joseph?" Jax asked.

"Not a clue. But I have a feeling Cindy knows," Sky informed them while she continued to lead them through the building. They dashed up several flights of stairs when voices reached their ears. Sky immediately jumped to one side of the hallway and rushed ahead, their destination not far away.

They managed to reach Cindy and Ell without being spotted, but the thudding of boots and voices echoing through the halls told them they might have to fight their way back. They all paused and tried to comprehend the sight before them. Fragments of a strange web-like substance dangled from a huge hole in the ceiling, and hundreds of bodies, mixed with broken mechanical spiders, littered the floor. Even more disturbing to Sky was the way it appeared Cindy was biting Ell. Cindy's mouth was wide open over Ell's upper leg.

"Keep watch," Sky ordered, snapping everyone out of their shock at the scene. *Come on Ell and Cindy hurry up!*

A conversation between several solders grew louder and louder as they approached Sky and the others' location. The military structure and their words indicated they were on edge and ready for action. *Probably a result of all the bodies.*

Sky motioned to Jax and Fenster to take up positions on the other side of the entrance. Sky waited against the wall on the opposite side and retrieved two short black sticks from inside her jacket. She cast her spell and disappeared, and Fenster and Jax did the same.

"Let them enter," Sky whispered.

The patrol continued up the hall, checking each room with trained tactical precision.

Loud bangs echoed through the floor when the soldiers kicked in doors and threw debris around in order to conduct their sweep of the area. Their spotlights flashed around the hall like broken strobe-lights.

A frequent "Clear" or "Check your corners" grew closer and closer until the squad reached Cindy and Ell.

"What the heck," gasped one of the first soldiers.

"Sarge, you need to come have a look at this," another spoke into his radio.

"What is that thing?" asked the first, shining their lights on Ell and Cindy.

"It's alive, whatever it is. It's breathing."

"What about that girl?" the Sergeant asked.

Before the soldiers reached Cindy, Sky attacked. She didn't want them to interfere with Ell helping Cindy, and if they moved her too soon, Sky didn't know what would happen. Sky let the entire group pass into the room before she pounced on them. Whirling a stick in each hand, she exploded on the soldiers like a raging poltergeist. She kicked out legs and struck the surprised soldiers with her sticks on their arms, heads, and midsections.

A terrified few who attempted to flee from the unseen attacker, crashed into the invisible Fenster and Jax.

"We're under att…"

Sky silenced the sergeant's plea by sending him off to slumber-land with a hard blow to the head.

"Do you need assistance? Sergeant, I repeat. Do you need assistance," rose from his dislodged head set.

"I don't think we have much time before more troops arrive," Jax stated, appearing in the doorway.

"We may need to hit them from an easier spot in order to defend our backs," Sky suggested, materializing out of the air and shooting a look at Fenster, releasing his invisibility spell.

"I'm on it," the large man responded, and scampered out the door and down the hall.

"Sk—Sky," Cindy's weak voice spoke.

"Cindy!" Sky leaped across bodies and debris to support a weak-ened Cindy who rolled away from Ell. "I've got you." Sky caught her in her arms.

Ell lifted his head to glance back at them. Sky reached out and touched his leg. *Great job, my large friend. Are you able to move?*

I'm good to go. I can carry Cindy, Ell rolled onto his stomach and rose to his feet.

"I'll get Fenster," Jax stated and rushed to find him.

"How do you feel?" Sky asked.

"Weak, but better. Thanks to Ell" Tears rolled down Cindy's pale-gray cheeks. "I'm so sorry. I didn't mean for it to go this far."

"Hey, look at the bright side: you single-handedly took down one of, if not our enemy's strongest, location." Sky smiled in an attempt to light-en Cindy's spirits. Sky wanted to keep Cindy positive and get her to Yelka as soon as possible.

"How do I look?" Cindy asked.

"Well…"

"The truth." Cindy struggled to drop a hand on Sky's arm while meeting her eyes.

"You could star in one of your world's zombie movies—as a perfect female zombie." Sky grinned, still trying to keep the mood light.

Cindy actually snorted, and the corners of her mouth turned upward for a brief moment before she started to cry again. "Thanks." She hic-cupped between sobs and laughter.

"Let's go home. You'll recover." Sky patted Cindy's hand.

"I know where Grandpa is," Cindy uttered. "He isn't well-guarded because his captors are here."

"That's news we need to relay to the others," Sky replied.

They decided to have Fenster carry Cindy instead of Ell, because Ell's back brushed the tops of the door frames when he passed through the building. Not to mention the fact Ell was a terrifying vision to any troops they should meet. With Ell in the front, followed by Fenster pack-ing Cindy, Jax and Sky brought up the rear. Voices, boots, and crashes echoed through the building, indicating more troops were searching the building for resistance or those needing help.

Ell surprised a squad coming around an intersection, prompting Sky to throw up a defensive shield to protect Ell from automatic weapons fire. She held it until the men had spent their clips and then turned Ell loose on them. Ell chased them down the hall before returning to lead the group back to the gateway.

They sped as fast as they could, knowing the squad Ell scattered would have announced their presence to the others. They navigated the halls, expecting to run into strong resistance at any moment. They rounded a corner and spotted Lita poking her head out of the room with the gateway.

"Hurry." She waved them forward before disappearing into the room.

Before they could reach the safety of the gateway, hundreds of troops appeared at the end of the hallway ahead of and behind them. The soldiers cocked and leveled their weapons at them, forcing them to stop short of making their escape. They all raised their arms above their heads.

"Keep moving towards the door," Sky hissed, and the group continued to walk closer to the exit.

"Everyone is free to go, on one condition." a voice called out from the crowd of soldiers in front of them.

"What's that?" Fenster asked?

"Your leader agrees to fight me!"

"Who, me?" Fenster's deep voice rumbled.

"No, *not* you. I'm talking about the blond witch in the back," the voice stated as the crowd parted to let a man through.

"You want to fight *Sky*?" Fenster laughed his deep voice reverberating off the walls. "Do you have a death wish?"

"Keep moving towards the door," Sky hissed again, forcing the group forward.

"Do you really think you can make your escape if I give the order to fire?" the man asked.

"Do I have your word my friends can go if I fight you?" Sky called, working her way around Ell to the front. "What guarantee do I have these soldiers will honor your orders after you're dead?"

"I will let your friends enter the room now if you stay behind." Agent Tanner stepped through the crowd to face Sky.

"Take Cindy and get out of here." Sky waved the others toward the door.

"No," Jax protested. "I...we aren't leaving anyone behind."

"Cindy needs help, *now*. Take her to Yelka. She knows where Joseph is. I will be all right. Go help Joseph, while their attention is here,"

Sky ordered, and the group started down the hall towards the door while Sky remained behind.

"I've been hunting you for a long time," Tanner sneered. "And I've trained all my life with the best instructors, for this day."

"If you consider a year a long time? And we shall see how good your training is." Sky smirked with her pale beautiful face. The others continued to inch their way to the exit.

"I thought you were more talented than that. Do you not recognize your superior when you meet him? I've chased you across galaxies and worlds without number. Your master sent me to collect you. Your new friends hid you well. I learned patience working my way through the ranks of the most uninformed people on this miserable planet. Careful not to reveal myself, until now. I suspected I had found you with the old man, but wasn't sure until our meeting at the convenience store," Tanner stated.

Sky's mouth fell open and her eyes grew wide. "M—my master?"

"Yes," Tanner continued to meander down the hall towards her. His eyes remained locked on Sky's. No one else mattered to him. "You re-member his name, of course?" A smile spread across Tanners face.

"H—his name?" Sky's stomach contracted into a tight not. It couldn't be, her past had caught up to her.

"Zmaj, your master. You were his favorite and he wants you back. Preferably alive. Apparently he cannot resist your beauty," Tanner in-formed her.

When the others reached the door to the room where Lita and the gateway waited, they all glanced back at Sky. She met their stares for a moment and then motioned them into the room with her hand. She wait-ed until they were no longer in the hall.

"He lost his control over me. I have a new master now," Sky stated.

"Ah, the old man. So, he has the object of your affection," Tanner stopped as if pondering this new information.

"No, I have the object. He gave it to me. I am my own master. So even if he found another, I have one, and he can have no power over me anymore," Sky said.

"He—gave it to you—willingly?" Tanner's face reflected shock.

"Yes, so you can leave—alive—and tell Zmaj, I won't be coming back." The smirk returned to Sky's face.

Tanner bent over and placed his hands on his temples as if fighting the pain of a severe migraine headache. He remained in this position for a few moments and then stood tall once more. "Unfortunately, that is unacceptable. If he can't have you alive, I'm afraid he wants you dead."

"He's going to be very disappointed. He's going to lose another servant." Sky smiled.

"You're sure about that, are you," Tanner said, a fire burning in his eyes.

"Rules?" Sky smiled.

"Do you think I would obey any?"

"No, just checking. Goodbye, Tanner," Sky stated.

"Veen, actually, but I now prefer Tanner. And goodbye, Sky." Tanner tipped his head, and the fire in his eyes spread to cover his body in a blue flame that flickered and pulsed all over the outline of his frame.

"You know why you prefer it? It is your free name. Even though you aren't free, you want to be, and this new identity gave you a small taste of that. You could let it go," Sky urged, lowering her center of gravity to ready herself against the coming attack.

"You know I can't. You were once in my place," Tanner started toward her.

"I know. I'm sorry." She frowned.

"I'm not. An evil grin spread across Tanner's face. "I return you and I am free. I told you. You are his favorite."

Tanner exploded down the hall towards her, faster than any foe she had faced in a long time. She dropped to her back and let him fly by, crashing uncontrollably into the soldiers in the hall behind her. Screams from the wounded issued from those who took the brunt of his blow as it broke bones and smashed bodies. He paid no heed to the injured and rushed back towards her.

He attempted blow after blow in the form of kicks and punches, which Sky blocked and dodged. Tanner swung a wicked hook that just missed Sky as she ducked, while his knee came up and caught her on the chin. Lights popped in front of her eyes, but she reached out and caught the foot of his raised leg. Straightening her body, she lifted him head first into the ceiling, breaking lights and support structures. As he dropped to the floor, he brought his fists together and hammered them into the top of Sky's head, buckling her knees.

Sky kicked his legs out when he hit the floor, and caught him across the chin with an up-kick from her other leg, sending him backwards down the hall. A little dazed, she sprang to her feet and prepared for another attack.

The fire burning along his frame flared brighter with his anger. It rose in height, then gathered into large burning balls of fire covering his hands. He swung his arms at her like windmills, launching curse after curse towards her.

Sky put up a shield to block the incoming fire bombs, each exploding off her spell in a shower of sparks. The shockwaves pushed her back towards the soldiers at the other end of the hall, who had taken cover around the corner. Only their heads poked around the corner to watch the fight.

Sky cast an invisible spell across the floor as Tanner pounded her shield with a fire storm. The dancing flames and ricocheting fire ignited parts of the hallway, choking the air with smoke. Tanner advanced toward Sky while bombarding her with everything he had.

Tanner continued to press against Sky's shield by closing the distance between them, pushing her back with his spells. She let him step into her net of magic, unaware, before it was too late for him to retreat. Sky dropped her shield and ducked, avoiding his scorching fire. She brought her hands together and yanked back quickly as if setting a hook in a biting fish. The magical net ensnared Tanner's legs and jerked him off his feet.

Sky snapped the magical net like a whip, slamming Tanner into the walls, the ceiling, and the floor. The surprise move, and the severe beating Tanner absorbed every time Sky hammered him against brick and glass, left him struggling to counter. He launched the occasional wild curse, trying to get lucky, but all missed their mark.

Knowing Tanner would not yield, Sky showed no mercy, collapsing portions of the ceiling by taking out walls with Tanner's broken body. Finally, when her energy level started to wane, Sky released Tanner onto the floor in front of her. His body was bent and broken at awkward angles and his breaths came in raspy struggled gasps.

"F—finish it." He swallowed, looking out from the slit of one eye, the other completely swollen shut.

"I don't want to kill you," Sky said, squatting down in front of Tanner. "I would prefer you go back to Zmaj and tell him you couldn't find me or you killed me in such a way there was nothing left to return."

Tanner's arm cracked back to its normal position and shot out, his hand clamping down on her throat. He snapped the fingers of his other hand, causing the troops on both ends of the hall to return with their automatic weapons pointed at Sky. "I can't do that," Tanner's voice grew stronger as more disturbing cracks echoed through the halls and he rose

to his feet. He continued to squeeze Sky's throat, choking off her air. A ball of blue flame appeared in his other arm, which he held high in the air. "Now, you die."

Sky punched upward into the elbow of Tanner's arm holding her in place while he attempted to stab the deadly fire into her belly. The blow snapped Tanner's already broken arm, and he released his grip. His fire ball fist continued towards her gut. Hopping back and curving in her stomach, Sky pushed Tanner's wrist down by making an X with her forearms. Then swinging his arm to the side, she rolled his burning hand around into an awkward position. The move forced him to bend over with his arm cranked up behind his back.

Sky blasted him in the face with a front kick, then caught his head behind her leg on its way back down and pulled him to the floor where she spun his burning hand around and forced it into his own chest. His spell burned its way through his body and fried his own heart. Tanner jerked violently for a moment, and then became motionless.

Sky stared down at Tanner's lifeless body for a few seconds and then lifted her head to see all the soldiers with their weapons pointed at her.

"Freeze," several hollered down the hall.

Sky checked the room with the gateway through a hole she had created with Tanner's body—to make sure everyone was gone. A smile spread across her face, "Even after what you just witnessed, you think you can still hold me?"

"Fire," an officer ordered, and Sky disappeared in a flash of light.

27

Hudich Lands

Joe and the others huddled around a motionless, Max trying to find a spell or medical treatment that could wake him. Joe fought the dizzying effect of the drugs he had been given to keep him sedated. Even though the minute Jax and Finster showed up to rescue him and had stopped the flow of the sleep agent through his IV, he still struggled to remain conscious.

A battered Sky rushed through the door to the third floor and all heads turned to see her.

"Glad you could make it," Finster uttered in his deep voice.

"Joseph. Whew, glad you're back. How are you? How's Max?" Sky joined the huddle.

"He's alive but in a comatose state, the same as Hudich," Yelka sang sadly, resting a hand on Max's chest.

"I'm fine, thanks to Cindy," Joe said. "After the mess and chaos she managed to create, Finster and Jax pretty much used the gateway to walk right in and take me out. She seemed to have detailed knowledge of where I was being held."

"Well, there was a little resistance, but not enough to matter," Finster added.

"And the fact we dropped into your room and snatched you out before more help could arrive, lessened the danger. Cindy also knew who the mole was, and she appears to have cleared out," Jax offered.

"Was Ell able to reach Max, like he did Cindy?" Sky asked.

"No, we tried that," Max's mother said. Her eyes brimmed with tears.

Ell, who stood close by, hung his head, unable to help a dying friend.

"He said all he could hear were screams and distorted fragments of spells and shouts of battle being waged from a great distance away. It was Max and Hudich fighting in an isolated world, with only bits of sound escaping," Joe stated.

Sky shifted and glanced around the room.

"Cindy is downstairs on one of the beds with her parents. She should be fine." Yelka's wide-eyed look revealed she wasn't sure that what she had just uttered was true.

"Do we know what happened to the book? Ell said Max was the last to have it," Joe finally asked after a long moment of silence, while everyone watched Yelka trying to reach Max.

"No. I didn't see it when I found him. That means it could still be in the hands of the wrong people." Sky frowned.

"Well, we know Hudich doesn't have it," Jax offered, motioning to the unconscious Hudich lying on the floor a short distance away.

"I'm thinking Max hid it in the complex. Only he knows where," Sky stated.

"I don't think there is anything I can do for him." Yelka looked up with a grim face, tears swimming across her lower eyelids.

"What?" Rachel shrieked.

"Rachel." Joe put a comforting hand on Max's mother's shoulder. "Max is doing battle with Hudich in a place we cannot help him. We need to see if we can help the others." Joe glanced at the chambers containing Martin and the others.

"I'm not sure of them either. They have been infected with a virus that has been mutated magically. I have never seen anything like it. The cold seems to keep it from spreading too rapidly."

"Hey, some of the scientists who did this may be in Pekel right now! They might have information that could help us," Lita suggested.

"That's worth a shot." Joe raised his eyebrows.

Joe had Jax and Finster take Max to his bed where his mother and Yelka could continue to care for him. He readied the gateway, collected weapons for him and the others, and supplies for the people they had trapped in Pekel. When Jax and Finster returned they accompanied him, Sky, and Lita through the gateway into Pekel.

They stepped out of the gateway into a rather large camp with their weapons at the ready. The group had moved to the top of the canyon where it would be hard for anything to reach them. The people huddled around fires and turned to meet them.

Joe, Lita, Finster, and Jax remained back from the group while Sky strolled right into their midst.

"What is she doing?" Jax asked out of the side of his mouth.

"Don't know," Finster whispered.

"We brought you more supplies," Joe stated when Jax and Finster dropped a pile of goods on the ground in front of the prisoners.

"Where are we?" several shouted.

"What are you going to do with us?" others questioned.

"That depends on how much help you can give us," Joe called. "Did anyone here…"

Before Joe could finish his sentence Sky marched the Vice President of the United States out of the crowd towards them. "Here's the man in charge." Sky shoved the Vice President, causing him to stumble.

"All right, all right. Will you tell this woman who I am?" the Vice President demanded angrily.

"We know who you are and what you've done," Joe answered condescendingly. "You have no power here. You're our prisoner the same as everyone else. If you want to go home, I suggest you help us."

"What am I supposed to do?" the Vice President complained.

"We want the scientists responsible for mutating the viruses used at that lab in Nevada. They injected some of my friends and we want to know how to cure them," Sky barked.

"How am I supposed to know that? I didn't oversee that sort of thing," the Vice President grumbled. "Besides, the virus will die on its own. Your people will get better."

"What do you mean?" Joe approached the Vice President.

"The people you sent me here with. They were all infected and they must have become immune to the disease, because they appear to be cured," the Vice President stated.

"They *are* cured?" Joe asked.

"Yes, ever since you brought us here. They grew better by the hour."

Joe exchanged a knowing look with Sky and they both spoke together. "They got better ever since we brought them here!"

"Get one of them," Joe ordered.

Sky rushed into the group with the Vice President and returned with a man. Besides a few cuts and bruises, the man appeared unharmed.

"I think we need to take him back with us," Lita offered.

"Watch him there for any changes?" Joe stated more than asked.

"Yep!" Sky agreed.

"Thank you for your help," Joe said and nodded toward the gateway.

"Wait," some of the people cried.

"You can't leave us here," they protested as Joe and the others, along with the once-infected man left through the gateway.

In about an hour, Joe and the others had transported Max, Hudich, Martin, and those still infected to a secure camp they had established in Pekel. Ell went along for additional protection, and Cindy and her parents decided to send her there to help remove some of the lingering effects of the magic she had let loose.

Jax brought in several of his men to secure the camp and keep watch over the man at Grandpa's house. Even though they chose a location away from the Trogs and all other known settlements, every one of Jax's men carried the most advanced weapons they had.

They removed Martin and their friends from the temperature controlled beds within an hour of transporting them to Pekel. The world's lack of magical power proved highly effective in stopping and reversing the conditions brought on by the magically altered virus. Even Cindy received benefits from being on Pekel, and her features returned to normal. Her skin color remained extremely pale and her eyes held on to the dark circles which had set in, giving her a strange ghoulish look.

Max and Hudich showed no change. They lay unmoving. Only the constant rise and fall of their chests indicated they were alive.

"What's *happening* to him?" Rachel said, more to herself than anyone else, while she sat in a chair next to his cot.

"I don't think it is anything like I just went through. Ell could communicate with me by touch, just like he always did. I wish I could help him. He did it for me you know." Cindy swallowed and wiped her eyes on her sleeve.

"Did what for you?" Rachel glanced towards her.

"Tried to take control of Hudich before I did. Ell told me they didn't think they could have brought me back if I had done it. I was trying to help Max by doing it. Instead, he did it for me."

"That's what best friends do." Rachel flashed a quick smile.

"Maybe we should just kill Hudich," Cindy offered right when Joe entered the tent.

"I don't think that's a good idea. Who knows whose mind the battle is taking place in? Killing one might kill the other." Joe frowned. "How are you feeling?" Joe asked Cindy.

"Exhausted, but better. It was a lot of work controlling an army." She tried to lighten the situation.

"I'll bet. Even though it was very dangerous, as I'm sure you now understand, you did manage to destroy most of this secret society's plans. Unfortunately, we didn't recover the book. If we could have destroyed it in time, we might have wiped out their power and control over the weak-minded of our country," Joe frowned.

"So, they maintain their control of the White House? They won the election?" Cindy questioned.

"Yes, I don't think they know where the book is because their influence diminished by millions of votes, but their plans to control the masses with lies and gifts worked. Only evil can cause people to give up their freedom for the promise of unearned comfort. In the end, they will have neither. They've filled them with hate against the rich, but what they don't understand is pulling down the rich will cause their standard of living to collapse as well. When you take away the producers you have nothing. You didn't happen to see where Max hid the book?" Joe asked.

"No, it took me time to organize help for him. By the time my troops arrived, Max no longer had the book." Cindy shook her head.

"I hope Max hid it well so they don't stumble across it before he recovers." Joe frowned.

"How are the others?" Rachel asked, trying to find some hope.

"Everyone is doing much better, and the man we took back to Earth hasn't shown any signs of a relapse. Yelka wants them to stay longer, for good measure," Joe stated.

Cindy put her hands to her mouth and gave a gasp.

"What?" both Joe and Rachel asked.

"I just realized that if—when Max and Hudich come to, Hudich will now have the spider venom in his veins. Doesn't that mean he will be able to do what I did? I will have given him more power."

"You may be right," Joe stated. "But alas, we have now successfully placed him back in Pekel with his life force in yet another world. He will be very weak. Even though he transported himself here magically three years ago when he murdered Frank, he won't be able to leave now.

I don't know how long he will survive in that predicament if he doesn't first return to where they found that magical gateway."

There was no change in Max or Hudich's condition over the next two days. The others appeared to have fully recovered except Cindy, who maintained her 'queen of the dead' look. Yelka gave the okay for Martin and the others to go home, and they put the once-infected man back with the prisoners they had trapped in Pekel.

Rachel and Cindy slept on cots in the same tent with Max, and Ell refused to go back to Svet until Max was better. Sky, Joe, Lita, and Cindy's parents went back and forth preparing operations and plans to retrieve the book should Max be able to give them its location. Cindy gave them detailed designs of the structure, down to the air ducts and even the broom closets.

Every couple of hours or so, Yelka and Lita showed up to check on Max's condition. Yelka felt a little put out because her magical tests were useless in Pekel, so she couldn't analyze Max's condition or try to help him much. Lita would repeat the same tests, even though nothing seemed to work. Then they would have Joe accompany them into the tent where they kept Hudich to see if there were any changes to his condition.

Joe had stationed several armed guards around his tent, along with alarms that would sound should he make any move. He fully intended to keep Hudich in Pekel this time.

The following morning while Cindy and Rachel ate breakfast, Max moaned softly. They both froze mid-bite and shot each other a look before glancing down at Max.

"Did you hear?" Cindy asked.

"He moaned. I heard it," Rachel answered and put down her plate. Both of them hopped to Max's side, while Rachel snatched up his hand. "He feels warmer."

Cindy reached down and touched his forehead. "Yes, he does." When she removed her hand Max's eyes snapped open.

"Mom, Cindy," he muttered, his eyes jumping back and forth between the two of them.

Tears started to roll down their cheeks.

"Max. You're safe," his mother sobbed.

"Welcome back." Cindy smiled.

"I've seen the One!" Max stated.

That night everyone sat around the dinner table at Grandpa's house, talking about the events of the past few months. Grandpa and Sky left Hudich at the location they had set up for Max, deciding it was better to keep him away from the others.

They caught Max up on the 'Dark Society,' as Cindy called them. How they maintained their control over the American people even though their powers had diminished. Max told them where he had hidden the book in the wall of the building. With Cindy's help, they pinpointed the exact location.

"What did you mean, when you said you had seen the One? Is this who we talked about a few months ago?" Cindy asked, causing everyone to be silent and listen.

"Yes. When I injected my blood into Hudich, I wasn't strong enough to take control of him totally. I had some influence over him, but he had more power over me. We kind of cancelled each other out. We fought endless battles in our minds. Hudich was slowly breaking down my defenses. It wasn't like where you dominated your subjects. Hudich was able to fight back and, believe me, he did. I had nightmares. I could feel myself slowly losing the battle. Even though I couldn't move my limbs, he was breaking into my mind more and more. I needed help because I was unable to free myself and I knew I couldn't communicate with you. I remembered we had talked about the One and I called out to him." Max stared off as if watching the events play over in his mind.

"What? So He came to you?" Sky asked this time.

Max noticed everyone's eyes glued on him.

"Yes, He said because I believed and because I had done a selfless act to help my friend." Max glanced at Cindy. "He could free me from Hudich's grasp if I believed it."

"So, obviously, you trusted him," Rachel said.

"Yes, He showed me things and told me to keep up the fight against evil. That He is coming and coming soon. Then I felt the connection to Hudich released. Hudich no longer had any control over me and I was so happy. That's when I woke up."

###

Max, Lita, Grandpa, and Sky dropped out of the gateway into a dark massive storage room about the size of a gymnasium. With the aid of their night-vision goggles, they could see everything as if the lights were on. The room didn't show any signs of the destruction that had taken place three weeks earlier when Max and Ell had fled from the magically transformed bear.

They waited in silence between the thirty-foot high shelves that filled the room, while Lita adjusted some controls on a small hand held detector. "There are alarms on the doors but no video, so we are free to move about without being noticed."

"I'm hoping the lateness of the hour lowers our chances of anyone actually needing to get anything from this room," Grandpa stated, looking around.

"Which way?" Sky asked.

Max poked his head out into the main aisle and glanced in both directions. On one end he could see garage-type doors and knew they needed to go in the opposite direction. "This way." He waved.

Max led them to the door on the side of the room. Everything appeared like nothing had ever happened. If Max hadn't been here to see it, he would have never known the wall had been collapsed.

"Where's your best guess?" Grandpa asked.

Max tried to recall everything he could about the events that transpired that eventful day. "Well, this door opens into a normal hallway. The creature dug his way through right at the height of the ceiling on the other side. This whole wall was ripped open several yards to the right. If they didn't find it when they fixed the room, the book should be about seven feet up and about eight feet away from the door."

Lita got out another smaller hand-held control. Using the shelf next to the wall as a ladder, she climbed to the designated height. While holding on to the shelf with one hand, she extended the other to the wall and placed the device against it. She slid the flat surface of the thing along the wall like a stud finder. It took her about fifteen minutes of searching to locate something in the wall that resembled the dimensions of the book. It was a lot closer to the door than Max had guessed, but at about the right height.

"I think this is it," Lita said.

"What are the chances we are going to set off the alarm by cutting into the wall?" Sky asked, constantly checking the door.

"I'll move the gateway to this aisle. I say we cut fast and then bolt," Grandpa said.

"I agree." Max nodded.

"Okay." Sky nodded.

"Cut it," Grandpa ordered.

Lita used another little tool to trace a strange florescent square around the item she detected in the wall. Then she slowly pulled it away from the wall and a green beam of light connected the wall to the device in a pyramid shape. She then tapped a button on the device, and the section of wall she had designated with the apparatus disappeared, revealing the book.

Immediately, a high-pitched, piercing alarm hurt their ears to the point it was difficult to function. Max caught Lita, who lost her hold in surprise, while Sky ran up the wall, grabbed the book, and directed everyone into the gateway just as the door to the storage room flew open.

Max cast a blocking spell as gun fire from the guards followed them into the gateway where Yelka shut it down. The third floor was full of anxious people. Max's mother, Cindy and her parents, Martin and Aunt Donna, Sam and Linda, and others waited for their return.

Grandpa held out his hand and Sky passed him the book. "It's time we end their source of power and get rid of this headache once and for all."

Everyone followed Grandpa through the house. Before he went out the back door he snatched up a can of lighter fluid and some matches. When he reached the barbeque pit, he threw the book in the round brick hole.

"You know we could use a spell to burn it," Max stated.

"It's a magic book. It might have some enchantments protecting it from magical harm. Better to do it the old fashioned way," Grandpa stated, dousing the book in lighter fluid.

Everyone stepped back while Grandpa struck a match and tossed it onto the book. A wail, like a tortured soul enduring unspeakable pain, filled the air. Everyone cringed as the flames consumed the old leather book. The horrible scream lasted for a couple of minutes until the flames turned the old pages to ash.

"That should limit their control over the people," Grandpa stated.

"What do we do now?" Cindy asked.

"We still need to fight. The war has only begun," Sky continued. "We need to discover all of Hudich's plans and stop them."

"Also, prepare for the One," Max muttered and everyone glanced at him in silence.

###

A week after they had recovered the book from the secret military base, the crash of breaking glass echoed through the house. Everyone rushed to the sound of the disturbance to see someone had thrown a rock through the front window. Max and Cindy dashed out the front door to see Larry and his gang racing their bikes down the street and out of the neighborhood.

"It was Larry," Max spat after he and Cindy entered the front room.

"What a loser," Cindy added.

"I'm not so sure," Grandpa responded, a strange look on his face staring at the rock for a moment. He then dropped the stone on the floor and sprinted up the stairs.

"What?" Rachel asked as Max picked up the rock and saw the writing on it.

Hudich left Pekel.

He showed the rock to Cindy and his mother before following Grandpa up the stairs. They found Grandpa inside the force field with Sky, Jax, and a few of Jax's men. They watched them all disappear through the gateway. Grandpa paced back and forth for about fifteen minutes before Sky and the others returned, shaking their heads.

When he finally lowered the force field, Max knew the answer.

"He's gone, along with the Vice President and a good number of the others," Grandpa said.

"How?" Max, Cindy and Rachel asked in unison.

"Those that remain said a space ship took them away," Sky responded.

###

Under the control of Brian, the alien sat the ship down in a clearing in the middle of the jungle. The canopy rocked back and forth from the wind created by the spacecraft's thrusters, blowing leaves and raising the frightened calls of animals.

A door opened and Hudich descended the ramp, followed by Alan and the Vice President of the United States. Hudich paused at the bottom and inhaled a large breath of air. "Earth." A wicked smile spread across his face. "I've waited almost two centuries for this day. The magic of this place will be mine to control. Now is the day of my reign. None will withstand me!"

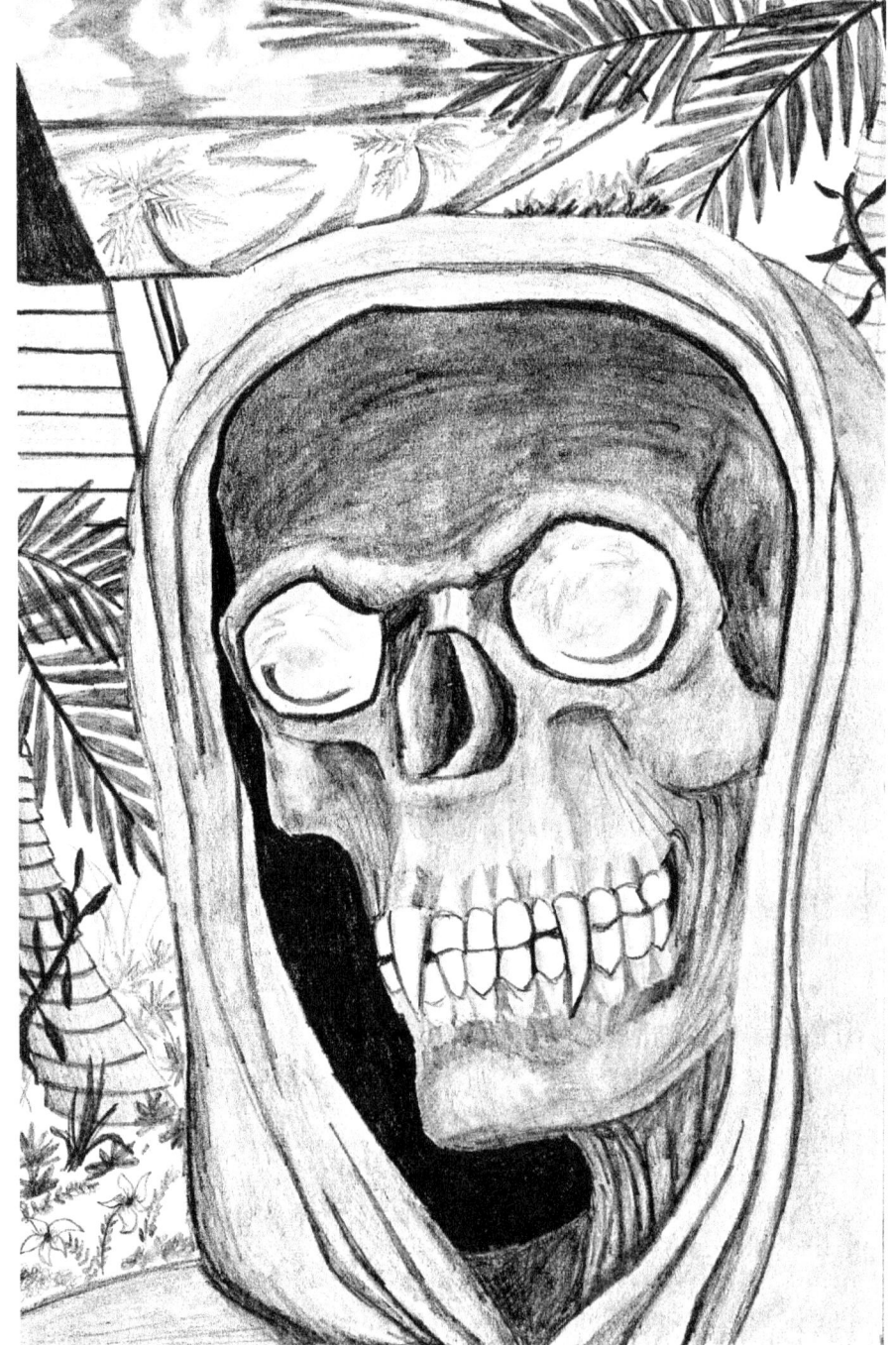

Spell Pronunciations and Definitions

The following words are from the Slovene language

Stress marks: [bold type] indicates the primary stressed syllable, as in news·pa·per [nooz-pey-per] and in·for·ma·tion [in-fer-mey-shuhn]

pridi (pri·di) [prē-dē] – Moves objects towards you.
zaspi (za·spi) [zä-spē] – Causes sleep.
prizgaj (pri·zgaj) [prē- 3g ī] – Use to create fire.
ugasni (u·ga·sni) [oo-gä-snē] – Use to extinguish fire.
premakni (pre·ma·kni) [prā-mä-knē] – Moves objects away from you.
vstani (vs·ta·ni) [oos-tä-nē] – Stops moving objects.
pochasi (po·cha·si) [pō-chä-sē] – Slows moving objects down.
izginem se (iz·gi·nem·se) [ēz-gē-n äm- sä] – Makes one invisible.
prikazi se (pri·ka·zi·se) [prē-kä-zē-sä] – Makes one visible.
izbrisi znamenje (iz·bir·si·zna·men·je) [ēz-brē-shē znä-menyē] – removes curses.
preselim se(pre·se·lim·se)[pre-se-lēm-sä] – Transports one to another world.
vrnim se(vr·nim·se)[vr-nēm-sä] – To return from transport.
odkri (od·kri)[ōd-krē] – Reveals something hidden.
razkrij zlo (raz·krij·zlo)[räz-krē-zlō] – Reveals a person who has been using evil magic.
razkrij dobro (raz·krij·do·bro)[räz-krē-dō-brō] – Reveals a person who has been using good magic.
unichi (u·ni·chi)[oo-nē-chē] – To destroy something.
vrtinchim se(vr·tin·chim·se)[vr-tēn-chēm-sä] – To twirl like a tornado.
zadravi (za·dra·vi)[zä-drä-vē] – To heal something.
oviraj (o·vir·aj)[oo-vēr- ī] – To block something.
beri misel (beri·mi·sel)[berē-mē-sel] – To read another's thoughts.
gori (gor·i)[gōr-ē] – To lift something up.
zakluci (za·klu·ci)[zä-kloo-chē] – To lock something.
zapri (za·pri)[zä-prē] – To shut something.
snezi (sne·zi)[sne-zē] – To create snow.
raztrgaj (raz·tr·gaj)[räz-tr-gī] – To break or tear.

Symbols and their examples:

ē bee
ä father
3 vision
ī pie, by
oo boot
ā pay
ō toe
e bet

James Todd Cochrane was born in California in 1969. He received his BA from Utah State University, where he majored in Business Information Systems with a minor in German.

A writer since elementary school, he published his first novel, Max and the Gatekeeper, in 2007.

The author writes part-time while working as a computer programmer.

BOOKS

Max and the Gatekeeper (Max and the Gatekeeper Book I)

The Hourglass of Souls (Max and the Gatekeeper Book II)

The Descendant and the Demon's Fork (Max and the Gatekeeper Book III)

The Dark Society (Max and the Gatekeeper Book IV)

Max and the Gatekeeper Book V in progress

NOVELLA SERIES (EBOOKS ONLY)

Centalpha 6 Part I

Centalpha 6 Part II

Centalpha 6 Part III

Centalpha 6 Part IV

Centalpha 6 Part V

Centalpha 6 Part VI

Centalpha 6 Omnibus

Centalpha 6 Part VII coming soon

www.ingramcontent.com/pod-product-compliance
Lightning Source LLC
Chambersburg PA
CBHW060759120626
46557CB00001B/34